'T. Jefferson Parker has carved out a niche for himself as the Hemingway of thriller writers.'

'If you're seeking a thriller ... is the writer for you.'
The Washington Post

'Some of the finest writing you'll ever read.'
Chicago Sun-Times

'This is gripping literary entertainment with a point.'
Los Angeles Times

'Parker has produced a body of work unsurpassed, perhaps unmatched, by any other contemporary writer of crime fiction.'
Kirkus Reviews

'No writer can match Parker when it comes to characters and mood. [He] is a brilliant craftsman and storyteller.'
The Providence Sunday Journal

'Since the days of Raymond Chandler, California has produced some of our finest crime novelists, and today the likes of Michael Connelly, Don Winslow and Joseph Wambaugh continue the tradition . . . Parker demonstrates again that he belongs in their company.'
Associated Press

'A pro, that's what T. Jefferson Parker is. His plots are intricate, keenly crafted, clearly mapped; his chracaters complicated, yet consistent; Parker is an ace.'
The San Diego Union-Tribune

'Three time Edgar winner Parker has created a memorable character in Charlie Hood, who remains a beacon of restrained hope in a world of despair and dark deeds.'
Booklist

T. Jefferson Parker was born in Los Angeles and has lived all his life in Southern California. He took a bachelor's degree in English from the University of California, Irvine, in 1976 and was honoured as a distinguished alumnus in 1992. He wrote his first novel, *Laguna Heat*, while working as a journalist covering crime and culture for the Newport Ensign. *Laguna Heat* received rave reviews, was produced as a movie and made the New York Times Best Seller list. His following novels, all located in sunny, southern California, also received rave reviews, have appeared on many best seller lists, and been awarded many prizes. His writing has been described as 'potent and irresistible' (L.A. Times) and 'resonant, literate and powerful' (Kirkus). His earlier Charlie Hood mystery, *The Jaguar*, is also published by Sandstone Press.

Also published by Sandstone Press

The Jaguar

THE FAMOUS
AND THE DEAD

T. Jefferson Parker

SANDSTONEPRESS
HIGHLAND | SCOTLAND

This edition published by
Sandstone Press Ltd
PO Box 5725
One High Street
Dingwall
Ross-shire
IV15 9WJ
Scotland
United Kingdom

www.sandstonepress.com

First published in the USA in 2013 by Dutton, part of Penguin Group
(USA) Inc.

ISBN: 978-1-908737-36-6
ISBN e: 978-1-908737-37-3

The publisher acknowledges subsidy from Creative Scotland towards
publication of this volume.

Cover design by Guilherme Gustavo Condeixa, London
Typeset by Raspberrymac Creative Type, Edinburgh
Printed and bound by Totem, Poland

For Thomas and Tyler

Am I the sea, or a sea monster,
That thou settesta guard over me?
Job 7:12

1

Rovanna strode into the convenience store by the dawn's early light. As usual he carried his Louisville Slugger, the barrel of it cupped in his right palm and the handle resting on his shoulder like a rifle. His back was straight and his gait purposeful. He wore cargo shorts, a black T-shirt, slip-on sneakers in a red-and-black-checked pattern. His hair was a white thatch and he could have easily been mistaken for a surfer, though he had never learned to swim. He bought his coffee and the Iraqi clerk handed him his change with a soft thank-you, "*Shukran.*"

"*Shukran jazeelan,*" Rovanna said.

He walked a different route home, noting the Granite Hills emerging into the morning around him and the light poles of the high school stadium growing staunch against the sky. More closely he watched the windows and doors around him because Anbar teaches you to watch windows and doors. It was a weekday in El Cajon, east of bustling San Diego, and the neighborhood had that just-getting-started hum.

He came to his street, a narrow avenue of older homes, spiked fences, and grated windows. Some of the trees had grown large. The pit bull that lived in the yellow ranch house growled murderously at him and Rovanna took a dog biscuit from his pocket. He cocked his elbow and flicked it as he might a dart, the biscuit arching over the wrought-iron lances of the fence. The dog fell heavily upon it.

Rovanna lived in a small guesthouse behind a sagging larger home. He walked along the gravel driveway that led to his house, passing his small blue Ford, which was dirty and plastered with large sycamore leaves. He stopped and studied the front door and the windows on either side of it, their plastic blinds drawn. At the porch he turned left as always, rounded the side yard, passed the bedroom and the water meter and the sun-hungry hydrangeas, then went right along the padlocked toolshed and the sliding glass door with the flannel bedsheet nailed inside. He turned the corner and stepped back onto the porch.

Inside he patiently checked each room, then sat on the Salvation Army couch with the Louisville Slugger propped handle-up beside him. The bat was wooden, clean, and waxed, and it shone slightly in the poor light. His front door was half open and he drank his coffee while he watched the light grow through the screen door. It was winter and the towering sycamore in the yard between the two houses was nearly naked, only a few big leaves still hanging on to the branches on this cool morning. The space heater glowed in its corner. There were paperback thrillers in shelves along the walls and newspapers and magazines piled on the floor, all paled by dust.

Rovanna watched the man come around the side of the main house out front and start up the gravel drive toward him. He carried what looked like a medical kit and he moved as if he was familiar with the property. He wore a gray fedora and a navy suit buttoned over a white shirt and a light blue tie. Rovanna heard the gravel crunching, then the thud of shoes on his front porch. The man stood framed by the screen door and raised his fist to knock.

"That's exactly far enough," said Rovanna.

"I'm Stren, consulting physician for the Superior Court in San Diego. I hope you have a minute."

"For what?"

"I'm reviewing your Firearms Rights Restoration application and I have some questions."

"You shouldn't have taken away my guns to begin with."

"I didn't take away your guns. The court did."

"I didn't hurt anybody."

"Not seriously. Though quite frankly, the court was also concerned with you hurting yourself. The psychiatric hold was for your protection, as well as the safety of others."

"So do I get them back or not?"

"You need to answer some questions. May I come in?"

Rovanna took the bat by its handle and moved across the small room. He unlatched the screen door and backed away. The doctor stepped inside and removed his hat. Stren was a small man with a ruddy complexion, short black hair, and eyes the same blue as his necktie and pocket square. His eyeglass frames were black and oversize and from certain angles the lenses magnified his eyes, such as now when he looked at the bat. He was familiar but Rovanna couldn't place him. Stren sat on the plaid, misshapen couch and set his medical bag beside him, then his hat atop the bag. He crossed his legs and looked around the room as if he were confirming, not discovering. From a breast pocket of his suit coat Stren brought a trim black notebook and a shiny black pen, which he uncapped and readied. Rovanna sat across from the sofa in a white resin lawn chair. There was an oddly low coffee table between the two men, littered with fast-food wrappers and a half-full plastic gallon bottle of vodka.

"How have you been?" The doctor's voice was resonant in the small room. He offered a compulsory smile and studied Rovanna with lively blue eyes.

"I'm taking the meds. I'm on full disability. I eat well enough. I stay home mostly. I walk around the neighborhood for exercise."

"With the bat?"

"I always have the bat. It's not as good as a gun but it's something for protection."

Stren nodded and wrote something down. "Tramadol and Zoloft?"

"They're in the bathroom if you want to see."

"Please do bring them out."

In the bathroom Rovanna grabbed the two bottles in one hand and brought them back to the doctor and dropped them with a rattle onto the doctor's lap. Stren lifted them one at a time, positioned the labels, and wrote in his notebook. "How much alcohol do you drink?"

"Two vodkas per day. Maximum. It's not a problem."

"What size?"

"The medium-size cups with superheroes they give out at Mr. Burger. Lots of grapefruit juice and ice."

Stren looked intently at the vodka then at Rovanna. "Voices?" he asked.

Rovanna suddenly felt angry and ashamed. These emotions could hit fast and they almost always arrived together. The anger felt like a mug of scalding black ink upended inside his brainpan. The shame just made him want to become very small. "No."

"Dr. Webb at Naval said you were hearing voices from radios, addressing you and you only. When the radios were turned off."

"I don't have radios anymore."

"Dr. Webb said you considered these voices to be your friends. So, that is what I am asking about. Voices speaking only to you. 'Friends,' as you called them."

Rovanna took a deep breath and exhaled slowly. "I got rid of them. I took the radios to the Salvation Army. All of them. Look around."

But Stren only let his gaze wander Rovanna's face. "Or did you put them somewhere you could easily get to—say, in the garage, or in the toolshed out back?"

"I did not."

"May I look?"

"Fuck yourself. Okay. So they're in the shed. I locked them in there so I wouldn't have to hear them. Maybe you should take *them* away, too."

"Let's move on."

Rovanna felt his anger steal away, then circle back. "You say you work for the court? Where's your ID?"

Stren reached into his jacket pocket and removed an envelope with a county seal on it. Rovanna took and opened it. Inside was a sheet of San Diego Superior Court letterhead stating that the undersigned was in the employ of the court and as such would be granted all rights and courtesies due an officer of said court. The seal on the sheet was embossed. At the bottom were the scrawled signature of Hon. Betsy Lambeth and the neatly composed signature of Dr. Todd Stren.

"You can't be a real doctor with a signature like that," said Rovanna. His anger was abandoning him. He handed the envelope and letter to Stren, who slipped them back into his pocket. "Why would Dr. Webb tell you those personal things about me?"

"It's my job to recommend whether you get your guns back or not. I'm the consulting psychiatrist. Dr. Webb and I work together and share medical information. He's a big fan of yours, Lonnie. He believes in you."

At the sound of his name, Lonnie Rovanna felt the familiar knot form deep down in his throat. It was painful and he knew it well. It was the aggregate of all his sorrows and regrets, a lifetime of bad actions and misdeeds large and small—everything he wanted to be rid of, or at least forgiven for. All of these, compounded into a hard sedimentary lump. Shame. Even something so minor could summon these things out and bring them together: a kind word, a smile, a small gesture. He had no idea Dr. Webb was a big fan of his. He sat forward and rested his elbows on his knees and looked down at the beaten braided rug.

"Do you still hear demons in the walls?"

"Occasionally."

"Have you ever seen one?"

"No, sir."

"Do the men with similar faces still follow you when you walk your neighborhood?"

The knot in his throat was painful now so Rovanna raised his head and took another deep breath. Why had Webb revealed these things about him? Why had the good doctor sold him out to this soulless judicial bureaucrat? The Identical Men all had the same face and the same clothes and the only reason he knew that there were five of them was because he'd actually seen them together, trailing him down the streets and sidewalks, in the park, and even, occasionally, waiting for him right here in the living room of his own home. Five men. Identical clothing. Same face. The quints from Washington, D.C. Maybe Langley. Or maybe hell itself. "Yes," he said softly.

"Do you consider yourself dangerous to yourself or others?"

"Absolutely not."

"Do you consider yourself sane?"

"Pretty much so, yes."

"I see that your larynx has constricted. I know this can be painful. And there are tears ready to come out. Are you ashamed?"

"Yes." Rovanna lowered his head and dropped his gaze to the floor again. His tears came faster than he could wipe them away, hot drops born of the aching knot in his throat, tapping on the old rug and his canvas sneakers.

"Now, this is important, Lon. I need to ask you about the bodyguarding. I understand that early last year you were hired to protect Congressman Scott Freeman."

At the word *Freeman*, Rovanna shivered. After a long minute his tears finally stopped and the clench in his neck relaxed a little. Now his shame was beginning to leave him, too. Without anger and shame he felt abandoned and uncontrollable, like a boat without crew or rudder. "He hired me. I protected him a few times. I'm not licensed but I'm good at it because of my military training and experience. When my firearms were taken away I couldn't get more jobs with him. That's one of the main reasons I need to get my guns back."

"How many were confiscated?"

"Twelve."

"Of what type?"

"Handguns and legal assault-style semiautomatic rifles."

"For work as a bodyguard?"

"To protect Representative Freeman."

Stren sat forward. "When was the last time you saw him in person?"

"After the last big rain."

"Three weeks ago, then. Late January."

"He was at a rally in El Centro," said Rovanna.

"And you had no gun?"

"No. They'd been taken. But I wasn't hired to protect in El Centro."

"Yet you were present. Do you have a personal relationship with Representative Freeman?"

"No, only as a politician. I never talk to him except about security. His staff, I mean. Obviously. I talk to his staff."

The doctor was quiet for a while. When Rovanna looked at him Stren was neither writing nor looking at anything determinate, just gazing out through the screen door, his magnified pupils large and black, gorging on the new morning light.

"Then why did you go to the rally, if not to protect him?" asked Stren.

Now Rovanna was silent for a long moment. "I . . . I thought it would be good to be seen."

"By him?"

"Yes. As a future potential bodyguard. A bodyguard again, I mean."

Stren sat back. "I'm confused about something here, Lonnie. Scott Freeman does indeed represent your district, the fifty-fourth, which is the southeasternmost district in the state. He's a proponent of immigration reform, tougher gun-control laws, and decriminalizing marijuana. He's considered very liberal. Some say radical. His recent book has raised the ire of the right-wing, Tea Party types."

"So?"

"So, Dr. Webb tells me that you are precisely that type. You are vehemently against everything Scott Freeman stands for. Yet Mr. Freeman hires you to carry a gun, and stand close by and protect him."

Rovanna rubbed his hands together then set each one palm down on a knee. "I don't mix politics and business."

"Everyone does. Tell me, have you been hired to guard other politicians, or perhaps celebrities of another kind? Actors? Athletes?"

"No. Scott Freeman was my first job. But I know there are other people who need me. That's why I need my guns back. Personal security is a growing business. I want it to be my career. I want to get a letter of recommendation from him someday. So I can protect other people."

Stren looked at Rovanna, then wrote something down and underlined it. "Have you ever dreamed of using one of your guns to save the life of Representative Freeman?"

A ripple of embarrassment went through Rovanna, then indignation. He looked through the screen door to the sycamore tree. A big leaf fell. It came down faster than Rovanna expected it would, an old leaf, folded in, hugging itself on the way down. "No one can control their dreams."

"Have you ever imagined using a gun on him?"

"I've imagined worse things than that. But you can't control your imagination either."

"Have you ever just *wanted* to shoot him, Lon?"

"I really don't like you using my first name. It's for friends and you're no friend of mine."

"Isn't Representative Freeman due to make a public appearance in the near future?"

"Later this month. A Sunday. He's signing autographs at the Alternative Book Fair in San Diego."

Stren pursed his lips and nodded curtly, then he flipped his notebook shut and capped the pen and returned them both to his coat pocket. He leaned elbows to knees and looked at Rovanna. "Thank you for your time and honesty. I'll be writing my letter of recommendation later today. Of course, the final decision will be left to one of the judges and this could take some time. The courts are terribly backed up at the superior level."

"What are you going to say?"

"I haven't decided. But, in the meantime . . ."

The doctor straightened, set his hat on his head, tilted it back at a casual angle, then brought his black leather medical bag to his lap and opened it. He held out the sides with both hands and stared down into it for a long moment, then reached in. Rovanna expected a syringe and vial, or maybe a sample packet for a new prescription drug, or maybe a form to sign. Or one of the dread orbitoclasts used in lobotomies. He even imagined a cobra, because, just as he had said, he could not control his imagination, and a cobra had just crawled into his mind.

Instead Stren pulled a firearm from the bag, then set the bag aside. He balanced the gun in his small hands, framing it like a salesman for Rovanna to behold. It looked like a common, medium-size, semiautomatic handgun, although Rovanna had never seen one exactly like it. The finish was stainless and the grips were checked black polymer, and it had a slightly plump and heavy look.

"What is it?"

"The Love Thirty-two."

"Love?"

"The manufacturer was the old Orange County outfit, Pace Arms."

"I never heard of them."

"Saturday night specials. Pace Arms was run out of business not long ago."

"Why call it Love?"

"Something to do with history." Stren reached into the bag and pulled out a sound suppressor, which he screwed onto the end of the barrel. Then he pointed the barrel down and with his left thumb and forefinger depressed two buttons on either side of the frame, near the back end of the weapon. Out popped two short rods connected by an end piece. The doctor then extended the assembly, like the telescoping handle on a piece of luggage. Rovanna heard it lock into place. A skeleton butt, he thought, to brace in the crook of your elbow when firing. Truthfully, it seemed more like a gimmick than something you'd need.

"It's fully automatic," said Stren.

Not a gimmick at all then, thought Rovanna. The doctor pulled a very long magazine from his bag, and Rovanna could see the glimmer of the brass and copper within until Stren pushed it up into the handle of the gun. It snapped into place with a sharp click. The bottom half of the magazine protruded from the handle in a gently lethal curve.

"Thirty-two caliber ACP," said the doctor. "Fifty rounds in one five-second burst. Or, several shorter bursts. Or, you can choose semi and just squeeze them off one at a time. Subsonic, of course, and practically silent. The casings hitting the floor make as much noise as the gun."

Stren took his sky blue pocket square and wiped down the weapon. He ejected the magazine and wiped this also. When the Love 32 was whole again, he dabbed away once more with the silk square then set the gun on the couch. From his bag he took a box of ammunition and a spare magazine and put them beside the gun. He pushed the square back into his coat pocket, zipped shut the doctor's bag and stood.

"I'll recommend that your constitutional rights be restored," he said. "Though quite honestly I don't think your chances are good. It will take time for the court to decide. There is nothing wrong with you, Lonnie. Sometimes friends are all we have. And voices speak to all of us at different times. Listen to them and do what you think is right. As a human being you are free to decide. Anyone who tells you differently is trying to enslave you. In the meantime use this gift to protect yourself and those around you and to advance the ideals you believe in. I cannot force you to accept this gift. You are free to reject it at any time."

Rovanna watched Stren walk back down the gravel drive. The doctor turned and tipped his hat, then disappeared around the main house. The lump in Rovanna's throat had returned, and he realized how badly he had misjudged this man. He sat on the plaid couch and looked down at the Love 32 for a long while before picking it up.

2

Charlie Hood's first big undercover assignment began with a nine-teen-year-old girl living in a small town in Russell County, Missouri. Her name was Mary Kate Boyle and she had first told her disturbing story over the phone to a girlfriend recently moved to Los Angeles, who happened to have just read a piece in the *Los Angeles Times Magazine* about a cool G-man.

The G-man was the Special Agent in Charge of the Bureau of Alcohol, Tobacco Firearms and Exlplosives in Los Angeles, and Mary Kate took a very long Trailways journey to come find him. In conversation Mary Kate got the *A*, *T*, and *F* correct but kept getting the order wrong, calling the bureau FAT. It was her first time away from her little piece of Missouri.

The SAC heard her out before handing her down the line to an ATF-led task force working guns along the Mexico border. She told of four men—three of them Russell County deputies—who were stealing confiscated evidence and selling it. Mostly guns and drugs. Of course any cash they just put in their pockets. This had been going on for over a year. Three of them were headed to California to do some business, hoping to find some drug cartel "beaners" with money to spend. The city of El Central was the place to be, they had told her. They wanted to find straw buyers. Cash, cash, and more cash, all that profit from the drugs the cartels sold. Plus one of the deputies had a friend in El Central with a restaurant that had the best burritos in the world. So they could eat there for cheap. You know how cops are. Oops.

All of this she had overheard, in pieces, during the last months of her senior year of high school. Last week she had been assaulted by one of those men, beaten sharply, and thrown out of his double-wide. His name was Lyle Scully, Skull for short, the leader. Now here in the ATF field office in Buenavista she sat, skinny, fair, and freckled. Mary Kate had an eye swollen up the color of a plum and a deep continuous split in both lips, but still she talked more than a little.

"And I don't think too high of that kind of treatment. Skull says I was born trash and will stay trash and it may be true. That sure didn't stop him making me pregnant, now, did it? God knows it took him long enough and I thought maybe a ring would come attached. It didn't. His divorce is long finalized. So I got the procedure. And now I'm here in California and that's behind me and I'm not going back. Never. Except maybe to get some things. I always wanted to rent one of them U-Haul trucks and just drive away from Russell County. I like the ones with the palm trees and waterskiers on the side. I'm going to be an actor, model, or nurse, whichever happens first. I told all this to your boss up in L.A. and he told me you're the people who can get things done down here."

Hood kept notes but mostly he just listened. He was a Los Angeles County sheriff deputy assigned to the ATF Operation Blowdown task force. The people in this room were part of his Achilles team, Mary Kate notwithstanding. Fourth year now for Hood. He thought of ATF not so much as Alcohol, Tobacco and Firearms, but as GDT—Guns, Dust and Treachery. ATF was chronically understaffed and the case-load was heavy, but scandal had further lowered the bureau in the public eye and sent its supporters in high places running. Certain ATF supervisors had implemented some bad ideas in an operation dubbed Fast and Furious and gotten bad results. Even before this calamity, ATF had been an easy political target but now it seemed nearly friendless. Hood had always thought that, just for starters, ATF had it rough because most Americans *liked* alcohol, tobacco, and firearms—and disliked regulation. Hence the agency was spooked and defensive. He chuckled when Mary Kate called it FAT. But Hood enjoyed the work because there was action, and he felt it was necessary work. Hood wanted to be necessary. He was a Bakersfield boy and he had served in Iraq, Anbar Province. He was thirty-four, tall and loose, with an open face and strong eyes.

"El Centro?" asked Janet Bly. Janet had been the senior agent of this Achilles team and still seemed to think of herself as such. Last month ATF had brought in a more senior agent, Dale Yorth, who now sat at the head of the table with an eager look on his face. He'd come in from Miami and the team jury on him was still out.

"Yep. Skull said El Central, pretty sure." Mary Kate dabbed her lips with a tissue.

Hood saw the still unhealed split and felt bad but he also thought that a beating and an abortion might in the long run be a fair trade for escaping a life tied to Lyle Scully. The womenfolk in her part of the world tended to bear the brunt of things, or so he'd read and seen in movies. But Mary Kate would have to stay escaped, of course. Would have to *want* to stay escaped. People had surprising needs and default settings.

"What happened to the fourth guy?" asked Bly.

"Went missing three months back. Not a trace. Disappearo."

"Do you know what contraband they have to sell?" Yorth asked.

"Not exactly. But there's plenty of crank since a lot of it's cooked up right there in Russell County. It's high-grade stuff so far as that kinda thing goes. I tried it once and didn't like it. Then there's always plenty of bud to be smoked. Heroin's still pretty popular but the pharmaceuticals are taking it over. Two guys broke into like four Jefferson pharmacies in one weekend, helped themselves, but the state police sent the videos around and guess what? The crooks were from our own neck of the woods. So the Russell County boys busted their butts. Skull and his team grabbed most of the evidence when no one was looking and him and his crew sold almost all of it. Right out of Skull's truck, he said, like a roach coach for drugs. Also I know they got lots of guns. Most of them were stored in the property room, some for years. I know this from Skull. And a course they're supposed to destroy the guns once the trial's over but Skull worked it so the paperwork for destroyal got sent but he took the guns himself. Don't ask me what kind or how many. Except once we all went out the woods so they could try out this new gun they got, and it was a big honkin' thing that had legs on one end and a big round doughnutlike thing on the top. Loud. And heavy, even for Skull who is approximately two hundred pounds of solid muscle. He laid on the ground and fired. Then he got up and braced it on his hip and had to put some back into it. Shot up a bunch of watermelons. I don't like guns any more than I like crank, though I don't see any harm in putting food on a table, which a course ain't what a gun like that gets used for."

"Legs on the end?" asked Hood. "A bipod?"

"Yeah, the far end, like two legs. For when he laid down and shot."

"And a black doughnut? Do you mean a drum attached on top, flat to the frame of the gun?"

"That's what I mean, valentine." She smiled, then winced and brought the tissue back to her mouth. "Ouch. That's what I get for funnin'. Story of my life."

He smiled back and shook his head. And thought, *An old Lewis Gun?* Not exactly state-of-the-art weaponry, though it was a bruiser. It was the only machine gun that he could think of with an ammo pan on top. Belgian. It was a popular machine gun in World War I, and into World War II, but they hadn't made one in seventy-something years. Of course, if Pace Arms could make a thousand Love 32s in Orange County, anything could happen. He'd seen pictures of the Lewis Mark I, and a total of one in the flesh, in his entire life.

"Where do you think they'll go when they get here?" asked Velasquez. He was the youngest of this team and the only one with a master's degree, which was in economics.

"To a motel I guess," said Mary Kate Boyle.

"And to get the best burritos in the world," said Hood.

Yorth leaned back and set his hands behind his head. He was a big man with short yellow hair that was dark at the roots. "You know the name of the restaurant?"

"I'da told you if I did. How many burrito restaurants can there be in El Central?"

"Probably twenty Mexican restaurants," said Hood. "That's just a guess."

"Call Skull and ask him which restaurant, Mary Kate," said Yorth.

Hood saw the tick of worry cross Mary Kate Boyle's face.

Janet Bly rolled her eyes and groaned.

Velasquez tapped his fingers on the tabletop.

"Why not?" asked Yorth. "Call him on your cell and tell him things are just fine in here in Russell County but you miss him. You just want to talk. Hoping you're okay, Skull. Just reach out. Get him talking to you. That's all."

"I ain't doing that."

"If you want Lyle locked away safe in prison, you better consider it. Because if you don't cooperate with us, our chances of putting these boys away go way, way down."

"I still ain't calling him."

Yorth stared at her. "What about testifying in court? You told the SAC in L.A. you'd do that."

"Testifying is one thing, but sneaking up on a man you're done with is something else."

"You started sneaking when you bought that Trailways ticket, Mary Kate."

Mary Kate colored and looked down for a moment and took a deep breath. When she looked up again, she had sharp anger in her eyes. "That isn't sneaking. I never asked Skull to steal. I told him not to. I didn't ask him to go bragging on and on about it. And I didn't ask to go out to the woods to shoot that big old machine gun. And I didn't ask—"

"For the cool stuff he bought you with money you knew he'd stolen," said Yorth.

"Knock it off, Dale," said Bly.

Mary Kate stood and slung her bag over her shoulder. Hood and Velasquez stood, too.

"There wasn't that much cool stuff involved," Mary Kate said. "I took a bus here to help and you call me a whore. You're as big an asshole as Skull ever was."

"Sit down," said Yorth. "I was out of line."

"I'm outta here and you can't stop me." She looked at each of the other three agents in the room. "You, you, and you got my number." Then she aimed her battered face down on Yorth. "You don't."

"Way to handle a cooperative informant," said Bly.

Yorth shrugged. "You've got her number."

"Christ, Dale, put her back with *him*? She should stay as far away from that guy as possible. Look what he did to her."

"Then we have a difference of opinion. I cleared the idea with L.A. Now, here's what these heroes look like." Yorth handed out photo prints and bios of the cops, and mug shots and a criminal record of the third man. "I've sent these to your phones."

Hood squared his sheets and looked through them. Two pictures of each bad guy per page, along with brief descriptions. The great leader, Lyle Scully, two hundred pounds of solid woman-beating muscle, had a shaven head and a goatee, and was a thirty-year-old sergeant-detective. Sgt. Brock Peltz was fifty-one and heavy. Clint Wampler looked chimplike, with big ears and small eyes and an early Beatles pageboy. Hood thought of his own pronounced ears. Clint was twenty-seven and unemployed, with convictions for driving under the influence, aggravated assault, and burglary. He'd done a year. Hood also saw that nineteen-year-old Clint Wampler had been questioned in the torching of a Russell County post office on April 19 of 2005. The FBI had charged two known associates but not Wampler. "That was the ten-year anniversary of Oklahoma City," said Hood. "When Wampler's buddies torched the post office in Russell County."

"I see he's got like-minded friends all over the country," said Bly. "Militiamen in Montana, the Minutemen here on the border, and the good old Aryan Nation boys out in Idaho. Even the Covert Group— the old guys who wanted to poison a small town with ricin. Apparently he's been in touch with them, too."

Yorth groaned. "But not with Islamic extremists? They should throw in together and share expenses. Islamamerica, how's that sound?"

"That's ridiculous," said Bly, then she muttered, "least I hope it is."

This got a brief laugh. In the ensuing near silence the agents pored over the images. Hood heard the central heat come on. Two or three times a year Buenavista was the hottest place in the nation, but in February the little border town could get cold.

"So then," said Yorth. "Where do we find Skull and his merry band?"

"Maybe through an informant we *haven't* run off," said Bly.

"I hear you, Janet," said Yorth. "I hear you, I hear you."

"The Palomino Club in El Centro," said Velasquez. "It's popular with narcos and straw buyers. So are the El Pueblo Restaurant and the Fuzzy Dice bar."

"There's the Monterey Restaurant on Main Avenue," said Hood. "They have a sign out front that says something about their burritos. 'Best in the west,' or 'world's best' or something like that."

Yorth smiled. "Has ATF ever gotten anything that easy?"

"L.A. should have the phone-tap warrant by this afternoon," said Bly. "I'll badger them, as I'm so good at doing. Then there's the gun stores. These guys might just watch the customers come and go, pick out a likely buyer, and make an approach. They'll want to get in and out and back home to their families and illustrious careers."

"Charlie Diamonds should be that buyer," said Hood. "He's been in all those clubs and restaurants and stores, and others. He's made some small legal buys. So now he needs a machine gun. And more. He's a familiar face and a fat wallet."

Bly nodded. "I like that idea."

"I do, too," said Velasquez.

Yorth locked his hands together behind his head again. "Ready to fly, Charlie?"

Hood smiled and the diamonds of his left canine caught the light.

3

Hood drove to the Monterey Restaurant in El Centro, just under an hour from Buenavista. The sun-blasted sign had faded from yellow to a kind of opaque cream and the lettering from black to pale gray, but BEST BURRITOS IN THE WORLD was still visible. He used the drive-through and parked in the shade facing the Monterey, the windows of his Charger down. Hood was a muscle-car guy and he liked it that ATF had a deal with Chrysler. The Charger had civie plates and black paint and plenty of get-up-and-go, though the Imperial County sun had no trouble finding it.

In the rearview he checked his diamonds. Five. They shined wicked cool and perfect for an arms dealer. Two months ago when they were installed, Hood was surprised by how different he felt: piratical, subversive, and an odd combination of marked and free. For those first two weeks his tongue had found the hard little chips every waking minute, reminding him of his new self. They were of course removable by a dentist.

He had also gotten on loan from ATF a diamond-studded Rolex. And grown his hair long, which added to his sense of separation and newness. He wore suits in pale shades, tailored to obscure the holster and weapon at the small of his back and his ankle gun. He wore striking shoes, often two-tone. Over the weeks it had become easier and easier to be Charlie Hooper—one dapper, unmistakable, and certainly unorthodox businessman. Hood was warming up to the tooth bling and the hair, which was almost to his shirt collar.

Using the rearview mirror again, Hood tilted his chin down and ran his hand under his forelock and lifted the hair. He studied the slender knife scar. It was nearly six inches long and nearly perfectly aligned with his hairline. Because it had been treated promptly by good doctors and sutured from the inside, the scar remained low profile, understated. His new long hair easily covered it. It still itched occasionally. When the cut was first made, it had bled terrifically, just as it was intended to, allowing a bad man to get away. Veracruz, Mexico, *M. Doblado* street. Four months ago. *I'll get back to you on this one, Mike*, thought Hood. *I will get back to you.*

Hood enjoyed his lunch. He didn't find the Missourians at the Monterey, but the burrito rocked.

He went down the street to Buster's Last Stand and talked to Buster about purchasing twenty-thousand rounds of .40 caliber. He balked at the price and wondered out loud why .40 caliber had gotten so popular lately.

"Latest answer to the same old question, Hooper," boomed Buster. "Stopping power and how many cartridges you can fit in a magazine."

Hood gave him a dismissive look. "Buster, you know I buy and sell. I've got a collector back in Virginia, licensed for automatics. Wants old machine guns like his great granddaddy might have used in a war—full size, not the subs. Operational, not replicas. Something with the smell of history still in the barrel."

"We don't do much full-auto here. I'll keep my eyes open, though. Try Crossroads of the West. It's in Texas this month."

"Sure. Good show."

"Always a big 'un."

Hood gave the man a card with "Charles Hooper/Firearms/New and Collectible/Ammo/Reloading/Accessories/Licensed" embossed on it and a phone number and website address handwritten on the back. No federal firearms license number was on it. "This is just in case you lost the last one. Let me know if you find some good old machine guns."

"Hooper. I can come off that price a little on the ammo. Five percent. Best and final. You pick it up here you'll save a fortune in shipping."

Hood gave the man a disappointed smile and walked out.

Three more gun stores, no Skull. He went to Walmart and bought Beth a bottle of her favorite wine, the best box of chocolates he could find, and a flagrantly sentimental card. He had been trying extra hard to please her these last few months yet he'd come to feel obvious and exposed, like a magician who'd revealed a trick and the trick would no longer work. He knew she felt the same. Walking back to his car he saw the sun setting on this late winter day and felt a deeper chill settling in.

Hood took a seat at the Palomino Club, well drinks half price. He was apparently the first customer of the evening. He set his hat crownside down on the stool beside him and gave the bartender a brief smile. She was a hard-faced Latina in a black-sequined Palomino Club tank top, a brief skirt, ankle-high boots. "Suzy" with a z and a y, said her nameplate.

Hood nursed a beer and talked to Suzy about the economy. El Centro had been hard hit and had one of the highest unemployment rates in the nation. Six years ago she'd been selling real estate, she told him. Those were the days, no credit/no problem, she was too busy selling homes to even take a vacation. Then all of a sudden those days were gone. There were tracts of new homes not getting sold, other tracts not even getting finished. Now they were nothing but brandnew ghost towns, tumbleweeds blowing down the dirt streets, security guards trying to keep out the vandals, coyotes running through in packs like wolves.

Suzy had a smoky voice, like another Suzanne whom Hood had once known. And high cheekbones and dark eyes, like hers. In the dusky light of the nightclub Suzanne Jones wasn't hard to imagine.

Hood let his memory drift across time. It glided easily, a skiff on a glassy bay. Five years ago, he thought. *Then all of a sudden those days were gone.*

Suzy went quiet and looked hard at him. "What do you do?"

"I buy and sell vintage cars, mostly American made. And other things that people want."

"Such as?"

"I do some firearms. Licensed stuff, all legit. Nothing goes south. It started as a hobby, actually."

"Hmmm." She lifted a tumbler of what looked like sparkling water, and looked over the top of the glass at him. "I've got a colorful little three-eighty. County wouldn't give me a permit to carry, but it's in my purse and I don't care who knows. I walk out of here at night with tip money, it makes me feel better."

"Let's hope you never have to use it."

"You don't sound like a gun dealer."

"What's a gun dealer sound like?"

"Well, he'd be curious what make and model I chose."

"Suzy, *colorful* was kind of a giveaway. How about a Sig P two-thirty-eight? With the rainbow titanium finish. That's the one the Gun Bin puts in their front window, with the purses and boots and accessories. Chances are, you bought it there."

She smiled again and this softened her face and seemed to bring light into it. "Okay. So you're a dealer. Another beer?"

"Next time."

She swept away his empty glass and dunked it into the rinse water. Hood stood and counted out his money, then pulled his phone off his belt and leaned closer to her. "These three gentlemen should be here in El Centro right about now. I'd appreciate a call."

Hood handed her the phone and she scrolled through the six shots. He set a Charlie Hooper card on the bar.

She looked past the phone at him. "I thought you were a cop. I shouldn't have told you about my gun."

"Your secret is safe with me, Suzy. If and when you'd like to purchase another sidearm, let me help. You might want real stopping
power someday."

She gave back the phone and glanced at the card. "I've *got* real
stopping power when I'm not slinging drinks and wearing whore's
clothes."

"I can see that."

"If they come in, I'll call. *Charlie Hooper.* It doesn't say anything
on your card about vintage cars."

Hood put a finger to his lips, then set the gambler on his head.

She gave him a minor smile, then walked away, waving over one
shoulder. Suzanne Jones, he thought, walking across the dining room
of her ranch house, Valley Center, California, August 2008.

Hood was made pensive with this, but the Fuzzy Dice was loud and
cheerful with a younger clientele, a mix of Anglo and Latino and even
a group of Asians in a booth. Some jocks from San Diego State stood
at the bar in their Aztec clothing. There was gangsta rap and *banda*
on the jukebox and a small dance floor crowded with intimate couples. Hood smelled the perfumes and colognes and the hair products
and the high-pitched smell of alcohol. He ordered a beer and sat at
the far end of the bar, near the bins of cocktail garnishes and napkins.

Just after eight o'clock the three men from Russell County walked
in, the beefy Peltz in the lead, followed by thin Clint Wampler. Next
came Skull, head shiny and held high, eyes hard. Last came El Centro
businessman Israel Castro, a man well-known to Hood.

There was a mirror behind the bar. In it Hood watched as two
young couples stood in unison when the Castro party approached
their table, swiftly gathering up their drinks to abandon ship. Israel
smiled and shook hands with one of the men.

The last time Hood had seen Castro was four years ago, in the
dead of night, the rain pouring down on a little border town called

Jacumba. Hood had caught a bullet in his back that night. He remembered the cold, mule kick of it knocking him into the mud as it went through him. He'd lost consciousness believing he was dying.

But I'm alive, he thought. I am not dead. Neither is the past: It's swarming all around me.

When Castro went into the restroom, Hood walked out of the Fuzzy Dice and got into his car. He set his hat on the passenger seat, then rolled down the windows and called Yorth. An hour later the four men came out. Castro got into a silver Ford Flex with dealer tags and the three others boarded a red Jeep Commander with Missouri plates. Wampler drove. Hood followed them three cars back to the Pueblo Lodge on the east side of town. It was an older motel with freestanding concrete-block casitas painted pumpkin orange and a sign out front with an arrow that lit up one bulb at a time, drawing customers in. The Commander swung in beside a white F-150, raised with big tires. Hood continued past the entrance and headed for home.

4

Awaiting his grand inquisitor, Deputy Bradley Jones slouched in a conference room chair, legs crossed and boots on the table beside his hat, rounding off his snagged left thumbnail with a pocketknife. He was twenty-two years old, clean-cut and good looking, a second-year patrolman. He had been a rising star with the L.A. County Sheriff's Department but was now a falling one, suspected of involvement in the L.A. drug trade, and more. By all signs that he could gather, LASD was going to eat him alive and enjoy doing it.

Lieutenant Jim Warren, Internal Criminal Investigations Bureau, came through the door, set a laptop on the table, and sat across from the young deputy. He wore pressed jeans and black wingtips and a crisp white shirt. His face was craggy and brown and his hair was a gray buzz cut. Bradley knew that the feared Warren came from a checkered background: Decades ago he had founded the Renegades, a gang of mostly white deputies, some of whom did some bad things to people of color. Warren had turned them over to Internal Affairs, but caught the brunt of the backlash and the hostility of his own department. Years later he became an Internal Affairs crusader, and Bradley figured it was his atonement. Bradley put him at seventy if a day and wondered why he hadn't retired over a decade ago as most cops would have. How much did atonement did Warren need?

"Feet on the floor, son."

"Sir."

Bradley put his feet down and Jim Warren squared the laptop and opened it. "Tell me about Carlos Herredia."

"Not again."

"Why not again?"

"You think if you make me repeat myself enough times I'll finally say what you want to hear."

"Just once more, Bradley. I'll listen better this time."

Bradley spun through Carlos Herredia's well-known bio: nicknamed El Tigre, head of the North Baja Cartel, fingers deep in L.A. drug distribution through Eme and the Florencia gangsters. Mota, junk, meth, coke, murder, kidnapping, extortion.

"And enemy of the Gulf Cartel," said Warren. "Don't forget that."

"What's left of the Gulf Cartel. I'll tell you this one more time—I've never favored Herredia's cutthroats in L.A. over the Gulf's cutthroats in L.A. The way I do things here is simple, sir: A gangsta is a creep is a punk is a dirtball. They're all the same. So I don't play favorites on patrol. And I resent you self-righteous dinosaurs making me out to be a bad guy. Of course I don't mean you, personally, Lieutenant Warren. Personally, I respect and like you."

"My lucky day."

Bradley folded the blade down and slipped the knife back into his pocket. He gave Warren a flat glance then focused on the repaired thumbnail.

"I've got sworn testimony against you, Brad. Octavio Leyal knows Herredia's organization from the inside. He says Herredia pays you to leave his L.A. distributors alone and focus on the Maras and Eighteenth Street, who are teamed up with the Gulf. He says you're a courier for the cash runs south, taking Herredia's money back to him. He says he's seen you in Baja, at one of Herredia's compounds known as El Dorado. Quite a place, according to Leyal."

"I know, sir. But Leyal is a low-level criminal and a liar. You want to believe a prison snitch over a second-year deputy? When did you sell your soul?"

"Easy now."

"There's nothing *easy* about this. Can't you just figure out what you're doing, then do it?"

"We're close. I do appreciate your cooperation."

"You want me to just walk away from the job? Well, I can't, because I have a pregnant wife and a son I'd like to feed. Oh, I made your watchers weeks ago. The new ones, the two men so bland looking I'm not supposed to know they're following me."

Warren looked over the screen at Jones and shrugged, then tapped something on the keyboard. "You're friendly with Eme and Florencia people here in L.A. Such as Rocky Carrasco. Whose son you rescued from kidnappers on your first day as a patrol deputy."

"I should *apologize* for that?"

Warren studied him. "You knew exactly when and where Herredia's men would try to buy a hundred machine pistols up in Lancaster. The Love Thirty-twos. One of the runners being Octavio Leyal."

"I was working an informant, a damned good one. All of it came from him."

"But you could never deliver your informant to us for questioning."

"He did what people under pressure do, Jim. He vanished. I've told you a hundred times, too."

Warren tapped the keyboard again. "Tell me about those two weeks you took off last October. Four months ago."

Bradley sighed and picked up his hat and slouched back down into the chair. The hat was the Corazón Espinado, a shantung Panama designed by Carlos Santana. His wife had given it to him. Bradley loved the graphic of the guitar stabbing through a human heart and considered the ninety-five-dollar cost a bargain. "One last time? I took Erin to Mexico. She was pregnant and exhausted from work and we wanted to relax. You've seen my passport with the customs stamps on it, so you know I'm telling the truth."

"You fished for tarpon and snorkeled."

Bradley looked at Warren for a long beat, then turned his attention to the hat in his hands. Finally he nodded and closed his eyes. Think up something pleasant, he thought. He imagined Erin, pregnant with his son and lovely. He imagined her onstage, belting one out. He imagined his home in Valley Center, the barn and the big oak tree. He imagined Carlos Herredia's compound, El Dorado, and its sprawling adobe house and casitas, and the pool that shimmered with cool salt water, and the golf course upon which Herredia happily cheated, and the thoroughbreds and the food and wine and the time Herredia had thrown Bradley's gift—an expensive fishing reel—into the air and blown it to bits with one round from a .50 caliber Desert Eagle handgun.

"Snorkeling and tarpon fishing in the Yucatán. You live large, Bradley. Don't you?"

"You exhaust my soul."

"Explain your riches."

"My mother left me a bundle and my wife is a popular performer. You know these things. I've told you. You've seen my tax returns—good enough for the IRS, I might add. If you don't believe my answers, make up some of your own."

"You know, Bradley, when IA kicked this investigation up to me, two months ago, I was pulling for you. I'd followed your ups and downs. I figured you were a spirited deputy, young and lucky. But the more I talk to you and the people around you, the more I think you're in it up to your eyes. Carrasco and Florencia, the North Baja Cartel. Your arrest and interview reports—ninety percent of your narcotics contacts comes from Mara Salvatrucha and Eighteenth Street, both lined up with the Gulf Cartel. Then suddenly you vanish for two weeks to the Yucatán with two more of my deputies, on a so-called fishing trip, and who dies in a gun battle five miles from where you're fishing? Benjamin Armenta, head of the Gulf Cartel and Herredia's biggest rival. All three of you deputies come home sick and beat up. You've got two teeth missing and your lips are split open, Cleary's got a broken nose and wrist. Vega has an infected arm and a thousand mosquito bites and she comes down with dysentery within the week.

Want to tell me about the great tarpon hunt again? Maybe add some truth?"

Bradley put his feet back up on the table. It disturbed him that in the last month or so Warren was apparently getting new and better information. Where? His friends, fellow deputies Caroline Vega and Jack Cleary, were also being questioned by the Criminal Investigation Bureau, and he wondered now if one or both of them might have finally made a mistake, or cracked. The truth was that none of the deputies had even seen a tarpon. For Bradley, those two weeks had been the longest and most miserable of his life, although he had finally gotten the only thing he wanted: Erin, freed from Benjamin Armenta, her abductor. Caroline and Cleary had gotten what they wanted too—some dark action and lots of cash.

Bradley looked at his shoes on the table. Ankle-high boots actually, expensive ones. Worry ate at him. Octavio was bad enough, but what if Caroline and Cleary were having trouble keeping their stories straight? Or what if Rocky was saving his ass by singing? Then there was another, far worse scenario, one he was almost afraid to consider: Charlie Hood talking his crazy brains out to CIB. Hood had also been a participant in the great tarpon hunt. But these days he reported to ATF, not LASD, and he'd stayed down in Mexico for another week, then quietly returned stateside to continue his furtive ATF work along the border. Which had left him off the sheriff's department's radar. Or was he? If Warren found out that Hood had been in Yucatán, then they were all dead in the water because Hood wouldn't lie. Hood was too square to lie. Hood had the goods on him in more ways than one. Hood was a self-righteous pain in the ass. If Hood was talking to Warren, Bradley knew he would fall hard and far.

So he told Warren again about the four of them fishing the Bacalar Lagoon, described the Hotel Laguna where they stayed and the Panga they rented and the fishing they did. Told him about the fight that he and Cleary got into with a half dozen very rough local fishermen who didn't care for gringo tourists fishing in their flats. He again described the food and the rooms, and the weather, and plenty of details, right down to which songs Erin played on a cheap guitar in a small cantina one night. And told again the story of dropping his camera into the dark warm water on the third day, losing probably fifty pictures that would have established his story better than did the Hotel Laguna owner who, speaking on a poor long-distance connection, was only able to loosely corroborate it.

"Why didn't Cleary or Vega bring a camera?"

"I told them not to because mine was waterproof."

"If it was waterproof, why didn't you jump in after it?"

"Did. Failed. Deep."

Warren was leaning against the wall now, arms crossed, listening. For a long moment he seemed distracted, then he came back, pushed away, sat back down. He looked unamused. He tapped away on the laptop, then turned the computer to face Bradley. Bradley saw the image of his mother, Suzanne, on the screen, an enlarged version of the photo on her Los Angeles Unified School District employee badge.

"It's been five years since she died," said Warren.

"I know how long it's been."

"You must miss her."

Bradley looked at him. "You have deep insight."

"My mother died when I was young."

"You told me that."

"Bradley, did Suzanne Jones really believe she was a direct descendant of Joaquin Murrieta? Or was that more of a marketing decision? Or maybe a delusion?"

"Marketing."

He looked at the picture of his mother for a long beat. Then he conjured the first time he had seen the head of El Famoso, Joaquin Murrieta, severed and preserved in a glass jar, hidden in their Valley Center barn. No delusion. He'd trembled.

"Marketing," Bradley said again.

Warren took back the computer and typed some keys and turned it around again for Bradley to see. Now his mother shared the screen with her alter ego, Allison Murrieta. Allison wore a black wig over Suzanne's wavy brown hair, and a black satin mask with a crystal fastened to the cheek. She held a small derringer up to her lips, as if blowing off the smoke. Bradley stared at the image. The picture was a hit during her crazy summer of '08. It was everywhere you looked. That was the summer that Allison held up fast-food places and boosted expensive cars and donated bags of cash to her favorite charities, posing mid-robbery for cell-phone photos from bystanders. The summer she'd run wild with Los Angeles Sheriff's Deputy Charlie Hood. The summer she'd died. Bradley hadn't looked at this particular picture in a long while. His mother and Allison Murrieta. Very different. But the same. Strange, he thought, for maybe the thousandth time, that in all of L.A., out of the ten million people in the county, not to mention the rest of Southern California, only one other person had seen the pictures of Allison and recognized her for who she really was. Charlie Hood.

"Do you believe you're related to an infamous outlaw? Do you feel that your blood is calling you into a life of crime? That you're battling your genetic destiny?"

"Don't be ridiculous, sir."

"Deon Miller's murder is still unsolved," said Warren. "And the witness description of the shooter matches you pretty damned well."

"It matches a million other young men in L.A., too," said Bradley. Miller was the young gangsta who'd shot down Allison Murrieta, believing he'd get a reward. Shotgunning Deon Miller had given Bradley genuine satisfaction, but it couldn't touch the loss of his mother.

"Bradley, I'm going to let you help this department. As of tomorrow you're assigned to the STAR Unit."

"No. I can't do the STAR Unit."

"You will do it or resign."

"Lieutenant, this assignment is worse than a demotion. It's everything I don't want to do."

"Report to Sergeant Gail Padilla in the morning up in Lancaster.

She'll be your supervisor. How bad can it be, Jones? You go out to the schools, you tell the kids to stay off dope and away from gangs. They look up to you. You tell them a story or two. Show them your side-arm. Show them what good people we sheriffs are. You hardly break a sweat. What could be easier?"

Warren turned the computer back, pushed some buttons, closed the lid. "We're going to do this one more time, Jones. But we'll have a polygraph examiner ask the questions. I'll let you know when."

He stood up and walked out. It was dark already and the night-shift deputies were rolling into the employee parking area in their pickups and Mustangs and Camaros and SUVs. He got into his Porsche Cayenne Turbo and gunned it when he hit the avenue.

His hands were tight to the wheel. His shirt billowed in the blast through the open windows and when the winter air had cooled his skin and calmed, if only a little, his riotous heart, Bradley pressed the back of his head into the rest and drove fast.

Three hours home in the evening traffic. And another hour forty to Erin, heavy with his child. Erin, fire of his life, his sin and soul.

5

Hood slowly climbed the dirt road to his Buenavista home. A sliver of moon faced him through the windshield and the serrated tops of the Devil's Claws reached into the black sky. The stars were radiant. He heard the gravel hitting the undercarriage of his car and when he topped the rise he saw that two of his three housemates were home tonight: Erin's SUV and Gabriel Reyes's pickup truck both sat in the dusty vapor lights. Beth would be home from her nightshift in the Imperial Mercy ER soon, unless catastrophe came knocking late as it often did.

Hood took his war bag and purchases and walked toward the stout adobe home. The night was cold by now and smoke rose from the chimney. Gabriel opened the door and two black mongrels heaved out.

"Bradley's on his way."

"This is twice in one week."

"I tried to talk her out of it but she agreed to see him. Beth's still at work."

Hood called the dogs and followed them inside. He set his gambler on the rack while Reyes took a quick look at the parking area, then closed the door and slid the deadbolt.

They sat in the near darkness by the fire, Hood with a large bourbon on ice, Reyes with a beer.

"We've got some new bad guys in town, Gabe."

"Tell me. I miss the action."

Reyes had been Buenavista's police chief when Hood moved here three years ago but he was retired now. He was a heavy-bodied man and he limped from a rattlesnake bite suffered years back. A widower. Hood had asked him to stay here with Erin while he and Beth were working. After the Yucatán fiasco, Erin had left Bradley and moved in with Hood and Beth to recuperate and have the baby. But Hood didn't want to leave her alone all day, pregnant and still half terrified by her kidnapping and bloody rescue. Thus Reyes. He was garrulous, alert, excellent in the kitchen, and capable with his old service revolver, on the off chance that Erin's tormentors might return. Gabriel said he spent his time hovering about the house as Erin wrote and recorded her songs, and joining her on walks in the pleasant mornings and evenings. Hood understood that these unusual living arrangements, coupled with her intense work in the ER, were taking a toll on Beth.

He told Reyes about the Russell County entrepreneurs leading him to Israel Castro.

"I'd like to pinch all four of them," said Reyes.

"Wouldn't that be fun? What do you know about Castro?"

Reyes recited the basics: Castro had grown up in Jacumba, saw his father shot down in front of his own restaurant, drug trade suspected but never proved. Family on both sides of the border. Relatives tight with the Arellano-Félix cartel in the early days. Castro into construction then building then real estate and property management. Later the Ford dealership in El Centro and a Kia-Hyundai place in Brawley—always does his own TV commercials, wears the sport coat with the fake jewels on it. Still has the restaurant in Jacumba—Amigos. Belongs to service organizations, big on charity.

"My San Diego cop friends suspect he's been laundering drug money for decades, but with so many legit businesses . . . hard to prove. He's smart guy, not a violent one. People like him. He was a San Diego Sheriff's reserve deputy for years. They also think he moved tons of heroin and cocaine north through Jacumba and Jacume back in the nineties when it was easy. They say Amigos used to crawl with narcos. Later he teamed up with Coleman Draper. But you know more about all that than I do."

Coleman Draper, thought Hood. An LASD reserve deputy who, along with his patrol partner, murdered two cash couriers up in the bleak Antelope Valley desert and framed an innocent man for the killings. All to take over a very lucrative cash run from L.A. to Mexico. Hood had trailed Draper to Castro in Jacumba. And almost caught up with them and the drug money that rainy night five years ago, but had gotten a bullet instead. A few days later Draper tried to finish him off and Hood shot him dead.

The past again, he thought. *Barreling right in like it's welcome.* "So what does Israel Castro need with stolen drugs and small-time crimescene guns? These Missouri guys aren't going to make him noticeably richer."

"Something more's going on."

Hood considered. He heard Erin in the back of the house, a door shutting and a sink running. Daisy and Minnie climbed off the couch and trotted down the hallway. The pipes in his adobe were old, and they telegraphed with groans and shudders the presence of those within. Erin was due in weeks but she still refused to see Bradley except for very brief visits, which she only allowed with Hood, Reyes, or Beth in attendance. The dogs invited themselves to all such meetings, positioning themselves between Erin and her husband, always facing Bradley, never quite sleeping.

Hood knew that Bradley despised him for this arrangement, but the whole thing had been Erin's idea. Although he did think it was a good thing. He himself despised Bradley's reckless endangerment of his wife, his prodigious greed and dishonesty, his crimes and arrogance and luck. Just four months ago he'd gotten her kidnapped and nearly skinned alive. Now it looked like LASD was about to cancel Bradley's ticket, and that was fine with Hood. Still, this was Bradley's second approved visit in a week. Erin was softening. Maybe ready to forgive, if not forget. He sipped the bourbon and looked out a window at the distant peaks faintly brushed by starlight.

"Got pictures of these new creeps?" asked Reyes.

Hood gave him his phone and while Reyes pawed back and forth through the pictures with a thick finger, Hood thought of Mary Kate Boyle and her big plum shiner, disappearing into the millions of people in Southern California. He had the nagging bad feeling that somehow she and Skull would reunite.

"When bad cops take over, it's the end of civilization as we know it," said Reyes. He handed back the phone.

"They're not taking anybody over."

"Too bad the girl won't cooperate."

"She's done enough if you ask me."

Reyes stood and yawned, then limped to the front door. He opened the deadbolt and looked outside for a long beat. Past his round shoulders Hood saw the stars flickering in the desert night. Reyes closed the door and locked up. "Anything new on Mike Finnegan?"

"Not for months."

"You'll find him again."

"Well, I won't stop."

"I believe in evil."

"I know you do."

"I saw it in him. You young people might think that's quaint. But I grew up with idea that evil walks and talks. It's a good way to see the world and the things that happen in it. And don't happen."

"I don't think of evil as quaint."

"They'll say you're crazy."

"Who will?"

"Everyone. The distracted and ignorant public you protect and serve. Your bosses and associates. You'll have to fight them off. And you still might end up believing them and not yourself. All you have is yourself and your faith." Hood saw the darkness brush Gabriel's face. "I like the way you hold on to things, Charlie. I like the way you grab on and worry them over and over again. I don't know about the diamonds in your tooth, but you're a good man and a good cop. You'll find him again."

In their bedroom Hood set the chocolates on Beth's pillow and put the bottle on her nightstand with the card propped up against it. Then he threw open the heavy window curtains, which left him facing not a window but a heavy steel door built into the wall. He pushed the combination code, then flipped a light switch and went down the stairs, his shoes twanging lightly on the metal steps. Sleek Daisy and stout Minnie impatiently clicked down behind him. At the base of the stairs was another steel door with a prison-style pass-through about waist high. This door he opened with a different code, then stepped into his new wine cellar.

Hood had built the cellar beneath his home at some expense, and it was only recently completed, though he owed twenty more monthly payments on the loan. He had sold his restored IROC Camaro to help pay for it. The four underground rooms were cold and high-ceilinged and there were no windows or doors but the light was incandescent and good. White walls—lath and plaster, hard as stone, not sheet-rock—and a textured concrete floor. High in the ceiling of each room was a steel grate, but no light came through the heavy grids. The cellar was only minimally furnished, with racks and a few bottles of red wine aging. A couch and entertainment center with a TV and some DVDs. There was a small bath and shower, a kitchenette, and one of the rooms had an empty bookcase and a double bed, made up.

He sat in a folding chair at a folding table in the bedroom and let his eyes wander the tabletop: a laptop, an external hard drive, an envelope containing eight eight-by-ten-inch photographs of Finnegan, a row of identical photo booklets containing four-by-six copies of the same photos. A coffee cup brimming with pencils, a pad of graph paper dense with notes and scribbles, a stapler. It was all very neat. He'd had to move his work space down here with the arrival of Beth,

Erin, and Reyes, but this had allowed him to discard the chaff and keep the wheat.

Hood looked up at the grate, beyond which was only darkness. He remembered Veracruz, and the quick grind of the knife blade against his skull, and the wash of blood that draped his eyes and blocked his vision while Mike fled down darkened *M. Doblado* street. Hood ran his finger along the scar and thought, *I've got room for you*. He looked into the amber twinkle of the glass and he sensed that he could become lost in it, and he wondered again if his sanity was eroding, and he told himself again—for what, the thousandth time?—that no, no, no, his mind was sound and his mission was clear and right. Just look at the neatness and order of the tabletop, he thought, a reflection of sound thinking. He reminded himself that he had seen what few had seen. This is why he had been given the scar. As a seal of authenticity. *I'll find you*, he thought. *And when I do, you will never so much as brush up against another person on this earth.*

Back in the living room Hood saw the flicker of headlights coming up the steep dirt drive. "He's here," said Erin. She sat at the far end of a long leather sofa, close to the fire, a Pendleton blanket over her. Even through the heavy blanket, her middle registered as a large, stout ball. Her face was pale and flushed and slightly fuller these last few weeks. Her hair shined red in the firelight. "Thanks again for waiting up for me."

"You know I don't mind."

"Beth should be home soon."

A minute later the motion lights outside the house came on and Hood saw Bradley's black Cayenne pull into the carport. The dogs were already at a window, up on their back legs for the view. Hood undid the locks and swung open the heavy wooden door, then walked back to the living room and sat.

Bradley swept in, the untucked tails of his shirt trailing, his face pinched and hollowed, eyes hard until he saw Erin. He held a long spray of cut red roses in one hand and a white plastic sack in the other. He stopped and stared at her in silence. He set the flowers on the sofa beside her, then slid a colorful box from the bag and broke it open and bowed somewhat formally to hand her a chocolate ice cream bar on a stick. "Happy Valentine's Day."

"Fudge Bars," she said softly. "My hero. That's Charlie sitting right there, in case you didn't see him. Maybe you should offer him one, too."

Bradley turned and took in Hood, then tossed him an ice cream bar. "Nice suit, bro."

"Thanks for saying so."

"You still look more like a cop than a gun dealer."

"You look unhappy. Did they fire you?"

"They're trying."

"Can't get used to you working for the North Baja Cartel?"

"Hood? I endure your piety only as a way to get into your home and visit my wife."

"If it was up to me, that door would still be locked."

"You'll make someone a sweet bitch someday."

Erin snapped her empty stick and set it on the wrapper beside her. "Can't you drooling primates shut it off for just one minute?"

"I'll be in the kitchen," said Hood.

He put the pops in the freezer and poured a light bourbon and sat at the stout wooden table. From back in the house Reyes's bathroom pipes thumped and whined. Hood listened to the soft voices coming from the other room. He couldn't hear the sentences, just fragments and syllables here and there, but the tone was of pleading and denying, apology and accusation. He looked into the living room where the couple faced each other from opposite ends of the long sofa, and he saw the firelight play upon their profiles—Erin's fine features and Bradley's tragic mask alike etched by light and shadow. He understood that Bradley would win this war because his need was larger. It was only a matter of time. He thought again of Bradley's mother, Suzanne, and the reckless need she had awakened in him. Maybe need was a kind of strength, he thought, though he had never heard it called that. Daisy and Minnie lay on the tile near Erin and facing Bradley, their muzzles to the tile but their eyes asparkle like bits of glass.

Using his phone, Hood checked his e-mail and social networks and his Mike-specific webpage but found only two new messages, chiding and familiar, from "Incipient Madness" and "Bonkers," which he suspected to be Mike himself. Nothing else. Not one sighting, not one lead, not even a crank reply to his endless inquiries in the ether. In the last few months, roughly half of his contacts had asked him to cease and desist. But there were always new contacts. New hope. New blood. He turned off the phone and slid it back onto his belt. When he looked up, he saw Bradley on his feet, leaning over Erin to kiss the top of her head while she slept.

Bradley walked toward the door, then stopped and turned to her, and from where he spoke Hood heard his words clearly. "Let me make a home where we can begin again."

He waited for her reply, but she didn't move. He stared at Hood for a long moment, then came into the kitchen. He went to the cupboard and took down a glass, which he filled from the tap and drank down. Then another. "Have you talked to Warren?"

"No. I'm letting you hang yourself."

"I appreciate that. An hour with Warren, though, and you could pretty much take me down. Isn't that what you want? Or are you just going to let me turn in the wind a little longer? Really enjoy the show before you sell me out."

"Sell you out. That's funny. Wake up. My silence is for her."

"Everything we do is for her."

"She's a good reason but a bad excuse."

"I hated the way you tried to take over my mother. And I hate the way you're trying the same thing with Erin. You've got the morals of a dog."

"Suzanne took over me. And Erin I'm protecting."

"From me. Protecting my wife from me."

"Yes, from you—someone arrogant and selfish enough to almost get her and the baby killed. Or have you forgotten that already, in your rush to reacquire what you want? You also betrayed her trust and broke her heart. Now you have to let her put it back together. It'll take time. And I'll tell you one more thing—it's not about Fudge Bars, bro."

Beth came home half past midnight. Hood held open the door as she trudged across the gravel, and he saw the exhaustion in her. She still wore her work scrubs and Crocs and one of her loose white jackets with "Dr. Petty" stitched on, meaning a busy shift. She had a heavy knit scarf around her neck against the chill. She stopped briefly to pet the dogs. "Still in your gun dealer duds, I see."

"Busy night. Erin's fine. Bradley was here. How are you?"

They walked in behind the animals and Hood shut and locked the door, then hung Beth's bag on the hat rack. She hooked the scarf next to Charlie Diamond's straw gambler. "We lost a boy to the canal to-night. Second one this year. We did everything—oxygen, trach, paddles. Flat. Eight years old. Father and mother carried him in on a blanket. He looked asleep. Heading north for a better life and the boy was yipping up at the moon like a coyote and he slipped right in. You know how fast it is."

"That's a loss. I'm sorry, Beth."

Her face looked calm but her eyes were bereft. "I am, too. Alright. So. Man. I need a long shower and I'm starved. What's to eat?"

"Got you covered."

6

In the bright cool of the morning Hood followed the red Commander from the Pueblo Lodge to Castro Ford. The El Centro traffic was light but enough for cover, and he drove past the dealership as the two Missouri cops and their young partner walked toward the showroom. They had parked up front, next to what looked like Israel Castro's new Flex.

Hood drove a block and swung around and parked in the Desert Donuts lot across from Castro Ford. He looked out at the Flexes, which he liked, and the hot new Mustangs, which he also liked, and the new Explorers, which he liked, too. The new Taurus SHO was extra cool, and even the new economy cars had stance. Ten minutes later he saw the three men hustling down the showroom steps, Clint Wampler eating what looked like a maple bar.

He followed them three cars back to the other side of town and Buster's Last Stand. He drove past and made a U-turn at the next stop sign and circled back. The three men were carrying in some of the boxes he'd watched them load from the motel room.

He drove to a convenience store where he bought a fancy coffee drink to go with the diamonds in his tooth. He wore a beige wool suit and the Borsalino gambler, and cap-toe, two-tone shoes that made an authoritative crack with each step as he crossed the parking lot of the gun store.

He strode inside Buster's Last Stand sipping the coffee, then slid his sunglasses into his coat pocket. He paid no attention to the three men who were talking with Buster across the handguns counter, but he nodded to Buster and Buster nodded back. He noted the heavyset woman at the checkout stand and strolled by to see her purchase: She was taking delivery on a semiautomatic AK-47-style rifle, and apparently filling out the paperwork to buy another one.

Hood cruised the ammo aisles, perusing various calibers and loads, mostly handgun and larger-caliber rifle cartridges. He could hear Buster's voice clear and loud: I'm not interested in any of granddad's heirloom junk but I'll take a look at what you got. Hey, Charlie Hooper! You come back for those forty cals?

Hood ignored him. Let them come to you, he thought. This was a favorite rule of his old Blowdown boss, Sean Ozburn, a crack undercover agent, always cool and never made: Don't be eager. Ozburn had been the best of them until Mike Finnegan tore him to shreds— mentally, spiritually, and finally physically. Oz's lovely wife, too. All of that, without even touching them.

Hood continued to ignore Buster and look at the ammo, noting that prices were leveling off. They had gone up dramatically after the 2008 and 2012 presidential elections, as had the domestic sales of new weapons from every major American gun manufacturer. Hood thought of Obama's first year in office, when the NRA and Fox News had told America that the new president, though possibly not a citizen, certainly wanted their guns—and America had listened. Hood had realized that fear was good for the news business, and for the entertainment and weapons industries as well. Fear drove sales. Fear of gangs, fear of government. Fear of terrorists, fear of gun control. Fear of Islam, fear of socialism. Hood wondered what the NRA's next marketable crisis might be. He'd seen a scary and entertaining zombie movie recently, which depicted more ammo being shot up in two hours than Buster could sell in a year.

He went back to the entrance/exit and tossed his empty coffee cup into a trash can festooned with popular Zombie Bob targets. *Eureka*, he thought. The Bobs had been shot up pretty badly but what was left of them drooled and grimaced from the canister. The heavyset woman, now wearing rhinestone sunglasses, had finished her next purchase order and she now waddled toward him with the boxed assault rifle cradled in her arms and a black rhinestone-studded purse balanced on top. "Get the door," she said.

"*Con permiso.*" Hood tipped his hat and held open the door for her, noting which car she was headed for and easily memorizing the vanity plates. Then he unracked a shopping cart and pushed it back to the ammunition aisle. He loaded in five ten-box cases of the .40-caliber shells. This would set ATF back some scarce money, but the western division had gone to .40-caliber Glocks, so the ammo would be useful beyond its moment here as a good stage prop.

He toured the store briefly, threw a package of Zombie Bob paper targets into the cart for good luck, and stopped where the four men stood looking at him. A small arsenal of used weapons rested on a folded camo-patterned blanket placed atop the counter to save the glass. Hood looked at the guns but not the men.

"Granddad's heirloom junk is right," he said.

"Except that nobody asked you," said Skull.

"He has a point, Mr. Hooper," said Buster. "And I'm glad you found some ammo. But weren't you after a lot more than that?"

"At your price this is all I can afford. Luckily it's for an immediate, short-term app. A mortal thing." Hood smiled slightly.

Buster gave him a confused look. "Ring it up, then?"

Hood looked up from the guns and into the faces of three men one at a time. "So what happened to old Granddad, anyway?"

"None of your business, Twinkle Tooth," said Brock Peltz. He was taller and heavier than Hood had expected.

Young Clint Wampler laughed. He wore a peacoat and had the same pageboy bangs as in his mug shot. "He died defending this country from people like you."

"I have no idea what you mean by that," said Hood.

"Grandpa's goddamned dead is what I mean," said Wampler.

"Gentlemen," Buster said.

Wampler again: "I mean this country can't live without no shit-faces but not principles."

"Clearly," said Hood.

"Mr. Hooper, why don't we just step over to checkout and ring up those shells?"

Hood looked at Skull. "How much do you want for the saddle rifle?"

"Hey, hey, hey!" boomed Buster. "Posted private property so no trespassing! This is my store and I do the buying and selling."

"You'd get your tithe, Buster," said Hood.

"It's a Winchester Ninety-two," said Skull.

"It's a Winchester Ninety-two knockoff made by Rossi. No shame in Granddad being value-minded."

"Three hundred," said Skull.

"I'll give you two hundred if you throw in the scabbard."

"*Gun Trader's Guide* has it at two-fifty. Gun alone."

Hood hefted the heavy little carbine, worked the lever, checked the chamber and magazine, lowered the hammer with his thumb. He brought a white handkerchief from his coat pocket, wiped the butt plate clean, then shouldered the weapon. "I always liked cowboy guns."

"I'll go two-fifty," said Skull. "And twenty for the scabbard, which I got no use for without the gun. That's the price the guide says."

Hood lowered the gun and with his hankie wiped what he had touched, then set the gun back on the blanket. "Sell it to the guide, then."

"Beat it, fruit loop," said Peltz. "We've got some business to do."

Hood glanced up at him, then back down at the guns. He studied them for a long beat. "I do have some homosexual clients."

"In New York you could marry one of them," said Skull. The other men laughed heartily.

Young Clint Wampler's face was filled with glee. "That's because you want to be one."

Hood smiled. "I'm sorry, young man, but I have trouble grasping your ideas. Just let me say that my customers, homosexual or not, need more than these rusty, small-bore playthings. Buster, let's cash out these targets and ammo."

"You got her."

Hood turned the cart around in a wheelie and headed for the checkout counter. "That fucker's fuckin' fucked," he heard Wampler say. At the register he paid cash.

"Sorry, I guess," said Buster.

"Don't be. Lowball the living daylights out of them. And do let me know when something more substantial comes your way. My Virginia collector is still hot for those vintage machine guns. And you still have my card, I trust."

"Got it somewheres."

Hood gave him another one.

Thirty minutes later Hood was at the El Pueblo waiting for his breakfast. He checked his e-mail and website and Facebook page and found one potentially legitimate message: *We need to talk. Lonnie R.* Hood didn't recognize the name. Lonnie had not included his phone number or a return address of any kind. The waitress poured him more coffee. After breakfast his phone rang and he was hoping for Lonnie R. with a red-hot tip on Mike. The voice was rough and familiar. "My name is Dirk Sculler. We met at Buster's half an hour ago."

"The wild bunch."

"Sorry. They get excited."

"I'll recover."

"Buster told me you want an operational machine gun. For a collector. Full size, not a sub."

"Plural if I had my way. And vintage. World Wars I and II. For a history buff."

"I might be able to do that. I checked out your website. Good enough. And your card says licensed but there's no federal number. Maybe you can explain that."

"I don't put it anywhere some fool might try to use it. I put it on the FTRs if I have to."

"If you're licensed you *do* have to."

"Some things are easier without paperwork, Mr. Sculler. If you've never filled out an ATF firearms transaction form, take my word for it."

A pause, then: "Forms are deal breakers for me, Mr. Hooper."

"The seller is always right."

"Maybe we understand each other."

"Possibly."

"I might be able to get you a Lewis Mark I."

"I might be able to buy an operational Lewis Mark I."

"Oh, it operates." Skull chuckled.

"Condition?"

"Very good."

"Would it come with the pan magazine and front bipod stand?"

"Both."

"How much?"

"Five thousand cash."

"That's too high."

"Four thousand. Try getting a quote from the *Gun Trader* on that old thing."

"Try someone who deals in Class Three, such as myself. It's not worth over twenty-five hundred unless it's gold plated or never been fired. The gold-plated part is meant as humor."

There was a long silence. "Let me think about it."

"You could ask the chimp in the peacoat what to do."

"He only looks harmless. Don't call him a chimp to his face."

"Keep a leash on him."

Hood finished his breakfast. The restaurant was nearly empty and the jukebox played a *narcocorrido* in which two corrupt U.S. lawmen gun down a fourteen-year-old Tijuana drug courier who had tricked them out of a thousand dollars. The two young narcos that Hood had seen here the night before were one booth over from where he'd left them, in their ostrich boots and python belts and black Resistols. They looked skinny and weathered and out of place. *Sinaloans*, thought Hood, straight from the mountains, here in the *Estados Unidos* to do some business. Hood read *The San Diego Union-Tribune* and had more coffee. He was just counting out his tip when the rhinestoned assault-rifle woman barreled from the lobby in to the dining room and settled into the booth next to the businessmen, who self-consciously ignored her. Hood slipped out and in the parking lot he looked again at her car. It was a black Caddy with vanity plates that said, YO YO 762, the numbers suggesting the popular 7.62 mm round for which the AK assault rifles are chambered.

Skull called as Hood was crossing the parking lot. "Three grand."

"I'll look at it with twenty-seven fifty in mind."

"You'll like it. I've got a couple of AR-fifteens, Czech made, full auto, two MACs, and an Uzi. Sweet, sweet stuff."

"Not at this time. What else?"

"Else? Well, the pharmacy is always open."

"Not my deal."

"Terrific crank and lots of good prescription downers. Mexican heroin, strong and black. Hash that'll melt your face."

"I'll think on that."

"People are strange. Who do you supply? North Baja? Sinaloa? Whoever pays best?"

"Door number three," said Hood.

"Are you a cop?"

Hood chuckled. "I only get accused of that by people who watch too much TV."

"That's not an answer."

"You sound like you're preparing an entrapment defense. I like that. It makes you seem trustworthy."

Hood leaned against his Charger and watched the entrance of El Pueblo.

"I've got access to fine, fine things," said Skull. "I just need a good man to lay them off to."

"Let's just date for now, Dirk. Get to know each other. I'll look at the Lewis, and if I like it, I'll have the money. Somewhere public."

"Walmart public enough for you? If so, be in the parking lot at noon. I'll call with details. What car will you be in?"

Hood told him and clicked off and called Yorth.

"Right on, Charlie," he said. "Make the buy and ask for more. I'll have the cash and wire waiting."

7

An hour and fifty minutes later Hood's Charger growled into the Walmart parking lot. He drove to the far end, near the home-and-furnishings section, and parked. The wire was built into his cell phone, invisible and impossible to find without destroying the phone. The cash was a messy booklet of small bills folded over once and shoved into the left butt pocket of his trousers. Before leaving the Buenavista field office, he had locked his Glock and holster in the trunk and made sure his ankle gun was loaded and ready. The winter noon was cool and blustery, but Hood felt hot and edgy and he ran the AC on high.

Skull called ten minutes later and told Hood to pull into a handi-cap space in front of the market section, near the main entrance. When a red Jeep Commander drove past behind him, Hood was to pull out of the space and follow.

"I'm not leaving the lot," said Hood.

"I'm not asking you to."

"Keep the monkey on his leash."

"He's my secret weapon."

"Is he for sale, too?"

"Hooper. We're going to back into our parking space. You don't. You park face in."

Hood pulled into the handicap space, left the engine running. An old man limping toward his truck glared at him, and from behind his sunglasses, Hood placidly gazed back. Seconds later the red Com-mander had rolled past him and Hood pulled out and followed. The Jeep rolled along hesitatingly, as if the driver couldn't decide his course. Hood wondered if they were arguing. He knew that these men were as much on edge as he was because, as Ozburn had often noted, all gun deals had one dangerous thing in common: guns. Ozburn had also told Hood that on an undercover buy, if something could go wrong, it would. If Plan A failed, then go to Plan B, and there was never a Plan C.

The Commander wandered toward an exit then turned out into the far and uncrowded recess of the lot. A low painted concrete wall ran the perimeter and the Jeep backed into a space where a paloverde tree cast a small pool of shade on the asphalt. A sun-blanched Chevy Astro van slouched in the next spot of tree shade, several parking spaces away. Hood waited and watched. The Commander's windows were blacked out, but through the windshield he could see Clint Wampler behind the wheel and Skull riding shotgun. If Peltz was in the back, Hood couldn't see him. Hood figured he was in the raised F-150 he'd seen at the hotel, and when he looked around for it, there it was, not two hundred feet away, beyond the Astro, backed against the same wall. He pulled in and shut off the engine and got out as the Commander backed to a stop. On the far side of the Commander, Skull's door slammed and a moment later the liftgate was wheezing open on its pneumatic risers.

"Come on over, Charles."

Skull lifted a dirty green blanket and Hood looked down at the Lewis Gun. The pan magazine was in place and the worn bipod legs were extended. "Must weigh thirty pounds."

"Twenty-eight," said Hood.

"It's not loaded."

Hood looked up through the smoked Commander windows to see a small stout woman pushing a stroller toward them. She wore a pale yellow dress and her skin was dark. Plastic shopping bags of merchandise dangled heavily from the stroller handles. Three small children followed in tight formation. She seemed to be looking toward the Astro. The driver's side door of the Commander swung open and Clint Wampler slid out with a smile on his face and a pistol in his hand. He looked at Hood and jammed the gun into his belt, right up front where it would show, then walked a line that would intercept the woman with the stroller.

"Go ahead," said Skull. "Pick it up if you can."

Hood swung the gun up and out and pointed it at the wall. It was very heavy and not balanced well, and Hood knew that it had been made to be fired from a prone position or mounted to an airplane. The best he could do while standing was to hold the grip with his right hand and let the butt extend beneath his armpit and hold on to the cooling shroud with his left. He wondered how many seconds of fire it would take to melt his hand to it. Not many. He looked past Skull's shoulder at Wampler, nearing the woman and children.

"What's the imbecile doing?" he asked.

"He'll just run them off."

"She's heading for the van. Probably trying to go home."

"I'd agree."

"Then why doesn't he just let her go?"

"He won't hurt her. He gets results because he looks cute but isn't very nice."

"Can you control him?"

"Not really. So what do you think of the machine gun?"

"Have you fired it?"

"Heavy rain, man. It's a thirty-aught-six, but it feels more like a fifty cal. You're talking six hundred rounds per minute, and it's accurate at a thousand yards."

Hood watched as Wampler stopped and set his feet widely and hooked his thumbs in his belt. He spoke but Hood couldn't hear the words. The woman stopped and answered. The children closed ranks, practically hidden behind her. She pointed toward the van. Wampler said something and she raised both hands and Wampler stepped closer.

"You want the gun or not?"

"I want it."

"Put it back in the Jeep and we'll take care of business."

Hood hefted the Lewis Gun back into the vehicle. Wampler was walking back toward him with something in his hand, and the family was hustling purposefully for the Astro. The woman moved at a near trot and the stroller bounced across the asphalt and the children were strung out single file behind her. When Wampler came closer, Hood watched him drive a large red apple into his face, heard the crack of the bite breaking off.

Hood looked at Skull, pretending that there was no such person as Clint Wampler. From his trouser pocket he dug out the slab of bills and handed them to Skull. The big man counted them patiently as Hood watched the family pile in to the van.

"Pleasure," said Skull. "I'll keep in touch if you'd like."

"I'd like some submachine guns and good autoloading handguns."

"I've got the two ARs, two MACs, and that Uzi, all dressed up and nowhere to go. That would be nine thousand. I'll bring some handguns. Got some dandy home-defense shotguns, too. Big-ass ten gauges, drum fed. I'll call."

It dawned on Hood that Skull and company had a line on weapons far deeper than the property room at their cop house. With friends like Israel Castro, what was the surprise? Mary Kate Boyle didn't know half of what her beau had been up to.

Hood unlocked the trunk of his car with a key fob. Wampler heard the lid click open and he stepped over and raised the lid and looked in. At the Jeep, Hood covered the Lewis Gun with the blanket, then carried the whole package to the Charger trunk and set it in.

"Gimme that blanket back," said Wampler. He reached into the trunk just as Hood slammed the lid and it trapped the tip of Wampler's left middle finger. Clint shrieked and grimaced and the once-bitten apple wobbled out of sight under the Commander. Hood found the fob in his pocket and hit the trunk lock. When the pistol appeared in Clint's free hand, Hood kicked it away and it clacked and skidded across the asphalt.

"Shit, Hooper!" said Skull.

Hood pulled the key fob from his pocket. "Dirk, collect his piece and get into your car and I'll let him go."

Wampler was on his knees behind the Charger, gnawing out curses and alternatingly trying to work his fingertip from the trunk or lift the lid. Blood ran down his arm and off his elbow to the ground. Skull gathered up the gun and climbed into the Jeep. Hood hit the unlock button and the lid clunked open and Wampler whirled free and charged. Hood was ready and eager to fight this one out, but Wampler stopped short, breathing hard, and clutching his bleeding finger. "You'll pay," he hissed. "You muckerfuthin' loser."

Soon Hood was back at the field station in Buenavista booking the Lewis Gun and using a computer program to transcribe the digital recording of him and the Missouri profiteers. The recording was of forensic quality. *Buster told me you want an operational machine gun . . . forms are deal breakers for me, Mr. Hooper . . .*

"Nice work, Charlie," said Dale Yorth. He held the Lewis Gun down low against his hip and made machine guns noises, spraying imaginary bad guys. "When you get the buy set up for the submachine guns and pistols, we'll get the takedown team in place and pinch these rancid creeps."

Hood looked up at him. To Hood, Dale Yorth was the combination of boyish adventurism and deadly adult mission that constituted law enforcement at most levels. Hood had long watched these traits ebb and flow, rise up and retreat, in himself and in others, often at odd and unpredictable times. As part of a takedown team, he had once been led by a senior agent who hummed the old *Hawaii Five-0* theme as they ran through a parking lot, guns drawn on armed felons. Hood believed that these traits were good things for lawmen, so long as they were balanced by sound judgment.

*   *   *

After writing his reports Hood drove back to Castro Ford to see if Israel's Flex was parked up front again. It was. Hood parked in the same spot that the Missouri men had used. He exchanged pleasantries with three salesmen waiting outside, one of whom looked disdainfully at the Charger and accused Hood of going over to the dark side. This got a laugh and Hood joined in. He could hear the pneumatic rasp of the power tools and the clank of steel coming from the service side and thought they weren't bad sounds at all.

In the showroom he admired a very hot yellow Mustang, a loaded Flex, and a little Focus that gleamed like a jewel. The fierce showroom lights made them look not only beautiful but somehow eternal. There was a bin of soccer balls right there by the Mustang, their colored panels the same hot yellow as the Mustang, with CASTRO FORD SAYS YES! emblazoned on them. Hood occasionally thought that if his law enforcement career was to end he might sell cars.

He wandered past the sales cubicles and the service hallway and the awards case and found Israel Castro sitting, back turned, at his desk in the last office. He took off his hat and rapped on the door frame. "Coleman Draper."

Castro swung around. "Who the hell are you?"

"Easy does it. Charlie Hooper. I worked with Draper at LASD."

Castro looked at him for a long moment. He was balding and powerfully built and his expression was of curious distrust. He wore a short sleeve shirt and a necktie. "You a cop?"

"Reserve. Like Coleman. We had some of the same friends, on and off the force. He spoke highly of you."

"I'm reserve, too. Imperial County. Come in."

Hood sat and Castro called for coffees. When the pretty girl had come and gone, Hood told Castro about meeting Draper back in '08 when Coleman's German car repair shop came recommended. They'd talked, found common interests, including cars and law enforcement, and Draper had later introduced him to the captain who ran the LASD Reserves. Hooper joined up for the action and the badge and the contacts. A year later, Coleman was gunned down by a deputy on his own force.

Castro nodded, his doubtful eyes roaming Hood's face. "What brings you here?"

"Just business. I'm buying and selling." He gave Castro one of his Charles Hooper cards. "It's all squeaky clean. No toys for boys. Nothing going south illegally."

"Do I look like I need a gun?"

"That's entirely up to you. I've been in San Diego for a few months now, moved down from Seattle after L.A. I'm touching base with my contacts, just working the field. As I said, Coleman liked you a lot. He told me about when you guys were young in Jacumba. Amigos Restaurant and all. I always wanted to meet you. Now seemed like the time."

"You're not just looking for a deal on a car, are you? Because if you are, you're in the right place."

Hood smiled.

"I miss Coleman," said Castro. "He saved my life and I saved his. Boys. He did things his own special way. Know what I mean?"

"I'd never met anyone like him. I haven't since."

"Alright. You want a car, see me and I *will* make you a deal. And if I need a shooting piece I'll come see you."

"I buy, too. If you know legit people with high-end firearms."

"Why would I?"

"Coleman said you were full of surprises."

Castro stood. "That's me. I'll walk you out. I want you just take one quick look at the new Taurus. Totally redesigned last year—they out-Germaned the Germans. Initial Quality? J. D. Powers went batshit over these things."

Later that day, as he wrote up his report in the field office, one of his cell phones rang again. "Hood."

"This is Lonnie Rovanna."

"Hello, Lonnie."

"I saw Mike Finnegan. He was Dr. Stren, from the Superior Court in San Diego."

"When?"

"Two mornings ago. I was on your website months back. I like to check in on, well, unusual . . . searchers. Like you. I enjoyed the way you described the changeability of Mike. I believe people can be not what they appear. That they can change. That they can have several names and personalities and professions and lives. I believe this happens all the time. And I saw him. Mike. He has black hair, not red. And big glasses. It took me a couple of days to realize where I'd see him before. It came to me in a dream, in fact. But there's no doubt he's the same man as in your pictures. So, I'm doing what you asked. I'm contacting you."

"Where was he?"

"Here in my house. El Cajon. He came to talk about my firearms being returned. They were taken away without just cause."

"May I come talk to you?"

"When?"

"I'm leaving Buenavista now. Give me your phone number and address and an hour fifty minutes."

8

Hood sat on a white resin chair in Rovanna's living room. The house was old and small and had the dusty burnt breath of the space heater that glowed orange in its corner. There was a layer of dust on everything—on the paperback thrillers grown plump with age and use, and the newspapers and magazines piled everywhere.

Rovanna sat on a slouching plaid couch with a baseball bat leaning against the pad beside him. He allowed Hood to place a digital recorder on the low coffee table between them. Then Rovanna spoke briefly of growing up in Orange County, California, his service overseas, subsequent troubles adjusting back to civilian life, a suicide attempt, and a later assault on two Jehovah's Witnesses. The police had arrested him and the court had committed him involuntarily to a hospital for evaluation. He was able to keep up the rent because of his disability checks. When he got home, his guns were gone. Lonnie Rovanna seemed straight to the point and factual.

"Iraq?" asked Hood.

"Two rotations. Mahmudiya District, then Anbar Province."

"Anbar and Hamdinaya for me. Infantry?"

"Five Hundred Second, Hundred and First Airborne."

"Which battalion?"

Rovanna looked at him levelly, took up the Louisville Slugger, gripped it like a batter, then set it back down. "First. Bravo Company, First Platoon. Triangle of Death. We found PFC Tucker and PV2 Menchaca after the rag heads tortured and beheaded them. They put IEDs in one of their crotch cavities. That was oh-six. Then I deployed again a year later, but after the triangle I was already a wreck."

Hood nodded. He remembered clearly that 1st Platoon of Bravo Company—Rovanna's outfit—had suffered terrible casualties in the so-called Triangle of Death. They had been isolated, outnumbered, terrified by videotaped beheadings circulated by the insurgents, and castigated by other B Company platoons. Four of them finally snapped, raping and killing an Iraqi girl and her family. It had been one of the darkest and most reported episodes of that long, dark war. But Hood also knew that Rovanna and his men had not discovered the bodies of the soldiers Tucker and Menchaca—that was 2nd Battalion. This atrocity had been reported in agonizing detail as well. As a part of NCIS, Hood had studied both of the terrible incidents as points of both personal and world history. Now these two events occupied dark compartments in his psyche, as Hood figured they must for many of the enlisted men of the 502nd Infantry. So how could Lonnie Rovanna get them mixed up?

"I was earlier," Hood said.

"The first deployment was the worst. Misplaced my mind. Still looking for it. Don't know how I made it through that last rotation. But I got out, got meds and a good doctor. I'll be fine. I filed my Firearms Rights Restoration application about three weeks ago. Dr. Stren came three days ago to ask questions. He's assigned by the Superior Court. He had a signed affidavit from a judge. He interviewed me, wrote in a little black notebook, and said he would be writing up his report later that day."

"What did he ask you? What did you talk about?"

Rovanna went to his kitchen and returned with two large superhero drink containers from Mr. Burger filled with ice and a plastic half-gallon bottle of vodka, new. He sat back down and cracked the seal and unscrewed it and poured half a glass for each of them. They touched the cups and drank. Hood felt the cold liquid burn down. He looked outside to the dirt-speckled Ford Focus in the gravel driveway and the big sycamore looming beyond.

Rovanna talked about Stren's prying, know-it-all attitude, and his interest in Rovanna's state of mind and behavior, his curiosity about the radios that Rovanna had locked away in the toolshed out back, and about his medications and alcohol use. He told Hood that his personal physician at the VA, Dr. Webb, had told Stren many private things about him—hearing voices from unplugged radios and demons in the walls, being followed by five men with identical clothing and faces. Rovanna said that Stren predicted his Firearms Rights Restoration application would be denied. Rovanna shrugged, then drank, then looked out the window to the sycamore standing almost leafless in the waning afternoon light. Hood studied him, trying to vet Rovanna's words and his grossly faulty remembrance of the war and the thousand-yard stare with which he now gazed outside.

After a long minute Hood pressed on. "Why did they take your guns away?"

Rovanna drank again, then told Hood in more detail about his assault on the Jehovah's Witnesses, who were quite possibly imposters. People were sometimes not what they pretended, he said with a bitter smile, like this Finnegan or Stren man. Rovanna spoke more informatively about his suicide attempt—flinched at the last second—then brushed aside his thick blond hair to reveal the brief scar above his right ear. "So after the Witnesses they put me in the loony bin for two weeks of evaluation. They always take your guns away when that happens."

"What did you use the guns for?"

"Oh, nothing really. They mainly just stayed under the bed in their cases."

"You didn't brandish them to the men posing as Jehovah's Witnesses?"

"Naw. No time. Slugged one and tackled the other. Neighbors ratted me out."

"Did you use the bat?"

"I didn't own a bat until they took my guns."

"What kind of guns?"

Rovanna declared them, twelve in all, semiauto assault-style rifles, semiauto handguns. He gave makes, model numbers, calibers.

"Describe Dr. Stren in more detail."

Rovanna addressed the navy suit and white shirt, the matching blue tie and patch, the small black shoes, the old-time gangster hat like Virgil Sollozzo wore in *The Godfather*.

"You said he wore glasses."

"Big ones. Greek billionaire glasses. Or that movie director. They made his eyes bug out. He's little, like I said. He has a deep, clear voice that seemed too big for this room. He wrote with a black pen in a black notebook. And that's about it. I think I've told you everything I can think of about him. Now, Mr. Hood—it's your turn to tell me what *you* know."

Hood declined a refill and told Rovanna how he'd first met Mike Finnegan in the Imperial Mercy Hospital in Buenavista. Mike had been hit by a car while changing a tire out in the desert, and was nearly killed. Broken bones, severe concussion, serious internal damage. He was in a full body cast, head to toe except for one good arm. Mike had been carrying Hood's address and phone number in his wallet. He claimed to have gotten the information from a mutual friend who worked part-time for Hood's Los Angeles County Sheriff's Department. He said he sold bath and shower products in L.A.— Mike Finnegan Bath was the name of his company. For a man who had cheated death just a few days earlier, Mike was lucid and humorful and apparently unpained, Hood said. Mike had asked him to find his daughter—she had run away before and Mike was sure she had run away again. He even had a possible address for her but now, well, he wouldn't be getting out of bed and walking anytime soon. That's what he said he'd been doing out in the infernal Imperial County desert, Hood told Rovanna—looking for his daughter. Lovely, troubled Owens.

"He's a good actor," said Rovanna. "You should have seen the way he looked at me. And around this place. Just like a doctor. You can't tell him anything he doesn't already know. The only thing he got wrong was his signature. Doctors can't write, they can only scribble. His signature looked like something an engineer would have—perfect slant and perfect letters."

Hood poured himself a short second drink. He told Rovanna that Mike had broken out of his body cast and walked out of intensive care a few days later. Checked himself out of the hospital, paid ninety thousand in cash for his treatment.

"Broke out of a full body cast with half his bones broken?"

"Correct. I saw the remains of the cast. He'd ripped it off with his bare hands, dressed himself, and left. Scared the hell out of the nurses. The security camera caught him getting into his daughter's car."

"Those five guys who follow me around? I call them the Identical Men. They tried to tell me they were IRS. Like I'm going to fall for that. They're *not* IRS. They're Langley. Pure and simple. Or worse. I think Finnegan could be with them. They all have the same attitude. They try to treat you like a piece of shit. Same with the Jehovah's Witnesses. Like they know God himself. Like they're going to introduce you to Him. They're all part of the same game, Mr. Hood. They're all out to control our minds. They'll use radios, they'll hide inside the walls, they'll change and morph and lie."

"A year later Mike was in Central America, posing as an Irish priest named Joe Leftwich," said Hood. He thought of the utter destruction that Leftwich had wrought upon his friends, the Ozburns.

"No surprise."

"Where did he sit?"

"Here, where I am. I sat where you are."

"Did he leave you a card? Or any way to contact him?"

Rovanna blushed and shook his head and looked down at the worn oval rug. "I forgot to ask. He didn't offer. Sorry. You could just call the court."

"Did you see his car?"

"No. I can't see the street from here."

"Did he give you anything?"

Rovanna looked up. "Give me? You mean like . . ."

"Anything."

"No. No. He didn't give me anything. Nothing."

Hood watched Rovanna's eyes lose their conviction and his gaze find the frayed carpet again. "He just said he was going to write up something to help me get the guns back. He said my chances weren't so good."

"But he didn't give you anything?"

When Rovanna looked at him again, Hood saw the anger in his face. And something along with it he couldn't quite ID—sadness maybe, or guilt. "I said he didn't. Is there any way to be more clear on that?"

Hood nodded absently.

Rovanna again took the bat in his hands, choking his hands all the way down. "What is that supposed to mean?"

Hood stood and Rovanna leaned forward to stand also. But Hood put a hand firmly to his shoulder and pressed him back down to the couch. He took the bat from Rovanna and set it beside him. Hood walked into the kitchen and looked around. Having been invited into Rovanna's home, pretty much anything in plain sight he could legally take a look at. But there was nothing unusual in the small, poorly lit kitchen. He thought of another poorly lit kitchen, in Mike Finnegan's Veracruz flat, where they had fought and Mike had run the knife along his scalp. He remembered the bony grind of the blade, a sound he would take to his grave.

Hood came back into the living room and saw Rovanna staring down once again at the floor. Hood could sense the disorder in the younger man, the teetering imbalances inside him. He wondered, *If Finnegan would tear apart a young, strong, faithful man like Sean Ozburn simply because he could—then what might he do with Lonnie Rovanna?* Hood walked down the small dark hallway and poked his head into a bathroom. It smelled bad. He turned on the light and saw the counter dirty with soap scum and toothpaste and the white-brown toilet bowl and the water-stained tub choked at its drain by hair.

The first bedroom looked unused. He couldn't legally open the closet but he did anyway. A few clothes hanging. Scores of wire hangers. Some old sneakers on the floor. Nothing unusual. Nothing under the bed but dust balls. Back in the hallway he looked in to the living room and saw Rovanna looking back at him.

"I'm almost done, Lonnie."

"Okay."

He walked into the second bedroom. He smelled the unwashed sheets, cut with a popular antiperspirant. There were posters of baseball players and beautiful actresses tacked crookedly to the walls. A bookcase rested along one wall, its bottom shelf fallen at one end, the volumes slouching precariously but still contained. He read some titles. Then more. Half were paperback thrillers. But of the sixty or so volumes, the other half were accounts of the American wars in Iraq and Afghanistan. Hood had many of the titles in his own library.

Rovanna stood in the doorway with the bat over his shoulder, his hands low on the handle.

"I'm not a threat to you," said Hood softly.

"It's time to go, though."

"I really want to thank you for what you did. Mike Finnegan can be imposing and sometimes downright scary. You did well with him. He didn't crack you. You did the right thing when you called me."

"Good-bye, then."

"Did you serve?"

Rovanna colored deeply and Hood saw his hands relax around the handle of the bat. "What makes you think I didn't?"

"You got your battalions mixed up."

"Easy, if you experience the level of fire that I did."

"No, Lonnie. Very hard to forget your own battalion, whether you go through heavy fire or not. I see your books here. You read a lot.

You strike me as more a student than a soldier." Rovanna looked down for a long moment, then shrugged.

"I don't care that you weren't in Iraq, Lonnie. It doesn't matter one bit to me. You don't need to be a soldier to be brave. I was there and I'm not one ounce more brave than you."

"It's just too bad I'm crazy."

"Yes, it is. I'll be walking out now, Lonnie. Careful with that thing."

Rovanna backed into the hallway, and when Hood came to him, he offered his hand and Rovanna let go of the bat to shake it. His grip was strong and damp.

"If you remember something, call me," said Hood. "If Stren calls or comes again, call me immediately. He's evil, Lonnie. He will hurt you."

"I sensed that."

"If you want to just talk, call me. Really. I mean it. I always have time to talk. I like baseball."

"I have prayed and have never been answered. Not once."

"I've never been answered, either. I think that's the way it's supposed to be."

"There's supposed to be more in this life."

"More what?"

"More good."

Hood clasped Rovanna on the shoulder, then walked past him into the living room and out the door.

The San Diego Superior Court clerks were getting ready to close for the day, but Hood badged his way through to the chambers of the Honorable Fritz Johnson. Johnson was an older man with brisk gray hair and prying eyes and mounted game birds everywhere: turkey, pheasant, quail, chukar, band-tailed pigeons. "We've never worked with a Dr. Stren. I assign the psychiatrists from Sorrento Valley Medical and he's not one of them. Why?"

Hood briefed the judge on an apparently troubled young El Cajon man, Lonnie Rovanna, who claimed to have been visited by Dr. Stren, with regard to his Firearms Rights Restoration form.

"No," said Johnson. "Rovanna's doctor is Darnell, not Stren. There is no Stren at Sorrento, unless he's brand-new. At any rate, he wouldn't have seen Rovanna without my knowing it."

"Rovanna claimed to have seen combat in Iraq. And says he's being treated at the naval hospital."

Johnson shook his head. "Those are delusions."

"I thought so."

"I guess if you're ATF, you're interested in his guns."

"I'm more interested in the doctor that doesn't exist." Hood took one of his Mike Finnegan photo albums from a side pocket of his suit coat. Each album contained six images of Mike, four-by-six inches, housed in clear protective plastic. He handed it to Judge Johnson, who flipped through it quickly and chuckled.

"He was a janitor here for a while last year. Did a good job and didn't steal one thing. I haven't seen him in months. Never asked his name. We talked bird hunting, among other things. He used to run his family's vineyard up in Napa Valley, or so he said. There were valley quail and mourning dove to be shot. I remember he knew the Latin for all these birds. Odd, for a janitor. Is this him? Stren? Yes? Well, kind of odd he'd show up as a bogus psychiatrist. If you want to know more about him, talk to Kim out front. She'll know who we contract for janitorial."

Kim gave him a contact and number for La Jolla Custodial. On his way home Hood called and got right through. He talked to one of the managers, then sent him his clearest Finnegan photo over the phone. A moment later the manager called back to say he'd never seen or hired such a man.

9

That evening and part of the night Hood sat at the desk in his wine cellar, using his Justice Department–issued laptop to flesh out Lonnie Dwight Rovanna. Hood was privy to the fine and various databases to which U.S. Marshals have access. It took just a few minutes to find Rovanna's basic biography: He was born in Los Angeles to an aerospace test engineer and a high school counselor. His Stanford-Binet IQ was 126. He was now twenty-nine years old. He had grown up in Orange County, California, attended public school until age sixteen, then . . .

Then it was as if Lonnie Rovanna had fallen off the edge of the world for ten years, only to resurface three years ago in El Cajon. And during that decade, Hood could find no prison time, no military service, no credit agency records, no filings with the IRS. The gap smelled institutional. He poured a bourbon and called an old friend in Sacramento who owed him one good favor. It was a long conversation. By the end of it, Hood was reading Lonnie Rovanna's state mental hospital records on the laptop screen.

At sixteen, Rovanna had suffered his first psychotic episode, which lasted three weeks. Neither parent had a history of mental illness. His original diagnosis had been brief psychotic disorder, but less than two months later he again reported delusions and hallucinations, and exhibited disorganized speech and behavior. After two years in a private hospital, psychotherapy, and antipsychotic medications, Rovanna's diagnosis was changed to schizophrenia, paranoid type with a delusional disorder, grandiose type. He was admitted to a San Diego–area state hospital at age eighteen and remained there for eight years. Medications and treatment had had positive effects, according to two of three doctors. Three years ago, when changes in California law enabled him to get a monthly check and qualify for state-assisted housing, Rovanna had found the rental in El Cajon.

None of which had shown up on his background check when Rovanna purchased a semiautomatic nine-millimeter handgun shortly after leaving the state hospital. Hood knew that the biggest problem with the mental health component of background checks was that nobody cooperated—state agencies shielded mental health records from one another and from county and federal agencies, including the FBI; not all branches of the military fully disclosed the mental health histories of their soldiers to state or other federal agencies, either, and some didn't disclose any at all. Not even government background checkers had friends in every state capital. It was no surprise to Hood that Lonnie Rovanna had illegally purchased four semiautomatic assault-style rifles and eight handguns in the last three years—people like him sometimes fell through the cracks.

Hood exited the state health records and went back to a California law-enforcement-only site that had links to DMV. Rovanna had purchased and registered a used Ford Focus one year ago.

Hood called him. "I just wanted to thank you again for letting me know about Finnegan."

"He's not a good man, Mr. Hood."

Hood heard a TV in the background, then the rattle of ice in a plastic cup and liquid being slurped. He sipped his own drink and commented on mankind's nearly universal addiction to alcohol. Rovanna chuckled and said he'd had his first drink at twelve and instantly recognized a lifetime companion. By fourteen he was shoplifting the stuff and selectively pinching from his parents' prescription sleeping pills. Hood told Rovanna that he hadn't missed much by not fighting in Iraq. The insurgents were ruthless against the Americans and their own people, he said. He told Rovanna about some of the investigations he did. And about playing tennis in Baghdad inside the

Green Zone, where he helped organize a tennis league of soldiers and local Iraqis—they even had an Olympic hopeful, but he'd been assassinated for cooperating with the Americans. Rovanna asked intelligent questions and listened patiently for the answers.

"I played Ping-Pong a lot," said Rovanna. "Every rec room in every loony bin in California has one. No pool tables though. They're afraid we'll skewer each other with broken cues. Isn't that a hoot? They worry about us with pool sticks, so they cut our brains away. Mr. Hood, can I tell you my deepest fear? My very deepest fear is of Dr. Walter Freeman and his orbitoclasts. It's difficult for me to say that word out loud. The tool I refer to is a long, slender piece of steel they use to perform lobotomies. It's sharpened on one end like a small chisel, and the other end flares into a heavy butt about the size of a quarter. This is where, after they've inserted the blade between your eyeball and your brain, they tap it with a mallet to get it in. Then they move the orbitoclast back and forth to sever the prefrontal cortex in the frontal lobes of the brain. Dr. Walter Freeman performed the first prefrontal lobotomy in the United States. My body shivers when I hear his name. It literally quakes. Truly, it did just now. And listen to this, Charlie Hood—that first prefrontal lobotomy performed by Freeman was on a woman named Hood! Alice Hood. *Hood.* Funny how all things circle back sooner or later, isn't it? How they connect to form a pattern. I hear her voice sometimes, oddly enough—Alice's. Now the story gets even stranger, Charlie. Later, Freeman simplified the prefrontal into the transorbital lobotomy for patients in insane asylums. It was a cost-cutting measure. There were around six hundred thousand asylum patients in the nineteen-forties. He wanted them all to have lobotomies. Freeman got rid of the need for cranial drilling and anesthetic by using electroshock, much cheaper, then going in behind the eyes. So what had been a surgical procedure became an outpatient office visit. Freeman drove a van around the country, from mental institution to mental institution, performing lobotomies and giving lectures on his miracle procedure. He called his van the 'lobotomobile.' He charged twenty-five dollars for each one. He personally did three thousand four hundred of them, though he was never trained as a surgeon. His partner finally left the practice because of the cruelty and overuse of the lobotomy." Rovanna went silent for a long moment. Hood heard the ice crunch and a loud swallow. "Say the word *orbitoclast*, Mr. Hood. Hear the way it lends itself to clear, syllable-by-syllable pronunciation, the way the tongue strikes the palette just behind the front teeth, not once but three times. *That*, Mr. Hood, is what I live in terror of. Of Freeman and men like him, of horrors sold cheaply and pushed upon all."

"I understand your terror, Lonnie. But lobotomies are not performed anymore."

"Don't be naive. There are many forms and manifestations. Remember Alice Hood."

"Do you have information I don't?"

"The more I think about Stren, the more I think he's linked to Dr. Freeman and of course to the Identical Men. It makes sense if you think it through, one connection at a time."

"I'll write down those three things—Finnegan, Freeman, and the Identical Men. I'll see if I can connect them like you do." Hood wrote them down on a legal pad.

"Are you mocking me? You think I'm crazy."

"I think you're at a disadvantage but still in the game, Lonnie."

"What do you mean by that?"

"That you can get better. Look at the progress you've made since the hospital years. You've got your home and a car. You might be able to get some work you like. There's nothing stopping you."

"Like when they hire defectives to be greeters or push brooms around the big discount stores?"

"It's just work, Lonnie. Work is good. It puts you in the world again. You'd be good in the world, I think. Otherwise it's just yourself and all the things that torment you."

*   *   *

Hood took his own advice and drove out to Castro Ford in El Centro. He didn't expect to see Israel's Flex parked out front, and it was not. He drove along the parts-and-service yard and the used cars, then the rear of the staging lot where the new cars were brought in from the plants. There sat a tractor-trailer rig, its double-decker ramps loaded with twelve new cars. A silver Flex, freshly washed and agleam in the bold dealership lights, was parked up close to the prep bay. There were lights on inside and one of the rolling doors was open. Hood drove a hundred yards, then swung around and parked on the sandy shoulder of the road. He pulled his camera from behind the seat and brought the staging area into focus. The telephoto lens was powerful and the picture very clear.

Castro came through the rolling door of the prep building wearing chinos and a bright aloha shirt, trailed by a tall man wearing an olive suit. Last came a shorter man in a white short-sleeve shirt with a blue Ford patch on the front, jeans, and work boots. Castro and the tall man stood away from the trailer as the short man climbed up into the cab and lowered one of the ramps.

Hood heard the hydraulics moan and saw the glittering new Fords, still in their white protective wrap, descending to the ground. They strained against the straps. The truck driver climbed back down, then got into the white Fusion at the far end of the lower ramp and backed it off the platform and into a place near the prep building. Castro and the tall man pitched in with the front cars—another Fusion, a Ford Taurus and two Lincoln MKZs. Then the short man backed out the last two Milans, one blue and one a dark red. When the top double-decker ramp had been lowered and relieved of its cargo, twelve new cars waited in two neat rows outside the prep bay. Hood timed it at twenty-four minutes and he shot eight pictures.

For a moment the men stood facing the cars. They seemed to be discussing what to do next and through the telephoto lens Hood saw that all three were talking at once and gesticulating at the cars and the prep bay to make their points. The tall man looked Mexican and his olive suit hung expensively. He seemed angry and impatient. The shorter man was nearly bald and he had a thick mustache and an open, humorful face. Castro looked as if he were trying to give orders. Hood had the idea that they'd never done exactly this before, that the situation was different, or maybe altogether new. But how many thousands of factory cars had Castro Ford received in its twelve years of business, Hood wondered. How many hundreds of tractor-trailer deliveries had the short man made? What was the suit doing there? What was the controversy?

A few minutes later Castro and the short man had moved six of the cars into the prep building while the tall one smoked and looked on with an air of disapproval. He checked his cell phone. Then they gathered inside and the roll-up door clattered down. It was 10:42 P.M.

There was a row of windows high up on the prep bay, but Hood had no way of getting up there to look in. He watched the building and tried to keep himself from running his tongue over the diamonds in his tooth. The scar at his hairline itched and he scratched it. He was hungry. Half an hour later the door rolled back up and the men moved the six Fords back into their places on the hydraulic double-decker ramp of the trailer. The other six they moved into the prep bay and the door went down again. Nothing more happened for an hour except that bugs flew in and out of the dealership lights and bats flickered in and out after them. Hood watched, wondering whether Beth would be home on time and whether he had enough croutons for the salad. And why Castro and his men were so touchy about a delivery of cars.

10

Late the next morning Bradley stood before Mrs. Perez's sixth-grade class at Lincoln Elementary School up in the Antelope Valley, north of L.A. This was high desert, where a constant wind whistled through the housing tracts and blew flotillas of plastic bags against the windward walls and fences. Antelope Valley was serviced by LASD's Lancaster Station, and was considered a Siberian assignment by most deputies. Bradley looked out a window at the flat brown grass of the playground as he tried to answer the question.

"Well, I've never shot anyone on duty because I've never had to," he lied. "The goal of any good deputy is to do his or her job without resorting to force."

"What if someone pulls a gun on you?"

"You waste 'em!" offered a skinny boy.

"No, you try to talk to them," said Bradley. He wanted very much to agree with the student. You can't talk to a surprised kidnapper with a gun in his hand. "Circumstances change quickly and you have to keep up. Things get complicated fast. It's like a game. Like . . . I don't know. I'm not being clear here. Sergeant Padilla, maybe you can weigh in on that one."

Bad verb choice, he thought. Padilla easily tipped the scales at two hundred. She glanced at him. His headache was back. The room on this cool morning was heated to what felt like ninety degrees. The children were alert and attentive and annoying. Padilla droned on about appropriate use of force and limits of restraint and last option and the like. Bradley watched a dirt devil unravel across a field. He imagined Erin in a Max Azria dress years ago when they'd ditched a party down in Baja and taken a midnight stroll on a beach and made love standing up in a sand dune.

"What if they pull a knife on you?"

"Don't mess with no blade," said the skinny boy again. "That's what my daddy says."

"He's a wise man," said Bradley.

"Not wise enough to stay outta prison!"

Bradley thought of Erin now, her middle distended, just days away from making him the proudest father on earth. How could he have fallen so far, from a world in which Erin loved him even in the sand dunes of Baja, to one where she was scarcely able to look at him without pity or anger or amazement at his self-absorption and greed? He felt cursed and singled out for tragedy. And worse yet, unlucky.

"I'm sure he'll be out of the can soon," he said, then looked at Sergeant Padilla. "Sergeant, I'm going to take a quick break. Just get a sip of water outside."

"You stay right here, Deputy Jones. We are just about done."

Padilla spoke in the cheerfully condescending tones of some elementary school teachers. She covered the three signs of drug and alcohol abuse, pedestrian safety on the wide new boulevards of the Antelope Valley, and dealing with suspicious adults. Near the end of the period she told the students about Maslow's pyramid of self-actualization, where once your basic needs are met you can then be free to strive for excellence. And a career in the LASD, she pointed out, was a wonderful base on which to build your life.

Outside in the soon-so-be-busy hallway Padilla stood before Bradley and launched a finger into his chest. "I don't care what kind of a celebrity you think you are. I'm a superior, and when I say jump, you ask how high. Got it?"

"Ma'am yes ma'am."

"And quit staring out the windows. You're worse than the children."

*　　*　　*

After shift he waited in a bar off Highway 395 in Adelanto. It was the nicest place in town, though still a hellhole, he thought. From the booth he could see the old motel still boarded up, its sign lying in the rubble of broken asphalt and bottle glass that was once a parking lot. The wind had blown the tumbleweeds up against the security fence and they looked like they were trying to get inside. He looked up at the sign by the highway: WELCOME TO ADELANTO, CITY OF UNLIMITED POSSIBILITIES. He caught his reflection in a window and noted that his hapkido-toned shoulders and arms were flattered by the uniform shirt, but his eyes looked heavy and dead. *The STAR Unit*, he thought. *Maslow's pyramid. What happened to my life?*

Mike Finnegan came in a few minutes later, dressed for golf in a lemon yellow shirt, green pants, saddle shoes, and a red newsboy cap with PGA stitched in gold. He had a white sweater tied around his neck against the high desert chill. He came to the booth with a smile on his face and the sound of his cleats clicking on the floor.

"This is the first time you've actually invited me anywhere since your wedding," he said as he climbed into the booth. Mike was a short, stout man. He took off his hat and Bradley saw that Mike had again changed his hair from its usual red to black. "After all these years! It makes me very happy."

"I'm not happy. I'm at the end of my tether. All tethers."

"Talk to me."

They ordered drinks from a wispy blond with tired eyes and no smile. She was chewing something as she took their orders and still chewing it when she brought the drinks back and set them out. Two men came in and looked at everything in the room except Bradley. The Blands, he thought. CIB's trusted watchdogs. He waved at them and they looked briefly his way.

"Friends?" asked Mike.

"Department watchers. Criminal Investigation Bureau."

"No wonder you're not happy."

"They're just a small part of my trouble. Although when I caught them loitering near my home I felt like *shotgunning them both*." He said this loudly so they could hear. They ignored him and took a table on the far other side of the room. Bradley marched over and slid a fiver into the jukebox and chose the six loudest, fastest songs he could find.

Back at the table he sat and looked into Finnegan's optimistic blue eyes.

"I am here to listen and help," Mike said.

Bradley gave a heated description of CIB's treatment of him—the endless interviews and accusations, the watchers near his home in Valley Center, the watchers shadowing him while he was on patrol, the CIB prying into his banking, tax, and phone records, the threat of a polygraph, his new assignment to the STAR Unit.

"STAR Unit?"

"Success Through Awareness and Resistance. It's for students. It's actually a good program," he said without conviction. "Keeps the kids from being taken advantage of."

"That's important."

Bradley sipped his beer and looked out the dusty window at the traffic moaning up and down 395. And of course his thoughts turned to Erin again: He remembered time they'd driven up that highway to Bishop, where Erin and the Inmates played the Millpond Music Festival. They'd taken a few days to go camping high up in the Sierras north of there. He pictured Erin with her little ultralight spinning rod and reel, catching trout in a lake, the way the high-altitude light turned her hair to radiant copper. Now a boxy-looking vehicle buzzed up 395 trying to outrun a big rig, and it was the same color as Erin's hair had been in that brief but eternal moment. He'd taken her picture. What a face. What a smile.

Then he began talking about her. His voice softened and he looked down at the tabletop as much as he looked at Mike. His heart felt so full yet so constricted. It felt good to let some things out. He had no one in life to speak to, really, except his wife. His brothers were scattered; his father missing-in-action, as he always had been; his mother a ghost. Erin was his best friend, now alternatingly tolerant and furious at him. He told himself it was her hormones but knew it was more than that. When he thought of his soon-to-be-born son, Bradley felt the tears well up in his eyes. He felt locked out of fatherhood, robbed of his natural right to protect and nurture, extorted out of something that should already be his.

When Bradley was finished, he looked up into Mike's hopeful face.

"What do you want?"

"I want my wife to love me. And if I can get those assholes over there off my case, I can operate again. And if I can, I can provide everything Erin needs. Both things are connected. I want it to be like it used to be."

Finnegan studied him frankly. His small freckled hands were folded over each other on the tabletop. "These are not small things. You are twenty-two years old. You have a powerful bureaucracy on your trail—men who know how to inflict harm. And you have lost the love of your wife. I can't make Erin love you."

"I know that."

"But I can help get you the *possibility* of escape from your predicament at work. And perhaps through that freedom, you could woo her back."

"That's what I want. I can work with possible."

"Bradley, do you truly believe that I can help liberate you from your tormentors at work?"

Bradley thought, *What I truly believe is I'll try anything to get what I want.* "Mike, without you I wouldn't have gotten Erin back from Armenta. I never thought I'd see her again. I've come to realize what you did for us. You and Owens both. So I genuinely thank you. I believe that you can help me again. I'm here to ask for your help."

Finnegan was standing and had already dropped a ten on the table. "Let's take a short drive, Bradley. Enough of these big-eared Blands."

"Blands? How do you know that word? I never called them the Blands in front of you."

"Bradley, your thoughts are as loud as those trucks out there, especially when they're about Erin, or your career. I can explain later. But now, *vamos!*"

Mike drove a nicely restored 1953 Chevy pickup, fire engine red, aftermarket pipes. They rumbled several miles up Highway 395, then out a dirt road that led past a Vietnamese Buddhist meditation center and wound back into the hills. Mike sat up ramrod straight on a pillow and Bradley could see that the toes of his saddle cleats were all that touched the brake, gas, and clutch. With his small hands at ten and two, Mike warbled on about the corruption that shut down the city of Adelanto a few years ago, how the cops were taking money and freebies to turn their backs on prostitution and gambling going on at the now-boarded-up motel, and how some of the city councilmen were taking bribes for business favors, and there were backroom real estate deals involving usurious mortgages and people of color.

"I was five years old then," Bradley said idly. He wondered what Erin was doing right now, what were her exact posture and movements and thoughts.

"It was an easy project, considering the handsome, long-term returns," said Mike. "There were gambling losses, loan sharking, foreclosures, ruined marriages, blackmail, drug addiction, violence petty and not, untold heartache. A murder or two. Even venereal disease has its own wonderful little half-life. Too bad it all couldn't last. You saw the old bordello. Technically a motel. Now nothing but dust. But those were three bountiful, beautiful years. All it took was a few ambitious citizens, a stuffed ballot box to put them into power, and *wham!* Bradley, remember this: If you can secure one politician and one member of the law enforcement profession, you can go *bonkers* in a small town. One thing leads to another to another. Everyone comes to see how easy it is to get what they want. It's social fission. Things explode. Look at Bell, Maywood, Vernon! It's my happy little circle of corruption."

"What did you do back there in Adelanto, Mike? Personally. I mean, exactly what did *you* do?"

"Me? Oh, mostly just brainstorming. The city manager was one of mine. Just pure good fortune that I ran across her years prior. She came up in the net, as I like to call it, long after I'd partnered with her father. Who, by the time his daughter was running Adelanto, was locked up in Corcoran for a very squalid domestic murder. I didn't see it coming. One of the dark spots on my curriculum vitae. But then, I gained her in the deal, didn't I? She was a blessing I didn't see coming, either."

Bradley checked the side mirror but through the swirling dust he saw that the road behind them was empty. He remembered now that Mike, for as long as he had known him, had often seemed to find humor, and sometimes even joy, in human travail. "What value is it to you, Mike? Crime and suffering?"

"Executive summary? There were two brothers who lived hidden in a forest near a village. One was the King and the other was the Prince. In the beginning they disagreed about control of the people in the village. The King wanted to give them laws and demand their worship. The Prince wanted to let them create their own laws and worship whatever they wished to worship. You see, they both *loved* human beings. They saw human beings as the future of not only the village but the whole earth. So the King banished the Prince from the forest to the desert. The King remained hidden in the forest and sent his representatives into the village, disguised as people. The Prince from the desert did likewise. Then the village became a state and then a country, then the world. This story is oversimplified. But it is a convenient and truthful way to understand the world around you."

"But I asked about the crime and suffering you seem to enjoy."

"When faith in the King is undermined, people are freed from his control. People can then choose. We who work for the Prince know that our best tool is chaos, but our goal for you is not chaos at all, but choice. Choice. Freedom. Liberty. Man came into the world free and

the King bullied you and stole that freedom away. We work in op-
position to his slavery. We hold humankind in the highest esteem. We
love and respect you. You are our image and ideal. In a very real sense,
we worship you. So we work tirelessly to help you get your freedom
back."

And you're crazy as a shithouse rat, thought Bradley. He nearly
laughed but managed to get out his next words convincingly, with
feeling. "You . . . you're the devil?"

"We rarely use that word, but yes. I'm one of many. And there are
angels, too, and they have us outnumbered roughly ten to one. We are
all representatives. Agents, if you prefer. Worldwide. We're compara-
ble to two multinational conglomerates. Though we wouldn't be
among the largest in terms of employees."

Bradley looked at Mike and tried to apply the word *devil* to a
small man dressed ridiculously and thought, *Why not?* A devil dressed
for golf? What better disguise? Mike always looked ridiculous. Maybe
that was how he managed to get around so easily. But try as he might
Bradley could not swallow the idea. *Still,* he thought. *Tell him anything he wants to hear. Let him believe that I believe.* "What do you
mean *partner*? You've used that word around me before."

"Partnership is the deepest personal and professional bond we can
offer you. To become a partner requires three things of you and one
of me. The first of your requirements is belief."

"Belief in what?"

"In yourself and in me. Second, there's a simple vow. Much like the
pledge of allegiance that students used to say at Friday morning as-
semblies. But it has to be spoken with the aforementioned belief or it
means nothing."

"Lay it on me, the vow."

"We call it the Declaration of Parity. It goes like this: *As the equal
of God, I renounce Him. I am the judge of right and wrong and of
beauty. I am the author of law. I am man. I am free.*"

"That's all a person has to say?"

"No. Truly believing, and then having declared your parity, you must ask me to be your partner. If I accept, then we are partners. I can't do the asking. That's a law of nature, of course, which neither man, devils, angels, nor God can delete or modify in any way."

"Can I change my mind later and un-partner?"

"Of course. We're not gangsters! Making up your own mind is what we're trying to promote. That's our number one goal, simply stated. So you can change your mind about anything. Though honestly, it's never happened."

"Not once?"

"Never to me. My partners have all been very, very successful. I try my best to get to them by age eleven, and I have rigorous standards. The single best prognosticator for success as a partnered human being is ambition. This is where everything begins. Second greatest? Appetites—*indulged* appetites. Third? Perfectionism. I look for monstrous, gigantic egos linked closely to a sense of entitlement and possessing a simple can-do attitude. I never partner with the mad, I simply won't. They sadden me. I use them occasionally, but never long-term. I do have associates who haven't been so fortunate with partners, but we all have different standards. It's all about judgment and luck. Enough of that, though. We'll have plenty of time for shoptalk, Bradley, if we decide to do this thing."

"Who is stronger, the King or the Prince?"

Finnegan looked over at Bradley with a frankly optimistic expression. Then he turned his attention back to the road, which had gone bad by now. He downshifted with a growl from the pipes and guided the truck through the ruts and around the rocks. "The King is stronger and has more angels, but they are not strong enough to defeat us. Think of the contest as elemental: fire and water, or wind and rock. They influence each other endlessly but there is no end to either, no finality."

"Are angels and devils evenly matched?"

"Very closely matched, pound for pound. We identify one another largely by smell. Very doggy. Close proximity weakens both parties. But as I said, they outnumber us considerably. They're much better organized. Look at the thousands upon thousands of churches and synagogues and mosques. They provide endless options for contact with men. Endless opportunities for observation and of course persuasion. We've got nothing of the sort."

"Why not set up some Satanic churches?"

"They go nowhere. Because we have no goodies or punishments, no carrots or sticks. We have nothing to offer *but* freedom. True freedom terrifies most of mankind. They would much rather have specific limits. God commissioned the concepts of heaven and hell through his poets, just for such people. These concepts give you easy-to-understand, obtainable goals. He still commissions them. Propaganda constantly needs to be updated. But there really is no heaven or hell. Thus, we offer no ten commandments except as each man decides them. What we want, finally, is for you not to need us. The final freedom, if you will."

Bradley studied the foothills around them, dotted by mines and collapsed frames that looked like piles of splinters and great rusted iron contraptions slouching here in the pitiless sun for over a century. Of course he didn't believe anything Finnegan was saying, but just hearing such blasphemy made the adrenaline flow. He'd never heard a more invigorating symphony of bullshit since some Scientology dweebs cornered him one night in a club where Erin was performing. So now his ears were ringing and his heart beating fast. *Tell him what he needs to hear.* "What about that night in Baja with the knife? When you cut my palm and yours, and we traded blood?"

"That was the yearning of an old man to enlist the faith of a young man. Sorry. I'd had a nip or three of that tequila while you were out in the pasture, and I was suddenly wildly romantic. But truly, I've made blood pacts before and there is something to them. Maybe they're nothing more than theater. Call me silly and sentimental but I swear . . . I *feel* something when the blood of a fine strong human being meets my own. I feel as if . . . as if . . . a river has met the sea."

Alright, thought Bradley, *he's clearly and spectacularly insane.* Get what you want from him.

"Don't think such things," said Mike. "I can't help you if you don't believe in me."

"How can you do that? Like the Blands? You think you can hear my thoughts?"

"A journeyman devil can hear human thoughts from thirty feet away, so long as those thoughts are clear and emphatic. If a person thinks visually, we get the images too, like watching a TV. Very difficult in a crowded room filled with conversation. Very easy in a vehicle, even one with those wonderful glasspacks I put on this thing. Don't you love that sound?"

"What else can you do, Mike?"

"Gosh. It's a pretty modest portfolio, really. We have more physical strength than men. Ask Charlie Hood, but more on him later. Much more on him, as a matter of fact. We have very high levels of energy and don't need much sleep. Tremendous tolerance to pain. We heal very quickly. But we have only minor powers. For instance, we can cause people to dream certain dreams. We don't have to be nearby, as with the thoughts. But there are dangers. Because once a dream is inserted, we can't control a person's *reaction* to the dream, so in the early days there were lots of backfires. We rarely do any dream work these days. We can will into being minor temporary ailments such as headaches, itchy skin, nausea. Conversely, we can also induce mild euphoria—a sense of optimism and power—in most people. This euphoria is a common thing during the first months of partnership, though we're not exactly sure why it is. Some believe it's something akin to the feelings of purification after baptism, perhaps, or the obscene ecstasies of Pentecostal types. It seems to come from the partners as much as from anything we do. We want our partners just as strong and happy as they can safely be. We discourage sadness and depression in both partners and the general human population—they are counterproductive. We're not quite immortal, though we are very durable. That's our greatest strength, really: We *last*. That's about it. People think that devils can possess a human, or that we wait for you in fiery pits, or turn into monsters. No. What we mainly do is listen, and talk, and suggest and persuade. We make arrangements. We introduce people to other people, in hope that useful things will result. I told you once that I introduced your mother and father because I wanted a certain *you* to be born. That is true. And now, here we are, talking about partnership. Partnership with you has been a vision of mine for many years, Bradley, many years before you were born. From Murrieta to Suzanne to you. One of my precious bloodlines. One of my families. Not that your mother was a partner. She really had no interest in the grander forms of mischief. She was a passion of mine because of her history, her line. Murrieta, El Famoso, was a remarkable, phenomenal man. And I saw that she could give him to me again, in you."

Mike guided the truck up a narrow two-track to a level shelf of tailings. They got out, the tailings aglitter in metallic blues and greens, crunching underfoot like loose jewels. Mike traded out his sweater for a small soft-sided cooler with a strap, which he slung over one shoulder. "It's a bit of a hike now," he said.

"To where?"

"To where you will hear something that will help you understand and adjust. You will not see, but you will hear. I hope one sense is enough to satisfy you."

"Understand and adjust to what?"

"I love your curiosity, Bradley. You will need to listen and learn. But first, follow. Simply follow."

11

Mike set out across the rocky slope, heading up. In spite of his small size he moved quickly and Bradley found himself losing ground and having to work to make it up, only to lose it again. The faint path finally vanished altogether and they picked their way through rocks that got bigger as they climbed in elevation. Soon the rocks were as tall as Mike himself and he stopped fifty yards up and looked down on Bradley, face flushed and smile wide. "You've got to get back to the gym, Brad!"

"I am back in the gym."

"We're getting there!" He turned and scrambled through an opening in the boulders and by the time Bradley got there Mike was a hundred yards ahead, and higher still, inching up a huge rock like a green, yellow, and red starfish. In the thin desert air Bradley could hear the screeching of the golf shoe cleats against the stone and the echo of Mike's voice. "This is the only way over! But this is the worst of it, I promise!"

Bradley finally topped the same rock, then picked his way down the backside of the hillock. His duty boots were not bad for the terrain, and his uniform trousers were designed for physical activity. The afternoon air was cooling already and he felt the tingle of his drying sweat.

He looked out at the mine at the base of the next hill. The entrance yawned, framed by rusted steel girders. He saw no roads or paths or game trails, no evidence that the mine had had a worker or even a visitor in a century or more. When he got there Mike was sitting on a big boulder near the opening. The soft cooler sat beside him.

"Look behind you at the view," said Mike.

Bradley turned and looked out across the desert, Adelanto faintly twinkling in the distance, the ribbon of 395 stretching from its dusty beginnings in the south all the way north to where it vanished. He could see the shiny steel plates of the solar plant swallowing sunlight through the dry, clear air, and the faint dome of the correctional facility.

"Bradley, I brought you here to give you a small piece of hard evidence of what I am, and what you can soon to be a part of, should you want to. You are among the most suspicious and least-trusting men I've ever met. Some understand me instinctively, through their hearts, such as Joaquin. But you are a man of the senses. You have to see and touch and smell. Because of men like you, there is actually a fourth step you must take if I am to help you and we are to become partners."

"I figured there would be a catch."

"Not really a catch. But, yes, as I explained, you must believe in me and make the Declaration of Parity. You must ask me to be your partner. But the fourth rule of partnership is that you must be fully aware of what I am. You must *know* who you are dealing with. As they say in American jurisprudence, you must be able to assist in your own defense."

"That's covered under belief. You already said your first rule was belief."

"Some men can never believe until they know. That's why we have rule number four. I have heard your doubts very clearly and loudly, Bradley. Way out here there's nothing to compete with them. They're coming to me static-free, as by fiber optics. They are as clear to me as carrier pigeons winging across the Veracruz sky. Shall I *quote* you?"

"Quote me."

"*. . . crazy as a shithouse rat . . . a devil dressed for golf? why not? what better disguise . . . he looks ridiculous but maybe that's how he manages to get around so easily . . . let him believe I believe . . . he's*

clearly and spectacularly insane . . . tell him what he needs to hear . . .
an invigorating symphony of bullshit . . . Scientology dweebs . . . Do
any of those pithy phrases ring a bell, Brad?"

"That's just a parlor trick. Like Uri Geller bending spoons."

Mike shrugged and slid off the rock and went to the mouth of the
mineshaft and bent forward, resting his hands on his knees as if he
were about to jump in.

Bradley looked at the little man, then down into the cave opening,
a dark and ominous thing to a lifelong claustrophobe such as he was,
and his mother and her ancestors had been. He saw, within just a few
feet of the mouth, nothing but blackness. A wisp of dust raised by
Mike's golf shoes hovered in the sunlight above the hole. The dust was
bright and hopeful, but unmeaningful to Bradley, compared to the
eternal blackness of the mine. He thought of being locked in the trunk
of his own car a few months ago, of the terror that had risen up inside
him there in the dark confines.

Mike's voice was sudden and loud. "Beatrice! Bea! It's Mike. Yoo-
hoo."

Hands still on his knees, Mike turned and looked at Bradley with
a mischievous grin, then turned back again to the hole. "Bea, I know
you're down there!"

Bradley looked at the back of Mike's red PGA cap, and his compact torso snug in the yellow knit shirt, and his little round rump
packed into the green cotton-poly golf pants. He pictured himself
skipping forward and knocking Mike in with a flying axe kick. At this
thought Finnegan turned again, with a hard look of assessment on his
face. "Be careful what you think," he said. This time his smile was not
one of mischief but one of knowing.

"You're not impressing me," said Bradley. "Let's get back. I'm tired
of your horseshit and I don't want to be your partner."

"Beatrice? I've brought some things for you. Incoming!" Mike re-
trieved his soft cooler and took it to the yawning mouth of the cave.
He unzipped a compartment and pulled out a bunch of chocolate

bars, a common and popular brand, and held them over the darkness and let go. Bradley watched them vanish, heard them ticking against the rock on their descent.

"Beatrice Ann, I want you to meet Bradley Jones, one of El Famoso's descendants. He's a fabulous young man and we're about to embark on what I think will be a very long and very profitable *partnership*. Yes, you heard me correctly. So, I just wanted you to say hello to him. I wanted you to tell him exactly what the stakes are when we talk about belief and partnership and angels and devils. He still thinks it's all something I make up for my own amusement. Speak up, you vapid little virgin. Say hello to Bradley Jones, you angel you!"

Then a voice came from the depth and darkness, and when it first vibrated into Bradley's ears, his legs lost their strength and he went to one knee on the hard, sharp ground. It was as if he'd been struck by an invisible hand. The voice was faint but clear, louder than conversation but not a shout. There was agony in it and pleading and anger. Its surface was hoarse with disuse and silence. "Bradley Jones, do not let Mike deceive you. El Famoso was a vicious murderer, a horse thief, and no part of a gentleman. Like him, you will suffer beyond your ability to imagine suffering. Look what the world did to Joaquin, partner of the great Mike Finnegan! And to Rosa and Chappo! Save yourself and your loved ones. Nothing on earth is worth his price. God and His angels wait to embrace you. We love you more than you know."

Mike turned and looked at Bradley again. "That's exactly what I thought she'd say. She really does need some new material."

Mike jammed a hand into the pack and brought out in succession a fistful of meat sticks, two bags of pork rinds, three red apples, then dropped them all back in. He pulled up a six-pack of cheap canned beer, which he dangled by its plastic binder for Bradley to see. "Odd, but these are the things she has come to enjoy. In ninety-four years it's come down to this unhealthy, processed crapola. Except the apples. I've thrown her homemade bread and real butter and honey and delicious smoked fish and fresh fruits and vegetables from around the world but no, she likes pork rinds and meat sticks and budget beer. Not that she needs these things. She needs no food or water to live, just as I wouldn't need them if I were down there. But these are treats and they taste good and you know what? She is my sworn and eternal enemy, but I do like and respect her. Look at all an angel must live without—the same as we devils. And century after century she remains feisty and tireless, though utterly without humor. Sometimes I feel sorry for her. Beatrice Ann? Fore!" Mike pushed the sixer back in and zipped the cooler shut and swung it out over the mineshaft and let it go. Four seconds later Bradley heard the light whack of it glancing off rock, then another, fainter with depth.

"We had a kind of Geneva Convention years ago," said Mike. "To get these situations under control. For a while there was much too much of this, very distracting for both sides. Now there's a hundred-year max on agent-by-agent detention, absolutely no torture beyond the boredom, heat and cold, and the obvious challenges of hygiene. So I'll have to get her out in six short years. In the meantime I've heaved dozens of blankets down there, good ones, real Pendletons with Native American symbols woven in. And bushels of meat sticks and gallons of beer, and antibacterial hand wipes by the case. Costco. I just can't quite bring myself to hate her."

Her voice wavered up from her private hell again. "Bradley? If you don't ask him to partner, he cannot destroy you. By the laws of God and the world He created, Mike Finnegan cannot destroy you. He can't even damage you in any significant way. He can only cajole you into damaging yourself and those around you. Whenever a devil comes to you he wants much more than just you. He is after your family, your descendants, your entire narrative upon the earth. Resist him. Refuse him. Any place of worship can help you. Any priest or pastor or rabbi or imam. Any spiritually cognizant person. Stay *away* from him. Read your Bible. Keep it near you. Strike him with it, or even wave it at him and it will make Mike nauseous."

Mike shook his head and smiled at Bradley, then called down. "Bea, you really are such a prude! But enjoy the treats and I'll be back someday soon. Are you still sleeping almost every night now?"

"Yes. Sometimes for over an hour. There's just literally nothing to do down here but pray. So after you get used to it, sleep begins to seem interesting. Dreams are revealing. You learn so much about yourself. Especially what you cannot do. Your weaknesses. You learn what you are *not*. I feel more like a human every day."

"Still dreaming that you can fly, little angel?"

"Every night I dream that I can fly."

"Can you still recite the complete Psalms?" He looked at Bradley and smiled wickedly.

"One through one hundred fifty. That's nothing, Mike. You know the hours I put in on them."

"Yes, I do. Well, until next time, Beatrice Ann, my ancient and eternally dried-up virgin angel, you take care and try to behave yourself down there. If God had made you with the wings that human beings give you in art and literature, you could flutter out of there like a big bat."

"I'm not so big anymore, Mike. Pretty much just skin and bones. There are so many things I wish I could do. Thanks for the gifts. Somewhere in the center of your hideous soul there is a flicker of goodness and light."

"Don't be saying things like that about me, Bea. They have a new word for that kind of thing now: *dissing*. Well, new to you, anyway. It means disrespecting."

"My nature won't allow me to respect you, Mike. But the apples and meat sticks really do go well together. And I'm happy that, in some strange way, you like pleasing me."

"Until we meet again."

"Pray to God, Bradley! Pray to Him!"

A moment of quiet fell upon them. Bradley watched three vultures wheeling in the sky high above and felt a net of crazy fear settling over

him, as if dropped by the big black birds. Then the entombed Beatrice
Ann let out a wail that made the hair on his neck rise, and his heart
flutter. It was not a scream or a moan but a high-pitched keen, corpo-
real yet disembodied, both flesh and spirit. It cut the clear dry air for
many long seconds. Bradley heard the animal in it, the fear and
mourning, the abandon and fury. Very gradually it faded, as if she had
fallen deeper into the abyss but never stopped crying out.

The fresh silence was long and brittle. Mike sighed and stepped
away from the mine shaft and looked at Bradley. "Stand up straight.
Don't ever again take a knee for anyone, especially not her ilk. Not
even for me. You have between here and my truck to organize your
thoughts and beliefs, and then tell me what you want to do."

Bradley rose and stepped forward to the shaft and looked down
into it. Then he turned to Mike and the small man did not appear ridiculous at all in spite of his bright clothing; he looked condensed and
capable and he had an expression that Bradley had never seen on him,
something dark and cruel and controlled. Bradley started down the
mountain. His legs were uncertain and his feet were cold. The sun was
bright and low in the west and with every step Bradley told himself
he had not seen what he had seen, nor heard what he had heard. But
for the first time in his life he could not believe himself, could not
override his senses with his will. All truth seemed new now and all
warranties expired. He veered off behind a bush to pee and check his
cell phone. *As the equal of God I renounce him,* he thought. What a
thing to believe and to say.

"Speak to me," called Mike from behind. "Speak to me, my fine,
wayward son of Murrieta."

"As the equal of God, I renounce Him," he muttered without looking back, his words buried in the sharp tumble and clatter of the rocks
as he sidestepped down the mountain. But he felt a sudden power of
heart, coupled with a confidence that he hadn't felt since the bloody
shootout in Yucatán four months ago. It was like the sun breaking
through dark clouds. His body and muscles and blood felt strong and

young again. His eyes saw very clearly. He took a deep breath and felt his lungs expanding with the cool clean desert air. "I am the judge of right and wrong and of beauty."

"Louder, Bradley! And with conviction. I can hardly hear you!"

Bradley shouted out the words and Mike caught up with him and they headed down the mountain.

12

The next afternoon Mary Kate Boyle waited at the bus stop across the street from the Buenavista ATF field office. It struck her as funny that the big bad ATF had a little cluster of offices inside the Imperial Bank building. It was a reflective glass building, two stories high, with an investment company and an accounting firm and law offices and who knew what else. Downstairs there was also a café that had good muffins and expensive coffee.

The day was sunny and cool, not sticky humid like back home. A very old Native American man sat unmoving at the other end of the bench, arms crossed and head lolled forward far enough for his chin to touch his chest. His eyes were closed and he had neither moved nor apparently breathed since she had come off the eastbound bus and sat down two minutes ago. Her phone rang again, and again it was Skull.

"I told you not to call, Skull. I wasn't *kidding* when I said I was done with you. I am *done* with you. It's over. You can't treat a girl like that. You just can't." She clicked off and glanced at the old man as if for approval. "Right?" He didn't move.

Near the end of her first week here in Southern California, Mary Kate was beginning to feel invisible but at least she wouldn't go hungry. For a skinny girl, she loved to eat, especially spicy food, and the zesty fast-food options here whipped her stomach into forest fires of appetite. Just seeing the graphic posters and signs made her want to order: the Angry Whopper, the Flame-Thrower Encharito, the XXL Chalupa, Spicy Chicken Crispers. The establishments: Del Taco, Pollo Loco, BK, and more, everywhere she looked. They put the bland Russell County DQs and Hardee's to shame.

Just two days ago she'd been down to her last two hundred bucks and change, and maybe one more week on Amy and Victor's couch if she was lucky. So she'd borrowed Amy's car and applied at temp agencies from L.A. down to San Diego, but she couldn't type except to text, wasn't handy with computers, and she had no high school diploma on account of chronic truancy while trying to keep up with Lyle and his bad-boy ways.

But yesterday a dapper young Latino had hired her on the spot at a KFC in downtown San Diego where she'd gone in for a snack, and after the three-hour lunch shift, she'd found a by-the-week hotel room not far away. By late afternoon she'd returned Amy's car, then come all the way back to San Diego on the bus. Trailways again. Her room at the Winston Arms was a dive but most the dives wouldn't take women at all so she felt lucky. And she could pretty much eat all she wanted at KFC, which made her feel good about both her present and her future. Mary Kate had gone hungry as a little girl and it was a feeling she never wanted to have again. Ever. It made you feel weak and worthless and it took away your fight.

At KFC she was "front of shop," which meant taking orders, bagging them up, and running a cash register. Just a few minutes ago, on her bus trip here to the ATF office in Buenavista, she'd seen a help-wanted sign at the In-N-Out Burger. They had better food than KFC except for the mashed potatoes and coleslaw, but the idea of her working in Buenavista and Skull being a few short miles away in El Centro didn't feel right at all. If their paths crossed, she might be able to convince him that she had come here because she missed him, because Skull had large ideas about his charm and desirability. He also might suspect something and just flat-out beat the truth out of her. Or worse. Her phone vibrated again and she saw the number and didn't answer.

A minute later she stood and looked down at the native. " 'Til we meet again, chief."

"Never answer a phone."

"You ain't kidding."

*   *   *

The lobby was spacious and the floor was shiny black marble with glittery shavings of something in it. The security guard was a large muscular man with a scarred but not unfriendly face and a very crisp blue uniform. He was armed. His nameplate said OSCAR. Mary Kate signed in and Oscar gave her a hard look as he dialed the phone.

Charlie Hood led her back to his cubicle and pulled out a chair for her, then sat behind a small desk. On the desk were a computer with a rolling-river screen saver and a cup of coffee on an electric warmer. Mary Kate had called Hood specifically because he was cute and had diamonds in his teeth and no ring on his finger, and because his boss, Dale, was a fool. "He's been calling," she said. "Skull. I thought you'd want to know."

"Have you talked to him?"

"Twice yesterday, twice today."

"Does your phone have GPS?"

"It's your basic flip, comes with the plan." She held it out and Hood took it and checked it over, then handed it back.

"No GPS. Skull thinks you're in Missouri?"

"I don't ever know what he thinks. Last time he called I didn't answer. His voice does kind of send a chill down my spine."

Hood nodded. "You can help us. It's up to you."

"I wouldn'ta called you if I wasn't ready to help. I get the feeling he'll keep calling me 'til you put him away."

"If you can just let him believe that you're in Russell County, you'll be safe and he might get loose with information."

"His Achilles tendon is that he brags."

Mary Kate watched Hood unlock one of the file cabinets that stood beside his desk, and rummage through a shallow cardboard box. His hair was dark and long and it fell over his forehead when he leaned down. He wore strangely alluring suits and shoes, but when he smiled it was uncomplicated and boylike despite the showy diamonds. He brought out a small digital recorder and opened the back and spilled out the batteries. He got a new package of triple A's and took two. He did things patiently and seemed to concentrate.

"Do you ever put him on speaker when you talk?"

"If I'm busy."

"If you can put him on speaker without making him suspicious, and use this, we'll have his words, too."

"For court?"

"We can't use them in court. He's got an expectation of privacy. We can use them to help us find and arrest him, though."

"I got a job at KFC in downtown San Diego."

"I'm glad to hear that. So you were serious about staying in Southern California."

"I was serious about the movie star, model, or nurse. I kid a lot but not about the important stuff. I'm at the Winston Arms downtown and it's a real pit."

"Maybe you'll make some friends, find a roommate or two."

"In San Diego they got the Old Globe Theatre, and a theater in La Jolla that wins awards. *Jersey Boys* got started there, not in New Jersey like you'd think. And *The Wizard of Oz* got written on some island near San Diego. The book, not the movie." Her phone rang and she checked the number. "Skull."

Hood pushed a black button on his desk phone and a red button on the digital recorder. "Answer and put him on speaker."

She sighed softly, answered, and went to speaker. "I got one hundred percent of nothing to say to you."

"Don't hang up. I miss you, Mary Kate. That's all I have to say. I wish I was back there with you. California isn't all it's cracked up to be. Doesn't look like it does on TV."

Hood had a half smile and he was nodding. He looked to her like Spider-Man and she wondered if she looked like Mary Jane next door. She let a beat go by and thought again how truly easy it was to act so long as you believed your part. "Russell County looks just fine without you in it. You never even said you were sorry."

"I am so darned sorry, honey."

"You know how much that hurt? You should see me now."

"I'd do anything in the world to make you feel better."

She winked at Hood. "Well, that's easy to say from two thousand miles away."

"Come on out. I'll pay for the ticket and we'll be together. We were meant for that, Mary Kate. You and I both know it."

"And the worst hurt was I trusted you, Skull. I was so fooled and surprised when you started hitting me. I had your baby inside."

There was a long silence. Mary Kate watched Hood, who was staring at the recorder intensely enough to hypnotize it.

"I can make it right again."

"It wasn't right to start with."

"Mary Kate, sometimes a man does things he regrets. I regret everything I did wrong to you. With all my heart. I'll be home soon. I'll make us right again."

"Sounds like my invite to California just got canceled."

"Where are you? What are you doing? What are you wearing? Did your lips heal up yet?"

Now Mary Kate let the silence grow again. She glanced at Hood and smiled slightly, though her lips still hurt. She winked at him again because she was about to deliver some very crafty words. "Lyle? I'm tired of talking to you. How 'bout you talk to *me*? Tell me something that won't hurt. Where are you? You making any money out there? Have you sold anything or not?"

"It's going okay. You know that big-ass thing we took out to the woods? The watermelons? I got us some good money for it. There's other sales pending. And we're about to get some new . . . items. Friends of mine out here, from the service. They got military stuff from the Naval Weapons Station. Big stuff, big money."

"You mean like bombs?"

"I could say MANPADS but that might not mean much to you."

"Nope. But I'm happy for you." Mary Kate reached across Hood's desk and took a pen out of a coffee cup and wrote on his legal pad: "See? Has to brag."

Hood smiled. The diamonds glittered. But Mary Kate could tell something had just hit him, and hard.

"You always had good luck, Skull."

"Luck enough to get you."

"Those days are most insuredly gone."

"I don't want them gone."

"Then when you coming back?"

"When the job is done, honey."

"I do not qualify as your honey anymore. We were on brand-new footing as of the second you hit me."

She heard Lyle sigh. As a bully he had no endurance. He had very finite levels of patience and forgiveness. When they were gone was when he started hitting people or whatever else was handy.

"I gotta go now, Mary Kate. I love you sure as the sunrise. I'll be home soon."

"Maybe I'll be here and maybe I won't."

"I'll bring you something."

"What?"

"Something nice. You like a necklace or choker or something? They got the Walk of Fame up in Hollywood, maybe I could find something there."

"Get me a Spider-Man doll," she said, looking at Hood, who of course didn't get the reference.

"Since when do you like Spider-Man?"

"What I'd really like is for this shiner to go away and my lips to stop bleeding every time I try to smile."

Mary Kate punched off her phone and watched Hood as he turned off the recorder. "It feels good to get a little even with that sonofabitch. Play his own kinda game right back on him."

"You're good."

"I can act, alright. Since I was born, Mom said." She saw that darkness cross Hood's eyes again.

"A MANPADS is a Man-Portable Air-Defense System," Hood said. "It's a guided shoulder-fired missile. They're not hard to use and you can take out a commercial airliner from five miles away."

"Who'd want to do that? Oh, damn, stop—that was *utterly* idiotic. I'm getting hungry-dumb."

"Transcribe the conversations with Lyle if you can. At least keep notes after you talk. Call me after every one. Don't press him and don't call him unless you feel him losing interest. Make him call you."

Mary Kate studied Hood's earnest face, his clear steady eyes, and thought she saw something of the boy he'd been and of the man he would become. She sensed secrets and resident obsessions. "Charlie, I've been dreaming Double-Doubles. Can we go to the In-N-Out down the street? I'll pay."

Hood pushed the recorder toward her. "Rain check? I've got paper to push."

"That sounds exciting."

They stood and Hood looked down at the computer screen and moved and clicked the mouse. From this angle Mary Kate could see the change in the color of the monitor light but not what was on the screen.

"What was the name of the fourth man? The one who disappeared?"

"Officer Pat Parsons."

Hood nodded and rubbed his chin with his thumb and forefinger. "This morning the Russell County Sheriff reported his body found out by Birch Springs."

"Miles of hollers out there."

"Gunshot. Foul play suspected. Coroner can usually tell a suicide from a homicide."

Mary Kate's heart stuttered a beat and she felt darkness falling over her thoughts. "I don't think Lyle and them are capable of that."

"Why don't you?"

"Just what my gut says." She watched Hood's calm eyes rove her face and she saw full well that he was looking at her shiner and her split lips. "Anybody that gets their heart involved can make a mistake. Whether you work for KFC or FAT."

"That's the truth. It's good you're helping, Mary Kate. You're doing the right thing. And just so you know, it's ATF not FAT."

"I'm funnin'. Last call for In-N-Out."

"Sorry."

"See you around, secret agent man."

"I'll walk you out."

She left him in the lobby standing behind Oscar's desk, both men looking at her with such gravity that she wanted to laugh but did not.

13

After dark Hood got a large coffee and drove out to Castro Ford in El Centro. Again he parked off the street behind the parts-and-service yard. He sipped the coffee and turned the news down low and looked through his camera at the new-car prep bay, which was open and well lighted. Two men he didn't recognize were peeling the protective film off a shiny new Taurus. Beside it was a stunning Explorer painted a metallic cobalt blue, still partially wrapped in white. Across the expanse of flat sand desert that separated Hood from the dealership he could hear the sound of the Mexican music playing from the radio while the men worked.

Half an hour later he drove around to the front and parked again in one of the guest spaces. Israel's Flex wasn't there. Hood wandered through the showroom, coffee in hand, admiring the new cars, then walked past the financing cubicles and past the just-closing service center. He found a restroom, then took the EMPLOYEES ONLY door that let him into a hallway that led to the parts and used-car offices and the new-car intake area.

Hood walked across the compound, toward the spray of light coming from the intake bay. He came through the rolling door and nodded at each of the men, then approached the Explorer and stopped. The older of the two men slung a shop rag over his shoulder and walked to a workbench and turned off the radio. The other, young enough to be his son, continued peeling the film off the Taurus.

"What I can help you?" asked the older man. His hair was curly and gray and his face etched by the sun.

"I'm interested in this Explorer."

"You talk to sales. We are not sales."

"Does it have the same gas-guzzling six cylinder as the old one?"

"No. Is V-eight. Now you go to sales. They make you a very good deal."

Hood walked around the car, frowning, fingers to his chin. When he had completed his circumnavigation the older man was still there, his polish rag still over his shoulder. Hood nodded and turned his attention to the two Lincoln MKZs and two Ford Tauruses that he'd seen delivered here a few nights ago.

He pointed. "Better mileage if I got one of those."

"You decide, then go to sales." The old man shrugged, then took his shop rag in hand and turned the radio back on and returned to the Taurus. Hood listened to the *banda* ballad, heavy on the accordion and tuba. He sipped his coffee and strolled closer to the Zephyrs and Milans. To him they looked showroom-ready, right down to the fresh tire black and the MSRP and Monroney labels. He threw open a driver's side door and leaned in. The smell was terrific. He pulled the trunk and hood latches and had a look at the engine first. It was amazing how densely packed the compartment was. Around back he lifted the trunk lid and thought of Clint Wampler's finger, and noted that the spare was not in its well but rather lying out in the open. The cover was loose and out of place. He pulled it up out of curiosity and saw the empty declivity where the spare would sit and the big bolt and plastic nut to hold it fast. He saw the dusting of off-white powder in the well, and he glanced over at the hardworking men before running his finger through it, then touching it to his tongue. The dust was cool and bright and a moment later the tip of his tongue was numb. *I'll be damned*, thought Hood.

He looked through the other Zephyr and the two remaining Milans and he found another dusting of cocaine in one of the trunks, this time in a small tool compartment. He slammed the trunk lid authoritatively. He used the bathroom and strolled back through the bay. He found the delivery whiteboard propped on a long table between a water dispenser and a very stained coffeemaker. He saw that the Zephyr/Milano shipment of days past had originated at the Hermosillo Ford Plant in Mexico. He wondered if that was where they loaded in the magic powder, or if the new Hermosillo cars made another stop before Castro Ford. The next Hermosillo delivery was set eight days away at nine thirty A.M., a Saturday.

Hood returned to the Explorer, wrote down the VIN in his notebook. "I really want this car," he told the older man.

"Then you go to sales."

"I might need financing."

"Go to sales and they give you it."

"Maybe I need to think about it. The GMC Yukon gets better mileage."

The man shook his head and turned his back to Hood and went back to his job.

Hood walked back through the dealership building to the showroom and paused again to check out the new Mustang. Over invoice but sweet. He stopped to talk to one of the salesmen about the Explorer back in the intake building, explaining how *Consumer Reports* had said buyers could sometimes save a few dollars by buying a vehicle that hadn't been totally prepped yet. The salesman offered to bring it around for a drive, but Hood said he was in a hurry. He drove away, then circled back a mile down and parked behind the dealership again, with a view of the new-car intake yard. The rolling doors were still open, and when he rolled down his window, he could hear the radio sounds lilting across the desert toward him.

He reclined his seat slightly and rested his head and watched. He called his mother, which he often did during surveillance. She was angry at the staff of her husband's board-and-care there in Bakersfield because they'd stopped trying to give him solid food of any kind and Douglas was "wasting away." Hood's father had been struck hard by

Alzheimer's five years back. It seemed as if he'd live on forever like that, sound of body but stripped of mind, until the stroke. Since then, just a downward slide—partial paralysis, atrophy, cardiopulmonary decline, infection. He recognized his wife and son only occasionally and, when he did, he was venomous in his complaints about the care they were taking of him. He loathed and feared the staff people, hated the food. Hood let his mother vent and tried to be comforting. He felt bad for her because she had loved her husband and pledged to endure with him in sickness and health, and that pledge was irrevocable. Three of Hood's several siblings still lived in Bakersfield, so at least she got some help, and Douglas got some company. Hood dreaded his visits, felt numbed by the dying, ghostlike oldsters and the knowledge that his turn for this would likely come. And his dread shamed him because the furious heap of skin and bone upon the bed before him, growing lighter by the week, was his father, who had been a funny and generous and gentle man, and Hood had loved him.

Hood saw the young man come to one of the rolling doors and grab the rope and pull it down. Across the desert and over the music he heard the metallic clanking and one rectangle of light was replaced by darkness. He told his mother about Buenavista's new Walmart and the surprisingly cold and wet winter they were having, and the un-usual amount of seismic activity in Imperial Valley, but said nothing about world current events. She read no papers and watched no news and had little interest in the world outside her husband's care, the garden in her backyard, and her two now-aging Chihuahuas. Hood warbled on about Beth, working hard but saving lives at the ER, and how he cooked for her when she came home and they traded tales of the day, how it was tough to figure out a good meal when you only knew how to cook a few things, but really the secret was to buy good ingredients and not overcook them. He watched the big man pull down the second rolling door. "I love you, Mom. I'll be up soon to see you and we'll visit Dad."

"When?"

"I'll be tied up this weekend. Maybe next."

"I have you down for next. I'll make sure your room is clean. Beth can have Mary's old room. I got a list of things I need for you to do."

"Terrific. I love you. Good night, Mom."

The young man pulled down the third door and the last rectangle of light was gone. Hood sat awhile longer, watching and thinking, feeling sadness for the world and the people in it.

14

Rovanna stood outside Neighborhood Congregational and read the weekly message off the marquee: HE KNOCKS BUT WE MUST OPEN. He followed the cement walkway to the front door of the church, which was set deep within a roofed portico. It was evening and already dark and through the wheel window above the transom he could see the colored spokes of light coming from within the church. He turned and scanned the street behind him. The traffic was sparse. An older woman stopped beneath a streetlight so her dog could do his business. Rovanna drew the Love 32 from his Windbreaker and knocked on the door of the church with the sound suppressor. He waited, then tapped again.

He turned the knob and found the door unlocked and pushed it open. He backed flush against the wall and saw the dog woman watching him. She stared a moment, then yanked the leash and the dog sprang out of its squat after her. Rovanna saw that the woman ran stiff-legged and that her shoes had thick, low heels. A long moment later he pointed the machine pistol up, then swung himself inside. The door shut behind him. The narthex was poorly lit but he could make out the worship program holders on the walls and the coatracks and the line of yellow light between the push-handled double doors. He passed through and stood inside the sanctuary, saw the pews waiting, the chancel with its simple railing, the altar overseen by a wooden cross that was lit by hidden spotlights in the ceiling above.

"Hello. I'm Lonnie Rovanna. Is anyone here?" He heard the echo of his voice and thought the choir must sound good here. He heard the muted squeak of his sneakers as he walked the polished hardwood aisle toward the front of the sanctuary. He stopped where the pews began. "Is anyone here?"

He heard a thump from somewhere behind the pulpit, where the choir would sit, and a man stood up and looked at him. He was young and stocky and dark-haired, dressed in jeans and a short-sleeve white shirt. He wore tiny reading glasses that sat far down his nose and he held a screwdriver in one hand. "Yes. Good evening. Can I help you?"

"I've come to . . . ask a question."

"Oh? Well, I'm trying to get this outlet rewired before tomorrow, but I'd be happy to take a break and talk. I'm Steve Bagley, one of the ministers here. Lonnie, did you say?"

"Yes."

The minister set the screwdriver on the communion table, slipped the readers into his shirt pocket and replaced them with a full-size pair of eyeglasses. He raised his head a little for a better look at Rovanna. "Oh, Lonnie, what is that you have in your hand?"

Rovanna looked at the machine pistol. "This?"

"Put it down. Or away. Is it real? Why is there a silencer on it?"

"Don't be alarmed. It's only for self-protection. There are some very bad men who want to do bad things to me. Five of them, to be exact."

"Put the gun away. It is not necessary or welcome here."

Rovanna opened his Windbreaker slid the Love 32 between his belt and his jeans, then snapped the coat up again He looked down at the conspicuous protrusion of the handle and the big curved magazine against his jacket.

"Are the police after you?"

"No, sir. I have committed no crime."

"This is very unusual."

"Trust me," said Rovanna. In the good light from above he saw the changes of emotion playing across the minister's face. The last one to register was a skeptical optimism.

"Okay, please sit," said Bagley, extending his hand toward the pews.

Rovanna sat in the front row, first bench to the left of the aisle. The minister sat on the first of two landings that separated the sanctuary from the chancel. He rested his elbows on his knees and the light from above reflected off his glasses and Rovanna thought of Stren.

"I'd like to know why God won't answer me," said Rovanna.

"Perhaps he has."

"I've prayed almost every day for my whole life. Quietly, mostly to myself, but sometimes out loud. Starting when I was a boy. Sometimes in church and sometimes just wherever I happened to be. I always prayed for a good job and a good woman and to be a good man and to do God's will and for peace on earth and for peace in my own mind. And I haven't heard one peep back. I don't have any job at all now, and I'm insane, and I'm twenty-nine years old. I haven't been with a woman in four years and before that it was three. A good man? I don't feel that I am a good man. I served my country, honorably, in Iraq, but does this make me good? I killed men I didn't know. I have no idea what God's will might be, unless it's the things that happen every day right in front of me, but when I look at those things I don't see anything close to peace on earth. What I pray for the hardest, and maybe this is selfish, but it's for peace in my own mind because my mind has always been a mess. Filled with voices and visions and ideas and most of them are not happy or good. But God never sent me any peace of mind. He just sent more voices and visions so far as I can tell. Now, I got this thing I want to do. It involves this gun. There are plenty of reasons to do it. It has to do with taking back the country. Our country. And I want to know if God wants me to do it or not."

"I can assure you that God doesn't want you to use that gun on any living thing."

"Why won't he tell me that himself?"

"Lonnie, the Lord doesn't always answer directly. And he doesn't always give us the answers we want to hear. What the Lord offers is steadfast love. This never wavers. It is constant and manifest in all the things around us, in every living thing and things not living. It is our duty on earth to listen, and to hear God. He speaks in a voice that is not always a voice we understand."

"I've had terrible dreams lately."

"Satan can send dreams as well as the Lord."

"The Bible says, 'To he who has much, much will be given. And to him who has little even that shall be taken away.' ' "

"This a statement of faith, not of material things."

"It's an accurate statement of the way God has treated me in this life."

Rovanna heard the double door open behind him and he turned and looked the length of the sanctuary. A young man in a dark brown suit walked in and nodded then sat in the back row, followed by another young man—same suit, shirt and tie, same face. Rovanna felt his heart break into a gallop and he wiped his eyes with both hands but the men remained.

"Are you alright?" asked Reverend Bagley.

"Don't worry. I've seen them before."

"Who?"

"The men in the back row. There are five of them and they are identical."

"Are they there right now?"

"They follow me for coffee some mornings. They sit on my patio furniture in the backyard when the weather is good. They crowd into my living room when it's cold out because I have a space heater. But you know what? They never used to come around when I had my guns. They only come out when they think I'm not armed." Rovanna smiled conspiratorially and tapped the gun butt through his coat.

"Would you be willing to see a doctor?"

Rovanna glanced at the men in back—all five were now seated in the ultimate row. Then he turned to the minister and whispered, "I have doctors. Too many. They prescribe medicines that do nothing but cloud my mind even worse than it's already clouded."

"You need more help than I can give you."

"I came here to speak to God, not you. You can go back to fixing the outlet if you want."

"I want to pray with you, Lonnie."

Rovanna looked at the men, then at the minister. He gestured toward the door beyond Bagley, at the back of the chancel. "Does that lead outside?"

"To the sacristy first. Then, yes, there's a door to the courtyard and the banquet hall and classrooms. Close your eyes. Let us pray together. Our Father who art in heaven, hear the prayer of Lonnie Rovanna, and grant him the sound of your blessed voice and the comfort of your love . . ."

Rovanna listened and closed his eyes and ran down a dark path between dark trees under a black sky suddenly bursting with fireworks of many colors, some huge and some very small but all of them were flowers made of sparks. The sky writhed in color. Then the sparks fell into the shapes of faces and these began to turn slowly within the wheel of heaven and they looked down on Rovanna but he could see by their expressions that these faces were preoccupied with the cares of giants because in fact they were giants, so they could not see him and they did not know he was here . . . *and grant to Lonnie Rovanna some of the great peace only you, in your forgiveness, can give . . .*

Rovanna heard the Identical Men moving behind him and he stood and opened his eyes to see three of them coming up the center aisle toward him and the other two splitting off for the far sides and every one of them brandishing a gleaming orbitoclast. He leapt forward and pushed Reverend Bagley to the floor of the chancel, then dragged him by his shirt collar to the communion table and told him to stay down. He turned, unsnapping his coat and pulling the Love 32. He fired a short near-silent burst into the closest man in the center aisle, blowing his feet out from under him and landing him on his back. Rovanna heard his sharp cry and the wallop of his body hitting but no more than a muted tapping sound from his gun, followed by the twinkling bounce of the empties on the floor. The Identical Men moved fast. He found the next one over his front sight and fired three quick single shots, which sent him sprawling back into the fourth row pew, kicking a hymnal and a batch of tithe envelopes into the air. The third center-aisle man tried to stop but his shoes slipped on the worn wooden floor and he slid toward Rovanna with the orbitoclast catching the light and Rovanna put him down with a rattling ten-shot fusillade.

Rovanna looked down at the writhing Identical Man, then turned to the minister, who stared up at him wide-eyed from under the communion table. The Reverend Bagley aimed a thumb back toward the door to the sacristy. "Don't shoot, Lonnie. I'm going for that door!"

"I have you covered!" The words were scarcely out before the minister jumped to his feet and ran through the door and slammed it behind him. Rovanna turned on the last two men. They had stopped and seemed uncertain what to do. Rovanna felt his soldier's heart take over and was not one bit uncertain what to do, charging the man on his left, who was closest, taking him down with a short burst, then cutting through the row of pews toward the last Identical Man who had turned and fled for the exit. He had just gotten his hands onto the door bar when Rovanna cut him down. He slumped and Rovanna saw the tight pattern of .32 caliber ACP rounds left in the white door among the sloppy red halos. Silence fell and Rovanna heard nothing but the beating of his heart in his ears and the short rapid draw of his breath. *Speak to me speak to me speak to me. Help us help us help us.* He closed his eyes and listened to the slow deceleration of his heart and the gradual settling of his breathing, but he did not hear what he had come to hear. There was no voice from God, not even a whisper, only the silence of His great indifference, followed by the whine of a distant siren.

15

Hood watched the *News at Eleven* segment on the malicious defacement of an El Cajon Congregational church by an apparently delusional man with a machine gun.

"He walked right into the sanctuary with the gun drawn," said Reverend Steve Bagley to the camera. "I was there doing some electrical work before going home. I asked him to put the gun away and he put it inside his coat and zipped it up. We sat and talked. We tried to pray but he claimed he saw five men enter the church, but there were no men. I crawled under the communion table when he started shooting. The gun was almost completely silent. I didn't know what he was doing at first, until I saw the plaster and wood flying where he was aiming the gun."

The story cut to close-up footage of the bullet-riddled sanctuary door, then the bullet-pocked walls, then a pew chewed by automatic fire. The reporter was a tall blond woman who held a mic in one hand and pointed out the holes with the other.

"Now, the gunman identified himself to the minister here as *Lonnie Rovanna*. A check of the *phone book* here confirms that a man with that name *does* live in an El Cajon neighborhood within *walking distance* of Neighborhood Congregational Church. San Diego police have not been able to locate the man and they are urging anyone with information to call nine-one-one or San Diego police at . . ."

One hour and twenty minutes later Hood cruised Rovanna's street in his Charger. Lonnie had not answered his phone and Hood had left three messages. Overhead a San Diego police chopper circled and dragged its beam of light across the streets and yards and rooftops. He saw a stakeout plainwrap parked in front of the main house and another across the street, two men visible in each car. He slowed but didn't stop.

There were still cops and news crews there when Hood walked into the roofed portico of Neighborhood Congregational Church. A detective stopped him at the door and Hood produced his badge. "You guys find him yet?"

The detective eyed him. "No. ATF. You didn't sell him the machine gun, did you?"

Hood smiled. "You're not half as funny as you look." He walked past the detective. In the sanctuary Reverend Bagley answered more questions and squinted into a videographer's floodlight. Hood stood in the middle aisle, halfway to the chancel, and saw the pattern of bullet holes in the main door and another on one wall. The hardwood floor was marked with small circles of white chalk where the brass had been found and photographed and booked as evidence. He knelt and let his gaze wander beneath the pews but the light was poor and he didn't find what he was looking for.

When the news crews hustled out, Reverend Bagley sat down with a sigh in one of the pews near the back. As he approached, Hood saw him stifle a yawn. "Long night," said Hood, sitting down the pew from the reverend.

"Took an hour for my heart to quit racing."

"I guess it's a semi-happy ending."

"I never thought he was going to kill me. Funny. I just never thought that about him. What I thought was, *damaged goods*."

"Young guy? Tall and slender? Blue eyes and thick blond hair?"

"Yes, yes, and yes. I've described him a dozen times tonight. And he still hasn't changed!" Reverend Bagley studied Hood's badge in its holder. "I didn't know the feds had diamonds in their teeth these days."

"They're optional." Bagley smiled. "Reverend, just one more time.

Tell me everything that was said and everything that happened." Hood set a small digital recorder between them.

Half an hour later the Reverend Steve Bagley set his hands on his thighs and looked down at his watch. "I believe I've done my heavenly and civic duties today."

"Tell me again what he said he was planning to do. It's very important."

"He was vague. I can't remember the exact language, but he said there was something he wanted to do that involved his gun. He said he had many reasons to it. He said it was about taking back the country. Our country. And Lonnie wanted to know if God approved of his plan or not. And I said God does not approve of you turning that gun on any living thing."

Hood considered these words and what they might mean. Political, he thought. Take back the country. Everyone was saying that, it seemed. Back from the left. Back from the right. Back from godlessness. Back from religious zealots. But not everyone had a silenced machine gun. A public slaughter? An assassination? With permission from God to open fire?

"What do you make of it?" asked Bagley.

"It sounds ominous to me."

"Me, too," said the minister. "The man was seeing things. Using a machine gun on imaginary enemies. Do you know him?"

"Some. We've met."

"I can't believe he lives just a few blocks from here."

"Reverend Bagley, I'm going to ask you four last questions."

"I am tired."

"Tell me once more what the gun sounded like."

"It made a rapid chattering sound. But muffled. It sounded toy-like."

"How many shots did he fire? I realize it's only a guess."

The reverend stood and looked at both walls, then the door. "Fifty. One hundred."

"Did he reload?"

"Not that I saw."

Hood wrote down the numbers, then put his pen and pad back in his pocket. "Where do you turn on the lights for this sanctuary?"

"There are switches up there, by the sacristy door, and on the other side of the double doors, back in the narthex. I need to lock up now, Agent Hood."

"I want to turn the lights up high for just a minute or two."

"I'll do that while I lock up."

Bagley went through the bullet-pocked double doors and a moment later the lights on the sanctuary came on strong. The reverend came back in and watched him. Hood slowly walked Rovanna's route, as the reverend had described it. He stopped at the little circles of chalk on the floor and he looked under the pews again. Then he walked all the way around the pews to the other side, where Rovanna had fired the second time. At these circles Hood knelt and put his face low and looked along the plane of floor. He stood and looked across the pews to the first shooting station. He squatted again and let his vision roam the flat horizon of the hardwood floor, studded with pew feet bolted to the floor. "That's where he cut through," called Bagley. "That's about right. I was watching at that point." Finally Hood's gaze landed on the shiny brass object of his desire, having rolled, as casings sometimes do, surprisingly far from where the cartridge is fired. A moment later he had it on the end of his pen—.32 caliber ACP—a relatively small center-fire load, common and affordable. Just as he had feared. He let it slide into his coat pocket. "Thank you, Reverend."

"Good night, Agent Hood. I hope you find him. Soon."

Hood backtracked to Rovanna's neighborhood and parked across from the main house. The surveillance cars were still in place and Hood could see the outlines of the lawmen inside. The police helo was still in the sky. He dialed Rovanna's number again and got the recorded message.

Tapping his phone lightly on the steering wheel, Hood waited and wondered if Lonnie Rovanna had used a Love 32 for his rampage. Reverend Bagley's description certainly fit the Love 32, and it was chambered for the .32 caliber ACP cartridge. If so, where had he gotten it? Hood pondered the confluence of Rovanna's Love 32—if that is what he had used on Neighborhood Congregational—and Rovanna's visitation a week earlier by Mike Finnegan posing as a doctor with the power to return Rovanna's confiscated guns.

Hood took out his voice recorder and found the part he wanted to hear again. *"He said it was about taking back the country. Our country. And Lonnie wanted to know if God approved of his plan or not. And I said God does not approve of you turning that gun on any living thing."*

He set the recorder on the seat and rolled down the window when one of the detectives walked up. Hood held out his badge holder and used it to push aside the flashlight aimed into his eyes. "Easy, Detective." With the light out of his face Hood saw that the cop was tall and wore a SDPD Windbreaker and his shield on a lanyard: BENSON.

"Hey, a real G-man."

"No Rovanna?"

"I don't see him. Do you? Let me guess—you're after his silenced machine pistol."

"Good guess."

"Do you know him?"

"I interviewed him two days ago. Part of an ongoing investigation. Do you?"

"Local color. The state hospital cut him loose a few years back, some new program. He was quiet for a while, then he roughed up some Jehovah's Witnesses who knocked on his door. We took away a dozen guns. Apparently we missed one. Somehow he'd flown through the background checks with flying colors. Now he walks around with a baseball bat. We told him, one bit of trouble and the bat goes, too. He's actually a nice guy until something sets him off. Must have been a doozy, based on the what he did to the church. The reverend was lucky he didn't catch a bullet."

"His car is gone. How long did it take your officers to get here?"

"Not long once they talked to the minister and found out it was Rovanna. By then, though, no man and no car. How come ATF is interested in him?"

"Connections to some bad actors."

"We don't see silenced machine pistols every day."

"It amazes me what people can get their hands on," said Hood. "And, Benson, don't make some dumbass comment about letting guns walk."

The detective shrugged and looked back at his unmarked car. "Maybe three's a crowd here, Agent Hood."

"Yeah. Good luck."

"You got a card? I'll give a courtesy call on this if you want. I got an ex-brother-in-law with ATF. You guys earn your money."

Hood wrote his cell numbers on the back of an ATF card and handed it to the detective, who gave Hood one of his cards in return.

16

The black town car glided to a stop in front of Bradley Jones's Valley Center ranch house, the dogs closing around it barking but never touching the car. It was two days later, just before noon, and the sun hung in a blanched, cold pre-storm sky. Bradley sat at the long picnic bench on the covered deck. He had worked his four tens for the week and now had three days to himself. The call had come to his cell this morning just before sunrise: Chief Miranda Dez would be there at noon. The meeting would take one hour. *Wonderful*, he thought. She had taken the bait. Either that or she'd bring some big deputies and arrest him.

A large uniformed deputy held open her door and Dez stepped onto the drive, straightened, and glanced up at him through her aviator sunglasses. She was forty, fit, and handsome, and reminded Bradley somewhat of his mother, Suzanne. It was more her attitude than appearance. She turned slowly, looking around the property. Her black hair was pulled back in a taut French roll. She wore a tailored tan winter-weight uniform with a necktie rather than the patrol-ready open-collared blouse and T. Her badge was polished, her chief's collar stars were bright, and her tie clasp and nameplate were perfectly horizontal in relation to the necktie.

She strode into the thicket of dogs without acknowledging them. They sprang and skulked out of her way and she climbed the steps to the porch. She carried a laptop in a black leather case. Bradley stood and pulled out the picnic bench opposite his and she set the computer on the table and sat.

"Where did you ever get the money to afford all this?"

"My mother and some good investments."

"You wouldn't think a schoolteacher and part-time car thief would be worth millions."

"She was smart."

"Smart enough to get herself shot and killed? Jim Warren at CID has other explanations for your . . . comfortable lifestyle."

"My mother's life is a past thing, Chief Dez. Jim Warren is a good old man with bad ideas. I hope you didn't come here to talk about them. I hope you're here to talk about our futures."

"Our futures. Good. But can you find me a cup of coffee here in the present?" She nodded down to the deputy who was still standing beside the town car. Before going inside, Bradley watched him get in and drive to the far side of the parking area, which was shaded by an enormous oak tree and had a nice view of the pond.

He set two mugs of coffee and a quart of milk on the rough, old picnic table. Dez already had her laptop up and booted and she positioned the machine so they both could see the screen.

"First of all, Deputy Jones, where did you get this stuff?"

"It was shot on location in the states of Baja California, Campeche, and Yucatán, Mexico, four months ago."

"By whom?"

"Mexican law enforcers. The real ones, not the corrupt ones. There were several shooters. I can't reveal my sources until later. The point is, the footage and images are authentic and untouched by editors or editing programs."

"Tell me what I'm looking at." She slid the mouse across to Bradley

"This is Charlie Hood. He's one of our deputies, on loan to ATF. A very distant acquaintance of mine."

"He was involved with your mother."

"Here he's involved with a crooked Tijuana cop named Rescendez. You can see the Jai A'lai Palace in the background. Hood doesn't know there's another TJ lawman working a cell phone camera from one of their police cars."

"What are the other cops looking at?"

"This." Bradley clicked the mouse and a picture of a duffel bag filled the screen. It was zipped open and there were bricks of plastic-wrapped cash inside. One of the bricks had been opened to reveal the hundred-dollar bills.

"The TJ cops are on the payroll of the Gulf Cartel," said Bradley. "The money is drug profits, collected in the United States. Hood drove it south. Remember, this was a few days before Benjamin Armenta was killed in the shootout."

"Armenta's money."

"Correct. Now, here's Hood in Juárez. The guy on his right is Valente Luna and the fat guy is Julio Santo. Both Ciudad Juárez cops, both button men for Armenta." He clicked the mouse and the screen went to video. Like most of the video and stills on this memory stick, this clip had been shot from fairly far away by Mike, but he had used good equipment. Hood and his friends looked like small players on a small stage and Bradley felt Zeus-like looking down on mortal Charlie Hood. "Now, here they are leaving Reynosa."

"Where's Santo?"

"Killed in a shootout about five hours previous."

"Why no pictures of that?"

"I have no idea. I was not the cameraman. My informants tell me that Carlos Herredia's people found out about Hood and the money. Unfortunately, they sent mere children to take it away, and Hood and Luna killed all five of them."

Dez took off her sunglasses and set them on the table. "How could Hood have slipped off leash like this?" she asked.

"When he attached himself to the feds, it gave him a chance to do what he wanted. Which, apparently, was to go private and upriver."

"Unreal."

"Real."

"How much money is he carrying?"

"Beats me," Bradley said with a smile. "They said a million but I wouldn't know."

Bradley clicked forward through a series of still photos taken at some distance: Hood and a boy walking toward a city during high wind and rain; a shelter in a small Mexican town, where the boy hugs a woman; Hood and Luna waiting on a rooftop while a helicopter comes down from a troubled black sky. "This is the village of Tuxpan, just after Hurricane Ivana went through. Hood got swept away and came up with the boy. Next up, Mérida. See, he's heading south still, toward Armenta."

The next video showed Hood on a busy street, buying from vendors, looking around, apparently nervous. The palms swayed with post-Ivana wind and puddles of standing water pocked the old colonial streets. "Luna is at the hotel with the money," said Bradley. "They took shifts guarding it. Now, these next shots are of a camp in Yucatán, a few miles from Benjamin Armenta's castle."

"That's where the Mexican Army stormed in and killed him."

"Not exactly. The men you will see next are soldiers of the North Baja Cartel—far, far from home. With orders to take the Castle and murder Armenta. Watch."

The camp wasn't much more than a crude opening in a thick jungle. As the video rolled, Bradley saw the first sunlight coming down through the trees, and the dirty, exhausted faces of the men. They cursed at the cameraman in Spanish, gestured. The camera caught the SUVs, partially hidden from above, under cut fronds and branches. Then the camera panned left, where at a distance Charlie Hood and Valente Luna could be seen, trudging after a young man along a trail toward the camp.

"Hood's got a shotgun over his shoulder and no money," said Dez, looking at Bradley.

Mom's eyes, he thought. Not how they look but how they see.

"He was never going to give it to Armenta in the first place. Neither was Luna."

"Then where is it?"

"At the hotel in Mérida."

"So there's been a change of plans."

"I'd say so."

The next video was shot from an airplane, its engine working away with a high-pitched whine. There was a bounce to the picture and its subject was some distance away. Slowly it came into view, a multistoried building and compound surrounded by dense jungle.

"Armenta's fortress?" asked Dez.

"For another minute or two."

The airplane overran the compound and a moment later it had turned around to approach again. Several men, each carrying a compact pistol with a sound suppressor, emerged from the green and advanced across a road toward the structure. "They're sneaking in," said Dez. "In broad daylight. Because their weapons are silenced." The camera zoomed and Charlie Hood grew larger as he ran from the jungle. The shotgun was strapped over his shoulder. When a man ran into a courtyard and leveled an assault rifle at him, Hood blew him down with a burst from the silenced pistol.

"This is just goddamned unbelievable, Bradley."

"Keep watching."

The plane made another pass. The cameraman had switched to a still camera with a strong telephoto lens: Hood exiting the castle through the front door, Luna behind him.

"Armenta is already dead by now. Hood and the rest of Herredia's hired cutthroats murdered him while he was playing accordion in a recording studio. They shot him up good and blew the accordion to pieces, according to one of the castle servants."

Then came video of Mexican Army troops swarming the compound from one direction while an assortment of civilians—black domestics dressed alike in gray, people wrapped in white robes and balaclavas, a tall angry priest and his frightened young novitiates—fled the castle and vanished into the jungle. Bradley stole a look at

Miranda Dez; she was transfixed by the spectacle. The last half minute of video showed the castle stewing in flames, smoke billowing all the way up into the camera until the screen went black.

"Pardon this," said Dez. She fished a pack of cigarettes from a boot sock, pulled the matches out from behind the plastic wrapper, and lit up.

"Something to calm you down," said Bradley.

"I'm not really sure what to say." Dez stood and walked to the railing and looked down at the many dogs. Only Call, the unrivaled leader of pack, was allowed up on the deck proper. He lolled in a sunny spot out past the overhang with his eyes open and on Dez. She blew a plume of smoke that hovered, then thinned to nothing. She looked out over the rolling hills of Valley Center, toward the creek and the Indian property on the other side of it. He thought of his mother standing right about there, the same tilt of head and line of jaw. Finally, he thought, I've found it: a way to punish Hood for taking her body and a piece of her heart, and leaving her unprotected in the world. "And I'm not really sure what to do."

"Get Warren off my back and deal with the real bad guy here. How can you not?"

"Warren thinks you were part of this Armenta thing."

"You just saw with your own eyes that I wasn't. I was in Yucatán with my pregnant wife and two good friends—fishing. Sometimes a coincidence really is just that. No matter how many times I tell Warren, he refuses to believe me. That's where you come in, Chief Dez. You're on the CID oversight panel. You can talk to the others, and redirect Warren's pathetic investigation of an innocent deputy. Get them off me, especially the watchers. Now. Every time I turn around, there they are. Turn Warren loose on Hood. In return, you'll have this recorded evidence to get started, and my full cooperation. And the full cooperation of deputies Caroline Vega and Jack Cleary, both in good standing, both of whom were there with me at Bacalar while Hood was gunning down Armenta. They'll corroborate my story from the top down."

Dez tapped some ash over the railing. "You're the most manipulative young man I've ever known." Bradley shrugged, reached down, and ran his hand over Call's sleek, hard head. "Do you hate Hood for carousing with your mother? I wouldn't blame you if you did."

"You're not qualified to not blame me."

"Then I'll retract that statement."

"In fact, I feel sorry for Hood," said Bradley. A strangely delicious warmth swaddled his heart. Lying was a genuine pleasure at times like this. Wickedly genuine. "He was a good man and he's lost his direction and clarity. His windmills are devils."

"Devils."

"Ask him about them."

Dez stubbed out her smoke on the underside of the top rail and let the butt drop to the ground. "I'll take that thumb drive back with me. The panel should see it. Undersheriff Counts isn't a fan of Warren, not since the Renegades scandal. And he's been dubious about the Jones investigation from the start. He'll see this my way, and the sheriff himself will lean with him. They're tight. Warren's men won't follow you again."

"I feel like a window has been opened."

"How much money do you think Hood has made off Carlos Herredia over the years?"

"Scores of thousands. Maybe hundreds. Maybe you'll be able to tell me someday."

Dez stood in front of Bradley and looked up into his face. "If this is some kind of frame, or if your intel doesn't wash, or if I begin to suspect your motives or your honesty, I'll give Warren the green light to take you down."

"I'm going to sleep at night, in spite of all that."

"You're a strange one, Jones." Dez put her sunglasses back on and looked out to her driver. "Isn't your wife due soon?"

"Next week."

"Congratulations."

Bradley smiled and nodded. "I'm truly blessed."

"Fatherhood will make either a man or a fool out of you."

After dinner Bradley went into the barn and lifted weights, then rode the stationary cycle for an hour plus. His muscles buzzed. He'd been missing the hapkido training but now it would be easily affordable again, thanks to Israel and certainly Mike. And Dez! What great good fortune, he thought. What a team. After the weights, arm heavy, he hit Ping-Pong balls against the raised half of his table, concentrating fully. When he'd had enough of this he tossed the ball and paddle onto the workbench and pushed a hidden button. With a whirring sound, the Ping-Pong table and the wooden rectangle of floor on which it stood rose into the air on hydraulic lifts. He'd taken them off trash trucks he'd stolen from the city of Escondido years ago. He climbed down the stairs into his vault.

He opened one of the four heavy safes just to see what was inside, though he knew. He admired the nearly four hundred thousand dollars inside, and the two cigar boxes filled with expensive wristwatches he'd bought for pennies on the dollar from a couple of his smash-and-grab friends. There were two jewelry boxes also, each crammed with treasures for Erin, similarly purchased for peanuts from bandits more daring than he—diamond brooches and ruby chokers and sapphire earrings and gold and gold and gold. The other three safes were comparably stocked.

He opened and checked them also, running his eyes and fingers over the bricks of compressed cash, the jewelry and old silver dollars, some loose gemstones waiting to be sold or set. He liked to see his loot in mild disarray and casually stored, more or less heaped, like a pirate might do. He lifted a wad of necklaces, mostly gold and pearls, then dropped them back to the safe bottom. There was even a cigar box that held the first few items he'd shoplifted, as a ten-year-old. He opened it and looked in at the baseball-card bubble-gum packs, now hardened and cracked within, the jawbreakers, pocket knives, toy cars and plastic reptiles, the tube of BB's, and the miniature skateboards.

Pleased, Bradley locked the safes, then walked over to the long table that stood along one of the walls. There were three colorful serapes spread upon it. He carefully pulled each one away and let them drop to the floor. Then he looked down on remnants of his history: Joaquin Murrieta's walnut-handled six-guns in old hip holsters; a bulletproof vest made for Joaquin by a French-American blacksmith in 1852; Joaquin's journal; the leather-bound journals written by various Murrieta descendants, including his mother, during the century and a half since his death, all of them filled with lawless exploits and seductions and great bravery and generosity, and no little violence. And of course Joaquin's severed head was there, too, still in the jar in which it was originally displayed after the shootout at Cantua Creek— the charge was one dollar to see the head of the bloodthirsty murderer and horse thief, Joaquin Murrieta!

Bradley ran his hand over the smooth leather of the holsters and the cool handles of the revolvers. He lifted his mother's first journal, begun when she was ten years old, and read out loud her opening line for maybe the thousandth time: "Dear Children, do I have a tale of adventure for you!"

A tale of adventure was right, he thought. He pictured her and set the journal back with the others.

Now Bradley beheld the head. It was pale and roughly severed. The original preservative was brandy but this eventually had been replaced with isopropyl alcohol, then formaldehyde. It had yellowed, slightly. The face was vaguely handsome, as Joaquin had reputedly been in life, but his famous wild black hair had fallen out through the decades and now lay at the bottom of the jar. Sometimes he looked noble to Bradley, and sometimes only hapless and forlorn.

He tapped it twice and watched the head sway and the hair lift and lilt. *How could you have been everything they said you were?* Bradley wondered. *They said you were a real man. But they also said you were only imagined. They said you were short and dark. They said you were tall, blond, and blue-eyed. They said you murdered for fun. They said you were generous and kind. They said you were loyal to Rosa. They said you seduced hundreds. They said you died young and were beheaded. They said no, it was a friend of yours who was beheaded. They said you lived and died very old with your head still on and a large family all around you. So what am I supposed to make of you, El Famoso? You're my history, but which history? How do I discover what I am when I know so little truth? What should I do with you? This is the twenty-first century, dude, and nobody needs a head in a jar. Especially a head that may or may not be what it's said to be. What am I going to tell Thomas about you? Mom got driven half crazy by that question—she worried for years what to say to me and my brothers. Should she tell us the truth? Tell us lies? Tell us nothing? Tell some of us some things and some of us other things? She agonized over it. Because she knew that I would fall for you. She knew I had something that she had, and that you had. Something waiting to be set free. Something wild. She died undecided. You must understand what a problem you are to me, Joaquin. Maybe I'm better off without you. Has knowing you made my life better? Well, you've helped me become reckless, brave, and rich. Yes. I've murdered several men, though I might add that they all deserved it. I've stolen. I've stolen a lot. I am steadfastly dishonest, manipulative, and self-serving. I've deceived and endangered the only person I love. And of all those things, the only one I regret even a little is the last—what I did to Erin. And here I am, doing it again. Hell, she doesn't even know about this place, and all the things I've done. So, Joaquin, why should I keep you around? Haven't you had enough? What does my son need with you? What good are you to me?*

Bradley went to the workbench and poured a neat Scotch. He brought it back to the table and clinked the glass to Joaquin's. "To the river that carries us all," he said. "Run long." Then he covered Joaquin back up.

17

In the morning Oscar the security guard offered a minimal smile as Hood held his ID to the door lock on the ATF hallway. Hood got coffee and went to his cubicle and began reading still another ATF Form 3310.12, used to report multiple sales of semiautomatic rifles in Southwest border states. Hundreds were generated each month. It was attached to ATF Form 4473, the Firearms Transaction Record. Dealing with such forms made him drowsy.

Bly had requisitioned them from Buster's Last Stand and it wasn't hard for Hood to find what he was looking for. He wondered why Yolanda Drumm, the rhinestoned AR-5 buyer, needed a new 7.62 mm assault rifle every week for the past four weeks running. And why, before the new reporting rules, she had needed two, sometimes three rifles per week. Once, four. Well, clearly, for the Sinaloans, Hood thought, or other deserving patrons. He yawned.

He wrote down Drumm's address in El Centro, and her phone numbers, and her credit card number. If they could catch her selling to the wrong people, they could take out one small supplier, one tiny contributory to the Iron River. She probably made fifty bucks a gun, maybe a hundred. Hood's counterparts in Mexican law enforcement called this small-time gunrunning *contrabando de las hormigas*— contraband of the ants—but when the many ants were added up, their trickles became a big part of the river.

From the government numbers Hood saw, he conservatively figured that the flow of guns from the United States to Mexico was between a thousand and fifteen hundred a month. What he'd seen with his own eyes—there were over six thousand federally licensed gun dealers operating along the border, roughly three per mile—put the number higher. One prominent think-tank estimate of two thousand guns per day seemed way high. But in a sense everyone was counting backwards, because the number of guns going south could only be extrapolated from the number of guns *found* in the south and traced back their origins. Many guns of course were never found, and many more were not traceable. So the numbers floated as numbers do, subject to interpretation and misinterpretation, often politically colored.

Regardless, Hood knew for certain that it was good luck running into Yo Yo and the Sinaloans at El Pueblo. They probably did their deals in the parking lot in back, or somewhere close and handy. Hood believed in luck. His cell phone buzzed and he liked the number he saw. He hit the digital recorder on his desk and answered.

"Hooper. It's Dirk Sculler here."

"The Lewis made my collector very happy."

"I had the weirdest dream last night. And when I woke up I thought of your customers, the ones you said didn't need small-bore playthings."

"Edge of my seat, Dirk."

"I dreamed of FIM-Ninety-two Stingers, straight from Raytheon, still in the crates."

"Certain people do dream of owning those."

"I'd like to meet just one."

"Let's get off the air for this conversation, Dirk."

"Meet me at noon at the Monterey Restaurant. Best burritos in the world, according to Israel Castro. And he *owns* a Mexican restaurant. You know Israel?"

"Every human being in Imperial County has bought something from Israel."

"That's him alright."

*   *   *

They sat back by the restrooms, away from the window. Hood set his straw gambler crown-down on the seat beside him. The restaurant was loud and busy. Hood got the carne asada "super burrito," which came loaded with guacamole, sour cream, and pico de gallo. He had a speedy metabolism and could devour such meals several times a day and not gain weight. Skull outweighed him by twenty pounds and his four-item combination plate was down to two before Hood had taken a bite. Hood looked around the room and tucked one corner of the paper napkin under his shirt collar. Today he was wearing a pale blue cotton/linen seersucker suit and a Jerry Garcia necktie that he didn't want stained.

"Where's the wild bunch?" asked Hood.

"What do you care?" Skull held his fork with the handle palmed and his thumb on top, lifting from the elbow.

"How's the chimp's finger?"

"Black. The tip's pretty crushed. The nail's gonna fall off for sure. I couldn't tell if he reached into the trunk before or after you started to close it."

"Before," Hood lied. "But I just couldn't resist."

"Yeah. He's a good guy, Hooper, and I guess you're not. Here's the deal . . ."

Skull talked softly and Hood leaned forward, ate, and listened: Two FIM-92 Stinger missile launchers, lifted from the Naval Weapons Station adjacent to Camp Pendleton by a pair of "enterprising friends." Two missiles to go with them, but more launchers and missiles possible. The weapons were the RMP variant, which use both infrared and ultraviolet homing systems. The warheads were hit-to-kill types with impact fuses and self-destruct timers. "They can knock a Cessna Citation out of the sky at five miles," said Skull. "Anything bigger is just that much easier. Eighty grand for the pair. Value priced." Scully gave him a wicked smile and his shaven head clearly reflected the ceiling lights. He had merry blue eyes and a black tattoo of barbed wire around his thick neck.

Hood nodded and gazed over Skull's shoulder to the sun-washed parking lot. El Centro was bustling and he could see the steady river of cars on the westbound freeway. The winter optics were clean and the day was cool. He leaned in and spoke softly. "I have some ideas, Dirk. But let me ask you something. Aside from friendly governments, these kinds of tools usually end up in the hands of religious fanatics, insurgents, warlords, cartel kingpins. Do you have any problems at all with these types of individuals?"

"I won't sell to rag heads. Just won't do it. Anybody else, well, the only problem I got is if the check bounces."

"That's what I figured you'd say."

Skull leaned back and looked around the room and didn't bother to moderate his volume. "There's plenty of people out there who could use what I'm offering. Any of these goddamned cartel beheaders and torturers, they'd love to shoot down a government chopper or a rival's jet or a commercial airliner. Just to make their point. Which is, well, I'm still not really sure what their point is." Beside them, a four-top of Mexican farmhands looked over at Skull and Hood. As did a well-dressed businessman and his female tablemate sitting catty-corner. "So, let the Mexicans lose their souls. They're not human anyway."

"That's not scientific."

"They're taking over this whole country. Look around you. And think it over, slick. Don't take too long. Nice suit. You see a lot of that poofy material in the south. Queersucker, something like that."

Skull stood and pulled two twenties off his roll and let them fall into the salsa bowl. He lumbered between the small vinyl tables and booths and pushed out.

Hood took his time finishing his lunch. Skull called, but Hood saw the number and let it ring. It was not yet one o'clock. When he was finished, he stood and walked out through the hostile stares.

Hood called Skull forty-five minutes later from the conference room of the ATF Buenavista field office. "The Stinger batteries crap out after five years, so none of the eighties-era stuff will do. I won't touch it."

"In the crates means new, Hooper. Christ."

"New, I've got interest at seventy grand."

"The price is eighty. Subtract it from your end, Hooper. You're not the only show in town on this one."

"I'm not coming alone with that chimp of yours on the loose. If we do this deal, I'll need to bring friends."

"Who and how many?"

"Two cartel *jefes*. The nonhumans you enjoy so much."

"End users?"

"*Sí.*"

"Show me the money, Hooper."

"Show me the toys."

Five minutes later Hood's cell phone received pictures of two still-boxed FIM-92 Stinger launchers, and two of the sixty-inch missiles they could fire. Each of the missiles was crated as well. Skull had included the day's *San Diego Union-Tribune* in the shots. The launchers were roughly one yard long, the diameter of a large orange, with fold-up telescopic sights and large battery packs underneath. Hood knew the batteries were crucial—they powered the missiles far enough so they could commence burning their own fuel and not scorch the gunner.

Now the Blowdown team—along with two agents just helicoptered down from L.A.—crowded around behind Hood to see the pictures. Velasquez ran out for a newspaper and Yorth lugged in a duffel full of cash, and a few minutes later Hood sent back two pictures of it back to Skull, *Union-Tribune* included. "Is this fun or what?" asked Yorth. He played air guitar to a Stones riff, windmilling his arm like Keith. "I love this job!"

Then he hustled to his office and came back with a one-way radio transmitter disguised as a smartphone and three tiny clip-on receivers all sprouting wires and earbuds. He said the mic was built into the body right behind the speaker, and it was supposed to be good for human conversation for roughly a thousand feet.

Hood clipped it to his belt, and when he walked outside the lobby and across the street to the bus stop and muttered to himself, his real cell phone rang. It was Bly, saying the radio reception was terrific; she could even hear the cars going by. Hood stood there a moment and looked out at the darkening eastern sky, then west to the orange spray of sunlight where the sun had just dropped behind the Devil's Claws. He thought of his home in Buenavista, somewhere out in that darkness beneath the mountains, and he thought of Beth. *Here we go*, he thought. He hummed a rocking tune from the new McMurtry CD. He felt the luck.

They all huddled in the conference room and Yorth laid out the basics: The two ATF special agents from L.A.—Marquez and Cepeda—would carry the cash and follow Hood in ATF's unmarked silver Magnum. They would be armed but not wired. The bust words were "kinda like a Steven Spielberg movie," Yorth's idea. It would tie in with the general theme of explosions and spectacle. In the event of a wire failure, or wire discovery, Hood would signal the takedown team by removing his hat. When the hat came off, hell would break loose. If he was inside or otherwise not visible, well, there was no Plan C—the team would move in when it felt right.

"Hood," said Yorth. "If by some stroke of luck we really can see you, please don't take off that hat just to wipe your brow or greet a passing lady. Don't do that, Charlie Diamonds."

"Got it," said Hood.

"When Scully calls, tell him you can go eighty grand. We've got a hundred in the safe. Let's bag and tag these dirtballs."

A few minutes later Hood caved on the eighty thousand and Skull told him he was smart. Skull set the callback for six o'clock. The next two hours sped by like minutes. The agents ate delivered pizza and watched TV, and Skull called at exactly six: Meet at the clubhouse at Buckboard Estates off the interstate in the southeast part of El Centro. Seven o'clock sharp. Skull said they'd leave the gate unlocked for Hooper and his cartel cutthroats.

18

"Buckboard is one of the new ghost towns," said Bly. "Brand-new six-bedroom homes, half of them with no doors or windows to keep out the squatters and coyotes. Swimming pools full of sand and tumbleweeds. They had just finished the first phase when the market crashed in oh-eight. God knows what kind of shape the clubhouse is in."

"One of Israel Castro's developments," said Hood. "Maybe that's where Scully got the gate key."

"How can we stay out of sight, then get in fast?" asked Yorth. "It's out in the frickin' sand. No traffic, no cars, or people."

"I used to run past that place when I lived in El Centro," said Velasquez. "There's a stone wall around it, maybe five feet high. We can use it. We can listen from the street side and they won't see a thing. Then, when it's time to go in, it's up and over."

"Can Hood's wire penetrate solid rock?" asked Bly.

"It's supposed to," said Yorth.

"We should set the receivers on top of the wall. The hat trick isn't going to work with us behind a stone wall and him inside the clubhouse."

"Good," said Yorth, humming the Stones song thoughtfully. "Mics on the wall for clarity."

A year ago Hood had driven through Buckboard Estates. It was exactly how Bly and Velasquez had described it. He remembered the houses standing in various degrees of completion, some only framed and others plumbed and drywalled. Some with roofing, others open to the sky. He remembered how the construction crews were still there, pouring and pounding and sawing away, even as the first-phase buyers were jumping ship and the FORECLOSURE and FOR SALE signs were sprouting up fast as weeds.

"When you jump the wall, one of you close the gate on them," said Hood.

"Good," said Yorth. "We'll need time to set up, but we're never going to beat them there now. We have to assume they're watching the area as we speak. So, what's across from Buckboard?"

"Cotton and more cotton," said Velasquez. "But there's a park-and-ride lot that doesn't get used that much, right across from the Buckboard entrance. There are always a few vehicles in it. We wouldn't stand out."

"Is there a traffic signal?"

"No. I'd remember that from my runs because I hate stopping for them."

"Perfect," said Yorth. "We can stage from there and jaywalk to the wall in the dark.

Hood looked at the L.A. agents. They looked badass enough to be cartel soldiers. What might cartel soldiers feel like doing before a big buy? "Do we still have that borrowed DEA dope in the safe here?"

"I just saw it," said Yorth. "What are you thinking?"

"Say we get there five minutes late, drive by real obvious, let them make us. We're on a standard paranoid security check, right? We loop back a few minutes later. We park near but not next to each other. All eyes on us. I wait a minute, then walk into the clubhouse, but Marquez and Cepeda stay behind because they're cartel killers and they're suspicious. They don't hurry and they don't walk into traps. They do what they damned well feel like doing, which is smoke some *mota* before the big deal goes down. All that's another ten minutes for you guys to get set. Then I go out and harangue them, try to hurry them along. They argue but finally bring the money inside. They reek of smoke. That's been another five minutes for you guys to get into position. And another reason for Skull and his friends to think they're dealing with real bad guys, not us."

"Janet, you remember how to roll a joint?" asked Yorth with a smile.

"I never learned, *Dale*," said Bly.

"I rolled my own cigarettes in college," said Hood. "I can muddle through."

This brought knowing laughter, cracks about inhalation, Slick Willie, Slick Charlie.

"Look, there's an earth embankment in front of the stone wall," said Velasquez. "Originally they had it irrigated and landscaped—boulders, succulents, and a lot of ocotillo and paloverde. But when the development went belly up, thieves took the sprinkler brass and the valves so everything died. They even stole the boulders and the good trees. So now . . . now it's a bunch of live weeds and dead bushes. It looks like hell but it's a good place to squat and hide. Same with the streetlights—the thieves cut down the poles with blowtorches, stripped out the copper wire and the conduit and took the light fixtures. It's good and dark out there now—a quarter moon. Once we're over the wall, it's only two hundred feet or so to the clubhouse parking lot. We can do this."

Yorth set half a brick of *mota* and a packet of Zig-Zags on the conference room table. The smell was green and junglelike and it reminded Hood of his murderous days in Yucatán just four months ago. "Go get 'em, Charlie."

Hood rolled down Imperial Avenue in his Charger. It was brawny and rigid of ride, like the IROC Camaro he'd had to sell in order to finance the wine cellar. He'd loved that car but the wine cellar was a necessity. Just this morning he'd run the Charger through the car wash, so now the black hood gleamed in the streetlights, and the reflections of the street signs rippled across it in yellow and red and blue. The engine growled. Adams to Fourth, then south again. In his rearview he saw the silver Magnum. He checked his diamonds in the mirror. The straw gambler waited on the seat beside him. He had a newly issued Glock .40 on his belt in back, a eight-shot .22 AirLite on his ankle, and a .40 caliber two-shot derringer that once belonged to Suzanne Jones in the side pocket of the seersucker coat, where it rested heavy as a railroad spike. He was hugely in the mood to purchase two shoulder-held Stinger missiles from crooked, crafty, girl-beating creeps.

One minute before seven he passed Buckboard Estates. The wall was rock and the gate was open. He came up a winding drive, past the parking lot, and stopped in front of the clubhouse. The red Commander and the raised F-150 were both there, backed up to the curb as if to stare at intruders. In the darkness the clubhouse looked large and had a spacious roofed patio out front. Faint light came from the building.

Hood watched the Magnum pull up behind him, then he continued right, past the clubhouse, following the drive. The streetlights had been blowtorched off near the ground and their gutted trunks lay about like fallen trees. The lawns were sand. The houses stood around him but they were little more than shapes. The windows with panes shone pale, and those without panes yawned blackly. Hood continued. He saw tennis courts thick with sand drifts, lines invisible, no nets. He thought of the Baghdad Tennis Club. There was a large, flat expanse of concrete with a huge black pit in the middle, and he realized it should have been filled with clean, cool water and lighted and surrounded by chaise longues and barbecues and umbrellas.

He stopped and turned on his radio transmitter and slid it back onto his belt. Looking down on it he could see the faint green LED that indicated power. Don't fail. His heart was thumping hard and steady. He pulled into a driveway with a NO TRESPASSING sign nailed to the garage door, reversed the car, and slowly drove back to the clubhouse parking lot. It was eight minutes past seven. Hood stopped and glanced back at the Magnum. He looked toward the wall and the open gate and saw nothing of the takedown team. The darkness is a friend tonight, he thought. He swung into a space and shut off the engine, then climbed out. He set the gambler on his head and checked his look in the window, then slammed the door with his foot. The Magnum parked five spaces down and the windows lowered.

"*Vámos, amigos.*"

"We'll wait. You check it out, *pinche gringo.*"

"I'll do that. I won't be long."

Hood ambled toward the clubhouse like a man with time on his hands. When he came to the bottom of the steps, he saw Clint Wampler standing off to the side of the building in his peacoat with a combat shotgun cradled in his arms. He had a hand on the grip and the white tape on his middle finger was luminous in the near-dark. "Good evening," said Hood. "How's the finger?"

"It's fine."

"Just bad timing. No hard feelings, I hope."

"You can call it an accident but that's like the kettle and the black pot. What are your greaseball buyers doing out there?"

"They don't trust you. Or me, for that matter."

"They brung the money?"

"Every cent."

"Go on in, Glitter Gums. If you come out before me getting a pre-arranged signal from Lyle, I get to blow your head off."

"Then I hope you have your signals straight."

"I'm praying for some kind of mix-up. A timing thing, maybe, like my finger. They happen all the time."

Hood pushed through a heavy wood-and-iron door and stepped into the clubhouse. The room was large and the ceiling high and there were double doors in the back. Near the center of it was an empty cable spool and on the spool stood two camping lanterns that gave off a whispering hiss and clean white light. Skull and Brock Peltz stood behind the spool, their faces beveled into light and shadow as if by stage lights. Skull had a pistol stuck behind his belt buckle and

Peltz wore a shotgun strapped to his shoulder. Four open crates rested on the spool between the lanterns. Hood saw the wooden nests of packing material and the glimmer of the hardware within.

"Where's the greasers and money?" asked Skull.

"The *amigos* are nervous."

"So, what, they sit out there and jack each other off?"

"I suppose."

Skull pulled a cell phone and said something, then clipped it back to his belt. "Get back out there and bring the money. Your men can stay where they are for all I care. You were the one who needed friendship."

"Well, the kid didn't shoot me so I guess I'm good."

"You're only as good as your money."

"Can I have a look?"

"Step up but don't touch until I'm counting my cash."

Hood looked down on the missile launchers. He could smell them, metal and gun oil and solvent. The missiles themselves were in long narrow crates, one beside each launcher, all of them nestled into the wooden packing nest. "They look like puppies," he said.

"You're fuckin' weird. Get the money."

"Roger. You've got the chimp in the loop?"

"He's expecting you."

Hood went back through the heavy doors and saluted Wampler on his way to the parking lot. He stopped near the driver's side door and spoke through the open window. "It's time."

"We're going to burn one."

"Suit yourself." Hood watched as Marquez held the joint up and lit it. He blew onto the lit end to get the stuff going and soon the smoke lilted into the air and began to drift out the windows. "The Stingers look new, just like they said."

Marquez passed the dope to Reggie Cepeda, who blew on it again and Hood saw the cherry glow. He looked back to the clubhouse for Wampler but saw only darkness. He glanced at the wall. "Let's do this," he said.

They walked back toward the clubhouse loosely abreast, Hood in the middle with the duffel. The last time he'd carried a bag full of money it was quite a bit heavier: one million dollars ransom for the life of Erin McKenna, Bradley's wife, to be delivered by Hood to drug lord Benjamin Armenta at his castle in Yucatán. Not much about that quest had turned out as Hood planned, though he and Erin and Bradley had lived to be haunted by those days. He remembered Mike Finnegan's Veracruz apartment, and the wet hiss of the knife across his scalp, and now here four months later in El Centro he felt his hat rubbing against the scar along his hairline. He pulled lightly on the brim to break the contact and felt a shiver climb his back. He glanced down at his transmitter and saw the green LED. Give me luck this time. Cepeda carried the joint and faked a big inhale, then flicked it ahead of him and ground it out on the way by.

19

Clint Wampler was not at his station. Hood's heart sped up. As they approached he peered hard into the darkness on either side of the clubhouse doors but saw no movement or glimmer of gun or flash of bandage. "The lookout's gone," he said. "The young guy." They climbed the stone steps to the covered landing and still Hood couldn't see Wampler. There was still the weak light coming from between the big double doors. He looked at each of the men and they nodded and Marquez unbuttoned his sport coat. Hood rapped hard on the door. "Money talks."

"Bring her in!" Skull called.

"Where's the kid?"

"What do you care?"

"I want to know why he's not out here."

"Because I'm in here, you dumb turd! Show us the money!"

"I like the kid where I can see him," said Hood.

"Then we'll sell these babies to someone else," said Skull.

"We're coming in." Hood took a deep breath and pushed through the heavy doors. In the brittle light of the lantern he saw that the crates were no longer open on the cable spool but leaning up against it, closed. Then all he saw was wrong movement: Skull and Peltz raising their weapons as their shadows mimed them from the ceiling, Clint Wampler springing in from the darkness beyond the lantern light, racking his shotgun.

"Police!" yelled Skull. "You are under arrest! *Police! Put your hands up! Good! Up!* And keep them there, you cartel beaners!"

Hood's hands were high. "I'm Charlie Hooper, ATF. We're all federal agents, Dirk. Put the guns down. You're *cops*? Then we have a big misunderstanding."

"Yeah, and the cavalry is coming."

"Don't turn it into a Steven Spielberg movie," said Hood.

"The fuck are you talking about?" said Wampler. "How come you said that?"

Skull squinted at Hood. Then, pistol still in hand, he gathered up two of the crates with his free arm. Peltz let go of the shotgun, which swung on its sling as he took up the second launcher and missile.

"Dirk Sculler," said Hood. "Be cool now. We're ATF. We've got our badges out in the cars. We're stinging you and you're stinging us. Guns down. *Guns down.* None of us wants to get shot over something like this."

"For nothing like this!" said Wampler. "Don't move or even dream about it." He scuttled in and squatted to snatch up the money, smiling up the barrel of his shotgun at Hood.

"I'm Marquez, ATF L.A."

"Cepeda, ATF L.A."

"I'm Jesse James," said Skull, sweeping by them with his gun still pointed at Hood's chest. "See you later, you wetback greasers."

Peltz and Wampler covered the agents as Skull put his pistol hand to the doorknob and pulled, keeping an eye on Hood. In the newly opened rectangle of night, Hood saw Yorth charging toward them with his sidearm drawn, Bly wide to the left and Velasquez to the right. Behind him, Marquez launched into Brock Peltz, who crashed hard into the door. Skull dropped his crates and was gone. Hood swept the pistol from under his coattail and went after him. From inside the clubhouse Hood heard a shotgun roar twice.

Skull was heavy but strong and he muscled through the darkness step for step ahead of Hood. Near the wall he stopped and fired three rounds that whirred past Hood's head. Hood went down, rolled over his hat, then popped upright again without ever stopping. Skull climbed the wall, turned and fired off two more rounds, then scrambled over. Hood made the wall and ran along it for fifty feet before he jumped it. He landed flat and hard and he could see that Skull had lost sight of him. The cop started across the street. A car swerved and the driver cursed furiously as Skull lumbered into the park-and-ride lot. Hood sprinted with all he had. His two-toned brogues were poor running shoes but his legs were long and he could see that Skull was slowing. He crossed the street without traffic and sprinted past Yorth's and Bly's cars. Skull ran to the edge of the dimly lighted parking lot and charged off into the darkness of a cotton field.

Now only the quarter moon showed Hood his way, but Skull's heavy breathing drew him closer. Hood could see him out ahead, plodding heavily between the rows. The cotton pods were just dabs of light in the broader darkness. Hood stayed a hundred feet back and a few rows over, keeping Skull's pace while the man tired. "Hey, Dirk—you can't outrun me and you've got no friends out here. Why not just drop the gun and we'll rest up a minute and head back? See what all the commotion was about."

He dropped to one knee behind a cotton plant just as Skull's pistol burped orange and a round whistled well to Hood's left and overhead. Then another round badly off to his right.

"We really are ATF, Dirk."

"I really wish you weren't." He had stopped and bent over, resting his hands on his knees, breathing hard. Sirens whined. "Me and the boys had a good thing going. Now I'm either going to get shot or arrested."

"Go with arrested, man!"

"Naw." Skull huffed upright and cupped his pistol in two hands and fired two more wild rounds, then he turned and barreled off down the crop row. Hood pushed off and followed. He saw two vehicles, light bars flashing, screaming down the street toward Buckboard Estates. Out ahead of him, Skull began to weave in and out of the cotton plants and Hood could hear the brittle snaps of the branches breaking. He couldn't get much closer without high risk of getting himself shot. Skull crashed through another plant and got himself realigned with a row and he pointed his gun behind him without stopping or turning and sent a bullet that cracked not inches from Hood's left ear. Hood pulled up and drew down. Skull's big body lurched in and out of his sights. "Drop the gun! *Drop the gun, Dirk!* I *am* going to shoot you!" Skull fired again without looking, then ran a brief, steady course and Hood heard him braying for air as he crashed through the cotton. Hood closed the distance easily, too easily, he thought, when Skull stopped and turned. Hood dropped into a shooter's crouch and held steady on Skull's big trunk. "Drop the gun, Dirk. Be smart for once in your life."

The big man took his air in big noisy gulps. The gun was at his side and he looked at it, then flung it toward Hood. Over Skull's exertions Hood didn't hear it hit. He stood and kept both hands on his pistol, taking long balanced strides right down the center of the row. Skull went to one knee, head bowed, his back and shoulders heaving. Hood was near upon him in an instant. "Don't touch the throw-down."

"There is no. Throw-down."

"Don't move either hand. Not one inch."

"Not gonna." Sucking wind, Skull looked up at Hood as he hiked his right pant cuff, and Hood saw the ankle rig and he took two long steps and kicked Skull in the chin so hard he fell over backwards and dazed. By the time Hood had rolled him over and cuffed him with plastic and removed the skinning knife from the scabbard on his belt and the switchblade from a pocket in his pants, Skull was snorting heavily, nostrils pressed into the fertile soil of Imperial County.

Hood heard the squeal of sirens leaving the clubhouse.

He aimed Skull through the open gate. Prowl car floodlights lit the clubhouse, and the colored flashers of the paramedics and fire-and-rescue units raked the walls. Hood heard a generator. In the parking lot he snatched up his hat and put it on and delivered Skull to two El

Centro cops, who roughly deposited him into the back of a car. One side of his face had swollen prodigiously and hate was in his eyes. Brock Peltz glared at him from the back of another police car.

The Blowdown team and six cops stood outside. Yorth looked stricken and Bly argued with a plainclothes detective. Hood could see Marquez inside, talking with a uniformed sergeant. Velasquez stepped away and Hood saw that he was breathing hard and his shirt was untucked.

"Wampler shotgunned Reggie. Paramedics made it here fast but it looked bad. No word."

"Where is that sonofabitch?"

"He lost us in the dark."

"Let me guess, with one of the Stingers. Out the back door."

"Yeah. I don't think he'll get far in this desert with two yard-long crates."

"He'll hijack the first motorist he finds."

"The cops have called up every available unit. There's a helo on the way from San Diego. There's no way that kid can get out of here."

"Did he get the money, too?"

"Not enough hands, apparently. It took Marquez a minute to take down Peltz and that's when Wampler got away. By the time we got there and saw he was gone, he was way in the dark somewhere. With a launcher and a missile. But Marquez got the money."

"Cepeda's that bad?"

"Shot twice and pretty close up, man. If it was buckshot . . ."

Hood stood at the entrance and looked into the clubhouse. The fire-and-rescue team had set up floodlights. There were more uniforms trying to figure out where to string the crime-scene tape, and a woman shooting video. Hood saw the launcher and missile crates on the floor where Skull had dropped them. He saw the blood-smeared floor were Cepeda had fallen, and the holes in the wall plaster where some of the shot had gone through. Big holes, he saw. Made for a man, not a pheasant. He saw that if he had waited a second or two to go after

Skull, he would have been hit. Suddenly Hood's adrenaline was gone and he felt ugly and tired and luckless.

For the next ten minutes Hood and Velasquez cruised southeast El Centro in the Charger, hoping for new luck. Just after nine o'clock, the police issued an all-units watch for Clint Wampler and a stolen white Sequoia. At the intersection of Imperial and Ross, he'd pistol-whipped the vehicle's driver, who confirmed that the carjacker was in possession of a pistol and two wooden crates.

Velasquez called Yorth at the hospital and Cepeda was critical and in surgery. Hood worked his way outward from the Imperial-Ross intersection in a series of right-hand turns. The wind stiffened and the night went cold.

They were quiet for a long while. Hood worked his way back toward the place where Wampler had carjacked the SUV, willing the white Sequoia into his field of vision. His heart sped up as a white Yukon sped across the intersection of Adams and Brucherie. Damn. "What if Wampler decides to use it for something spectacular?" asked Velasquez. "Because that's what guys like him want. To do something unforgettable. Because they themselves are so utterly and totally forgettable."

Hood nodded. He hadn't forgotten the Murrah Building catastrophe. He'd always remember the date because he was sixteen years old, learning to drive his father's pickup truck on a lightly traveled farm road outside of Bakersfield, when the news came over the radio. His dad had told him to pull over so he could listen. Hood had watched the anger building on his father's face and that anger Hood would never forget because his father was an otherwise gentle and generous man. *I hope they hang those fuckers*, he had said. Years later Hood's mother told him that his father had flown an American flag on the day they put the bomber to death.

"There used to be something in me like there is in Clint," said Hood. "When I was young, I wanted to make a statement and be a hero. But I had no statement to make and I had no idea what a hero was. There's nothing in the world scarier than a young man with bad ideas."

"Yeah. I get that." Velasquez answered his phone, listened silently, and punched off. "Reggie didn't make it."

Hood drove for a while in silence, doubling his willpower to conjure the white Sequoia with the murderous young man inside.

Velasquez asked him to pull over, so Hood steered the Charger onto the white, broad shoulder of the avenue. Velasquez set his head back against the rest and closed his eyes. Hood looked out at the stars and the cotton field and the windblown sand inching across the asphalt.

20

Rovanna holed up in the mountains where he didn't think the cops would look for him, a little village not far from San Diego called Wynola. Rovanna, meet Wynola, he thought. He got a weekly rate on a motel cabin because it was off-season and cold. The owner was in no way curious about him and she accepted his cash and his story of stolen ID. He signed in as Donnie Archibald. That first night he saw the eleven o'clock news story with the Reverend Steve Bagley. Rovanna saw now that it was careless to use his real name inside the church.

His cabin was small and mostly clean. He took in his suitcase, prepacked before the Neighborhood Congregational visit just in case of trouble. He waited until nightfall to bring in the radios, six of them, various shapes and sizes—two powered by nine-volt batteries, three by AC, and the other a hand-crank unit meant for emergencies. All of which he found amusing because they didn't need external power to be heard.

Now he sat in the darkness with the radios deployed around him and the Love 32 loaded with a full magazine and hidden under a bed pillow. His motel was built up close to the busy road, and there must be some kind of biker rally, he thought, because the Harleys growled and grumbled and roared at all hours, singles and pairs and big convoys of them twenty and thirty at a time. So the voices coming from the radios picked their moments to be heard. They were all soft, reasoning voices, two men and four women today, the opposite of yesterday. Though he only understood the English, the radios spoke several other languages that Rovanna recognized, and others not necessarily of this planet.

Later he walked to the pizza place and sat in the back, spiking his soft drink with vodka from a water bottle he carried in a cloth market bag along with the Love 32. The pizza was excellent. A woman dining alone gave him a hard look as she walked out. She was older than Rovanna but not old, and she wore a heavy black knee-length sweater and black gloves and leggings. Her hair was auburn, touched with gray. Avoiding her eyes, he noted her boots, old-fashioned lace-ups with low heels, something he imagined Belle Starr might wear. The leather looked ancient and worn of color, and could have been suede or finished, he couldn't tell, though the modern, lug-pattern soles looked new and squeaked on the floor as she went by.

He watched the TV for a while, then went outside into the surprising cold. As always he wore cargo shorts and slip-on sneakers but he did have his hoodie. He walked down the curving mountain highway, past his motel and a saloon and a beauty salon and a restaurant. The trees were high, jailing the quarter moon, and invisible patches of ice waited along the roadside. A pack of motorcycles snarled by. Rovanna followed a dirt road down into a swale surrounded by trees but open in the middle. He stood still for a while in the close darkness and listened. No voices out here. Not one. What a strange thing. He picked his way through the rocks and skidded where the road was steep and found himself locked in by the trees again, trees so high when he looked up he couldn't see the tops against the black sky. He heard the distant gurgle of running water. Down the slope he stepped and slid as the rocks clattered beneath his feet and the cloth shopping bag knocked against his leg.

Suddenly he found himself standing directly in a stream. The water was vividly cold and his sneakers were instantly soaked through. The water rippled over the stones sending up bright sounds—chirps and bell-like ringing, and the clear tinkle of glass. He had avoided bodies of water his entire life because he couldn't swim but now, hearing the water music, he felt no fear. He heard something behind him but when he turned he saw nothing. He put one foot in front of the other and walked into the current. The stones were smooth and extremely slippery. After a few yards he couldn't feel his toes. Then his feet. He stopped again to experience the voicelessness around him. The stream warbled and the highway was just a faraway hiss. He thought of the Identical Men and what had happened when they attacked him in the church and he felt that he had done the right thing. Stren's voice joined the stream and highway, a three-part harmony: *There is nothing wrong with you, Lonnie. Sometimes friends are all we have. And voices speak to all of us at different times. Listen to them and do what you think is right . . . use this gift to protect yourself and those around you and to advance the ideals you believe in.*

He waded farther upstream. His ankles were aching but not unpleasantly, because Rovanna could separate himself from himself at times, just observe. He heard rocks clatter behind him but when he turned, again there was nothing. Then another a voice broke through but it wasn't a voice he was expecting. He could see the owl hunched black in the sere branches of a cottonwood, and he could see the flat metallic eyes blink when it adjusted its head to better behold him. "Owl. Don't say anything more. Too much talk on earth. Plainly." Rovanna sloshed along until he was almost under the owl, then he stopped and looked up. The animal watched him for a long while. Then without warning its wings spread and it rose from the branch as if pulled by strings and disappeared into the blackness. Rovanna saw the feather spiraling down toward him and he caught it and put it in his bag.

Back at the roadside a car was waiting. It was a newer economy car like Rovanna's, but red. The passenger door stood open and inside Rovanna saw the woman from the pizza place. Her sweater was buttoned up tight, the cowl almost covering her ears. Her auburn hair had a coppery sheen in the weak interior light. "I'm Joan," she said, her breath fogging. "Get in."

Rovanna sat close because the car was small. The defroster was set to roar. Before shutting his door he looked at her face, which was grave and prettier than he had first thought. She did not smile. He glanced at her aged boots encrusted with brown dirt, one on the brake and one on the clutch. The car smelled faintly of cherries. He set his market bag on the floorboard and fastened his restraints.

The little car revved high and jumped onto the asphalt and sped up the mountain toward Julian. "Lonnie, you have no chance if you try to do this alone."

"Do what alone?"

"Survive. In the glove box there's a book, and your meds from the El Cajon house. Take them out. Put the pills in your pocket and the book on your lap."

Joan turned on the interior light, and Rovanna found the small leather-bound Bible and his Tramadol and Zoloft and did as she said. He saw the cherry-shaped cardboard air freshener on top of some maps. He looked at the backseats and saw the neatly rolled sleeping bag resting on a bed pillow, a laptop computer, two milk crates overflowing with electronic pads and pods and gadgets and cords and chargers.

She turned off the light. "First, you must take your medications. They work for you. Over time you can teach yourself to live without them. But for now you must take them or your mind will betray you into foolish actions."

"I left them behind in El Cajon on purpose."

"That was bad decision-making, Lonnie. Second, do not talk to Stren again. If he shows up, hit him with that Bible. Literally pound him with it. It will repel and sicken him. The Torah and Koran can be used also. Electronic editions are not effective. But, the most important thing you can do is to not stalk Representative Freeman at the Alternative Book Fair in San Diego."

At the word *Freeman*, Rovanna flinched inwardly. "How do you know about—"

"I don't have the time to explain myself to you in a way that you're ready to understand. But I know you. Believe me, I know you. It really *was* nice back there on the little stream, wasn't it? When you stood in that cold water and listened and there were no voices. For a short time, at least."

"I haven't experienced that in years—no voices for minutes on end."

Joan wound out the little four-banger on an uphill run. Rovanna watched the pines sweep past. She came up fast on a couple of belching Harleys, downshifted, and gunned the little car into the oncoming lane, passing them on a blind rise, then veering back into place ahead of them.

"I got a blue Focus," he said.

"These new economy cars are really something," said Joan. "The mileage and power and comfort. I put between eighty and one hundred twenty thousand miles a year on cars. This is like my third or fourth one."

"What do you do for a living?"

"Sales. Look, Rovanna, I can't take that gun away from you. You know, the machine pistol in the shopping bag at your feet right now. I'm not authorized to take it. But I can tell you this: You are a troubled man now being manipulated by a devil, and the final cost to you will not be the pain you inflict, but the pain that you will receive. It will be utterly unbearable and you will not survive it. Take your meds, read that Bible, and keep it with you always. Most importantly, stay away from Scott Freeman."

Again Rovanna flinched. It was a physical reaction to the word and the man it identified.

"Do not attend the book fair," Joan continued. "I implore you to leave that gun with me tonight. Just leave it where it is when you exit my car. If you are not strong enough to do that, then *do not attend the book fair for any reason.*"

"I'm not going to let some stranger take away my last gun."

"I didn't think so."

With this Joan braked and downshifted, then threw the little coupe into a tire-screeching U-turn that ran them onto the dirt shoulder, then back to the pavement. When they passed the bikers coming up the mountain, Joan honked her horn on the way by. She looked into the rearview and smiled as if she'd really shown them.

She pulled into the motel lot and drove to his cabin. Rovanna looked out where the headlights hit his front door. "Would you like to come in?"

"No, thank you."

"I want to thank you for helping me."

"I don't feel like I've done enough."

"I never feel like I've done enough."

"Bible. Meds. No Stren. No book fair. Pray, Lonnie, pray with all your heart. Start simple, with these seven words: *I thank and praise God. Help us.* That's all you need to say."

"Can I kiss you?"

"Open your door."

Rovanna unslung his harness and opened his door, then turned to kiss her only to find the sole of her lace-up boot planted in the middle of his chest. She pushed him out of the car so hard he flew halfway to the cabin before hitting the ground butt-first. He felt the strength of five men in her. He crabbed away, momentarily belly up and on all fours, then struggled upright, pissed off. He felt his anger and shame flare and his face flush. He marched forward and braced himself with one hand on the door frame in case she tried anything else and, without taking his eyes off her, he snatched his shopping bag from the floor mat.

"God will bless you if you let him, Lonnie Rovanna. He has spoken to you through me."

He slammed the car door and didn't look back. But he did peek out the cabin door half an hour later, just to see if there were tire tracks in the packed dirt where Joan had let him off. Hard to say. So he stepped onto the landing and looked down in the dim porch light and saw what could very well be the neat narrow tracks of an economy car. And he saw a two-orbed impression right where he remembered landing, hard, at least ten feet away from the car tracks. He thought of her astonishing strength and the smell of cherries. An incredible woman. She had known exactly what he was thinking while he stood in the freezing little creek. Still, he knew that he was not sane and that sometimes he saw things that weren't really there. Then, almost embarrassedly, he turned square to the porch light and looked down at his sweatshirt. There it was, plain to see, the proof he wanted—the dirty outline of her boot on his chest.

21

The following night, in the stately, chandeliered lobby of the Biltmore Hotel in Los Angeles, Mike greeted Bradley with a strong hug and a grand smile. His tuxedo was notch-lapelled and expertly fitted and somehow gave him added height. With Mike was his lovely associate Owens, inches taller than he was, in a sleek pewter-colored dress that matched her eyes. Pearls around her neck. Bradley hadn't seen her since she came to visit Erin, shortly after helping her survive the ordeal in Yucatán four months ago. He took her hands and kissed her cheek and glanced at the scars on her wrists and furtively inhaled the scent of her though he tried not to.

"I like your new dental work," she said.

He'd certainly needed it after Yucatán. "The new teeth complete my smile."

"And I like your conservative haircut. Are you an old-fashioned conservative, or just one of the new ones out to wreck the country?"

"I love this country. And look at you—the same old beauty you always were."

"Why, thank you. I hope you don't find it tiresome."

"Boys and girls?" Mike handed Owens a small silver flask and she smiled, then sipped.

Bradley took it and swirled and smelled it. Cream? Cucumbers? Mint? It was perhaps nonalcoholic and very cold, in spite of being inside Mike's breast pocket. Bradley thought of the absinthe bar he'd had at his and Erin's wedding down in Valley Center. What a night. And another day and another night and morning until the last celebrants were gone. Tents in the hills and all the guest casitas full and someone getting the fighting bulls drunk and letting them out of the corral. They'd made Bacchus proud. "What is this stuff?"

"Let's head down to the basement ballroom," said Mike, swiping back the flask. "We can hit the bar for an ordinary drink and work the crowd."

Owens fell arm-in-arm between the men. They swept down the broad stairway toward the downstairs ballrooms, and with each step Bradley felt lighter and more confident and even more clear in the head. What *was* that stuff? He felt like stripping to his briefs and diving off a ten-meter board. Just before hitting the water he'd arch his back and spread his arms and fly down to Buenavista, knock out Hood with a left uppercut and zoom back here with Erin on his back. For some reason a conversation he'd had with his mother came back to him now, word for word, their voices exactly as they'd sounded when he was five, like someone was playing a tape of it in his head.

"Exactly what crowd will be here?" asked Bradley. "The marquee in the lobby had New England Dental Association, Model Train International, and Western States Fabrication and Manufacture."

"The last," said Mike.

"People in your bathroom-products business?"

"Well, in all fields of fabrication and manufacture, Bradley." Downstairs Mike flagged a waiter and a moment later their three drinks arrived. Bradley got a Bombay martini up with a twist and told himself to go easy on the booze tonight. Mike had gotten him a room but his plan was to leave early and make Buenavista by midnight. He had a full tank in the Cayenne, a "maybe" from Erin, and a nine-o'clock phone call scheduled. He had no doubt that she would want to see him.

The ballroom was crowded and an orchestra played. There were tables set up for dinner but not many people yet seated. Some were dancing. To Bradley there seemed to be no dress code at all. On the men he saw tuxedos, dinner jackets like his own, suits and sport coats and slacks, open-collared shirts without ties, polo and rugby shirts, work shirts with names stitched on the chests, guys in aloha shirts and shorts and flip-flops. The women had a generally higher level of presentation—mostly dresses and suits—but he did see two women dressed in 1890's prairie calico and heavy boots; and three others in buckskins and moccasins festooned with beads and feathers; and two more wearing sheer bathing suit cover-ups over bikinis, and heeled sandals with rhinestones across the toes. He guessed the age range to be twenties to early sixties. No children. Mostly whites, Native Americans, Latinos and blacks, and a few Asians. There was a giant with razor-cut hair and enormous hands, dressed in a tuxedo, and two dwarves in tails. The room was loud enough with conversation to compete with the music. Entire groups burst into laughter. The laughter struck Bradley as knowing and ironic. Everyone seemed to know everyone and there were no nametags.

Bradley sipped the martini, lightly. He noted that nearly all of the guests were drinking highballs or apparently straight liquor and the waiters and walk-up bar were quite busy. Empty glasses were already stacking up on the bar top and bus trays. He also saw that many of attendees were drinking from silver flasks like Mike's, often offering the flask around to others, as Europeans offer cigarettes.

The three of them went from group to group, where Mike and Owens unfailingly drew warm hugs and hearty backslaps and words of good cheer. *Fantastic work down there in San Diego, Mike— wonderful!* Mike introduced him as Bradley Murrieta, the new partner in MFB—Mike Finnegan Bath—a man he hoped would help to "resuscitate MFB's wheezing bottom line." The conferees were polite but seemed slightly skeptical of Bradley, which was fine with him. Owens positioned herself at his side, and occasionally held his arm in such a way that drew looks.

Mike and Owens danced a waltz, then she and Bradley drew a brassy foxtrot and, when it was over, light applause for a dance well done. Bradley was struck again by her lustrous beauty and easy humor. Even now in the late days of winter her skin was tanned brown and smooth, and her black hair was wavy and shiny as obsidian. Silver gray eyes.

Bradley knew that Erin had spent many hours with Owens in Benjamin Armenta's castle in the Yucatán lowlands, where Erin was held for ransom for ten days. Owens was Armenta's mistress and Erin had distrusted her at first. But Owens had helped Erin preserve her sanity, and protected her and her baby from men far more wicked than Armenta. From that remote jungle fortress without computers or telephones, Owens had shown Erin how to communicate with her husband, at no small risk to herself. Owens had even helped Erin attempt an escape. Now as Bradley danced with her he was aware not only of her beauty but of her strange history—illegitimate daughter of a powerful Catholic monsignor; attempted suicide; devotee of Mike Finnegan; consort of cartel kingpin Benjamin Armenta; actress, cipher, and siren. What else was she, and what had she done and what did she want? Bradley understood that she was far more versed in life's shadows than he was, and therefore somehow his superior.

They dined at one of the eight-tops with a two-man extrusion-mold-making company based in Grass Valley, a patent lawyer from Fresno, and two tool-and-die honchos from the Bay Area. The conversation was arcane to Bradley, all about people he'd never met and events outside his experience. It was plain that they were all part of a huge, complex industry about which he was uninformed:

And I told Delmonico himself, right then and there, that we could help this man and why wasn't that enough? Isn't that what we're about? My prospect was a good-enough prospect—maybe not a brilliant man, but—oh, Bradley, can you pass the Thousand Island?

And:

We've got to quit apologizing, everyone. We need to be more confrontational. People crave it in this short, violent century. It's simple as that. Transparency and honesty. They need to know the facts so they can decide.

Or: *I've never seen such a tender being turn into such a producer.*

You should have seen the swath she cut through those happy Presby-terians! It just made me realize again how talent can hide in a person and how our job is to bring it out.

Bradley followed as best he could, wondering what a customer's history or this short, violent century or cutting a swath through Presby-terians had to do with fabrication and manufacture. He thought of the Los Angeles County Sheriff's Department social events and how it was all cop talk. How much of that would these guys understand? They probably had no idea what a 187 was. He wondered what Erin was doing. He pictured her sitting in that shadowy, low-ceilinged adobe living room of Charlie Hood's, could see the play of the lamplight off her fine face, and the round outline of their future alive inside her.

By the time dinner was over, Bradley felt tipsy with half the martini and one glass of red wine down, plus whatever Mike had given him from the flask. But he still felt solid, too. They made the rounds from table to table. The conversations became harder to decipher. *The miasmal soul I told Delmonico I had secured? At the last second of the final minute of the eleventh hour? Betrayed. Betrayed!* Bradley noted that practically every attendee was drinking far more than he was. He watched them carrying two empty glasses at a time to the bar, and two full ones away. The bus trays were overloaded and drinkers were setting their empties on the floor beneath the stands or on the stage or neatly along the baseboards of the walls. The waiters had given up stately attendance for old-fashioned hustle. Bottles were appearing at the tables, buckets of ice and stacks of clean tumblers. The giant delivered a case of something to his table, balancing it high over his head on his fingertips. Yet none of the conferees appeared in the least intoxicated to Bradley. Slightly more animated, but only slightly.

"We can certainly hold our liquor," said Mike, taking Bradley by the arm and heading to an empty table. Owens led a tall man to the dance floor and looked over her shoulder at Bradley with an oddly apologetic expression. The men took off their jackets and put them over empty chairs and sat with their backs to the wall. The giant swung by with a bottle of Scotch that Bradley recognized as rare and expensive and placed it in front of Mike with three glasses. His face was huge and bony but pleasant enough. He gave Mike a smile, then strode away.

"Bradley," said Mike, opening the bottle. "I'm worried for you."

"Don't be—things are good. The Blands are gone and Dez is pushing Warren into retirement. Hood's on the run and it's only going to get worse for him. Carlos has a new business plan for me, according to Rocky, but Rocky can't tell me what it is. And Erin? Well, I think she's coming around. I think I'm starting to add up to something in her eyes again. It's all coming together, Mike."

Mike poured them each a shot, held his glass up to the chandelier and twirled it. He looked pensive. "It's Erin. She is your love and your reason for living. What worries me is this—what if something happens to her?"

Bradley sipped the Scotch. "Nothing's going to happen to her."

Mike raised his eyebrows and looked away. "What if? Accidents? Disease? Enemies?"

"That's why I'm trying to get Erin back to Valley Center, like ASAP. I can protect her and the baby there. It's secure now. Nothing like that kidnapping will ever happen again. Me, her, and Thomas. The family unit. That's how it's going to be. I can feel it, Mike. She's going to come back to me. Soon."

"What if she doesn't? What if you don't know her heart as well as you think you do? You've been quite surprised by her thus far, correct? By her independence and anger and strength in resisting you? What if she moves further away from you with the birth of Thomas? What if all of her heart goes to him? This is commonplace in many women."

Bradley drank again and studied Mike's face. Mike looked concerned but crafty. Bradley surveyed the crowd and saw the same basic expression on every face in the room. Mike's worries about Erin and him were ridiculous, he thought. "Are these people all like you?"

"You could say that."

"Are a lot of them partners?"

"Very few. I applied for permission to bring you and it was granted. We keep the partners segregated until we or someone upstairs finds a synergy. Then introductions follow. Hitler and Himmler are a good example. But most of our work is far more subtle—thousands of couplings over the centuries."

"Upstairs?"

"Well, we here are only the foot soldiers. Journeymen. Both sides of this competition are dictatorships, basically—the only organization model that can really work on this scale. The King on one side, and the Prince on the other. Beneath them are clearly defined hierarchies. Of course the nature of devils is to rock the boat. So you can imagine the delinquency, trespassing, obstruction, and insubordination that go on between us mid-levels. Endless, really. It can get competitive. That's what almost everyone in the room is talking about by now—their work. It's shoptalk. These biannual rallies are our watercooler, our place to gossip and catch up and brag and berate."

"How do you drink so much booze and not show it?"

"We metabolize differently, which is necessary for very long life. Alcohol is only about one-tenth as strong as it is for you."

"What's in the flasks? Everybody's got one."

"What's in the flasks is a closely guarded secret. I can tell you it's all organic and is nonalcoholic. It's actually a mild antidote for alcohol, kind of an energy drink. It promotes clarity, confidence, energy, and even a small amount of generosity. It brings forth memories in startling detail. So, the more alcohol, the more antidote. It's a big standoff is what it is. We crave abandon but utterly detest being out of control. Just like people. Some of us practically live on the stuff."

"How does that potion stay cold up against your body like that for hours?"

"Cucumbers. And that's all I'm going to say about that."

Bradley wanted a good shot of the secret potion. Mike nodded and handed him the flask, and he drank the cool, sweet liquid. He remembered Mike's words during their visit to Beatrice in the mine: *A journeyman devil can hear human thoughts from thirty feet away, so long as those thoughts are clear and emphatic.* "You don't doubt me as you used to."

"No," said Bradley. He took another little sip and handed back the flask.

"That's good. We can't build except on trust."

Bradley felt a thorough sense of well-being easing through him, something whole and undefeatable. "I believe in you, Mike."

"I still hear small doubts."

"I could lie to you but what good would it do?"

"None. I truly hope that you and Erin can patch things up. I worry, yes. And I certainly do wonder if you and Erin will be able to see eye to eye on the raising of Thomas. You are very different people. In many ways you have opposing beliefs and values. This is my number one concern."

"We'll raise Thomas as we see fit. End of that story."

"Oh? And when you and Erin disagree?"

"It's called compromise."

"I'm tickled by your idealism, Bradley. Your mother had it, a big fat streak running right down her middle. Of course she hid it well but it gave her purpose. It allowed her to steal from the rich and give to the poor, and to herself. Joaquin? The same. Ideals pave the way for so many actions, both noble and atrocious."

"We'll work out what is best for Thomas."

"I wonder if you will tell him who he is, someday? Tell him of Joaquin and his generations through Suzanne and through you?"

Bradley held Mike's gaze. "I don't know. It tormented Mom, what to tell me."

"She came close many times. At night, when you children were asleep, she would go out to the barn in Valley Center and confer with the head in the jar. And read through Joaquin's brief letters. And write in her own growing journal. This was her secret life, but it wasn't a fantasy life, it was genuine. As Suzanne Jones—woman, mother, schoolteacher—she was only half. The other half is the woman that you came to know. So, will you tell Thomas who she was? Who you are? Who *he* is?"

"I'll know what to do when the time comes."

"I wonder what Erin would say about it. Certainly, she would leave you instantly and forever if she knew what you have kept from her. The head, the history, the fortunes you have plundered every bit as nimbly as Joaquin ever did. I'm impressed that you've kept her in the dark for as long as you have. But . . . I can't see her tolerating your most unusual truths. Certainly she would not reveal them to her first-born son. Erin would take Thomas and move to the Borneo jungle before doing that."

"I'm sorry you think so little of her. She's all I've ever wanted."

"Don't lie to yourself or me. What about the loot you so enjoy taking? The loot that compounds monthly in your safes under the barn? You want your treasures very badly, too. And you crave the excitement of snatching them. It's in your blood."

"We'll work it out."

"I have something to tell you. I want you to listen until I'm finished, and remain outwardly calm. I want no answer at this time. I only want you to *hear*. Can you do this?" Bradley sipped the Scotch and waited. Mike placed his hand on Bradley's shoulder. "Bradley, you will soon realize that you need a companion on your journey with Thomas. I want you to consider Owens. She is markedly fond of you. She is everything she appears to be—a beautiful, bright woman. Look at the way she dances. *Look*. I know her inside and out. She is not my daughter but my partner, as you may have concluded. I have never had a more loyal, agreeable, satisfying, and satisfied partner in all of my long life. She could bring all of these qualities to you. In order to do so she would need to break away from me completely and abso-lutely—Owens can only give herself to one purpose at a time. She is simply that way. It is her character, and one I cherish. But I would willingly transfer her to you. Owens and I have discussed this. She would make an exemplary wife, and mother for Thomas. She has depths that you do not have, and she would open them to you and to your son. She wants children of her own, with the right man, of course. In the long run, Bradley—and the long run is foremost on the minds of every being in this room—I want what is best for you and Thomas. I love Erin dearly as a sister and a friend but she is not an ally to me, except as she is an ally to you. If she is your enemy, she becomes my enemy and she will be engaged as such. If her heart remains hard against you, and if Thomas becomes the sole focus of her life, then you will become diminished by the rage and impotence of unanswered love, and Thomas will grow up to become a hesitant, coddled, insignificant man. You must consider the necessity of taking Thomas away from Erin and allowing Owens help you raise him."

"If you lay a hand on either of them, I'll kill you."

Mike gave Bradley's shoulder a powerful squeeze, then lifted his Scotch. "This is what I mean about rage and impotence, Bradley. This is why I ask you to consider this spectacular and devoted woman. I don't expect a decision from you now. *Enjoy* the birth of Thomas. Revel in young fatherhood. But there will come a day when my words and this offer will sound like music in your ears. That day may come soon or it may come later. So, don't forget, Bradley, that just as I sit here now with you, I will someday sit with Thomas, discussing our mutual projects and the bounties of life, long after your bones are in the earth." Mike released Bradley's shoulder and both men stood as Owens came from the dance floor toward them. Her dress caught the chandelier light in shifting facets and her body, perfect and trapped, rippled beneath them. "Behold. See. If I were a man . . ."

Bradley hooked his tuxedo coat off the chair and held the chair out for Owens. He slid it forward as her weight settled. "Pardon me."

"You will change your mind over time, Bradley," said Mike. "You most certainly will."

"Go to hell, Mike."

"I think I missed something," said Owens.

Bradley walked around the dance floor and through the tables, headed for the stairs. The orchestra started up "Smoke Gets in Your Eyes." The dwarves sat on opposite sides of an empty table, leaning forward and arguing loudly, an ocean of empty glasses between them. An old woman wearing a prim and very faded Victorian dress, one of the few old people in the room, caught Bradley by his shirtsleeve and thrust a silver flask at him. He swallowed some and gave it back her. She didn't let go of his arm. "I'm Eva. And Mike told me that you met Beatrice."

"Yes, I did."

"What did you think of her?"

"I kind of felt bad for her."

"Well, don't forget *what* she is. She'll be out in a few short years. There's always been lots of back and forth between us and the dullards we're trying to keep from ruining humankind. Mike is so swashbuckling sometimes, and darling, too, of course. I've never seen him happier than he is now. It's all your fault! I'm very happy to have you with us."

"Nice to be on the team."

"Your timing is pitch-perfect, and the West has always been the most interesting territory, bar none. And this economy is making people question everything they think they know. They're so angry and afraid and sometimes desperate. You wake up in the morning and can't help but smell the fear. It's the most delightful peacetime work environment I've experienced since the Great Depression." She reached up and pinched Bradley's cheek.

He stood outside where guests arrived and the valets dashed into the dark with tickets in their hands. He dialed Erin and while the phone rang he rocked up and down on the balls of his feet, feeling the strong flex of his calves, and recalled in detail, though for no apparent reason, flying a kite with his brother when he was five, a big blue

Chinese dragon with a six-foot wingspan and a long tail and big white teeth. They were at Huntington Beach on the twenty-second of August, 1991, the water was sixty-eight degrees, and the swell was out of the southwest. Now Bradley could clearly see that kite wobbling back and forth in the stiff onshore breeze, zigzagging higher and higher into the blue sky, slashing away with its great white teeth, and he could feel the pull of the plastic handle, and the warmth of the sun on his back, and the grit of the sand trapped between his skinny boy hips and his low-slung canvas trunks.

"Hi, baby."

"Brad. I was sleeping. How's the convention?"

"It's over and I'm on my way."

"No. I'm sorry. I'm tired and I want to sleep, just me and Thomas tonight."

Bradley said nothing for a long beat. He felt the optimism draining out of him like milk from a ruptured carton. "I'm very disappointed."

"Tired is tired. I wrote a song today. Maybe tomorrow we can see each other."

"When? What time?"

"Please let me sleep on it."

"But for tonight I could just curl up on the couch like I have been. Or on the floor in your room. Whichever you want. I wouldn't even wake you up."

"That's a really nice offer. But no. Not tonight, Bradley. Thomas is quiet now."

"That's really good, honey."

"I don't like your tone of voice."

"I love you."

"I know you're furious at me. You can't hide it. I'm sorry it's like this, Bradley. I don't know how else to get through."

"Let me be with you."

"Not tonight."

"I love you with all my furious heart."

She clicked off. Bradley stood for a moment in the cold February night, then gave his ticket to the cashier and paid the parking charge. He headed west to Sunset and the Whisky, where he had first seen Erin McKenna six years ago. She had been onstage with her first band, the Cheater Slicks, and he'd fallen for her before the first song of their first set was over. He was sixteen but looked nineteen, had a good fake ID and a solid vodka buzz. Two nights later he finally caught her eye and he had not let go. Now, heading for the front door of the Whisky, Bradley remembered their first conversation perfectly:

When you look at me it's like walking into a beautiful room. I'm Brad Jones.

That's a pretty thing to say.

I'm short on words right now.

I'm Erin McKenna.

After the last set tonight, we need to talk.

Oh, we need to, Brad Jones?

Yes.

What are you going to talk with if you're short on words?

I'll find something.

In honor of that memory Bradley had a vodka rocks, listened to the band, thought about Erin. Six years with her. He knew that thousands of men had seen her perform here in L.A., and half of them had fallen for her just as he had. But he had had the luck. He was the one who got her. She had given herself to him, along with her trust and love. She would soon give a child to him.

Mike's cool cucumber potion continued to stoke his memories, bringing them back in splendid detail. But his memories of Erin were not a comfort now; rather they were bitter torments of regret and frustration and of all that he had lost in her. Lost. Every beautiful remembered image cut him; every fond recalled word rang with impermanence. He drank two more vodkas hoping that his anger would soften but they only made it worse. He called her but she didn't answer. He headed out of town on the 101, then cut east on Interstate

10, which took him to Monterey Park, where the Los Angeles County Sheriff's Department is headquartered. He pulled into the parking lot of a Circle K he knew.

Looking back and forth between the storefront and the rearview mirror he tied a black bandana loosely around his neck. Then he set the lucky Santana Panama on his head and dropped the heavy .40 caliber derringer his mother had given him into the breast pocket of his tuxedo coat. He got them ready as he walked across the lot. He came out with a plastic bag stuffed with cash and a tall can of sweetened tea for the road and a promise from the face-down clerk not to get up off the floor for exactly five minutes. He had apologized to the terrified clerk and removed his wallet, added five twenties to the eleven lonely dollars inside, and worked it back into the man's pocket.

22

Yorth stood at the open side of Hood's cubicle with a cup of coffee in his hand and a frown on his face. He was haunted by Cepeda, and Hood could see it in his red eyes and the gray crescents under them and hear it in his voice. "I don't know why Washington has to choose times of crisis to make things even worse for us. But the SAC wants you in L.A. in one hour."

"For what?"

"He wouldn't say."

"Fine with me, but it's a two-and-half-hour drive even if you flog it."

"They're sending down a helo. It'll be here in fifteen minutes."

Hood raised his eyebrows. "Don't I feel special. What's up, Dale? Cough it."

"I don't know. Maybe they want to talk more about Reggie. Or Wampler or the Stingers."

"Why talk to just me?"

"I told you, Charlie, I don't know."

Ten minutes later Hood was tucked into a little Department of Justice Bell, looking down at the diminishing Buenavista Airport. The pilot introduced himself as a U.S. Marshal and those were the last words he spoke. Hood was taken not to the rather swank ATF regional headquarters in Glendale but to the westside Federal Building. He saw twenty-something chairs around the conference room table but there were only four people in them except for himself. He recognized two—a congressman from California, who was talking on his cell phone when Hood sat down. The other was Fredrick Lansing, acting deputy director of ATF, who shook Hood's hand and gestured to a chair but said nothing. *He's a long way from headquarters in Washington, D.C.*, thought Hood. Then he interlaced his fingers on the table and looked out the window at Century City and wondered if he should have stayed in the Buckboard clubhouse to help Cepeda handle Wampler instead of going after Skull when he bolted. Maybe then Cepeda would still be alive and Wampler would have bought the farm instead. Really, where could Skull have gotten to? Well, the same place Wampler had gotten, Hood thought: away.

Three of his four interrogators had laptops open on the table before them and small digital recorders beside the computers. A large monitor on a wheeled stand stood within eyeshot of everyone. The congressman spoke first. "I'm Representative Darren Grossly of California. Thank you for coming on short notice, Agent Hood. You must be rung out."

"I'm fine, sir."

"Any word on the Stinger?"

"None. Wampler carjacked an SUV ten minutes after he lost us. Now he's in the wind."

Grossly was a small man with wispy white hair, fierce eyes, and an offended manner. Hood knew him as a hard-nosed conservative from the middle of the state, a power player who seemed to enjoy competition and attention. He'd seen him on TV. Grossly played the outrage card quickly and well, haranguing at any opportunity against the federal government he was a part of and against liberal social views, including abortion and gun control. Hood was a registered independent. "That Stinger is good from what, five miles out? Blow a passenger jet to kingdom come?"

Hood nodded.

"That's a yes?"

"Yes, sir."

"They're recording is why."

"I see that."

"Then answer out loud please. Now, Mr. Hood, I didn't fly you or

Mr. Lansing or myself all the way here to talk about what happened out in the desert. I'm sure you and your ATF associates will make short work of this Wampler fellow. You have my complete confidence."

"We'll stop him before he sells or uses that thing."

"He's right about that," said Lansing. Lansing was an imposing man, gray faced and gray haired. His voice was deep and resonant. He was reputed to be intelligent and dour. His overcoat lay on the expanse of table beside him.

Grossly nodded and gave Hood a long look. "Randall, can you fire up that PowerPoint or whatever it is, and just start at the beginning?"

Randall was fortyish, slender, and dark haired, bespectacled. "Hello, Mr. Hood, I'm Randall Schmitz. I'm a Department of Justice prosecutor. Across from me is my associate, Grace Crockett, also a DOJ lawyer. I'm sorry this whole meeting came up so quickly and, perhaps to you, rather mysteriously. I know the timing couldn't have been worse with regard to what happened to Agent Cepeda. He gave his last full measure. So I thank you for being here at such a difficult time down in Buenavista. But, on the lighter side, I can tell you this is a very informal hearing. You are not being deposed. You will not be placed under oath. We are not here to lay groundwork for a finding or indictment. We are here to help Representative Grossly gather information about certain individuals and policies of ATF, which of course operates within the Department of Justice. Representative Grossly is on the House Committee on Oversight and Government Reform, as I'm sure you know. So, we're here to ask some questions and try to get some clarity on things. Specifically, we're interested in the smuggling of guns from the United States into Mexico in the summer of two thousand ten. Here—I may as well just start out with the physics of all this."

Schmitz used his computer to control the images on the large monitor. Hood had never seen the first few pictures but the lawyer's question was easy enough to answer. "Mr. Hood, can you identify this firearm?"

"It's a Love Thirty-two."

"Describe it, briefly."

Hood ran through the basics. Grossly's eyebrows knit dubiously upward.

"And these?" Schmitz continued.

"Crates full of the same, it looks to me." A charge of adrenaline went through Hood. Three years ago he'd seen such guns in crates while peering through a slot basement window of the Pace Arms manufacturing building. That was last anyone at ATF had seen Love 32s until some of them showed up in the hands of cartel *sicarios* one year later in Buenavista. But he'd never seen photographs of the newly manufactured, crated guns, except for the few he'd taken himself through that window and later included in his reports. These were of much better quality and taken up close. He wondered who took them and why, and how Grossly had gotten them.

"Do you know where these guns were made?" asked Schmitz.

"A thousand of them were made in Orange County, California, by Pace Arms. It's possible they made others at that time. Or have made them since."

"What time are you referring to?" asked Grossly.

"August of two thousand ten."

"To your knowledge, was ATF aware that Pace Arms was manufacturing these guns at that time and in that place?"

"Yes, sir. We opened an investigation into Pace Arms. It's well documented."

"And what did that investigation conclude, if anything?"

"We confirmed that Pace Arms was manufacturing the Love Thirty-twos. Because the gun is fully automatic, they're illegal for most people in California to buy, possess, or sell. We were building our case against Ron Pace and a Los Angeles County sheriff deputy who we believed was planning to transport the guns for illegal sale."

Next came pictures taken inside the Pace Arms production area. There were workers at the tables, and they looked at the cameraman, smiling with pride and admiration, as if they were in the presence of a celebrity. One of them had puckered his lips for a kiss at the moment the picture was taken.

"Pace Arms again," said Hood.

"And this?"

Hood watched the video. It showed the backside of the Pace Arms building, apparently evening but still light. Ron Pace and two Latino men—possibly two of the gunsmiths—were loading the Love 32 crates into the cargo hold of a very dirty motor home. Then came a series of still shots taken at night, showing Ron Pace and a pretty young woman loading more the gun crates into a Ford F-250 and a Dodge Ram. They were dressed in snappy travel wear, and looked as if they were packing up for a pleasure trip.

"ATF shot that video of the shipping dock of Pace Arms," said Hood. "That's Ron Pace, and his girlfriend, Sharon Novak. I think the others are the gunmakers."

"They've loaded three vehicles with crates of guns?" asked Grossly.

"That's what we thought."

"Thought?"

"Doesn't it look that way to you?"

"Keep watching."

Hood watched video of the dirty motor home trundling across the tarmac on a charter company landing strip at John Wayne Airport in Orange County. It climbed a loading ramp into the belly of a waiting CH-47 transport helicopter with Red Cross signage, which lifted into the air. An SUV came skidding into the picture.

"Airport security video," said Grace Crockett. "Is that one of you ATF agents in the Yukon?" She looked at Hood with a faux innocence. She had a sweet, almost girlish voice.

"It was me," said Hood.

"That's what we had deduced," she said. "Because all of your other agents were down near the Mexican border, correct?"

"Right. They followed the two trucks and I took the motor home on a hunch. There was also a van that left the loading dock, so at that point, we thought the weapons were divided up into four vehicles."

Grossly leaned forward. "You followed the motor home on a hunch. A hunch that turned out to be very damned right. The motor home had one thousand of these machine pistols in it. Yet still it got past you."

Hood looked back at Grossly's incredulous face. "I realized it too late. We were stretched thin and the helo was waiting."

"You seem smarter than that. Maybe you just did what you were told."

"Nobody told me to let a thousand machine guns get away. We were trying to stop those guns. When we pulled over the trucks down near the border, they were loaded with gun crates. But the crates were filled with clothing, mostly new pants. The load-in was a good stage play."

"*Pants?*" said Grossly.

"Mostly children's jeans. New ones. Different colors and cuts. Bradley Jones was driving the Ram. He said they were taking the pants down to Mexico for the poor."

"Did you believe Bradley Jones's story?" asked Schmitz.

"No. The charity work was just a cover. We chased the jeans one way and the guns went the other way."

Hood looked at Lansing and wondered where the moral support was. The big man sat back with his arms crossed.

Crockett spoke again in her sweet voice. "You know him, don't you? Jones. You're a friend and you attended his wedding."

"I went to his wedding. We're not friends, never have been."

"Why doesn't he appear in any of these pictures or videos except with the crates of pants?" Schmitz asked.

"I've been wondering the same thing," said Hood, though it seemed obvious that Bradley himself had a hand in this. "He was at the loading dock."

"Yet *you* appear," said Crockett. "And several other ATF agents."

"It was our case." Hood looked past Grace Crockett to the Century City skyline. In Iraq he had worked for Naval Criminal Investigative Service, which put him at odds with the soldiers he was investigating. Over the months he had come to know their distrust and contempt. Now he felt that same enmity coming from the people in this room.

"Who were your Achilles team partners in this?" asked Grossly. Hood named them while the representative and lawyers wrote. "Were you the only LASD sheriff deputy attached to ATF in Operation Blowdown?"

"Yes."

"And you'd been assigned to ATF for how long?"

"It was my first month."

"And on only your third day, you were involved in the shootout that killed Benjamin Armenta."

Hood said nothing. He had not fired on Armenta and he knew that Grossly must know this. The shooting had been covered widely by the media.

Next, the monitor showed various pictures of Mexican crime scenes, all containing Love 32s. The police officers and military men looked down on the bloody bodies and guns. Then came a video news clip from a Juárez shootout that showed masked gunmen firing automatic weapons that were almost certainly Love 32s.

The following video clips showed the weapons back in the United States one year later: police and ATF footage of the aftermath of a rampage in Buenavista that left three young men dead—and two Love 32s to be recovered.

"Buenavista," said Grossly. "Not the Mexican side. The American side. *Our* side. ATF let one thousand machine guns go south into Mexico and now they're coming back."

"Hold it," said Lansing. "A thousand machine guns got away." He looked dolefully at Hood, then to the congressman. "But we have seen no fault of ATF. We did not let these guns walk. This was not part of

Fast and Furious. This was not failed policy. Don't try to make us a scapegoat. I won't stand for it."

"Is that right? Then I'll ask Mr. Hood directly—who in ATF gave the orders on this investigation?"

Hood looked at Lansing, who stared back. "Sean Ozburn was the team leader."

Grossly gasped incredulously. "Sean Ozburn murdered three people, was mixed up in a Mexican cartel gun deal in L.A., and later died in an airplane *accident*. Correct?"

Hood nodded and felt fury that a man in such a high position could be so ignorant of what Ozburn and ATF had been through with regards to those thousand machine guns. What Grossly had said was true, but it was not the whole truth. And what Grossly chose to ignore was much larger than what he chose to see. "He was murdered. He lost his life in the line of duty. And you have the chronology wrong, also."

"Well, okay. We all see what we want to see, don't we?"

"I was just thinking the same thing."

"Then who was above him? Certainly Special Agent Sean Ozburn, young and zealous, was not calling the shots on all of Blowdown."

"That's above me, sir," said Hood. "I had no contact with upper level management at ATF. I joined the Blowdown task force in order to work along the border. I followed orders and did my job. If all you need is someone to hang, go ahead. Hang me."

"You're not big enough."

Hood looked at the representative but did not speak.

"I will look until I find him," said Grossly.

"ATF is blameless in this," said Lansing.

"ATF blameless? First Fast and Furious, now this? If you are blameless, then I have never seen a more inept governmental bureaucracy in my entire life. One thousand new machine guns flown out of the United States into Mexico under your noses? And you suggest to me that a murderous and perhaps half-crazy ATF agent doing deals on the side was responsible? I beg your pardon but that's not how things work. Things work top to bottom, not the other way around. And all I want to know is how far up the line did the real decision-making on this whole thing go? Who let it happen? I'm going to find out. I'm done here, people. Agent Hood, thank you for your time. We will most certainly be in touch."

23

Mary Kate Boyle rang up another Family Bucket Extra Crispy and took a handful of wadded bills from a very short woman who looked exactly as wide as she was tall. Mary Kate sorted the damp currency and made the change and when she handed it to the customer she had to bend over the counter and reach down. The woman waddled out with a white-and-red KFC bag in each hand, their bottoms scarcely clearing the floor. Tony, the manager who had hired her, helped another customer at the next register. He'd been shuttling between the front and kitchen all day but, now that early evening had come, he had to concentrate on the waves of hungry working people who hit just after five o'clock. Tony glanced very quickly at her, then away. He'd been doing that. Mary Kate pulled her cell phone from her apron pocket and checked the time, then put on a smile for her next customer.

Thirty-five minutes later she was at the Lowell Theater on Fourth, breathing hard from the long fast walk, trying to steady herself to read for the part of Curley's wife in *Of Mice and Men*. It was a Community Theater Players production, non-Equity. In the theater lobby she scanned through the brief story synopsis and character description of Curley's wife. She'd read the book twice, years ago. She had liked it that Curley's wife didn't have a name and wasn't allowed to exist outside of the way the men on the ranch saw her. But she knew that Curley's wife had a whole other existence, invisible and outside the written story, like many women where Mary Kate came from. Secret hearts, she called them. A good many of the women she knew had them. Some men, even.

Waiting in the near darkness she watched the other actresses read. They were doing the scene at the end where Curley's wife talks to Lennie in the barn. Mary Kate noted the training and skill and robust beauty of the real actresses. Several of them seemed to know one another. Still, after four readings, she saw that there were things about Curley's wife that these women did not quite get. They played her as a sexy tramp, but didn't give her true loneliness and her sharp fear that her life's possibilities had almost totally slipped away. Those qualities were what made her more than just Curley's wife, which is what the writer knew but his characters didn't. Mary Kate sensed she wouldn't get the part, especially with her split lips and black eye, though the wounds were healing. But the idea of not getting the part somehow calmed her. She felt good inside. She was out of the sticks and into a city full of terrific food and good people. Her pulse was normal as she waited, her thoughts drifting peacefully along with the dialogue, a sense of confidence settling in. Her *fight*. The one thing she knew she had a lot of. A lot more than most people could even see. It was hers. Only an empty stomach could take away that fight, and her stomach now was filled with fiery chicken thighs and mountains of coleslaw and those terrific mashed potatoes, and there was more where all that came from.

"Mary Kate Boyle?"

The casting director said he may or may not call. Later she met Tony and some of the other KFC crew at a diner in the Gaslamp District. It was not far from her fleabag hotel, and it was noisy and busy and had the buzz of a local's hangout. Tony bought beers for everyone because he was the manager, though he explained that he made little more than his cooks and front-store employees made, and put in twice the hours. Three of the cashiers were there, all about Mary Kate's age. Two of the cooks came by later. Mary Kate liked the cooks. They were Mexicans, like Tony. For the past few days during slow times at KFC, she would go back into the kitchen just to watch them work. She liked their coordination and athletic balance and goofy singing as they slid around the greasy kitchen floor carrying heavy pressure kettles—boiling with fat and chicken—from the flame-belching stoves to the drainers. They looked like they were roller-skating. They were a happy bunch of daredevils, sliding around like that, but she hoped they weren't just showing off for her. Don't want to be like Curley's wife, she thought. That story had haunted her since the day she finished it.

They shot some pool at the Rack and when it got late Tony walked her out. The Gaslamp was quieting now and the breeze off the ocean was up and Mary Kate buttoned her coat high and put her hands deep in the pockets. Out in front of the Winston Arms, Tony embraced her politely and waited until she'd gone inside. By the time she got upstairs to her window he was gone, and this was good. She liked him but didn't want him stuck on her. Her phone rang and she checked the number and didn't recognize it, except the area code, which was Russell County. "Hello?"

"Clinton Stewart Wampler here."

"Not you, Clint." She put him on speaker phone and turned on the recorder that Charlie Hood had given her.

"Why *not* me? Skull's in jail and Brock, too. They got busted by the feds. But not me. I got away. I got a plan and I need some help."

"How am I going to help you from way back here in Missouri?"

"You listen. I didn't just get away, I got away with a *missile*! I want to sell it for big bucks. And if I can't, I'll just blow something up. Like maybe an abortion clinic or a Muslim church or school or something. Southern California's full of shit like that."

She felt queasy at the words *abortion clinic*. "But why are you calling? What do you want me to do?"

Clint said nothing for a moment, then, "I want you to come out here and be my girl."

"While you blow things up?"

"Exactly. We'd be like a movie."

"I was Skull's girl."

"Why did you say that?"

"I'm not sure why. Something about how different you two are."

"But you're not his girl no more, right?"

"'No more' is most certainly right."

"Then what about me? I always was lookin' at you when I wouldn't get caught at it. Skull and you didn't know squat about my affections and overall designs for you. He was too old to understand your value. I'm young, Mary Kate, and I got a future."

Mary Kate Boyle said nothing for a long beat. She was truly flummoxed.

"Now when you come, bring all the money you got and a decent car."

"I can't afford a car."

"Then borrow one. Just get here. Take a Greyhound if you have to."

"What's in this for me, Clint?"

"*Forty thousand American-made dollars* is what I'll take for this here Stinger. I ain't saying one penny of it's yours but if you're with me it's gonna rub off. You know what I mean."

Mary Kate kept herself from laughing. It was funny to her that anyone could be as self-serving as Clint yet so confident in his success. Maybe that's how people like him got away with things. He'd never said much more than a word or two to her in the six months she was hanging with Skull's merry band. He looked about eighteen with the big ears and bad haircut but she knew he was older than that.

"Let me think about," she said. "I'll call you."

"You can't. I'm on a pay phone and I won't use it twice. When you going to make up your mind?"

"When I'm done thinking about it."

"Don't be taking all day. I got half the cops in the world out here looking for me. I think I've pissed them off. There's this one, Charlie

Hooper—tall asshole with diamonds in his teeth, the guy who set us up—I'm gonna do something special with him."

A chill rippled down Mary Kate's back. "Like what?"

"Like none of your business."

"If Skull and Brock got popped, how did you get away?"

" 'Cause Clint is smarter and meaner, that's how."

"I guess I believe that."

"I'll call soon. Don't' piss away the lifetime of an opportunity, honey. I've got a big heart for you. And plenty more."

"Yeah, yeah. I get that part, Clint."

"Skull said you got it real good. Now I'm the one loving you."

"You're not doing any such, Clint."

"I know you're gonna come."

She played the recording over the phone to Charlie Hood. It was very late but she thought this information might be important. Lawmen always wanted to hear about bad guys blowing up things like schools or mosques or clinics. Hood had told her a full day ago that Clint might call and she had thought that was ridiculous. Why would he call her? But now she knew and Charlie had been right. He was a smart guy. With diamonds in his smile. She wondered if maybe he was still in bed right now and if anyone was in it with him. It worried her that Clint Wampler wanted to fix Hood's wagon and had a missile to do it.

"So, Charlie, what do you want me to do?"

"Tell him you're on your way."

"Then what?"

"Set him up for us."

"I figured that's where you were going."

"Can you do it? There's always risk when you deal with people like Clint. He murdered a man less than forty-eight hours ago. But we'll keep him away from you. It can all be by phone. We won't let him get close."

"Promise?"

"Promise."

"Promise me another thing, Charlie."

"What's that, Mary Kate?"

"Aw, I don't know. Anything you want. Just funnin' with ya. My lips are almost healed up enough to smile again."

24

That Friday Bradley embarked on his first Baja run in nearly a year and a half. The evening was crisp and breezy, and the sunset was framed by towers of black clouds limned in orange. It was a glorious feeling for him to leave Rocky Carrasco's El Monte warehouse without the Blands tailing him. Heaven on earth. He kept checking the mirrors and smiling to himself. He wore the Santana Panama for good luck.

His heart was filled of nostalgic memories of such nights, and the hidden compartments in his Cayenne Turbo were filled with bricks of cash. So were the bottoms of the plastic tubs that otherwise held new clothing for poor Mexican children. The cash amounted to $412,500 and he'd end up with approximately $14,000 for himself. Of which he would lay off $2,000 each to Caroline Vega and Jack Cleary. All of it was Southern California drug profit for Carlos Herredia's North Baja Cartel.

He drove the speed limit south on Interstate 5, past the nuclear power plant at San Onofre and then along the hills of Camp Pendleton. To his right the Pacific Ocean looked plated with gold, which made him think of the silly gold-plated pistols that Herredia loved so much, which made him think of drug lords so he put on a recording of the song Erin had written in captivity four months ago. It was called "City of Gold," and she'd been forced to write it by Benjamin Armenta, one of Mexico's most powerful drug lords, as a way of gaining greater fame and notoriety for himself. Thus, it was a lowly *narcocorrido*, one of many such ballads commissioned over the years by cartel players in order to glorify themselves. But because Armenta came from Veracruz he'd made Erin write the song in the well-known *jarocho* style of that city. So, although the song told the story of a violent drug lord, it did so with exuberance, a lovely harp-decorated melody, a hint of Caribbean rhythm, and exotic percussion instruments. The dissonance between subject matter and sound somehow made the song beautiful.

Armenta had never heard the full version because Bradley had blown him into eternity right there in his own recording studio in his secret castle on the Yucatán. Erin had foretold such an ending in her song. What a journey that had been, he thought now, what an astonishing ten days of trying to rescue her from the hell that he had helped put her in. He remembered the moment he swung open the door to the studio control room and through the glass saw Erin at the piano, facing him, and Armenta standing with his accordion on and his back to Bradley. He pictured it all again: charging into the hushed tracking room, opening fire with his silent machine pistol, the window glass shattering and falling, the dozens of bullets that the bearlike Armenta took before he finally went down in a heap, draped over his instrument. Bradley turned the volume up and started the song again.

But by the time "City of Gold" was over so were his violent memories, and he was sobered again by Erin's continuing anger and distrust of him. He knew he deserved these things, and likely more. He had been a reckless fool and he had endangered her, Erin, the fire of his heart, his reason for being. How could he have been so stupid? How could he have thought a hidden room could possibly protect her from professional kidnappers and killers? How could he have allowed these men to have observed her, and himself, and their property, long enough to discern the weakness in their defenses? How could he have failed to electrify the perimeter fence of their Valley Center ranch, and install motion sensors and wire them to his central monitor in the bedroom? That fence was his Achilles heel and Armenta had somehow found it. *Never again*, he thought. *I'll never be that stupid and careless again.*

Still, in a larger sense, he had successfully gotten Erin away from her tormentors. That task had been on par with any labor of Hercules, in his opinion. A young deputy and a few friends, up against one of the most powerful criminals in the Western Hemisphere, on his own turf, on his own terms. Bradley had told her he would prevail. He had promised. And he had delivered. He'd taken her back to the home they had made and fortified it against further attack, so she could give birth to the life they had created together. He'd even come away with most of the ransom money. And after all that, still she had left him.

Now he pictured her in Charlie Hood's dusty hovel down in scorpion-infested Buenavista. What was she doing? Playing her guitar? Watching TV with fucking Charlie? Listening to the hobbled old cop's war stories? Hanging with Dr. Beth? He turned off the music and cracked his window for a moment and let the cold hit his face. Emboldened, he rolled the window back up and used the voice dial. When she answered, the sound of her made his heart stir. "You're a soundtrack I never want to end."

"You're full of it, Bradley."

"I'll always be full of it. Are you okay?"

"I'm fine. Are you?"

"Good. Driving to Escondido for some takeout. Long day. Can I come see you tomorrow? Around noon? You said maybe."

"I know what I said. I'm not sure yet."

"Is he moving a lot?"

"All the time. He kicks and hits. I can feel his little fists in there. The doctor predicts a stubborn and gifted person, but he's just saying that."

"Why wouldn't he be stubborn and gifted?"

She was quiet a moment.

"I miss you every second," he said.

"I miss you sometimes."

"Say that again."

"No. It's already passed."

"Ouch."

"Self-defense."

"It'll be caesarean, then."

"Well, *he*, not *it*."

"Dr. David better do a good job."

"He's done hundreds of them."

"I'm going to be there."

"You should be there."

"Amazing how cold your voice can get."

"It just follows the rest of me," she said. "But you seem stronger the last few days. Your voice and your attitude. You sound different. More positive."

"I'm bullish on you and me and the baby. Decide on the name yet?"

"I still like Thomas."

"Jones or McKenna?"

"You keep asking that. Still Jones. We're married. I'll honor it."

"Thank you. I'd like the middle name to be Firth. After your mom."

"She would be very proud of that."

Bradley looked out at the black ocean sprinkled with the lights of Oceanside. The Coaster train glided over the fog-misted marsh and he saw passengers reading in their seats, each passenger upright, individually lighted and alone. "I like that time we made love in the sand dunes. How can you make love in a sand dune? We did."

"And that laundry room up at Zach's that smelled like fabric softener and dryer lint and somehow it was so . . . just took my silly breath away."

"That time in Nordstrom."

"We used to have a lot of that," she said.

His heart sped up at the sound of melancholy in her voice. The sound of loss. It meant that she wanted him back, or soon would. Wouldn't she? "I dwell on it. I'll probably go to my deathbed picturing one time or another, what we did. Like remember—"

"I wish I could dwell."

"I could help you."

"I'm going to have a baby and I feel empty and alone."

"If I was there you would only feel empty."

"Very funny."

"What's the difference between a musician and a large pizza?"

"A large pizza can feed a family of four."

"It's important to laugh," he said.

"I'm trying to talk to you."

"I'll listen anytime."

She was quiet for a long beat. Bradley stayed at seventy down into Carlsbad. The smokestack at the electric plant wafted steam into a starry sky. "Did youth get wasted on us?"

"I don't see waste, honey."

"This whole thing. Didn't you feel golden for a few years? Just really . . . blessed and full, like the world was happy to have us in it?"

"I still do feel that way."

"I don't. I feel like I spent all my goodness. Pissed it away on a man who lied to me. Like I just got plain old *faked out.*"

"Guilty as charged. Again. But I've changed, Erin, for the better. You'll see it as our lives move forward. You and me and Thomas. But you have to let me up off the floor someday, girl. I'm no good for anyone down here."

"Noon," she said and rang off.

Beneath a foreign glow of moonlight he drove the last five miles to El Dorado, Carlos Herredia's compound. It was in the general vicinity of Cataviña, near the middle of the state of Baja California. There were several routes he had been brought in on over the years, some gated and heavily fortified, some roadless and nearly impossible to see unless you knew what to look for. Tonight the way was new. Two SUVs with shooting ports built into the rooftops led the way, and two more

followed. Dust billowed through the path of his headlights and surrounded the small convoy.

Coming up the last mile to El Dorado, Bradley felt a fresh wave of
nostalgia break over him. The lights of the compound lay sprinkled
on the hillside up ahead. And then he saw the spring-fed pasture for
the cattle. And there was the nine-hole golf course upon which El
Tigre so boldly cheated, and there the paddocks and hot walkers and
barn for his thoroughbreds. Then came the helipad upon which sat
not one but two immense transport helos and half a dozen smaller,
heavily armored gunships. One of the big helos was a CH-47, painted
over in Red Cross insignias, the one they had used to carry a thousand
automatic pistols down here to Herredia while Hood and the other
ATF morons were focused on boxes of clothing going south to benefit
poor Mexican children. What an operation that had been! Tonight on
the airstrip was something that Bradley had never seen before: a Lear
Jet, lean and proud and somehow smug.

At last he approached the compound proper, several stone-and-
adobe buildings low slung and countersunk into a boulder-studded
hillside. He saw the outbuildings and the lights of the swimming pool
and cabanas that Carlos had so often stocked with dazzling young
women that Bradley had always refused out of loyalty to Erin, though
in truth she was more lovely to him than all of them put together.

Another surprise waited for him as he swung into the large circular
cobblestoned drive: a transport truck and trailer filled to capacity
with glittering new automobiles. Herredia himself stood beside the
truck, wearing his usual uniform of shorts and flip-flops and a T-shirt
with a sportfishing logo of some kind. Behind him was old Felipe with
his eternal sawed-off shotgun. Standing with Herredia were two men.
Bradley's escorts broke away and he pulled to the curb.

Herredia strode to greet him. He was large and powerful, with
thick legs and a barrel chest and skin browned from long hours of
fishing. His hair was a curly tangle and he had an expressive face and
telltale eyebrows. He hugged Bradley with considerable strength, then

stepped back and clutched Bradley's face in both hands, using his thumbs to lift the lips as one might do to a horse. He turned Bradley's head one way then the other, up then down. "*En buen estado*. You are well repaired."

When the thumbs were finally removed, Bradley could speak. "The teeth are almost too good. But the lip healed up well."

"*Perfecto*. And with most importance, you are now free to be doing your work with me again. I must hear all details tonight at dinner, of how this became possible. I have a new jet. And tonight there are important guests here for you to meet. Come now."

Felipe had already laid his scattergun across the trunk of the Cayenne and begun stacking the bins of cash and clothes on a hand truck. Felipe had designed and welded the secret compartments beneath the floor of the storage area of Bradley's Porsche, as well as the front-end containers that could only be opened electrically, using a car battery. Felipe was small and goatlike and sharp faced, and he appeared very old but he moved with a lithe ease. Bradley knew that he would weigh out the bricks of cash and set aside his courier's fee, which was based on the total amount transported. Good couriers were highly valued in the drug world, not only for their honesty, which was a prerequisite, but for their ability to smell out dealers who had turned to informing. Bradley, as an LASD deputy with close friends in narcotics, had special powers in this area and had identified two such young men, who were no longer.

He stood off to the side of the big auto trailer and looked at the shiny new Fords. Even the dusty journey from the Hermosillo plant to El Dorado had not ruined the sheen of their paint where it showed between the protective sheets of white plastic, or the occasional glimmer of chrome. There were four Fusions, four Lincoln MKZs, and four Ford Tauruses, in varying colors. He wondered if these cars might have something to do with what Rocky was hinting about?

Herredia introduced the men not by name but by their positions in Ford Motor Company, Hermosillo Manufacturing Plant, Mexico. The young, tall one was the assistant director of quality control and the short, stubby one was the transport manager. Herredia said they had personally delivered the cars and were here to make sure the fourth and final leg of their new Fords' journey began well.

"For the U.S. market?" asked Bradley.

"Yes," said the transport manager. He was dressed in a crisp guayabara and jeans and tan lace-up work boots. "Hermosillo now has the highest quality rating of any Ford plant in the world. J. D. Powers & Associates have proven this."

"How come you brought them through Baja?" asked Bradley. "That means you had to trailer them south to Guaymas, then ferry them to Santa Rosalía, then trailer them all the way here. If you went straight north from Hermosillo to Nogales, it's less than half that distance."

The tall man looked coolly at Bradley and drew on a cigarette. He had a patrician face and a pale olive suit and a white shirt open at the collar. "What concern are our freight routes to you?"

"I'm just curious why you go four hundred miles out of your way."

Herredia stared dolefully at Bradley, then he laughed and his eyebrows shot up in a mirthful display. He turned to the men. "See? I told you my gringo partner has a sharp eye for opportunity. I'll bet that he already has a strong suspicion of why you bring your new Fords hundreds of miles out of their way to the United States."

"He can suspect whatever he wants," said the tall one. "He is a danger and I don't approve of this." He flipped his cigarette into the gravel and stepped on it, then walked around the trailer toward the compound. Bradley could see him between the Fusions, glancing back at him.

Dinner was an unusual banquet consisting only of meats, seafood, asparagus, and various alcohols, part of Herredia's slimming diet. He wanted to lose twenty pounds. Bradley had often seen him doing his two miles a day in the big saltwater pool out by the cabanas, though it looked to Bradley more like pounding than swimming. Herredia attacked the water as if it were the enemy.

At dinner the tall quality control assistant director, Arturo, argued that the Mexican drug cartels were stifling the common people with their violence and there would someday be a grassroots uprising against the cartels. Herredia boomed back that the uprising would be not against the cartels but against the government, which did little protect the people. Bradley sided with Herredia. The transport manager, Caesar, agreed that the people would eventually tire of cartel violence and there would be a popular revolt against someone.

"Using what as weapons?" asked Herredia. "Shovels?"

"*Corazóns*," snapped Arturo, tapping his fist against his heart. "Connected by cell phones."

Herredia leaned forward and Bradley saw his brows knit down over his dark eyes. "Arturo, your brave heart is angry because you believe you are a hypocrite. But you are not a hypocrite. I understand what the government does not understand, and that is that some of the people are dissatisfied. You, for example, are men of great ambition. Yet what does the government allow you to do with such ambition? Look around you at what I have made with my own hands and brains. You have two of the best jobs in all of Mexico but is that enough to satisfy you? To work for the great gringo makers of cars? To lick the shoes of J. D. Powers for thirty years? No! You want more. You demand more. So you come to me with your idea, not to Ford."

"Ford would not have liked our idea," said Caesar, smiling.

"You are wrong about the people and the *narcos*," said Herredia. "The people need the *narcos*. The people *are* the cartels. I have rebuilt churches from Tecate to Mulegé. I have built schools in Cataviña and Guerrero Negro and San Felipe. I have donated two million dollars for a hospital in Santa Rosalía. I have paid for medicine and operations and funerals and weddings and shrines for people I do not know. I have given millions of dollars to charities and churches. For every Mexican in Baja who tolerates the government, there are ten who love me."

25

That evening after dinner the men followed Felipe to the coops where Herredia kept his fighting birds. The building was a prefabricated metal structure designed for agriculture or light industry. It was coyote and dog proof, air-conditioned and heated for steady temperature. Felipe waited outside with his shotgun as the others went in. Bradley smelled the dank stink of feathers and the sweeter smell of the scratch on which the birds fed. The overhead fluorescents glowed down with faint shivers. Herredia was renowned for his fighting cocks, some of which were scheduled for battle the next day in La Paz, five hundred miles to the south. Thus, the Lear jet, Bradley had learned.

Bradley and the Ford men followed Herredia on the tour: first the incubation room, then the exercise runs, the sparring pit, then the various pens. Each rooster was separated from any others except for the breeding pairs. They were handsome birds, and bold of eye. Bradley had seen cockfights and hated them, hated the blades and the pain and the selling of bravery for entertainment. Though he also knew that solid money could be made.

On the way back toward the pool the Ford men talked with Felipe up ahead while Herredia fell back to walk with Bradley. Bradley looked out at the mountains, black and jagged. He had spent many nights here, all but a few without Erin, and therefore she was always poignantly in his mind at El Dorado because all he could do was imagine her and picture what she was doing. The cell phones wouldn't work and the satellite phones were a security risk, so virtually every night here was a night without her or her voice, a tribulation.

"Come this way, Bradley." They veered around the pool and cabanas and walked back to the drive where the trailer of new cars stood in the moonlight. "I need a driver for these cars. Caesar and Arturo have made the delivery only once and I believe they are not reliable. This trailer has very dependable state-police escorts to the border at Tecate. My friends at Mexico and United States customs will make sure that there are only minor inspections, if any. As you probably know, a trailer carrying new cars from a U.S. factory is not a thing of suspicion. In Mexico, it is a thing of pride. In the United States, it is the great Ford Motor Company. And not to be suspected. That is the beauty of this idea. Almost no suspicion. I'm surprised that Arturo and Caesar could think of it."

"What's in them?"

"Heroin and cocaine, packed solidly into the spare tires. And in the spaces created for subwoofers in the trunks. And in the tool compartments. We also created flat bricks, only eight centimeters thick, and glued them to form plates underneath each car, like an off-road vehicle. They are triple-wrapped against the dogs, and painted the same black as the chassis, and have genuine bolts driven into each corner. Very realistic. But there will be no dogs. It is just a precaution."

"What's the total weight?"

"One hundred kilos per car."

"A ton and a quarter. Half blow and half junk?"

"*Más o menos.*"

Bradley did a quick calculation on the street value of drugs contained in the twelve new cars—roughly twenty million dollars by the time the last diluted gram hit the streets of L.A. "Wow."

"The destination is Castro Ford in El Centro. A pleasant and relaxing three-hour drive from here! I know you and Israel are old and very good friends. We are new friends. The Tijuana Cartel has treated him poorly. He came to me. He is very influential in California. And we agreed that you would be a good courier for us. You have the class C license necessary in the United States. You are a gringo but you speak good Spanish. You can use your skills of bullshit if you are questioned.

You can use your sheriff's department badge should any trouble or controversy happen. You are made by God for this job." Herredia smiled.

"How often?"

"It is variable. Once a month. Then maybe twice."

"So I'd make the runs here on Friday evenings, but once or twice a month I would leave my car and drive the trailer back north."

"I will arrange for your Porsche to be waiting for you at Castro Ford. Israel will give you a complimentary wash!"

"Twenty million dollars, retail," said Bradley.

"I will pay you ten thousand as a flat rate. No matter the amount of product transported. Israel will pay you ten thousand more upon each delivery."

Bradley inwardly smiled at a minimum $240,000 a year of tax-free cash, for roughly four hours of work a month, driving the same home-bound route he'd be driving anyway. Herredia chuckled, then laughed. "Son of Joaquin!"

"That's me, alright."

"I can see by the light in your eyes that we have an agreement."

"We do."

Walking back toward the pool, Bradley wondered again at how his fortunes had begun to change so abruptly for the better, almost from the instant that he'd recited the Statement of Parity and asked Mike Finnegan to be his partner. Warren? Off his case. The Blands? Dismissed. Hood? Headed for genuine catastrophe. Herredia? Instead of punishing him for eighteen months of spotty service, El Tigre was heaving fresh fortune his way via Ford Motor Company, Mexico. Could all of this derive from his arrangement with Mike? Or were these upgrades largely just a matter of his own attitude? What could Mike really *be* other than insane? Yes, Mike had beautifully staged the Theater of Beatrice. But it was clear that the "angel"—most likely Owens using her actor's vocal skills—was not truly trapped in the mineshaft at all. There was probably a ladder bolted to the rock walls, or perhaps some kind of powered miners' funicular by which she came and went. But, Bradley thought, if Mike and his silly rituals were just a placebo that swelled his good luck, then so be it. His terrific reversals of fortune were almost everything he wanted in the world. *Except for Erin*, he thought. Erin. But this was all for her; his fortune was for her. And their son. And down near the center of Bradley's cunning soul he knew that Erin was coming around to him. He would win.

The four men drank and smoked cigars around the pool late into the brisk Baja night. Felipe with his craggy face and shotgun kept to the edges of light and darkness. There were six women—three Mexicans and three gringas, pretty and friendly and well dressed. Bradley was polite but uninterested and enjoyed Caesar's company and shoptalk about the Hermosillo plant. Caesar had a hopeful face and tone of voice, and he was a proud Ford man all the way. His wife's staggering gambling and shopping debts had led him to the other side of the law. Those, and his daughter's seemingly eternal college studies in the United States.

Herredia regaled them all with fishing stories of which he was the hero. Arturo in his olive suit drank heavily and extolled the virtues of ignorant, promiscuous gringas over wary, repressed Catholic Latinas. He danced with a gringa who wore a gold dress and she was nearly his height in her gay rhinestoned heels and when they finished he whispered something into her ear, then knocked her into the pool with a roundhouse punch. She looked like a mermaid gliding to the shallow-end steps and climbing out, sheathed in gold, bent in pain, the high heels still on. She gathered up a towel from the cabana and pressed it into her face as she ran in short steps, shivering, toward her guest casita.

Arturo said something about the way a wet dog shakes itself dry and laughed at his observation. One of the Latinas followed the drenched blonde and the other four women migrated to the cantina at the other end of the pool. Their anxious words and brittle laughter carried across the water. Arturo brought another bottle of tequila to the table and cracked the seal, then poured himself a shot. He pushed the uncapped bottle toward Herredia, and by some small miracle it slid to a stop instead of pitching over into El Tigre's lap. "Carlos," Arturo said. "I quit. I resign from this. I am ashamed of what I have become."

Herredia tipped the bottle and Bradley saw the downward furrow of his eyebrows as he measured the pour. *Watch out*, Bradley thought.

"I truly thank you for your friendship, Carlos," said Arturo. He burped. "But I am not the man I thought I was. I am an engineer. I am in control of quality. I have skills. I have no nerves for this kind of work."

"You had nerves enough for the many thousands of dollars I shared with you."

"You bribed me for the use of my automobiles," said Arturo. "Isn't that more accurate? In addition, I will pay you back."

"Don't lose your bravery now," said Caesar. "We're almost finished here. Señor Herredia only has to fly us home in his jet tomorrow. You drink too much, Arturo."

Arturo burped again and knocked back the shot. "When I drink too much the veil is lifted and I see the world for what it is—a cauldron of greed. I want to go home tonight. I want to sleep in my bed and wake in the morning without the stain of greed in my heart. I want to confess my sins to Father Patricio."

"*Confess?*" asked Herredia.

"Fully and truthfully."

"Fully and truthfully. I understand. But you can't go home tonight. My pilot is drunk and sleeping."

"We drove here. And we can drive home."

"We cannot drive home the trailer loaded with new Fords," said Caesar with a smile. "We have made a deal and they are going to El

Centro. And we would look crazy driving back to where the cars were manufactured."

Herredia studied Arturo in the short silence. "Go to the garage and choose a car to your liking," said Herredia. "The keys are in the ignitions." He gestured invitationally but in the candlelight Bradley saw the pronounced blackness of his eyes. Bradley sensed that he was reading a story that would end in blood. Herredia barked an order to the women and they trailed off toward the guest casitas, drinks in hand.

"You are coming with me?" Arturo asked his friend.

"No," said Caesar. "But I will prevent you from driving in your condition."

"I shall now be finding a car. Can it be a Ford, El Tigre? So that I can be assured of its quality?" Arturo swayed upright and zigzagged along the pool without falling in, then made it past the cabanas. Bradley heard the crunch of the drunk man's feet on the dry desert gravel.

Caesar tried to rise from the table, but Bradley stopped him with a hand on the man's shoulder. "I will stop Arturo from driving away," said Caesar.

"You will sit and stay," said Herredia.

Bradley watched old Felipe appear beside Herredia's chair as if by magic, and lean down close for El Tigre to whisper in his ear. Then Felipe hustled off, bandy-legged, unslinging the shotgun from his shoulder.

"Caesar," said Herredia, "We have arrived at a problem."

"I know it. He will kill someone on the highway at night. Or be killed."

"He will not get to the highway."

Caesar's hopeful expression had fallen away. He looked at Bradley as if for help.

"Everything Arturo has seen and heard here can be told to authorities," said Herredia. "He is made rotten by fear and he cannot be trusted with our secrets. Do you understand this?"

"He is a harmless quality control engineer."

"He is a foolish and greedy child. And you, Caesar? What are you?"

Caesar looked past Herredia, toward the garage, then back to his host. "I am interested in remaining alive."

Bradley looked up the drive to see Felipe and Arturo walking back toward the pool. They were little more than faint apparitions but Bradley saw that Arturo was weaving drunkenly and Felipe was well behind him. Felipe's cackle rode in on the breeze and the two men walked to the barbed-wire pasture fence and stopped.

"If I cannot trust Arturo, why should I trust you? You are as important a danger to me as he is. You have seen what he has seen. You know what he knows."

"His courage failed. Mine has not."

"But you are together. You two are a link in the chain. And the chain is only as strong as the weak link. Look how weak Arturo has turned out to be. He wants to go home and confess!"

"Yes. I see."

"And you are a part of him."

"But I am not weak."

"You say you are not weak." Herredia reached behind his back and set his Desert Eagle on the table, pointed at Caesar. It was a .50-caliber semiauto, bulky, gleaming, and incontrovertible. Herredia set his big brown hand upon it. "Your words are like drops of rain on the ocean. They fall and can never be found again. But this? This is how words are made to be real. You say you are not weak. This is the true maker of weakness and of strength. Not words."

"Why is it pointed at me?"

"It is judging you."

"What are the charges against me?"

"Weakness. Disloyalty. Betrayal."

"I am none of these."

Herredia lifted his hand from the gun and rested on his elbows, leaning toward Caesar. "Then use this tool to make your words real. You know what must be done."

Caesar glanced at Bradley again and Bradley saw the panic in his eyes. "How? How am I to . . . ? I have never touched a gun."

"It's the only way to continue your life, you fool."

Bradley followed Caesar's gaze to the Desert Eagle as he drew his own civilian sidearm, a compact nine-millimeter. He set this on the table in front of him with both hands upon it, in case Caesar tried to shoot his way out of this predicament, unlikely though it was. He caught Herredia's approving glance. Caesar placed both hands against his face and pressed against his eyes as if he could wipe this terrible moment from his vision.

Bradley looked out to the pasture fence. Arturo was haranguing Felipe but the old man, hunched and gnomelike, stood with his shotgun pointed at the quality control assistant manager.

"Murder," said Caesar.

"Weakness and strength. Loyalty and cowardice. These are only words that stand for something. But they are not what they stand for. They are all equally without meaning. You choose which ones are to be made real and then you make them real."

"He is a good man."

"He has treated you very poorly. He has forced you to the edge of death with his own weakness and shame. Yet El Tigre has seen a way for you to live."

Caesar looked toward the pasture. He wiped a tear from under each eye, then took a deep breath. "You just pull the trigger?"

Herredia offed the safety and placed the gun in front of the man. Then the tequila. Bradley tapped his fingers on the nine. Caesar drank deeply, then stood. "Only two months ago everything was good. There were no drugs hidden in our cars and my friend Arturo was not about to die."

"Think about your debts," said Herredia. "Think about a future that has great riches no matter how much your wife gambles and spends. Or how many degrees your daughter needs to have. Caesar, be a man. If you hesitate much longer I'm going to be very happy to shoot you both."

Caesar took up the .50 caliber and walked past the cantina and the poolside *palapas* and onto the road. Bradley could see him stop and look back, and beyond him he saw Arturo still gesticulating and Felipe with the shotgun on him. Arturo's voice, shrill and angry, came in fragments. Caesar trudged toward them and Bradley heard the road gravel rasping under his shoes.

"Will Felipé kill him?" asked Bradley.

"Only if he loses his courage."

Bradley watched Caesar approach the two men. There were still fifty feet between them. Arturo turned and said something and Felipe didn't move. Caesar answered, still advancing. Arturo spoke again and his voice ended on the upsweep of a question. Caesar began talking fast but Bradley could only catch a few words, something about the truck and getting back to Hermosillo and their *esposas*. Arturo exclaimed something to the old man and proudly slammed his fist to his own chest. He took one step toward the new Fords, then an orange blast from the Desert Eagle blew him like a rag into the pasture fence. He shrieked and thrashed a while, then his head sagged forward with the great exit of his life. His coat sleeves caught up on the barbs so his arms and body slid only partially free and he hung there, half in and half out of his coat, with the dark liquid blooming on his white shirt.

"Now *both* men can be trusted!" boomed Herredia.

Bradley watched as Felipe sprang forward and tore the gun away from Caesar, who did not move to stop him. The old man came scampering down the road toward them, his gargoyle face delighted in the moonlight. Bradley saw that Caesar had knelt and wrapped his arms around his friend. His lamentations arrived in a cadence broken by the breeze.

26

Bradley was ready set off at sunrise on three hours' sleep, sitting high in the tractor cockpit as Baja California came alive in the clean pink light. He'd always liked driving eighteen-wheelers, and was taught to handle them by one of his uncles, who drove long hauls for a living. At age sixteen, Bradley had stolen a big rig from a drunken operator at a truck stop. Just a joyride, really, though he had gone all the way to Reno. But this morning's ride was an even bigger joy: $24,000 stashed in a toolbox, another ten thousand cash coming at Castro Ford, followed by the greatest joy of all, Erin. He'd have time to buy her something nice.

He had a tall mug of strong Mexican coffee between his legs and the nine-millimeter holstered under the seat. Herredia waved like a proud father, two pretty women standing on either side of him, one of them the gringa who'd been knocked into the pool. Bradley picked his way through the first few gears, felt the great tonnage pressing from behind him like something untamed. Two gunships, four men each, rumbled along up ahead, and two more trailed behind. They'd get him as far as the first paved road, then the way north would be secured by various state police. Dust rose around him. The *cardón* cacti, tall and singular, passed his windows slowly, then less slowly, then not so slowly at all and El Dorado was gone.

He drove Highway 1 west through the spectacular Baja desert. The clouds were dark blue but through them sunlight slanted down in bright girders. The beauty of it fought his nerves to a draw. He listened to Mexican songs on the radio and thought of Erin.

Off Highway 3 he stopped in a village with a lovely old church because he suddenly wanted to say a simple prayer in the house of His Lord. Maybe mention poor Arturo. He set his hat on the seat beside him and climbed down from the tractor. He checked the pigtail, then walked the length of the double-deck trailer, eyeing the tie-downs and chains, three per automobile.

The church was of minor historic note because it was made almost entirely of copper. The door was copper-covered wood inlaid with a full-length stained-glass image of Saint Francis of Assisi. There were birds on his shoulders and a lamb and a lion at his feet. Bradley pulled open the door and stepped inside, smelled the soot and smoke of many candles, the decades of incense, the faint earthy scent of the pavers.

He sat in the back row of pews and looked at the simple altar and the communion table with its wooden candelabras and folded white towels. High on the chancel a bleeding Jesus hung on his cross. Bradley began the Lord's Prayer but as soon as he thought *Our Father* a wave of nausea broke over him and his face went cold. He felt dread. He bent over slightly and looked at the floor, reviewing what he'd eaten for breakfast at El Dorado: ham and eggs and tortillas and grapefruit juice. He had always had an iron stomach and was proud of it. The nausea passed so he knelt as his mother, a very lapsed Catholic, used to do on the family's rare excursions to church.

He began his prayer again, but he felt his stomach turning over and the cold flash of sweat on his back, and again he had to stop at *Our Father*. Bad ham? It had tasted fine. Too much coffee? That was hours ago. Maybe it was just the pressure of smuggling over a ton of drugs into the United States. And all that cash. If convicted he'd get, what, fifteen years? Twenty? He thought of the Blands. What if they really weren't off the job? What if Dez had changed her mind? Dread nagged him. Could this be some kind of delayed reaction to last night's murder of Arturo? Certainly not the first killing he'd seen, and he'd never had such a reaction before. Then he wondered if this might be Mike Finnegan's Declaration of Parity coming back to bite him.

Asinine, he thought. The second wave of nausea left him breathing faster and more heavily, and even when he straightened his back and felt all his weight being borne by his knees he couldn't quite seem to get his breath.

Movement on the floor beside him caught his eye and he looked down at the red diamond rattlesnake inching toward him across the pavers. It was very small, no more than eight inches long. Wide head, thin neck. It was nearly the same brick red as the floor, but its diamonds were outlined in white and black and its tail had black and white rings. The pupils were elliptical. The rattle was but two small buttons. Bradley was conversant with the behavior of some snakes, having lived on the Valley Center property for much of his life, where he had observed that in spring and summer the rattlesnakes were active, less so in the fall, and in winter were almost never out moving around unless it was very warm or very late in the season. This February activity was unusual. The day was cool. The snake approached slowly with its tiny tongue darting in and out and made small directional adjustments, but its course was directly at Bradley.

Suddenly the nausea hit again. Using the back of the pew in front of him Bradley pulled himself off the padded prayer kneeler and stepped into the aisle and stumbled for the exit. Outside he rounded the building and bent over with his hands on his knees in the cool shade. But the nausea passed again, and he straightened and felt the blood coming back to his face. Settling into his seat in the tractor, he had a headache but no longer felt sick. He glanced at Saint Francis of Assisi and wondered what had just happened in there.

By eight thirty, he had passed through both Mexican and U.S. customs with only cursory inspections. Both sets of officials had cheerful words about the high quality of the new Fords made in Mexico but neither asked why he'd driven nearly five hundred miles out of his way, or endured the tedious Guaymas-to-Santa-Rosalía ferry, instead of just crossing at Nogales. He felt safe in using his cell phone now that he was stateside, and his heart fluttered when he saw that Erin had left him not one but three texts. *Thomas turned! No caesarean needed! Due in eight days and I feel very happy right now!*

Shifting quickly through the low gears as he left the customs plaza, Bradley felt the great weight of his dread diminishing and he noticed that his headache was gone and his hands were no longer so tightly clenched to the wheel. El Centro was just little over an hour out. He set his phone on the seat beside him and voice-dialed Erin.

27

Hood cruised by Castro Ford and saw that Israel's Flex was parked up front. He continued down the street and made two right turns that brought him again to the back side of the lot, the parts-and-service yard and the new-car intake bay. The bay looked ready for the nine-thirty delivery—all three rolling doors up and Israel and two other men all standing out in the cool morning sunshine, smoking and checking their watches and kicking around one of the promotional Castro Ford soccer balls that Hood had seen in the showroom. Again he pictured a life as a car salesman should his law enforcement career not pan out.

He parked well away in the meager shade of a stand of greasewoods and rolled down the windows. The greasewoods gave off a clean scent but Hood knew from a boyhood of shooting doves from the shade of Bakersfield windbreaks that they were greasy and home to all manner of spiders, scorpions, ticks, and other biting things. Dug into the bank of fallen greasewood needles he saw a silk-lined cavern in which a fat spider sat. Then another. Looking through his camera he could see the men still horsing around with the ball, Israel apparently the best athlete. Hood shot a couple of pictures.

At 9:43, Hood saw the big tractor-trailer coming down the avenue toward him, the new cars catching the sun. He raised the camera and saw the Hermosillo Fusions and Ford Tauruses and Lincoln MKZs tethered tightly but still rocking slightly against their moorings. The sun was just high enough now to blast into the powerful lens of the camera, and Hood had to hold it low to get a look at the drivers.

There was only one driver this time. No man in an olive suit, no man in a blue Ford shirt. Just Bradley Jones, signaling his turn and throwing his weight into the downshift, sending a plume of gray smoke out the stacks above him.

Hood smiled and let the motor drive rip.

28

Bradley and Erin sat in the courtyard of Hood's Buenavista adobe. Bradley saw Gabriel Reyes loitering in the kitchen inside, peeking through the window intermittently at them. Bradley saluted him. He wondered what Hood was doing on this fine day. Working his ass off for not much reward, was Bradley's guess; probably wondering where Congressman Grossly had gotten such good documentation of the Love 32 fiasco from three years back. And wait until Hood got a load of Dez's Yucatán dossier, and a likely investigative exposé by his admirer Theresa Brewer at Fox News. Amazing how Mike could look and plan ahead. Not just weeks and months, but *years*. As he had done for his mother, Suzanne. And if Mike was to be believed, for many others. The biggest question about Mike was, could he be trusted? And the answer was, of course, *too late*.

"So, what are bathroom-products people like?" asked Erin.

"They vary."

"I don't like you spending time with Mike. No matter how many good things Owens has to say about him. I think the truth about Mike is closer to the way Charlie tells it. And he's got that scar to prove it. Was she there, Owens?"

"Of course. The two peas."

"Did Mike try to get you two together?"

"Of course not. Why would you ask that?"

"I always had the feeling that he wished I was her. So he'd have more control over you. She's very beautiful and mysterious. Are you tempted by her?"

"I'm tempted by you."

Her smile was faint but a smile nonetheless. Without asking permission he reached over and placed his hand over her distended middle. She closed her eyes. His heart was beating strong and hard. Sitting on the table near them was the Victorian-style wrought-iron birdcage and two blue parakeets he'd bought cowered together on a perch as far from the humans as they could get.

"Why parakeets?" she asked.

"Why not parakeets?"

"They don't look super happy."

"They're the happiest creatures on earth. These two are just afraid. It will take them a little time to get used to the new cage. Then they'll sing to you. See, they'll sing for you, the singer. They can live to fifteen. Thomas will be just about ready for his learner's permit."

She opened her eyes. Bradley studied the blue surfaces of them and wondered exactly what she was thinking. He told her about his last few days of working the STAR Unit. He talked up the value of the program for troubled as well as untroubled youth. He spoke highly of Gail Padilla. He thought of the $34,000 stashed in the spare-tire well of his Porsche, which had been waiting for him at Castro Ford. Not only waiting but washed, as Herredia had promised. It was good seeing Israel again after so many years, he thought. A good businessman. Then Bradley had a fleeting image of El Tigre and the two women standing there at El Dorado just six short hours ago.

"What are you smiling at?" she asked.

"The way the sunlight makes your hair shine."

"Gabe says it's the avocados he puts in the salads."

"You talk girl stuff with Gabriel?"

"He's got four daughters and four granddaughters."

Bradley nodded. "I hope to have daughters and granddaughters someday. What did Dr. David say this morning?"

"Everything is fine. Now that he's turned I can have him without a surgery. It's exactly eight days until he's due. I think he's going to make it real clear when he's coming. He seems . . . assured."

"I love you."

"You're immature and deceitful and reckless."

"Those days are over. Behold the new Bradley Jones." He took her hand and kissed the back of it lightly, then closed his eyes and let the winter sun warm his face. For the first time in four months, since her ordeal in Yucatán, Erin let her hand stay in his for longer than ten seconds. He felt his heart large in his chest and he knew his luck had changed and he knew he was going to write himself back into her book of days. He would be the best father in the history of Western civilization.

Back in Valley Center that evening Bradley took the dogs on a long run down to the creek on the far side of the property. He rode a noisy ATV with a toolbox in back and kept to the fence lines, checking the sensors and electrified wires. Never again, he thought, never again will someone breech this border. The dogs bounded along with him, all twelve, led by Call, a Husky–Saint Bernard mix. The dogs were all dragging their tongues by the time they got back to the house. The Labradors waded, panting, into the pond to drink chest deep, while the others lapped noisily at the edge.

Suddenly he heard someone calling his name from across the pond. The dogs heard it too and they stopped their drinking and perked their ears. The woman was older and small and from what he could see she was wearing an old-fashioned Victorian dress. He actually rubbed his eyes but it did no good. Eva. She waved and called out his name again and started out around the pond toward him. The dogs charged around the water toward her, led by Call, but when they reached the small woman she raised her hand confidently and they halted and some sat and some crept up to her but didn't quite touch their noses to her dress. Bradley came up behind them. "How in the hell did you get past the fence?"

"I jumped over it."

"It's eight feet high and electrified."

"I'm well aware of that! You do remember me from the convention, don't you? Eva?"

"Of course I do."

"For you." She slipped the silver flask from a slit pocket in the abundant hip ruffles of the dress and held it out to him.

"No, thank you."

"Drink the damned stuff, Bradley. I've got unhappy news for you." He took the flask and drank without taking his eyes off her. The flask and potion were both cold. "Mike is not happy with your behavior at the convention, or since. He believes you are spoiled, truculent, thankless, and selfish. Now, these kinds of disagreements do come up, and they usually resolve positively. However, during such standoffs, competitors often attempt to forge an advantage. Some of Mike's envious coworkers here in the Western Territory have decided to try just that. I have this on good authority. It's imperative that you refuse to speak to them or hear them out. They can't and won't coerce you in any physical way, but . . . well, you should know that they can be very, very persuasive. Especially with you soon to be so vulnerable. And for the first time."

"First time?"

"Becoming a father. They'll try to manipulate you using Thomas. But mark my word: What they really want is for Thomas to be theirs."

"That will never happen." He drank again and gave the flask back. She drank and pocketed it. He began to feel the confidence and clarity, the alert well-being that the potion caused. He felt his vision becoming stronger and his imagination more boldly visual.

"Do not negotiate with them. Mike has worked himself to the bone to provide for your family. They'll claim to be friends of his. They'll claim they have been ordered to replace him. They'll tell you anything to get you talking back. And, of course, they'll bribe you with pretty much anything you want. Say nothing. And, please, Bradley, don't mention me or this visit. I'm breaking a hundred rules just by jumping your little fence. Now, I'll leave you to yourself. Bradley. Dogs. Good evening."

Bradley took her offered hand—a cool, soft-skinned, bony hand—and he shook it firmly but he felt the unlikely strength in it. She smiled and turned and glided back into the thick chaparral from which she had apparently come. The dogs trotted along behind her and Bradley loped into the brush, too, in strong pursuit. But the manzanita and the scrub oak and Spanish saber were thick and high, and Bradley had not gone fifty feet before he lost sight of them. He heard the faint cracking of branches and brush far ahead. The dogs were not barking. He put his hands up over his face and plowed through. What there was of the trail soon narrowed to nothing and he was left to shoulder his way between the trees and stout strong shrubs. He could feel the branches scratching his forearms and cutting at the scalp of his lowered head. Finally he broke into a clearing and joined the dogs looking out at Eva, who was already far on the other side of the eight-foot-high, electric, motion-sensing fence—nearly a hundred yards beyond it, in fact—striding through a low grassy swale with a speed that Bradley could hardly believe. She turned and waved and a white van came rocking along the Forest Service fire road and picked her up. Call was as close to the fence as he had learned to get, watching her intently.

Late that night Bradley's cell phone buzzed from his bed stand. He saw Jack Cleary's number and answered.

"It looks like Warren flipped Rocky Carrasco," said Cleary. "They spent two hours in the Gallo in Cudahy today. My informant says she saw a voice recorder on the booth between them. Your name was spoken. And my ears in Warren's office tell me Warren can't wait for Dez to hear it."

"Rocky can hurt us. This is not good."

"We can hope he's just bullshitting."

Bradley thought it through. Rocky was a La Eme OG, respected, well off, well protected. An aging family man. He'd taken over the North Baja Cartel's L.A. franchise from Hector Avalos and he ran it well, employing the youngsters of Florencia 13 and kicking heavy taxes up to his old bosses in the prisons. He also allowed Bradley to function as courier to Herredia, a coveted and lucrative position. For which Rocky took a tithe from Bradley, of course. Rocky also had Florencia's 18th Street competitors dying to put some bullets in him, and at least one informant in his organization passing along damaging information to LASD. Thus making him vulnerable to Warren. Thus giving him the need for something solid to keep Warren happy. If Rocky was ready to sing in earnest, Bradley was cooked and he knew it.

"We'll hope that. I want updates before they happen. If your people can keep any closer eye on Rocky, we could use it."

"I'll do what I can do. You a father yet?"

"Soon."

"Love to Erin."

29

Rovanna walked onto the campus of SDSU when the San Diego Alternative Book Festival opened at ten that Sunday morning. He wore long pants and a different colored Windbreaker than at the church and a black wig he'd bought at a drugstore two days ago. He had on sunglasses and carried a free book bag, courtesy of KPBS. He had a backpack slung over his shoulders, as did many of the students in attendance. The day was cool and clear and Rovanna stopped to look at the roses just budding out in the open-air quadrangle near the bell tower. There were tables and booths set up throughout the quad, banners strung to advertise various publishers, a food area and a stage and the Children's Big Top. He got a festival schedule and a large coffee, then sat on a bench and let the sunshine hit his face.

He heard Joan: *The most important thing you can do is to not stalk Representative Freeman at the book festival.*

He heard one of the Identical Men: *You must act decisively, as an extension of impulse.*

He heard Stren: *Use this gift to protect yourself and those around you and to advance the ideals you believe in.*

He heard Hood: *If Stren calls or comes again, call me immediately. He's evil, Lonnie. He will hurt you.*

He heard a voice from one of his radios: *Exterminate Freeman!*

An hour later he saw Representative Freeman making his way toward the stage. Upon seeing him again Rovanna felt the familiar shiver, a physical as well as psychic reaction. Freeman. Orbitoclasts came to his mind and he was helpless to dispel the images until they were ready to depart on their own. Then he saw Dr. Walter Freeman himself, leaning over a patient, orbitoclast and mallet in hand. Rovanna closed his eyes, hard. Finally Dr. Walter Freeman was gone, and Rovanna's mind was at least partially his own again.

He watched the representative. This Freeman was an unassuming man, early forties, imperfect posture and a head of gray-brown curls. Again Rovanna saw the subtle similarities between him and the pictures of Dr. Walter Freeman. Scott Freeman's wife was with him, along with a young broad-shouldered man who had quick eyes. Today Freeman was dressed in jeans and running shoes, a work shirt, and a black blazer. He stopped and shook hands, talked, seemed to be in no hurry.

Rovanna stood and ambled toward the seats in front of the stage. The first few rows were already filled but there was plenty of room in the middle and rear, so Rovanna took off his backpack and sat in the very last row, the first seat on the aisle that Freeman would likely walk. Freeman would go right past him, no more than a few feet away. Rovanna set the book bag on the ground and the backpack on his lap and opened the large compartment and took out a pack of small doughnuts.

Identical Man: *When in the course of human events it becomes necessary to neutralize radical individuals, exceptional men will receive the call. You are an exceptional man.*

Hood: *You'd be good in the world, I think. Otherwise it's just yourself and all the things that torment you.*

Stren: *There is nothing wrong with you, Lonnie. Sometimes friends are all we have. And voices speak to all of us . . .*

Joan: *Do not talk to Stren again. If he shows up, hit him with that Bible. Literally pound him with it. It will repel him.*

Radio Voice: *Onward, Lonnie. Defeat Freeman in the name of free men everywhere. Do what you know you must do. History has left a space that only you can fill.*

Freeman and a small group came into the seating area. Lonnie turned his face away but watched him through his sunglasses. When the representative chose to walk around the seats rather than use the aisle leading directly to the stage, Rovanna felt the terrible anger surge through him. Doesn't that just figure?

As always, this anger was visible to Rovanna: a bucket of black liquid upended inside his skull, working its way down into his body, demanding violence. The anger would try to hold Rovanna hostage until he delivered such violence. The anger was far more frightening to him than any nightmare, even those of Dr. Walter Freeman, because he could not wake up from it, and he could not escape it and, yes, he could resist it but sometimes it was stronger than he was. And he would be forced to act.

Stren, from last night's dream: *You know the purifying fire of violence, don't you, Lonnie?*

Joan: *You are a troubled man now being manipulated by a devil, and the final cost to you will not be the pain you inflict, but the pain you will receive. It will be utterly unbearable and you will not survive it.*

Rovanna set the half-eaten doughnuts back in his pack. They rested upon the silver flank of the Love 32. The silencer was screwed into place, but Rovanna had not deployed the skeleton butt because it made the gun too long for the backpack. He folded his hands over the top and watched Freeman kiss his wife then spring onto the stage. The representative went to the podium as the crowd mostly applauded but also booed. Off to one side of the stage was a long table stacked with Freeman's book, *The Cost of Liberty: Paying for the American Dream.* The cover was a dollar bill waving from a pole, with the stars and bars of the American flag superimposed.

Freeman smiled and waved and buttoned his blazer, then waved some more. Three couples in the front row stood and shouted in unison, "Right to life! Right to life! Right to life!"

"The choice belongs to all of us," Freeman shot back.

Four people not far from Rovanna suddenly stood and shouted overlapping immigration slogans that were impossible for him to unscramble, though the words *illegal, criminal,* and *no scholarships* blasted through. They waved their fists in the air. Rovanna put his hands over his ears and turned back to the stage. Freeman had raised his hands for quiet and, odd as it seemed to Rovanna, all of the partisans eagerly sat down.

Freeman talked about American society returning to tolerance and a sense of fairness both at home and abroad. He said that good nations begin with good citizens, and the duty of the citizen was to be informed, open-minded, and skeptical. He said that the people must hold themselves responsible for the government they elect. He said that government should be smaller in the bedroom and bigger in the boardroom. He told an emotional story about people he knew, bankers and executives, reaping huge personal bonuses from bailout funds—tax money that all of us paid. This brought loud boos from all around Rovanna. Then Freeman told another emotional story about friends of his, a married couple in their forties, who decided to abort a child with Down syndrome. He said it was the hardest decision that they had ever made, it nearly tore them apart, but in the end they believed what they had done was moral and right. And that was why he believed abortion should be a choice made by couples, not governments. This brought boos from the front row and two of the couples rose to walk out. One of the men turned and raised his fist at Freeman: "Life begins at conception, you godless fool!"

Radio Voice: *Freeman is blasphemy! End him. End Freeman!*

Front Row: "You will not murder our babies! You do not have that right!"

Stren: *You are vehemently against everything Scott Freeman stands for.*

"I will never accept that right," said Freeman. "And I will give my all, all of my being, to ensure that only *you* have the right to choose what is best for you. No government can do that for you. Do not cede your individual responsibilities or surrender your right to choice to any government, ever. Now, can I tell you a little bit more about my book? Please. There are people who want to hear what I have to say."

Rovanna took his backpack and book bag and walked up the aisle. Freeman started telling a story about growing up in La Mesa. Without looking at him, Rovanna turned and walked along the front row, then took one of the seats vacated by the antiabortion shouters. It was still warm. He set the pack on his lap and placed his hands on top of it.

Stren: *Have you ever just* wanted *to shoot him, Lon?*

Hood: *If you want to just talk, call me. Really. I mean it. I always have time to talk. I like baseball.*

Alice Hood: *That man looks so familiar to me. I do not feel comfortable being this close to him.*

Identical Man: *Maybe this is Dr. Freeman's grandson, Lonnie! They look alike, don't they? Remember the pictures! Don't they?*

Representative Freeman was talking about the racially mixed neighborhood he grew up in, how the two main cultures—European American and Mexican American—remained separate yet mostly tolerant. Rovanna thought of his own neighborhood in Tustin, which was all white and very conservative in the 1960s. It was white-flight central. Most of the people were Republicans, and some were outspoken members of the John Birch Society. The world communist conspiracy was a highly discussed topic, as were Soviet atrocities, the United Nations, Cuba, fluoridation, bomb shelters, and the Beatles. To Rovanna as a boy, the list of fears seemed to go on and on. He became unhappy. Shortly before his tenth birthday he had started his first fire.

Now as he watched Representative Freeman talking about racial tolerance, Rovanna saw Dr. Walter Freeman bent to his task, orbitoclast in hand, like a knitting needle, probing the eye socket of his sedated but conscious patient.

Identical Man: *Now.*

Hood: *I understand your terror, Lonnie. But lobotomies are not performed anymore.*

Alice Hood: *Look at the doctor. He performs them still, every hour of every day.*

Radio Voice: *Freeman is a slippery character. Exterminate him!*

Joan: *It really* was *nice back on the little stream, wasn't it? When you stood in that cold water and listened and there were no voices.*

"No kidding it was," Rovanna answered softly, though he rarely heard his own voice and couldn't hear it now. He felt the black paint scalding down through him. He took the Love 32 from the backpack and stood and fired an automatic burst at Dr. Walter Freeman, then another one at his nurse and another at the big orderly who was already racing across the stage toward him.

30

Ten minutes later Hood got a call from Janet Bly, with a sketchy report about a political shooting on the SDSU campus. Bly forwarded a bystander's video to Hood's phone. Hood peered at the chaos onscreen—screams and a rush of bodies, then two men fighting over a gun, with a third man down and bleeding. "Channel Ten should have it any minute," said Bly. She sounded breathless. "That was a Love Thirty-two, wasn't it?"

"I think so," Hood heard himself say. Beth and Erin came in quietly from the living room, drawn by his tone of voice. The dogs looked at him alertly as he turned on the kitchen TV. They watched the special bulletin. Channel 10 had been covering the book fair for the six-thirty news, and doing a sidebar on Scott Freeman. What Hood saw took his breath away: a gunman spraying bullets at the representative and others. The Love 32 was easy to recognize, and when the gunman's wig was ripped off in the fight, Hood recognized Lonnie Rovanna. His heart fell. Yorth called next, then Frank Soriana from San Diego, then the SAC in L.A., then Fredrick Lansing back in D.C., who thundered into the phone: "*Was that one of your goddamned Love Thirty-twos?*"

"Yes, sir."

"*The ones that got past you and disappeared in Mexico?*"

"I can't answer that yet."

"*Answer it! What the hell is going on out there with you goddamned people?*"

Hood stayed by the TV with Beth and Erin. *Freeman*, he thought. Representative Scott Freeman. Dr. Walter Freeman, Finnegan, the

Identical Men. He remembered Rovanna's soft voice. *My very deepest fear is of Dr. Freeman and his orbitoclasts.*

Congressman Scott Freeman had been rushed to Sharp Medical Center with multiple gunshot wounds. He was alive, in critical condition. His wife, Patricia, had been wounded as well and was listed as serious. Freeman's assistant, who wrestled the gunman to the stage and disarmed him, had also been shot, condition critical. Three others, all book fair attendees, had been hospitalized and were listed as stable.

"The suspect is a Caucasian male, five feet ten, one hundred seventy pounds, in his mid-twenties. He is currently in the custody of the San Diego Police . . ."

Hood walked outside into the cool Imperial County desert. The dogs bounded out ahead of him. He watched the cloud shadows move across the flanks of the Devil's Claws and he wondered how Rovanna could have deceived him, how he could have missed the violence brewing inside the man. So much evidence: insanity, aloneness, delusions, violence, the bat, the confiscated guns. Hood had instinctively understood that Finnegan had given Rovanna something. He'd *known* it. He'd asked Rovanna more than once what Finnegan had offered him. Hood had thought that maybe it was only something for Rovanna to think about, something to be afraid of, or a task to do. Mike loved trading favors, tit for tat. It gave him control, a way into you. Now Hood realized that Mike had given him something much heavier. Something physical. And Rovanna had just used it on six innocent people at a book fair. Hood felt small and hapless and fooled. He had failed to listen to his own voice. He'd let it be smothered by his sympathy and sad affection for disturbed, delusional Lonnie Rovanna. "You should have listened," he muttered. He called the dogs, and when he turned to go back inside, his phone rang again.

"Hood, this is Detective Rich Benson at San Diego PD. We met at Lonnie Rovanna's home six days ago. That's where I am now. We need to talk. It's urgent."

By the time Hood was halfway to El Cajon, Scott Freeman and his assistant had died. Patricia Freeman was stable and the three wounded bystanders were soon to be released. The suspect in custody was identified as Lonnie Dwight Rovanna.

San Diego PD had Rovanna's house taped off and a half-dozen uniformed patrolman stood in the driveway near the front porch. The mayor stood among them, arms crossed, nodding. More officers stood along the crime-scene tape that ran from the main house to the fence of the house next door, talking with the media crews and the neighbors. Hood badged a sergeant as a photographer shot him, then he stepped over the tape and walked beneath the towering sycamore tree.

Benson and the San Diego County district attorney, Lisa Alex, met Hood on the porch and escorted him inside. Hood stepped into the familiar room and saw the dusty piles of books and magazines, and the slouching plaid couch and the white chair and the low coffee table between them. A police videographer came down the hallway behind a camera and a wall of bright light and a still photographer patiently framed a shot of the plastic vodka bottle on the coffee table, then set loose the motor drive.

Benson led Hood down the short hallway and into the unused bedroom. DA Alex came in last and shut the door. Benson looked forty, freckled and red haired, with big shoulders and a paunch. Lisa Alex was tall and slender and sharp faced.

"Tell me what you know about Rovanna," said Benson.

Hood told them about his web and social media search for Mike Finnegan, a man he suspected of being involved in illegal enterprises in both the United States and Mexico. Then about Finnegan's surprise visit to Rovanna as Dr. Todd Stren. He told them about his own interview here in Rovanna's home and the follow-up phone call he'd made later that night to the troubled young man. He told them what he'd found out about Rovanna's mental health problems. He admitted that he'd seen the indicators for possible violence in Lonnie but had no legal way of detaining him.

"Tell us about that gun he used," said Alex.

Hood told them about now-defunct Pace Arms of Orange County, the one thousand Love 32s smuggled south under ATF's noses three years ago, then the discovery that some of the guns had been brought back into the United States and used in drug gang killings.

Lisa Alex and Rich Benson looked at each other. "Let me get this right," said Benson. "Mike Finnegan—a bathroom-products whole-saler in L.A., who has no criminal or any other kind of record—is the connection between Rovanna, the guns, and ATF?"

"I think Finnegan gave Lonnie the gun he used."

Again the detective and the DA exchanged looks. Benson looked long at Hood. "Rovanna told me he got it from you."

Hood confronted their doubt with a slight shake of his head. "He hears voices. He's delusional."

"But you were here in his home just a few days ago," said Lisa Alex. "And he said you two talked at some length about Iraq, and this Dr. Stren and Mike Finnegan, and he said you drank vodka."

"Yes. He told me about the U.S. Army brigade that he never was a part of. And about the Identical Men who followed him, and the fake Jehovah's Witnesses he attacked. I didn't give him a gun. Don't make me say that again."

"Why would *he* say it?" asked Benson.

"Ask him," said Hood.

"We did, and he said you have been badgering him since your days together in Iraq. That you have been inciting him to political violence for years. And, lately, specifically toward Scott Freeman."

"He was never in Iraq. I only met Rovanna six days ago. But Lon-nie was phobic about a Dr. Walter Freeman. Walter Freeman was the so-called father of the prefrontal lobotomy."

Alex cleared her throat softly. "Mr. Hood, what in God's name are you talking about?"

"Lonnie conflated the two men—the two Freemans. I didn't stir him to violence. His terror of lobotomy did. Mike Finnegan did, and he supplied the instrument to carry it out. Lonnie thought Freeman was after him. He was fixated on the instruments and the procedure. Dr. Freeman's first patient was named Alice Hood. So, somehow, Rovanna associated me with her. And her with Scott Freeman as Walter Freeman. So he claimed to be Scott Freeman's protector, as a way of getting physically close to him. Delusion fed delusion. Rovanna heard voices, imagined people who were not real. I don't think anyone knew how crazy he was. I didn't."

"Clear as mud," said Lisa Alex, standing. "And unless the feds beat me to it I'm going to put Lonnie Rovanna on death row. If you supplied him that firearm, we may have a conspiracy and you may well join him on said row. If not, my office will depose you at some point and you may well find yourself on my witness list. All yours, Rich."

Alex marched out, leaving the door open. "You're a person of interest in this investigation," said Benson. "You know the drill. Don't leave California without notifying me."

31

Clint Wampler lay on his trailer bed in Bombay Beach, peacoat buttoned against the desert cold, head against the buckling wallpaper, watching yet another news story on the shooting of the congressman in San Diego. He thought, *The federal government sucks and Freeman deserved it.* The next story was of course about him and the "cold-blooded murder of Agent Reggie Cepeda." They showed the same picture of Clint they'd been showing for seven straight days.

He answered his phone to good news.

"Clint, I have a buyer at thirty-five thousand."

"It costs forty."

"It's a solid offer from a dependable client."

"Solid shit is what I call it." Wampler rang off and dropped the phone to the bed beside the .44 Magnum. Of course Castro called back ten minutes later.

"He wants three."

"I ain't got but one."

"He can go forty on the one if you can get two more at thirty-seven five."

"Nope. These things are hard to come by. If they're worth thirty-seven five, then they're worth forty. Tell him to go to hell."

"Let me tell you something about business, Clint. You have to learn to be flexible. You have to offer up a little bit to keep your customers happy. You take care of them and they take care of you. Sometimes you take a little more and sometimes you take a little less. This is how things get done."

Wampler did the math while Castro lectured him. "This is the deal, then: forty for one, thirty-eight each for two more. I need the money up front for the second two. I don't get 'em on promises and you aren't either."

Clint hung up again and dropped the phone and went to the front door window. He cracked the curtain and looked out at the late morning. He saw the dirt patch with the derelict cars, some up on concrete blocks, some resting on their wheels or rust-eaten brakes. Not a one of them less than thirty years old, he thought. He hated this place, hated living locked down like a criminal. But this hole was hard to find and cheap. And the old lady who took his cash was so blind she made him fish out the key with the TRAILOR tag on it, though not too blind to count the money.

And near blindness was a virtue because, even though the murder of the congressman in San Diego had knocked Clint out of first place on the news, Clint was still everywhere Clint turned. For two straight days after he'd killed Cepeda, he had made the front page of all four newspapers for sale outside the Bombay Beach convenience stores. He bought some to see what they were saying about him. His picture was shown and his name bellowed out on every news show he watched on the wretched little TV in his trailer, and every radio station he could get, from Yuma to San Diego, L.A. to San Bernardino. But even with the fresher dead congressman to prey on, they were still yapping on about the fallen hero, Cepeda, and showing his official fed mug shot and a portrait from his wedding day, over and over. And of course, most of the focus was on the growing manhunt for Clint Wampler, a militia-affiliated extremist who had thus far escaped arrest. The papers and TV kept showing his worst picture, the one that made him look like some kind of rotten-toothed sixties rock star, with stupid bangs and big ears and an IQ of ten.

In the few brief minutes that he'd spent outside this miserable aluminum refrigerator over the past three days, he'd personally seen more cops per mile of road than anywhere he'd ever been. It was like a convention of them. He saw local police, sheriffs from God knew how many California and Arizona counties, Highway Patrol, Tribal Police, even Fish and Game had units out looking for him. And of course ICE and Border Patrol in their SUVs. And then there were all the unmarked-but-still-obvious cars the feds were driving—Mercs and Chevys with little whippy antennas on top: FBI, ATF, DEA, U.S. Marshals. Even the U.S. Postal Service investigation service was after him again because of that post office fire back in Missouri, is what the TV said. He had also seen unusual numbers of small helicopters and low-flying aircraft. He had almost been trapped at a CHP checkpoint that, as if by a miracle, had shut down when he'd advanced to fifth in line, a pistol lying under a rag on the passenger seat of his second stolen car, his cool and clarity settling over him.

Looking out past the junked cars he saw the rutted dirt drive and the Jackalope Lounge sign, and beyond that the Jackalope Lounge itself, an almost windowless, low brick box decorated with Christmas lights. Quiet, this time on a Sunday. It sat just off a wide dirt road. Beyond the road was a white expanse of what looked like sand or maybe salt, then the flat silver mirror of the Salton Sea. The whole place smelled of dead fish and foul water, and there were screeching goddamned birds everywhere you looked. *Bombay Beach*, Wampler thought. Worse than anywhere in Russell County. Plus he was hungry and worried about going out for groceries and his money was running low. And his left middle finger might be getting infected because it got redder and hurt more every day. The pain made him think of spectacular ways to return it to its rightful owner: Charlie Hooper.

Thinking of revenge on Hooper gave Clint just a taste of that cool, clear feeling he liked. So he went to the middle of the small "living room" and practiced his draw. He was a pocket man, not a holster man—easier to conceal and easier to draw fast if you had the right jacket, which he did. The peacoat had wide slit pockets at perfect angles. He whipped out twenty quick lefts, then twenty rights, then twenty doubles. On the two-gun draws he alternated bracing left over right, then right over left for steadiness, none of that waving-'em-around bullshit like in westerns. Wampler liked short-barreled guns with flush or internal hammers that wouldn't catch on things. He turned around and went through the routine again. Not a snag or fumble. Gotcha. The best was doing it live, out in the woods by Little Creek, using the skinny poplars and willows for targets—if you could hit them, you could hit a man practically with your eyes closed. Plus it sounded great. Clint did another twenty draws each way.

Then he stepped into the "kitchen" and instead of drawing a gun with his right hand he whipped out his hand-made blackjack and rapped it righteously against one of the wooden cabinets. The weighted end left a quarter-size dent in the wood, just like it would leave on a skull, Clint thought. He hit another cabinet, harder, and this time the sap went all the way through and he had to wrench it back out through the ragged hole. When he finished his workout, his pulse and breathing were right up where he liked them and his vision was clear and sharp.

Half an hour later Castro called to say he could go the full forty thousand on a new crated Stinger. "And he'll front the money on the next two, at thirty-seven five."

"Fine. Deal. See how flexible I can be?"

"I vouched for you, Clint. I think you understand what that means."

Wampler felt flush and lucky, though still hungry. "Oh. And I want five thousand of my money to be in the form of a dependable used car, Mr. Car Dealer. A good one, not some fucked-up little economy car. I want it legal and mine. I also want a sawed-off shotgun and some ammo and a blanket to cover them up with. The gun, the car, and thirty-five grand gets you the missile. And seventy-five thousand more gets you double trouble. Or is it triple?"

"I've got a secure place we can meet."

"That's good, but I'm not moving one inch until I've got my money."

*   *   *

Five hours later Wampler parked his '09 Sebring in the Denny's parking lot in Fallbrook and stepped out into the cool winter air. He left the sawed-off shotgun on the backseat, covered in a bright yellow-and-black serape. The pistol under his Windbreaker felt useful and he was assured by the flat, hard combat knife strapped to his calf. His fingertip throbbed in the cold, same beat as his heart.

Skull's two Pendleton friends were older than Clint had expected. One short and one medium. They had tattoos and military haircuts and moved with brisk authority. They reminded him of Skull. The parking lot was dark but busy enough, and the friends had told him that Fallbrook had some sheriffs for patrol but not many. Wampler saw a security guard who seemed not to notice them. His heart rate always fell in dicey situations like this, and he saw things in a slowed-down kind of motion. For the two Stingers he handed over $50,000 in the backpack in which it had come to him. The other $25,000 was his end, already stashed in the car. The Sebring had a big trunk and the crates fit fine alongside the plastic bags of his cash.

Wampler shut the trunk and got back into his new $5,000 used car. The balance of $35,000 from Castro for the first Stinger sat on the front passenger seat in a steel navy ammunition box covered with the heavy wool coat he'd brought from home. He wondered again if he should keep Skull's and Brock's shares. With the blood of a murdered federal agent on their hands, it might be a long, long time until they saw the light of day. There was a question of honor, however. He had honor. Up to a point. One of the men was coming to the car so he drew his .44 and kept it in the dark and rolled down the window.

"More where those came from," said short, who called himself Skip.

"All the business I'm giving you, Skip, seems the price might come down some."

"Take a thousand off the next two, if that helps."

"Off each one or both?"

"Off each of however many you want, my friend. We aim to please. Where are these babies going?"

"If it mattered to you, you wouldn't be selling them."

"It's a big world out there, partner."

"That's why you need me. Cause I know where the customers are."

"You know how to find us."

Wampler rolled up the window and slid the big pistol under the coat on the passenger seat. With this part of the deal done he headed south again for El Centro. He stopped at a motel on the edge of Fallbrook and used the pay phone to call Mary Kate Boyle. "I got some money in my pocket now, Mary Kate. Where are you at? You there? What's that clicking sound?"

"It's my damned phone falling apart. I got to get something better."

"Where you at? Are you coming out here to California to be my girl or not?"

"I'm coming to California to see some friends. There's nothing in this about being your girl, Clint."

"But you are coming, now, aren't you?"

"Didn't I just say that?"

"I made the biggest deal of my life today. I got a new used car and thirty-five *thousand dollars* in it, every cent of it mine if I want it to be. All I got to do is deliver two more missiles and I'll have even more. I think I might be in the missile business for a while to come."

"I don't understand how you can make so much money so fast. Thirty-five thousand dollars and a car, Clint? Skull never made money like that in one day."

"Then you know it's Clint can take the best care of you."

"Where do you get 'em? You can't just buy missiles in El Centro, can you?"

"Like I'd tell you?"

"Did you go to El Centro like Skull said you were going to?"

"Maybe. Why are you asking so many damned questions?"

"I'm trying to talk to you."

Wampler let his suspicion run its course while he pictured Mary Kate Boyle. Last he'd seen her, one of her eyes was puffed up purple and her lips were cut. But she had a good figure and one of them alluring smiles when her mouth wasn't all swollen. He'd been pissed off at Skull for messing her up, but what could he do? You couldn't fight a guy that big. You could kill him but that wasn't fair. "I was in El Centro for a while. That's where Lyle and Brock got busted and I got away. I'm out of that desert now. Like I said, I've got my money and now I'll get myself a place to stay. A good place, not some trailer. You going to come join me in it or not, Mary Kate?"

"I don't know."

"You sound like you might could."

"I've got friends in San Diego."

"I ain't moving to San Diego, girl. We went to see some business contacts there. Too many people in that city."

"What kind of place you looking for?"

"What kind of place *you* looking for?"

"Someplace I don't get hit by Russell County hell-raisers, Clint. I've had enough of that for the next about hundred years."

"How about the beach? Chicks like the beach."

"It's up to you."

"I can't believe you're coming to see me. I feel happy about that."

"I never said it was to see you."

"It ain't what you say, MK, it's what you do. I got a real nice Sebring, decent sound and just about new. One of my friends out here, he owns a Ford dealership. He set me up with a good deal."

"What color did you get?"

"Kind of a gunmetal gray."

"Why'd he sell you a Dodge if he owns a Ford lot?"

"What kind of question is that? It's a used Dodge. What are you talking about, Mary Kate?"

"Shall I call you when I get to California?"

Clint thought about that for a short moment. "No. You don't call me. I call you. You driving or the bus or what?"

"Trailways. And I'll need to be picked up, Clint. I can't be dragging luggage all over San Diego."

"Clint's your man! What a great day this has been. How are those lips of yours healing up?"

"Not bad."

"So, whatcha wearing right now, Mary Kate? That black lacy top with them little shiny things on it?"

She hung up and Wampler laughed but didn't call back.

He met Castro off a dirt road near Jacumba to deliver the Stingers. The night was cold and the breeze hissed in the treetops. Wampler blew into his hands while Castro opened and closed the crates, then started loading them into a beaten-up old F-150. When Castro had pushed in the last crate and closed the squeaky tailgate, he started toward Wampler, reaching inside his sport coat. The pistol seemed to just appear in Wampler's hands, holding steady at Castro's forehead.

"Oh no," he said, stopping instantly. "I'll take my hand out slow, Clint. It's going to have a pack of smokes in it."

"Anything but smokes'll get you dead."

"Watch this." Israel pulled his hand from behind the breast of the coat, a half-flattened red-and-white package held between thumb and forefinger. He shook a cigarette into the opening and offered it to Wampler.

"Your hand ain't shakin', Mr. Car Dealer."

"I've had guns pointed at me before. So put it away."

Wampler spun the pistol around his finger with a gunslinger's flourish and a smile, then pocketed it and snatched the smoke. "How come you're driving that shitty old truck?"

"Less attention." Castro lit Wampler's cigarette, then one for himself. "I got some people who want to meet you, Clint. And I got a buyer for seven more of those Stingers at thirty-five grand apiece."

"You work fast."

"I work when there's work. Life is like that, Clint. It just goes along real slow, day to day, you get up, you get bored, you go to sleep. Then *swoosh*, off it goes in some crazy way you least expected. The trick is hanging on. Letting it happen. Letting it pay."

"You got all sorts of advice for me."

"I'm trying to be helpful. I have young sons. When they're your age, I hope I can offer good advice to them, also."

"Good advice? Like selling stolen missiles to a drug cartel?"

"Cartel? Good guess, I'd say. You've got a quick mind, Clint."

"I get ahead in life by taking the stuff I want. And I never took one thing from anybody who wanted it *less* than I did. The only difference is I'm smarter and meaner. And faster. Maybe that's the biggest and best difference about me. I'm *faster.*"

"So do you want to do seven more Stingers?"

"You just pony up seven times thirty-five and they'll be yours. Clint will take care of you." *Seventy-seven grand in the pocket*, he thought. *Seventy-seven grand!*

"Clint, I can do better than that. I've got a sweet new Explorer that just came from the factory. It's one of the most beautiful SUVs Ford's ever made. I'm talking the good V-eight, shift-on-the-fly four-wheel drive, traction control, cobalt blue, cream-colored leather, tow hitch with electric, premium sound, Ford's own electronics that beat the hell out of Bluetooth. Extra-dark tinted windows, navigation, off-road tires, and a free year of Sirius. It's something a young man like you could feel real good in. Women like the white leather and the blue. My plan was keep it for myself. I haven't even prepped it yet, but I'll let you take it as partial payment for five hundred over invoice. Just as a gesture of goodwill, Clint. Thirty-nine five. *Thirty-nine five.*"

Clint puffed on the cigarette and flicked some embers into the cold wind. "Plus you'll take this piece of shit Chrysler back, right? For the five grand I done already gave you for it."

Castro sighed and looked over at the Sebring, then back at Clint. "That's a nice little car for five grand."

"Then take it back and sell it for six."

"Okay, Clint. You have yourself a deal. You'll get exactly one quarter of a million dollars for seven Stinger launchers, seven missiles and the Sebring. Of that amount, thirty-nine thousand five hundred are the new Explorer. I'll have the fleet manager do the paperwork and I'll get one of the junior salesmen to deliver it to you."

"So the paper don't point to you."

"That's the way it works."

A new Explorer and sixty thousand, five hundred dollars, thought Clint. Not bad for a day's work and a few more hours tomorrow or the next day. *Mary Kate, you're gonna love me. Love me a lot!*

32

The next afternoon the Department of Justice sent Hood an economy-class e-ticket from San Diego to Washington, D.C., for early the next day. He would appear for testimony the following day, then fly home.

The flight was rough and arrived slightly ahead of a powerful Atlantic storm. Hood took a taxi to the ATF headquarters on New York Avenue, arriving in a darkness swirling with snow. He had time for a quick sandwich and a cup of coffee across the street before going in. He watched the bureaucrats and office workers bundled in overcoats and scarves bustling onto the Metro Red Line. He carried his overnight bag through the snow and into the building and went through the scanner, then gave his name at the desk. An intern met him and took him up. The building was new and sleek, with faceted glass walls and a feeling of openness even in the winter dark. The hallways and offices were laid out in angles that challenged logic and memory. From an upper story Hood looked down on the courtyard and the lights of the district muted by snowflakes.

Acting Deputy Director Fredrick Lansing stood as Hood came into his office. He hovered, sallow faced, then sat and pushed a thin stapled collection of papers to Hood. "Grossly's subpoena and your hotel for tonight. You're testifying under oath before the House Committee on Oversight and Government Reform at nine tomorrow morning. They'll want you to answer the same questions you answered before, and God knows what else. Tell them what you told them the first time and you'll be fine. So long as it's true."

Hood glanced down at the document. *You are hereby commanded . . .* "He wants someone to blame."

"He wants to hear the words *gun, walk,* and *ATF* in the same sentence so badly his face turns pink. He'll ask you again and again who gave the order."

"There was no order. We just came up short."

Lansing sat back and tapped a pen on his desktop, nodding. "You do understand the real reason why Grossly's so hot for this, don't you?"

"He wants our budget cut."

"That's not the end goal. The goal is to make ATF look either dangerous or inept—it doesn't matter which—and hold the attorney general and the president ultimately responsible. It's another way to discredit the administration. They're using you to do it."

Suddenly it dawned on Hood why it was him, and not Bly or Velasquez or Morris or any of the other agents involved with Blowdown who was sitting here. "You gave me to Grossly because I'm not genuine ATF. I'll be easier to blame and fire."

"It looks that way but it isn't."

"How can it not be?"

Lansing looked heavily at him. "Grossly was interested in you, particularly, Hood. Maybe because you're not ATF he figured you'd be quicker to point upstairs. He asked about you and we gave him some information. Since Fast and Furious, it's our new transparency with Congress. Fine. But it looked to me like someone whispered in Grossly's ear. He knew what questions to ask, where to look. Not all of those photos or video came from us, you know. So who supplied them? Grossly is a partisan and nothing more. He wants to beat down this president so his party can take over again. I'm a Republican. But he's the right wing at its worst. It's simple politics, Hood. You're a tool. So am I and so is ATF. And by the way, Janet Bly will be testifying right after you. Grossly subpoenaed her, too. Not Velasquez or Morris. You and Bly."

Hood looked through the window blinds and the black shiny glass to the district beyond. "When will you fire us?"

"When the timing is best. We might have to make a show of it, you know."

"Wash the hands."

"It plays outside the Beltway. Thirty years with ATF and I've never seen agents treated like this."

Hood looked through the window again to the darkness and the lights below. "You don't know how close we were to intercepting those Love Thirty-twos. We missed them by inches. Literally inches, when the transport chopper took off. We knew Pace and Jones were getting ready to ship those guns somewhere. We *watched* them load them in and we still missed. I think about it. I wonder about it. I dream about it. And I don't know what we could have done better."

"Tell Grossly. I mean it. Say it to him like you just said it to me."

Hood nodded, feeling patronized and abandoned and alone.

"Hood, I don't know what Darren Grossly and his committee know about Lonnie Rovanna yet. But when America learns that it was an ATF-surveilled gun that killed Congressman Freeman, all hell will break loose. A thousand guns lost in Mexico? One of them the gun that killed Representative Freeman? The agency tasked with keeping such guns from the hands of violent criminals? You can hear Grossly: Where are the rest of those guns right now? Where was ATF leadership when all this was happening? Where was the attorney general? *Where was the president?* Hood, your head will roll but it won't roll alone. I'm sorry. This is ugly business. The ugliest I've seen. I hate to see good men and women suffer in it."

The next morning Hood walked into Rayburn House Office Building Committee Room 2154 and looked into flashing cameras and the steady glare from the video lights. He wasn't sure this was how celebrities felt. He was led to the witness dock by a one of Grossly's aids, who sat him in the middle seat, which left him flanked by two empty chairs on either side. He was given a bottle of water. In front of him was floor, and a few yards away was an empty row of seats facing him. Behind this row was another, raised on a dais. Seven men and two women presided there, with Representative Darren Grossly in the middle. Grossly gave him a brief nod. Hood nodded back, then read the name signs of the others, recognizing most. The American flag behind them had been lowered in mourning for the fallen congressman, Scott Freeman.

Hood tried to ignore the photographers by looking out at the handsome walnut woodwork and the black leather chairs of the committee room. He felt self-conscious about the diamonds in his tooth, and resolved not to smile, which would not be difficult. His navy winter-weight wool suit was the best he owned. *Nine on one*, he thought, a baseball team against a boxer. Who's the underdog here? He turned and looked behind him to the spectator's gallery, gradually filling. Tourists? The curious? Committee groupies? When he turned to face forward again, a photographer was kneeling on the floor right in front of him, with a long lens aimed up at his face and the motor drive already clattering away. Hood smiled without opening his mouth, thinking, *This is the worst fucking day of my life and it hasn't even started yet.*

A few minutes later Grossly tapped his gavel with an amplified thud and called the meeting to order. He introduced Father Peter Dobson from St. Mark's Episcopal Church, who asked the participants to close their eyes and bow their heads in a prayer for Representative Scott Freeman and his assistant, Bruce Harbison.

Hood bowed his head and listened. Dobson had an intelligent and soothing voice that made it seem God would have a hard time denying his blessing upon the slain men. After the amen there was a long heavy silence.

Then Grossly cleared his throat but his voice cracked anyway: "Thank you, Reverend Dobson. Today continues our congressional investigation into the questionable and quite possibly negligent conduct of the Alcohol, Tobacco, Firearms and Explosives task force involved in Operation Blowdown . . ."

Grossly's introduction was long and thorough. He explained that the Department of Justice, within which ATF operated, was not a partner in this inquiry, but a focus of said inquiry. He accused ATF of "irresponsible actions." He suggested that the "highest levels of the DOJ were trying cover up those actions by stonewalling this investigation." Hood thought of Cepeda. He stared at the portraits behind the dais, wondering who the men were, remembering his first boyhood visit to the Haunted Mansion at Disneyland. Grossly's outrage began to build and his voice became louder and his face went from skeptical to doubtful to abashed, then back to skeptical as he introduced the ranking member of the OGR Committee.

The ranking member, Representative Collins, gave a much briefer opening statement, then looked over his sheet of notes and down at Hood. "Our first witness today is Charles Hood. Mr. Hood is a deputy with the Los Angeles County Sheriff's Department, currently attached to the ATF Operation Blowdown task force. This task force was established five years ago to prevent the illegal flow of guns from the United States to Mexico. Mr. Hood served our country as part of the U.S. Navy during Operation Iraqi Freedom, and he has been a Blowdown task force member for four years. Mr. Hood, thank you for being here today."

"You're welcome, sir."

"Mr. Hood, in light of the recent tragic assassinations in San Diego, I'd like you to open this hearing with a history of the firearm that was allegedly used in those murders, the so-called Love Thirty-two, an illegal fully automatic machine pistol manufactured in California. I understand these guns have a rather shady history with ATF. Then I would like you to tell us about your meeting, just last week, with Lonnie Rovanna, the accused assassin of Scott Freeman and Bruce Harbison. You did meet with Mr. Rovanna last week, did you not?"

"Yes."

"Okay, then. Let's start with the gun. Tell us about the gun that Mr. Rovanna allegedly used. We've got pictures up on the screens so we can all see what you're talking about. We're going to dim the lights for just a few minutes. Please proceed, Mr. Hood."

Hood heard the ripple of curiosity rise from the gallery behind him and he turned again to see his jury. From the wall a large monitor blipped on, with the bright image of a Love 32 resting on a black background. The gun looked fifty times life-size, like some futuristic contraption designed to orbit in outer space. The stainless-steel finish of the weapon glowed softly, and the powerful monitor threw light into the dimmed room. Brushed by that light, positioned directly below the monitor in the last row of mostly empty seats, sat Mike Finnegan. His hair was black and his eyeglasses were thick and he wore a dark suit. He seemed to be staring directly at Hood. Hood stared back. His vision was twenty-ten, last time he'd been examined. It was Finnegan, without a doubt. Even in the dim light. No doubt at all.

Hood turned to face his congressional watchdogs, hearing the cameras and looking into the video lights aimed into his face. He took a deep breath and looked back once again and Finnegan was gone. He faced forward, folded his hands on the table before him, leaned into the light and told his story.

33

One hour later it was over. Grossly thanked Hood and a marshal seated the next witness, Janet Bly. Hood stood and waited for her as she approached and he could see that she was stricken. The stress of ATF work had long ago hardened Bly's pleasant features, but now her faced looked weathered and her eyes were flat with distant fury. She took his arm and guided him away from the microphones to a quieter place near the gallery. "Good job, Charlie. I hope I can keep my cool, too. I didn't know you'd be here until Soriana told me. Did you know that no one else from Blowdown got subpoenas but us? I find that interesting."

"It's divide and conquer."

"They can't pit us against each other. It won't work. This is an embarrassing spectacle." Bly leaned in close: "Twelve years of this and I'm about *that* close to flipping them this badge."

"Don't. The Love Thirty-twos didn't walk. They ran. It wasn't our fault."

"Then why do I feel like a sucker?"

"Just tell the truth."

"But where's our backup? Where's Lansing? Where's the *director* for that matter? Where's the rest of ATF when we need them?" She let her eyes roam Hood's face, then looked past him toward the dais. She took his arm again. "I can't help you with Rovanna, Charlie. I can't speculate or make excuses. I don't know why you saw him or what you were looking for. All I know is one thing: I trust you. I've got to go. Caution, friend—there's some reporters lying in wait."

Hood stepped out of the committee room and looked past the reporters and around them and through the windows in search of Mike, holding up a hand and politely declining to answer more questions. They trailed after him anyway, shouting questions and shooting pictures and video as he worked his way to the underground that would take him to the Capitol Building. At his hotel across the street he collected his bags and the bellman told him all of the airports had just now been shut down for the storm. *Fine*, Hood thought—a stroke of luck? He took one of the last available rooms at a much higher rate and carried his overnight bag back to the elevator and into his new room. He changed into the casual clothes he'd flown out in and the chukka boots he'd sprayed liberally with waterproofing before leaving Buenavista. He bought an expensive overcoat and a heavy wool scarf in one of the hotel stores downstairs, then ventured outside into the storm.

He hustled across Pennsylvania toward the Metro entrance, leaning into blowing snowflakes that made no sound. The sky and the ground were white, and the buildings had lost their color and they looked like long-forgotten prisoners peeking out at the world. He made the Blue Line landing and climbed down the steps. The government had shut down and the cars were filled with workers heading home. Hood scanned the rows of faces, got off at Federal Triangle, and headed into the blasting wind toward the Capitol Building. He found his way back to the Rayburn House Office Building, trudged to committee room 2154 and looked in. A young man with a deep voice was talking about Mexican law enforcement being kept in the dark by American agencies. Hood looked around the committee room, noting the security cameras.

Down in the basement, just past the empty fitness room, Hood located the U.S. Capitol Police substation and badged Officer Donna Ford at the front desk. Behind her, he could see the monitor room with the live feeds coming through and other officers watching the screens. He asked to see the first-session OGR hearing videos from that morning.

"Was that your hearing?"

"Yes, it was."

"Can I ask you why you want to see our video?"

"I saw a man in the audience I want another look at. He's a person of interest back in California."

She studied him with frank suspicion, then rose slowly from her chair and went into the surveillance room. A minute later she came to the doorway and nodded him in. Sergeant Mark Herron sat Hood at a console and pushed some buttons and a moment later Hood was watching Grossly tap his gavel and calling the meeting to order. Herron asked where he saw the subject and pushed more buttons. The POV did a 180-degree switch and Hood was now looking over the backs of the OGR Committee members, toward the rear of the auditorium.

"He was right there, under the monitor," said Hood. "I saw him a few minutes after the meeting was called to order. Less than a minute later he was gone."

Herron ran the video forward. Ranking member Collins gesticulated rapidly without sound and Hood watched himself sitting stone-faced, looking up at him. Collins was still at it when Hood saw Finnegan come into view. Hood pointed and Herron slowed the video. Mike took a seat beneath the monitor, crossed his legs matter-of-factly and locked his fingers together and over one knee. He appeared to be looking at the back of Hood's head. A moment later Hood watched himself turn and look at Mike. The stare-down was longer than he'd remembered. Finally he turned back to the committee. Mike rose and walked out of the camera's view. Hood watched himself take a deep breath and turn again toward Mike, finding only the empty chair. Hood waited for Herron to burn some stills onto a disc, then pushed his way outside into the storm.

He trudged along Constitution past the Senate Office Buildings, but the snow was heavy and soon his boots were wet and his feet were cold so he found a Metro Blue Line station that took him out to Largo

Town Center and back toward downtown, where he switched to the Red Line to Bethesda and came back to try the Orange Line way out to East Falls Church. No Mike. Then Hood rode back again to the center of the nation's capital. The Metro cars were mostly empty in this storm, but Hood continued to watch and look and use his wonderful twenty-ten vision but he saw no Mike. He wondered if Mike had gotten out before the airports closed. The cold advanced on his hopefulness. He was zipped fully into the overcoat but his feet were mostly numb and his body shivered intermittently. The cars were surprisingly cold. The Green Line sounded lucky so he rode it clear to Greenbelt, staring at the faces of the other riders, but there was no Mike here either and he knew Mike would not be here and the other passengers averted his eyes and he got off near his hotel, he thought, only to find the streets were white prairies and not a single building was familiar. He faced into the wind and followed his feet. His waterproofed boots were soon soaked.

Sometime later he came upon a tavern where he ate ravenously and knocked back a couple of bourbons neat to warm the blood. The waiter said the storm was supposed to blow through within hours so air travel might resume sometime tomorrow. After dinner, Hood sat in front of the fire with a woman and her dachshund, which was curled on her lap and wearing a sweater. She talked about her granddaughter, who was second-chair cello for the Baltimore Symphony Orchestra and pregnant. He watched the flames and they took him away, outside himself, where thoughts could gain no traction and where there was no Charlie Hood. Freedom from himself was pleasant. He saw rivers and Beth's face.

Later, when his phone vibrated, he had a heart-dropping premonition that his father had died, and he was correct. The stroke had been massive and his death nearly instant. His mother was strangely composed and she didn't talk very long, having two more of her children to inform of this. She seemed fortified by purpose. Hood stayed by the fire long after the woman and the dog had gone. More bourbon. Midnight came and went. When he got back to his room and took off his boots, his feet were blue-white and as cold as a T-bone just out of the fridge. He pulled the armchair up near the heater and put on the dress socks he'd worn that morning. He thought of his father and remembered good things from his boyhood and let the tears come.

34

Bradley and Erin walked slowly across the gravel driveway on Hood's property. Her legs and ankles were growing heavy from bearing the weight of the baby and Dr. David had advised very light daily exercise such as this. The afternoon was cool and bright. Bradley turned to see Reyes watching them from the courtyard, the top half of his face just visible above the low adobe wall.

"He's worse than a bad conscience," said Bradley.

"He's a delight and I love him."

They came to the dirt road and started up the gradual rise. The slender stalks of the paloverde were green now and just starting to flower out. A tarantula hawk buzzed past them, flickering black and orange in the sun. They came to the crest and stood with the peaks of the Devil's Claws high and jagged to the west.

Bradley saw motion on the hills between them and the sharp mountains beyond. He saw two vehicles facing them on the hillcrest far away where no road or even trail was visible. They were parked a few yards apart, what looked like a white half-ton Chevy pickup truck and an older red Durango with its driver's-side door open. Two very small men sat on the hood of the truck, side-by-side, legs crossed. It looked to Bradley as if they were both looking through binoculars at him. Standing between the vehicles was a giant wearing a black sweatshirt, hood up. Bradley recognized the dwarves from the Biltmore and assumed that the enormous man was the one who had delivered Mike the bottle of Scotch. *What in hell*, he thought. Why? Spying for Mike? *If Erin is your enemy, she is my enemy and she must be approached as such.* Or, horning in on Mike's territory? *Some of Mike's envious coworkers have decided to try just that.*

"I've seen them before," said Erin. "Once where they are now. And once way over the opposite direction. East."

"You should have told me."

"I just did. Who are they?"

"I wish I had a rifle."

"God, Brad. They waved at me once. They don't seem to mean harm."

Bradley pulled his service pistol from the holster snug in the small of his back. He aimed one-handed and held well above the giant's head and squeezed off the round. A second passed, then a puff of dust rose from the slope behind the vehicles.

"Brad!"

The giant put his hands on his hips and it looked like the dwarves lowered their field glasses and spoke, then raised the glasses back again. Bradley thought he heard laughter reach him across the distance. He held a little lower and fired again. The bullet hit to the giant's left and short. Bradley guessed thirty feet off the mark, adjusted his aim and fired again. High and left, but closer.

Erin turned away and started down the road toward the house, but Bradley shot again and again. The first shot landed left. But the next one hit home with the familiar whap of a bullet hitting something solid and Bradley saw the giant flinch and step backward. Bradley lowered the pistol and watched the huge man. He seemed to be looking down at his middle, then he lifted the sweatshirt. Hood saw a patch of red on the man's belly. The giant let go of his shirt and looked at Bradley and spread his arms out in a gesture of, *really?* The laughter of the dwarves carried to Bradley on the cool, dry air and hearing it he felt a fear that was different from any he had known. It was cold and constricting and on the move. With it came a crushing remorse and the humiliating knowledge that he alone had brought these demons upon her, and upon himself.

The giant walked to the Durango and climbed in and sat with his long legs dangling out. He knocked his shoes together to get the dust off them, and closed the door. The dwarves scrambled off the truck and got in. Bradley emptied his semiauto at them, six more rounds: One hit the Durango door with a metallic ring and two more threw up dust close to the pickup, but the others were off. The giant waved out the window at him as the vehicles headed over the rise and one of the drivers laid into his horn.

He caught up with Erin as she waddled slowly down the road. He took her arm gently but his voice was hard with anger. "Mike's friends."

"What do they want?"

"Thomas."

She stopped and pulled her arm from his hand. "For *what*?"

"They're just like Mike. They use good people to create chaos and to amuse themselves. When the good people are used up and ruined, they let them self-destruct. They like to start with children. Those things back there are either helping Mike or trying take away his prize. Either way, they all want to befriend Thomas. They're all evil, Erin. They claim to be devils. They don't try to hide it. They want to make Thomas part of it. I made a deal with Mike. I took some stupid oath. It changed my fortune and something inside me. I'm utterly sorry and ashamed, Erin. It's all my fault. I've never been this sorry for something I've done."

He looked into her eyes as they searched his face. He saw the doubt in them and the fear. As she studied him, the doubt shrank and the fear grew. "What can we do?"

"Nothing right now. Don't ever talk to them, or to people you don't know. They won't use force. It's not their nature. They cajole. They persuade and deceive. They're serpents in our garden. They won't try to steal Thomas. They'll try to become our friends and get to him through us. Like Mike did."

"Mike. Do you believe me now?"

"I believe you now, Erin. You were right and I was wrong."

"Is there a place where they can't ever find us?"

"I don't know the answer to that. But I promise you I will find a way to make us all safe."

"I feel sick. I feel like when they kidnapped me. And you promised you would come."

He put his arm around her. His heart was beating fast. "I did. I came and I got you. Now, Erin, walk slowly with me. We're not in danger now. We're okay. We're okay. We're okay."

Cleary called when Bradley was halfway home to Valley Center. "Round two. Rocky and Jim Warren met at El Capitán lounge in El Monte yesterday. A two-hour lunch. Much intense conversation. Warren and Dez in conference this morning and your name came up. More than once. So did mine, and Vega's and Hood's. And Carlos Herredia's."

"I'll talk to him."

"Talk to Rocky Carrasco?"

"What else am I going to do?"

"I can think of one thing."

"There's a better way, Jack."

"Name it."

Bradley watched the paloverde flashing past and the flat desert greened by the winter rain. He hated this, thinking like some sociopathic gangbanger. Rocky had always treated him with respect and generosity. Of course, Bradley had single-handedly rescued Rocky's young son from a ransom kidnapper so there was not just good money between Rocky and himself, but good blood, too. "Talk to me, Cleary."

"Listen—my man called yesterday, halfway through the lunch. If we can get that kind of notice, we could take him on his way out. I know some Eighteenth Streeters who'd love to make their bones on Rocky Carrasco. Would they ever."

"No."

"And what's your better idea?"

"I'll come up with one."

35

Mary Kate Boyle watched Hood come into the Buenavista ATF field office lobby on Monday morning. He looked haunted and sucked of life, real diamonds in a fake smile. She looked at Oscar and even the big guard had an expression of brooding concern as he watched Hood. He led her back to his work cubicle and she handed him the voice recorder with her and Clint's last conversation. That conversation now seemed ages ago, but it wasn't her fault Charlie had been out of state and out of touch. He set up another recorder to make a copy, checking the available recording time and the battery like he always did with those steady, unhurried hands.

"Where you been?"

"Washington."

"I heard it snowed a lot."

"Lots."

She smiled and looked away, but he wouldn't look back at her. At least she could smile, slightly, without bleeding. She looked out the window to the waning light. It was winter but she could sense the season starting to lose hold. People out here had no idea what a real winter was. She liked weather. She thought of the long Missouri summer days, the sun on her body on that flimsy deck out behind Skull's double-wide.

Hood listened to the conversation, staring at the little recorder and occasionally looking at her with an approving glint in his eyes. He tapped on his computer keyboard and glanced at the monitor. He made notes on a yellow pad. She listened to herself explain to Clint what all the noise on her phone was as she was trying to get the recorder set up fast, then leading Clint on with the whole coming-to-California idea, and also doing a fair job of getting info for Hood on his car and the missiles and where he might be. She really was a good actor. She'd fooled Clint, and Clint was smart. Not book smart but crafty and alert, like a weasel. They played the tape again, then once more.

"I didn't want to press him for a phone number," she said.

"No."

"How'd it go in D.C.? You look like they shot your dog."

"It went okay, Mary Kate." Hood tapped on the keyboard again and again looked at the screen.

"You don't tell me much more about what you're doing than Clint does."

Hood looked down at his notes. "My father died after a long illness. It wasn't a surprise but it was still a shock."

"Oh, Charlie—I'm so very sorry for him and you."

"He had a good life. He was loved. Don't feel bad."

"I've never lost someone close. I know it's going to change everything about me. Ma says it's death that gives your life a shape."

"Good words."

"Did they send you back to D.C. because of that political murder in San Diego?"

"Yes. Someone needs to draw some fire. It's going to be me."

"You mean get blamed?"

He looked at her and nodded.

"I read the headlines on the newsstand paper this morning and it said that ATF—see, I didn't say FAT, now, did I?—had something to do with the gun that killed the congressman. They showed a picture of the gun. And of course the congressman. Agent Bly said some things. And then at the San Diego bus station there was one of those TV news loops on and they had a story about the assassination, too. They showed the same gun. And they showed just a second or two of you talking into a microphone in a big room full of important people. And later, Bly. But the sound was off so I couldn't hear anything."

Hood felt his stomach tighten. He pictured Representative Grossly's florid mask of outrage and heard his offended voice. "That gun got away from us during an undercover op four years ago."

"So you get blamed?"

"I get to be the face of blame."

"Like put you all over TV and magazines?"

"That's possible."

"I'm *trying* to get on TV and magazines."

He smiled and for the first time today it seemed authentic. "I remember you saying that you wanted to be a model or star. Or a nurse."

"I read for a part in a play last week. And I got it, Charlie. I *got* it! I'm still pinching myself. The director's a chick and she said she was going to work my black eye and the split lips into the character. 'Cause Curley's wife is a sexualized object and is punished for it. And since my face'll heal up before opening night, she's going to have makeup do me up like it just happened. So I can thank Skull for getting me the part."

Hood managed his second authentic smile in a row. "I'm happy for you, Mary Kate."

"Maybe you'll come see me."

"Maybe I will."

"I don't make any money. It's not an Equity play."

"Maybe it will lead to something better."

"Enough about me. How we gonna trap Clint?"

Hood turned the monitor her way. "Here's the Trailways schedule. We want him to pick you up in daylight hours so we can see what we're doing. We're in luck. There are arrivals through Las Vegas Monday through Saturday, ten thirty every morning."

"Maybe I could actually take a bus into San Diego. Make it more real and convincing?"

"I don't want you anywhere near the Greyhound station or Clint Wampler."

"You're a good boss, Charlie."

"Tell him Saturday, ten thirty. Five days from today. Less people downtown." Hood copied the Greyhound schedule on a noisy old printer and circled the Saturday ten thirty arriving from Las Vegas, like she was too dumb to remember it. He pulled a San Diego *Thomas Guide* from a desk drawer. "Let's go to the conference room. I want to bring Dale and Janet and Robert in on this—we can get your lines right and figure how this should work."

"I don't stay in any room with Dale. It's him or me and you can choose."

"He's not a bad guy. You embarrassed him."

"I embarrassed *him*? And he's not a bad guy? Don't you tell me how to interpret character, Charlie Hood."

"How about this? We'll leave him out but he's still not a bad guy."

"You just gotta win, don't you? Even if it's just a little something, you still have to win it. I understand that. I'm the same damned annoying way!"

It was dark by the time the meeting was over. Her shoes echoed faintly with Hood's on the marble of the ATF hallway. On his way past the security station, Hood rapped his knuckles lightly on Oscar's desk, so Mary Kate did, too. The big man offered her a withering look, then a smile. Under a deep purple sky they walked from the lobby to the intersection near the bus stop and she said good-bye and could tell by his expression that he felt bad leaving her there alone.

She buttoned up her coat and headed toward the old part of Buenavista because she'd heard the Mexican food at Club Fandango was the best. Of course she'd invited Hood and the two agents to go with her and of course they'd turned her down. There was a line with these people, she had concluded: They could help you if you could help them but that didn't establish anything at all personal. And Charlie Hood maybe didn't have a woman in his life but that didn't mean he had one flicker of interest in her. An SUV came up behind her going kind of fast and she moved over and turned her back to it and watched the thing whiz past, brand-new, beautiful blue paint job, looked like it was right off the showroom floor.

She climbed a gradual rise and the streets turned from asphalt to cobblestone and became narrow. The buildings grew older and somehow more interesting, and although many were simple flat-roofed rectangles, many were built with ornate arched doorways and cool-looking mud-brick adobe walls. One building had a plaque outside about it being in the National Historic Register because a man born there had distinguished himself in the War of 1812 and later become the vice president of the United States. There were iron streetlamps on curved stanchions that looked a hundred years old but she was pretty sure there wasn't electricity in Buenavista in 1913, so maybe these were added. Their light had a nice glow that showed off the crooked stone street. Above, the sky was the same dark desert blue as that swanko SUV, with small stars just peeking out then ducking back behind the darkness again like they were shy.

She entered a wide, flat circle with a beautiful old church and big shade trees and people sitting and walking. She liked the way that many of the young men were dressed, not like in Russell County at all—all hoodies and jeans with their butt cracks showing—and she saw that many were Mexicans, which reminded her that Tony, her boss at work who had Mexican blood in him, was always groomed well and dressed nicely compared to most of his Anglo counterparts. She had read that Latino American men spent twice the money on personal grooming products as other American men, for whatever this was worth. She read another plaque, which identified the church and explained that this area, called a *zócalo* in Spanish, was the center of Buenavista social life until the city had been divided into two sides along the border in 1848. Since then the Mexican side of Buenavista had built its own *zócalo* while this place remained a part of California and the United States.

She came to a marketplace where most of the merchants were packing up their wares for the day. She wondered why they moved so unhurriedly. Under the strands of tiny twinkling lights lay tables of big yellow grapefruit and tomatoes and oranges and lemons and avocados, flats of chilies, piles of onions and garlic. She was suddenly very hungry.

Soon she came to the lighted plaza with its restaurants and clubs and shops and galleries. Behind the buildings the mountain rose and above the mountain the moon was buttoned, not quite half full now, but very clear and bright. She walked past a bunch of expensive cars and trucks and a large muscular doorman and into Club Fandango. It was dark and reminded her of a saloon in a Western movie. A pretty hostess greeted her and suggested she dine in the cantina if she was dining alone.

The cantina was nearly empty this early and Mary Kate got her own booth. She ordered a margarita and the cocktail waitress asked for ID, so she presented the good fake that Skull had gotten for her so they could drink in public. Skull. Seems like a thousand years ago, she thought. What on earth did I see in you? Even with the straw, the salt on the margarita burnt her lip cuts, but only slightly, so she lifted the glass and muttered a toast to herself and drank the whole thing down in two gulps. She caught a glimpse of herself in a mirror and thought she looked goofy sitting there alone with a beat-up face and an empty margarita glass. So she ordered another, then her *arroz con camarones diablo* arrived. Even though the dish was already "of the devil," she had asked for extra spicy and indeed it was, an inferno of flavors and textures. It was hot enough to make her nose run and her whole lips burn, not just the cuts. She enjoyed it so much she ordered another. The waitress admitted it was her favorite dish also and brought her a complimentary margarita to help cool the fires.

Later back in San Diego she tiredly stepped off the bus and started the longish walk to her hotel. Her feet hurt. A light rain was falling and it was cold but nothing like Russell County cold. On Fourth, another blue SUV came sweeping past her, new and sparkling like the one in Buenavista. Even in the dark the cobalt blue was undershot with a wonderful metallic glow. Same truck twice in one night, seventy-five miles apart? Or two different vehicles, just a coincidence and nothing to worry about? *Two different*, she thought—*get a grip, girl*. She cut across the Gaslamp District and ducked into the Rack to find Tony and some of the other Kentucky Fried Chicken employees. They invited her for beers and no-slop eight-ball and she held her own against them, having spent some hours at this with Skull and Peltz and weird Wampler. All the while she kept her eye on the street outside, but the blue SUV never came by again and that was fine with her. Tony and Luis walked her to the Windsor Arms and when she got up to her room and looked out the window they were gone and a cobalt blue Explorer passed by, brand-new, no plates on yet, windows so dark she had no hope of seeing who was behind the wheel. Could be J-Lo or John Steinbeck or the man in the moon, she thought.

She turned off her lights and sat back from the window in a comfortable old chair with the bedspread over her and called Hood. He wasn't angry and didn't sound sleepy even though it was after one in the morning, and he kept her on the line awhile, talking her down in his calm, one-thing-at-a-time voice. She said her first thought on seeing such a truck three times was Clint Wampler, but he'd just gotten the new Sebring, so that didn't make sense. And she'd been fooling Clint real good over the phone. How could he know she was there? Hood was quiet for a moment, then he said she should file a police report in the morning—it was good to be on the record with things like this. He made her tell him several times exactly where she'd seen the vehicle. Then he asked who knew she was living in San Diego and she had to think about that one because really, she'd only told her mom and one brother back home, and of course Amy and Victor in L.A. knew because she'd stayed with them while she found a job. Hood wanted to know if any of them knew she was at the Windsor

Arms or where she worked. Yes, she said, she'd given them all her new address, and told them about KFC, too. Not a single call or text back, however. Hood seemed very serious about every detail and very concerned that she'd told her family these things. He asked her to text him numbers for her mother and brother, and for Amy and Victor, just as soon as they were done talking.

"Do not forget."

"I'm not an imbecile, Charlie."

"I know. But you're tired and worried."

"What if it's Clint and now he knows I've been here all along, leading him on? And what if he saw me going in and out of the ATF office, and he puts me together with you? You told me he was furious at you, for treating him like a moron and smashing his finger. He'll be triple furious if he knows we're a team."

"That's what we'll find out, Mary Kate."

"I like it when you say my name. Please talk to me now as an equal." He asked about dinner and laughed when she said it was so good she'd eaten two. He asked about the play she was going to be in, and he said he'd always liked *Of Mice and Men*, and that he'd seen the countryside in California where the story was set. They talked about how her work at KFC was going, and after a while she felt like this was a conversation with a friend or relative. The SUV did not return. After she hung up, she got the numbers from her phone and her tattered address book, then settled back in the chair facing the window and texted them to Hood. She looked out at the street after every few entries. The rain looked like the tinsel you'd put on a Christmas tree. Two hours later she woke up with the bedspread pulled up tight and her phone on the floor.

36

The next morning Hood arrived early for work, parked in the semi-secure tenants' lot, and pulled his war bag from the front seat of the Charger. He set it on the roof while he got his coat on and locked up, then used his reflection in the car window to adjust his felt fedora and snug his tie. He was wearing his best navy power suit and highly polished black Allen Edmonds cap-toes to ward off the sense of defeat that had hounded him since the death of his father and the OGR hearing. As he approached the stairs, a woman with a large microphone and a man with a video camera were waiting for him just outside the small lobby of the elevator bank. He recognized the reporter. The man was already shooting and the woman surged into Hood's airspace with a flourish of hair and lipstick. "ATF Agent Charlie Hood, I'm Theresa Brewer with Fox News in L.A. How are you today?"

"A little early to tell."

"What *can* you tell us about the gun allegedly used to kill Congressman Scott Freeman in San Diego last Saturday?"

"That's not our investigation."

"But you testified to Congress earlier this week about the gun."

"It's an automatic machine pistol made by Pace Arms of Orange County." Hood pulled the fedora brim low and stepped past them into the elevator lobby. But the woman followed him and the videographer was still shooting.

"Is it true that you personally *visited* the accused assassin, Lonnie Rovanna, just five days before he murdered Congressman Freeman?"

"I interviewed him as part of an ongoing investigation."

"What were you investigating?"

"I can't comment."

"Is it true that ATF lost track of one thousand such weapons in a botched investigation in two thousand ten?"

"It wasn't botched. We got outmaneuvered."

"But the guns went into Mexico, correct?"

"We believe so."

"And now, apparently, at least one has come back to kill a United States congressman."

Hood hustled up the stairs to the second-story ATF offices. The steel steps made a ringing sound that echoed in the concrete stairwell. He heard Theresa Brewer's footsteps behind him. "Representative Darren Grossly accused ATF of 'irresponsible actions' regarding these automatic weapons. He said the Department of Justice is, at the highest levels, quote, 'trying to cover up these actions by stonewalling' his investigation. Is this true?"

Hood stepped onto the first floor landing and turned to face the journalist. "I testified. I didn't stonewall. Have a nice day."

"Did you act alone?"

"We always work in teams. Good-bye. I'm going to go to work now."

"Before you testified, did your superiors at ATF ask you to protect their superiors? Maybe even the attorney general himself?"

"Don't be silly." Hood tipped his hat and unlocked the ATF suite with his nametag chip. Dale Yorth glanced at him from the watercooler in the hallway. Theresa Brewer was asking another question as the heavy door locked behind Hood. He made it to his cubicle, aimlessly enraged, his heart beating hard.

Yorth soon stood looking down at Hood over the low fabric partitions of the workspace. "Fox News?"

"They must have seen me on C-Span."

"So did everybody else. I'm so sorry about this, Charlie. Can I come in?"

Yorth sat next to Hood's desk in the crowded cubicle. He had a slip of paper in his hand. "I just got off the phone with San Diego. Frank's gotten interview requests from *The New York* and *Los Angeles Times*, *The Wall Street Journal*, *Time* . . ." He looked down at the paper. "Well . . . I couldn't write fast enough. They all want to know about the Love Thirty-twos and they all want interviews with you. Soriana referred them to Washington but you know damned well they'll be back. That *Union-Tribune* story yesterday really caught fire. Shit. Hold on." Yorth pulled his cell, checked the number and answered, then was quiet for a long while. "Yes, sir. Okay. Now that's a damned shame. He's here now. Yes, sir, I will. No, sir, he won't."

He hung up and shook his head. "Lansing just let IA loose on you, Charlie. You're officially jammed as of right now. ATF has to show that something is being done. So I'm to put you on administrative leave. The leave is paid—you just have to stay home and be accounted for. In a way it's good. It will let you dodge these reporters. You know how it is—they'll lose interest in a few days. Sorry, but this is direct from Lansing."

"Can I keep working?"

"AL is fully paid."

"It's not about the *pay*. It's about Wampler. For all we know he's still got that Stinger and he intends to use it."

"Do what you need to do, Charlie. Bust Wampler's ass. But I don't want to know about it. Just pick up the phone when IA calls. Be there. Act good. I'm on your side."

"I'm taking the laptop."

"I don't hear you."

Hood went to his office and called Mary Kate's parents and siblings. Only her brother knew of Clint Wampler at all, and he knew very little—just some badass punk from a few towns over. But they all admitted to having told friends and neighbors about Mary Kate's move to California. Her mother had to inform the school district, that was the law. Hood realized that scores of people in Russell County could know she'd gone to L.A. and the ones who knew her might assume she'd gone to stay with her old friend, Amy. All it took was one of them to be an acquaintance of Wampler and the circuit was complete.

When Hood reached Amy by phone in L.A. she sounded vague and dismissive. Hood smelled fear. It took a few minutes of earnest cajoling but she finally admitted that Clint Wampler had showed up at her apartment when Victor was working. He'd put his hand on her throat and demanded to know where Mary Kate Boyle had got to and said if she went to the cops he'd come back and strangle her and leave her for Victor to explain. *I'm real afraid*, she said. *Is Mary Kate okay? I shoulda called the cops. I shoulda, I shoulda.*

Hood told Mary Kate by phone, and for the first time in the several hours he'd spent with her, she was temporarily speechless.

"Where are you now?"

"Walking to work."

"Are you close?"

"Yeah, another two blocks."

"Good. Once you're inside, don't leave. Make sure you aren't alone there."

"Hard to be alone, with a crew of four."

"I'm going to make arrangements with a motel we work with in San Diego. It's a decent place. I'll send a cab for you at work and it will bring you there. Figure about one hour. Don't go back to the Windsor Arms. Don't pack. Don't panic. Just do your job and get into that taxi when it arrives. You're going to vanish for a few days, Mary Kate. Be invisible. Can you do that?"

"That hick bastard. I'm gonna lose my job and my room because of him? I got rehearsal later, you know."

"You'll get back everything. Right now, just stay invisible."

"I don't scare easy but he gives me the genuine creeps, Charlie."

Hood read the news to ATF Buenavista: The crazy with the Stinger was on to Mary Kate Boyle, and probably on to them, too.

An hour later Yorth scouted the parking lot for reporters, then Hood locked the laptop in the trunk of his Charger and climbed in. The car bounced into the bright sunlight of Buenavista. He drove toward Castro Ford listening to the reports of rain in San Diego and he looked out at the endless blue sky overhead. He felt betrayed but free. ATF would fire him soon and loudly, he thought: damage control. It was a perilous feeling to know how very small he was within the bureaucracy, how unimportant and discardable, a single-use man. He wondered if the Los Angeles County Sheriff's Department would can him, too.

He drove around to the rear of the dealership lot and parked in his usual place. He fished his camera from behind his seat and brought the new-car intake area into focus. All three rolling doors were up and he could see two men working on a white Taurus. There were three other vehicles waiting for attention but the dazzling cobalt-blue Explorer was not one of them. His heart fell a little. He heard a Tejano-style song coming from the prep men's radio.

Mary Kate called and told him she had walked right past KFC and checked into a hotel of her own damn choice, using cash and a fake name, and Clint was nowhere to be seen. Hood took the name and address and told her have food delivered and she said she'd already bought enough stuff at the market to last two days. She had a microwave and a pint-size fridge. And she'd talked to Tony at KFC, too, and he said he'd cover for her, no problem, just come back when she could and she'd have her old job. He'd offered to help but she hadn't told him squat about what was really going on.

"Don't rehearse tonight."

"It's an evening rehearsal and I'm going."

"He'll cruise downtown when you don't go back to the Windsor. Easy to spot you. Don't be a fool."

"I'm nobody's fool, Charlie Hood. Not even yours."

She hung up on him. Hood dialed but she didn't take the call. He drove around front and parked near Castro's silver Flex. The salesmen eyed him with a new humorlessness and Hood figured he'd been made. He headed across the lot to where the new SUVs were waiting but no salesman bothered to follow. He walked the rows of Explorers but the one he'd seen in the prep area—much like the one described by Mary Kate Boyle—was not there. He circled back and stepped inside the showroom to find that the display cars had been changed. He paused to check out the new black F-150 outfitted for off-road, a pink Fiesta, and a burgundy-colored Flex. The pickup stirred him.

"Hey, it's Charlie Hood, ATF's finest." Castro came toward him, tossing one of the promotional Castro Ford soccer balls from hand to hand. "Come back to buy that Taurus?"

"I had my eyes on a cobalt blue Explorer but now it's gone."

A shadow of doubt crossed Castro's face. "That's what happens to cars. Kind of like guns. They just vanish sometimes. I saw you for a few seconds on TV and I thought, man, I'm trying to sell that guy a Ford. Congress! You're a mover and shaker, Charlie. You should be thinking Lincoln Town Car, not Taurus *or* Explorer."

"You sold it?"

"To a very nice soccer mom." Castro spun the soccer ball on one finger, as if this confirmed his statement.

"Can you get another one?"

"Sure. But I can sell you a black one you'd like even better. Look, you've got black shoes and a black belt. Black is what a secret agent should drive." Castro shot the soccer ball into the big bin of balls over by the Fiesta. "Of course, since you're government you've got that Charger for free, right? So why do you need to buy an Explorer?"

"I need a car of my own."

Castro studied him. "No. I don't want to sell to you. Never thought I'd hear myself say that. What I want is for you to get out of my dealership. You proved on TV that feds are idiots. I don't sell Fords to idiots. Ford Motor Company didn't take fed bailouts either, like Chrysler. You deserve that piece-of-junk, government-subsidized wop Charger." Castro barged through the front door and stood with his hands on his hips, barking out at the salesmen. "Hey, men! You see this guy drive up again, call the cops, okay? Tell them Israel Castro needs their help with a trespasser!"

Hood tipped his hat to Castro and burned rubber on his way out. Down Interstate 8 he tried again and got Mary Kate to pick up. "Keep inside, Mary Kate. Please. And call nine-one-one if something happens—if you even *suspect* that something is happening. Tell them you're part of a federal investigation and you're afraid for your life. Then call me. I'm asking you to do this."

"I didn't think you cared."

"Don't go to rehearsal. Keep the deadbolt thrown and don't leave the room."

"I know what to—"

"Don't leave the room."

"Okay! Okay! Fine. I'll sit right here at this rickety little table and wait for a handsome man with diamonds in his teeth to come rescue me."

Hood said nothing, watched the ocotillo flashing past.

"You'd at least do that for me, Charlie. Right?"

"I would do that. Please, Mary Kate, stay low."

"Charlie, I'm a blacksnake crawlin' through the berry patch."

He drove up the steep dirt road toward his home. Cresting the rise he saw his home and the familiar carport and the Fox News van and Erin standing at the open front door, talking to Theresa Brewer while Gabe Reyes yelled and waved at the video guy, who was backing up slowly but shooting. The dogs bounded around, barking. Hood gunned the Charger and skidded to a stop in the gravel. The video shooter swung away from Gabe and captured Hood's brisk advance.

"Here's Agent Hood just now," said Theresa Brewer.

"No, Charlie!" called Erin. "It's okay!"

"Be cool, Charlie!" yelled Reyes. "I got this."

Hood was not only tall but fast and he covered the ground to the videographer before the man could get the camera down. Hood twisted it away and fumbled distractedly for the delete buttons as Daisy and Minnie herded and barked at the cameraman.

"These dogs bite?" he asked, backpedaling.

Erin waddled from the house wearing a loose muumuu, white hibiscus on a red background, both hands under her giant middle for support. "It's *okay*! I asked them to leave and *they were leaving*, Charlie!"

"And *you're* committing a crime," Brewer told Hood. "You're abridging the constitutional rights of a free press."

"You're trespassing, lady. Get out now."

Beth spilled out of the house wrapped in a bedspread, hair wild and eyes squinting, freshly wrenched from sleep.

"Who are you?" Theresa Brewer asked.

"I'm a woman who resents being awakened by trespassers. You should be ashamed of yourselves. Charlie, can you make these people go away?"

By then the dogs had the cameraman backed against the low stone wall. Hood strode over and called them off to no avail and gave up on the delete. He two-handed the recorder into the shooter's chest and the man managed to hang on to it and not fall backwards over the rocks. Hood dragged Daisy and Minnie by their collars into the house and slammed the door on them. He could hear them barking behind the heavy wood and adobe. The video guy ran for the van and Brewer scrambled away also, reaching back with her microphone to catch the last of the chaos. Reyes was on his cell phone, and Hood figured he was calling in his old buddies on Buenavista PD. Beth clutched the bedspread at her neck with one hand and helped Erin back up the steps to the front door. The Fox News van made a dramatic gravel-spraying turn.

"Don't miss *Fox News at Eleven!*" Theresa Brewer called out. *"I love your music, Erin!"* When Beth opened the front door, Daisy and Minnie bolted after the van in a yelping frenzy and chased it down the hill.

Hood looked for Erin's reaction. She was steadying herself on Beth's shoulder and looking down toward her feet. "Guys? My water just broke?"

37

Hood watched through a window as Dr. David delivered Thomas Firth Jones. Beth assisted in the birth. It took nearly two hours, but when it was over, Beth held up a robust-looking baby boy. Hood's eyes misted over when he saw Erin's face, dazed, exhausted but joyful. He'd never seen an expression like that on her before. Beth looked at him through the glass, hopeful and proud of her work. Hood thought he saw a glimmer of *maybe us someday?* in Beth's smile and in spite of the things that seemed to be collapsing upon him, the idea pleased him and he smiled back.

Thomas Firth Jones himself was seven-plus pounds, ruddy and wrinkled and doubtful. *Doubting Thomas*, thought Hood. His eyes were shut tight and his fists were clenched up at his mouth and the plastic bracelet was large upon his small wrist. His hair was fine and sparse, light brown. He didn't cry much after the shock of being born was over. He seemed to be recuperating. Hood wondered if he was even more spent than his mother. Thomas was outfitted in a white blanket and a small blue cap to fight off the chill of his brave new world, and he looked perfect in Erin's arms.

Hood stayed at the hospital, looking in on her but trying not to be a nuisance. For some reason the birth of Thomas made him think of his father, but the memory was not lugubrious or sad. The death of Douglas and the birth of Thomas, having come so close together, were just two more reminders that you get life for a while, then it goes somewhere else. So make the most of it. *Put that on my headstone*, thought Hood. Douglas would be buried in two days.

A couple of hours later Bradley, wearing his LASD uniform, came running down the hallway toward Hood and braked to a stop outside Erin's room. "We need to talk, Charlie."

"Ready when you are."

Bradley took a deep breath and stepped inside. Hood waited awhile, then looked in. Bradley had worked himself into the bed beside Erin, and Thomas was asleep between them. Erin was asleep, too. Bradley, up on one elbow, looked at Hood with unusual gravity.

They sat at a plastic patio table out in the hospital courtyard. The late afternoon was cool and they were alone. Bradley's uniform was crisp and clean, but he looked anxious, dark around the eyes and unkempt. "I'm a father."

"Congratulations."

"I feel different. Everybody said I would and I do. But not how I thought it would be."

"Talk."

"I partnered with Mike. It's a simple oath and he accepted. I did it to get his help. It seemed to have worked. Certain aspects of my life started to flourish again. Then I realized he wants Thomas. I'm in way over my head. You understand how dangerous Mike is?"

Hood lifted his hair to expose the knife scar. Bradley eyed it long and hard, and Hood saw fear in his young eyes. Bradley scooted his chair up closer and spoke in a whisper. "He hung around Mom and me for years. Since before I was even aware of him. When I got older he'd haunt the L.A. club scene when Erin was playing and I was there. He always knew things about people. Sometimes he seemed to know things he really couldn't know. Then he started coming up with things he shouldn't *have*—pictures of himself at a hanging that took place over a hundred years ago. And a bulletproof vest that he claimed once belonged to Joaquin Murrieta—and it really was old enough to have belonged to him. Mike and Owens gave it to us as a wedding present. Isn't that touching? Years of weirdness like that. Then, a few weeks ago he shows me pictures of you and the Blowdown team surveilling me at Pace Arms with the Love Thirty-twos. And he's got video of you down in Yucatán, lugging that ransom money around for Armenta. It's all there—the jungle, Armenta's castle, Luna, the Mexican Army, even you in his apartment in Veracruz. He can't *have* this stuff, Charlie. But he does! Get this: He can actually read my mind. He's done it more than once. Word for word, the exact words, the inflection perfect. And get this, too: He's got a woman trapped in a mineshaft way out in the desert above Adelanto. Beatrice. He says she's an angel— one of his enemies—and he's had her down there in the mine for ninety-six years. Ninety-six years! Mike says devils and angels live ten to twelve times longer than men and you can't kill them. They don't have to eat or drink. I heard Beatrice's voice. She wasn't hysterical and didn't seem afraid. Apparently, they pull this kind of shit on one another all the time. She pleaded with me to resist him and save my soul. Mike threw her meat sticks and beer and teased her. At first it blew my mind. Then later, he said something that made my scalp crawl. He said I should take Thomas away from Erin and raise him with Owens."

"No court would let you take him from Erin."

"What if there *is* no Erin? I'm afraid for them, Charlie."

"You should be."

Bradley nodded and stared off. Hood saw the tremble of his chin and the wet shine of his eyes and he saw how much it hurt Bradley to have placed them—his wife and his just-born son—so far beyond his ability to protect them. It was the first time Hood had seen Bradley put anyone truly ahead of himself. "God, I'm a fuckup."

"What is Mike trying to do to me?" asked Hood.

"He wants to ruin you."

"Why?"

"Ruin and chaos delight him. He told me that you *came up in the net* through Mom. He chooses promising people to befriend and use. He chose me because of my lineage. You saw Joaquin's head in the barn, so you know what I'm talking about. Other people, just good regular ones, he torments for the fun of it and to stay busy during slow times. People like you."

"And the Ozburns. They were good people, Bradley. He tortured and destroyed them, without ever touching either of them. Is Grossly one of Mike's partners?"

"I don't think so."

"Did he point Grossly at me?"

"Did he ever. First Mike posed as a doctor to give Rovanna one of the Love Thirty-twos. Then he used 'dream insertions.' He said he inserted the same dream into Rovanna twice a night for three nights running. That's the maximum, or the waking mind devalues the dream and it will soon be forgotten. In the dream, you gave Rovanna the weapon and told him to defend himself and his ideals with it. Rovanna told the cops he got the gun from you. Mike tipped Grossly through a friend in Washington, and Grossly's office pried loose the police interview tapes."

Hood thought of Rovanna's terror of Dr. Walter Freeman and lobotomies. Freeman inserts orbitoclast. Finnegan inserts dream. "Where did Grossly get the interior photos of Pace Arms and the Love Thirty-twos?"

"From Mike."

"But Mike was in a full body cast at Imperial Mercy Hospital when those pictures were shot."

"Owens took them."

Hood remembered the starstruck smiles and the puckered lips of the Pace Arms gunsmiths—hamming it up for the pretty woman with the camera. *Owens*, he thought, *shilling for Mike again*.

Bradley looked at Hood with a punished expression. He wiped his face with his hands and took a deep breath. "I did more than give Theresa Brewer your home address. I gave Dez all the stuff Mike had of you down in Yucatán. Mike shot some of it from a little bi-wing airplane. I shot some of it myself. One of Mike's friends in the Mexican Army, an officer, contributed some video of the raid on Armenta's castle. Owens shot some."

"And you're not present in a single frame or image of what you gave to Dez."

"Correct. Mike edited me out. I've told CIB a thousand times I wasn't there—I was tarpon fishing a few miles away. So long as Caroline Vega and Jack Cleary back me up, I'm solid. I look innocent and it looks like you trafficked a million dollars in drug profits to a Mexican drug lord."

Hood wondered at the depths of betrayal in Mike and in Bradley. "I did it for Erin."

Bradley nodded. "I know. I know. Hood . . . I'll do what's right. I'm ready to do what's right."

"Start by telling Erin the truth."

"Like what, Charlie?"

"Everything. Start with Murrieta. Then tell her about the cash you've been delivering to the North Baja Cartel for the last four years. It took me awhile to put it all together. But I investigated those Lancaster murders back in oh-nine, the North Baja Cartel cash couriers. I found out that Coleman Draper and Terry Laws murdered them to take over the delivery route. Good money, short hours. After Coleman killed Laws, he took on another partner. I didn't suspect it was you until you put a bullet in Coleman. At first, I thought you were watching my back. Then I realized you were taking over the cash run for yourself. You doubled your take without him."

Bradley looked vaguely sickened. He glanced at Hood, then away.

"Something had to explain the way you lived, Bradley. Everybody saw that you had too much. Erin told me once that you always worked Friday nights and Saturday mornings so you could spend Sundays and Mondays with her—she never gigged on Mondays. She was proud that you'd do that. But a friend in payroll told me you've only worked four Friday P.M. or Saturday A.M. shifts in the whole time you've been a deputy. So, Friday nights had to be the Baja nights."

Bradley sighed but still didn't look Hood in the eye. "Yeah, those were the Baja nights."

"Tell Erin about the thousand Love Thirty-twos you sold to Herredia. Tell her about the deal you made with Mike. Tell her about last week, when you brought cocaine across the border in new Mexican-made Fords. The ones you delivered to Castro. I've got *you* on camera for that one."

Bradley groaned.

"Part of her putting herself back together is sorting out your lies from the truth. You have no idea how much trust she wasted on you. So help her out, Bradley. Tell Erin who you are and what you've done. She knows the basics already."

Bradley sat back and looked down at the plastic table. Hood saw the flush on his face. "If I do that, I'll lose her. Then I won't have anything."

"Sure you will—you'll have that little streak of decency you were born with. Grow some, Bradley. It's time. And help me take down Mike."

"How?"

"Owens is the key."

38

Later Bradley sat near Erin and Thomas as they slept. He listened to the hum of Imperial Mercy Hospital and looked at his wife and son and wondered how he could feel so far from them when they were actually just a few feet away. But now that his small family was real, just when his direction should be clear, he feared that he would lose them. Maybe to Mike Finnegan. Maybe not. But lose them he would, when Erin learned the truth. He pictured a cat trying to hold on to a wet glass globe, claws scratching for a purchase that could not last.

He watched them sleep and wondered what it would be like to confess it all to her—what he had done, his history, his ill-gotten treasures, his deal with a devil. Was it really time? *Grow some. Tell Erin what you've done.* Then Erin would complete her banishment of him. And if Hood told Dez the truth of what had happened in Yucatán, the LASD would certainly fire and possibly prosecute him. He imagined prison, and what it would be like when he got out, trying to be a weekend dad, a man not with a wife and son but a man with mere visitation rights to what had once been his. He could not convincingly imagine such a life.

In the evening Bradley took the elevator down to the lobby and walked out to the parking lot. The sun had set and the eastern sky was purple and dotted with bashful young stars. He fished the pack of smokes from his sock—deputies were not allowed to carry tobacco products while in uniform—and lit it with a match. He called Owens and told her the news.

"Is he beautiful?"

"He's very beautiful."

"Does he look like you?"

"He doesn't really look like either of us."

"I am so happy for you. I am proud. You'll be a strong and good father. And Erin will be a wonderful mother."

"I want that."

"I'll tell Mike that Thomas Firth Jones is now among us. He'll be glad to hear this."

"We need to talk. Face to face. No Mike. It's important, Owens."

"He told me what you two were discussing at the convention before you made your exit. What he said about me is unflattering but true. I can be traded."

"Can he be traded?"

She was silent for a long beat. "That's a dangerous idea, Bradley."

"Hear me out."

"Name the time and place."

39

Wampler stood on the deck of his Imperial Beach apartment, peacoat buttoned, considering the Pacific. It looked heavy and dangerous, big, frothy slabs of ocean banging against one another, all mixed up. The wind huffed and howled and two skinny kids in black wetsuits paddled around. Looking to his left, he could see Tijuana with its first lights of evening coming on. The property manager had told him that this complex was the last one south on the California coast—next stop, Mexico, just a few hundred yards away. She said the river between the two countries was filled with sewage and poison and don't go in it. She also said the new wall and the bad economy were keeping a lot of the Mexicans out, but keep your apartment and garage locked or your stuff will get ripped off, no doubt.

Wampler stared out at TJ. He liked the idea that he could walk down the shoreline dragging his new kayak behind him, then paddle it across a tidal channel and just minutes later be in Mexico, far beyond the reach of American cops. Not a bad feature for a man who'd murdered an ATF agent and was now taking down scores of thousands of dollars selling Stinger missiles to Mexican cartels, dollars that would be sealed in plastic bags in the hold of the kayak, along with a gun or two. His emergency exit plan.

Clint took a deep breath and tasted the thick salt air. He felt a shrewd pride that he had been able to pull himself out of poverty from one of the poorest places in America and make something of himself. Mr. Clinton Stewart Wampler regarded his Pacific Ocean.

Mary Kate would have dug this, he thought. He'd kept her in mind as he rented it. Beach right here. Romantic Mexico right next door.

Her own furnished and clean apartment, with a refrigerator that wasn't loud and didn't drip, a gas heater instead of a stinking electric plug-in, windows covered with blinds rather than plywood and aluminum foil like Skull's flop. Sunshine three hundred days a year.

Too bad that Mary Kate was now in for a slightly modified program. He pictured her cute little face and was still pissed that Skull had messed it up for him. But even more pissed at her for sneaking around Buenavista with ATF agent Glitter Gums Charlie Hooper, all the while pretending she was back in Russell County getting ready to come be his girl. Pissed wasn't even the word for it. Clint thought they needed a new fuckin' word for what those two made him feel. Sweet revenge it would be. A package deal.

He got a sixer of premium beer from the stainless steel fridge and went downstairs to the garage. He used the remote to open the door and stepped inside, then closed it quickly so as not to advertise the new Ford Explorer.

It was beautiful. It was part of his reward for the last seven Stingers. Unfortunately, the cobalt blue beauty was also of interest to Charlie Hooper, according to Castro. And therefore of interest to every other law enforcement agency in America, Clint had to figure. So he had bought a cheap used Kia Something or Other—cash, private party—for his day-to-day transportation needs. Parked it on the street.

Now he used the Ford key fob to unlock the Explorer and he climbed in and pulled the door closed. God, the smell. He turned on the premium sound. The fancy subscription radio had a whole station dedicated to good, hard, head-banging death metal, which was what he liked. Israel Castro had had his guys install a subwoofer in the back and it truly throbbed. No charge. Clint broke off the first beer and set the rest on the passenger floor mat, not on the milk-white leather. He ran his hand over the seat instead and thought of MK and felt the music rattling his bones. Someday he'd get to drive this thing wherever and whenever he wanted. He checked his look in the rearview and was startled by the self-shorn and self-dyed hair, a styling disaster of divots and whorls and wrong angles and flubbed-up cuts, all shiny white. *Platinum Frost.* He patted the mess but it did no good. Truly, he didn't care.

A nap and three beers later he drove the Kia out to Alpine where he met two of Castro's men in a casino parking lot—Clint's choice of places, and far from Imperial Beach because Castro and his men were getting harder to trust. But the money was there and right. It was heavy and packed in two cloth shopping bags, and Wampler said not one word to the bagmen other than "hey" and "see ya." The deal was for four more Stingers at $35,000 each. Way up I-15 north he got off at Gopher Canyon, used the darkness to break off his $44,000 and stash it on the backseat floorboard.

By ten, he was in Fallbrook, where he forked over $96,000 for four more Stingers. Skip and his muscular buddy loaded the crates into the trunk and that was that. Clint stopped at the pay phone he'd used before and called Mary Kate. He'd made his plan and it was important to keep up appearances. "You coming into San Diego tomorrow morning or not, MK?"

"Yes. The bus is on time. So here I come."

"Where you at right now?" Snuggling up to Charlie Hooper? Runnin' your little pink tongue over them diamonds?

"Just left El Paso. What's the matter with you?"

"What is the matter with me, Mary Kate?"

"You don't sound very happy is all."

"I got a lot to deal with."

"Everybody does."

"What everybody *don't* have is a goddamned army after 'em, like I do. What you're gonna do is get off that bus and walk across the street. It's Sixth Street, I looked it up on a map. And then you're gonna stand right there and wait for me."

"What if it's raining?"

"It don't rain in San Diego."

"Weatherman says big storm tonight."

"Then use an umbrella, MK—shit, how hard you going to make this? It's like we're already married and sick of each other."

"We're about as far from married as two people can get."

"Just get to San Diego and we'll figure it out."

"Don't leave me standing in the rain, Clint."

"Do what I said, *Mary Kate.*"

"Now you sound mad."

"Maybe you'll cheer me up."

"Remember this is about me visiting California, not me visiting you."

"Over and out."

Wampler hung up and drove toward Jacumba to deliver the product to Castro. He felt humiliated by MK's betrayal, and infuriated by the arrogance she showed in thinking she had fooled him. For a few miles everything he saw through the windshield was outlined in red. Seeing red through the windshield of a goddamned Kia, he thought. He would put Mary Kate Boyle in her place. He looked forward to it. And really, what she had done to him gave him an advantage over Hooper, and Hooper was what he wanted most. By Lake Cuyamaca the red was gone and he had begun to feel that good cold clarity settling back over him.

This time the delivery was at Amigos, the restaurant Castro owned. Castro had told him it was out of the way and safe and to park around back by the kitchen Dumpsters. Clint pulled up and two dark burly men in white straw cowboy hats came from the kitchen toward the Kia. He let them get close, then fully extended his arm through the open window and pointed the semiauto at them. "El-stop-o right there-o, amigos." Clint smiled slightly as he heard the sound of their boots braking on the old asphalt. He saw Castro trot from the kitchen toward his men, then shove between them, his hands out beseechingly, shaking his head.

"Clint, you're going to get yourself killed for no reason someday. Just by being who you are."

"They look closer to being kilt than I do."

"They're our friends, Clint. Friends with money to spend. Man, that's quite a hairstyle."

Wampler did a fancy gunslinger twirl and retracted the pistol, though it was difficult with his arm-room constricted by the window. "Go to hell if you don't like it."

"I do like it."

"Maybe I'm a little on edge. I can't even drive my brand-new Explorer there's so many cops out there, all looking for me. But it's no problem going the speed limit in this Jap piece of shit."

"It's Korean and well built. Considering."

"Good—I'll make you a deal on it." He threw open the door and stepped out. The two big men regarded him without expression but Wampler caught the disdain in their eyes. He hit a button on the key fob and one of the men lifted the trunk lid. Clint thought again of Charlie Hooper and what he'd done to his finger with the trunk of the Charger. Hard to believe that Mary Kate had really teamed up with that diamond-toothed sonofabitch. How many ATF people worked in the Buenavista office? How many of them would be waiting for him at the Greyhound station tomorrow morning?

He raised the finger and looked at the dirty white tape around his fingertip. Soon as he changed the tape it was dirty again. Below the tape the finger swelled red and shiny and there were no visible wrinkles or marks because the skin was taut. And hot, he thought. It felt microwaved. Lucky he could still shoot with it. One of the Mexicans was looking at him and it took Clint some real willpower not to draw his gun again and shoot him.

When the two men had loaded the crates into the pickup truck

Wampler lugged out his $44,000 grocery bag from the back of the Kia and looked at the men. "You wanna do the windshield, go right ahead."

He followed Castro back into the noisy restaurant kitchen, then down a dark, short hallway and into a good-size office. It was furnished with futuristic leather-and-stainless-steel sofas and chairs, a glass-topped desk, and an art painting that to Clint looked upside down.

"That thing worth any more'n the paint that's on it?" he asked, nodding at a framed swirl of thick red and black, lighted by its very own beam from a hidden ceiling lamp.

"I took it in trade. Here." Castro sat behind the desk and produced two twinkling glasses and a bottle of Scotch. He filled each glass halfway and pushed one toward the open chair across from him. Clint set the money on the floor and, still standing, drank the Scotch, then clanked the glass back onto the desktop. He heard the Mexican music playing in the cantina and the distant ring of plates and flatware. "That finger of yours looks bad."

"Maybe you could get me a doctor that can make a house call and not rat me out."

"I can do that. But first I want you to listen to an idea. I'm going to reach into my coat now . . . can you handle it?"

"Try me."

Castro reached into a coat pocket, then set a tight roll of bills on the glass top of his desk. Clint picked it up and flipped it into the air and slapped it back to the desktop. "What's it for?"

"I'm sorry you can't drive the Explorer, but I'm glad you're not. I don't know how Hooper put you and it together. Maybe he was bluffing me. But it doesn't really matter, because you don't want ATF after you. And I don't want them after me."

Clint felt that cool, clear feeling starting to come back over him. "Everywhere I look there's some cop."

"You have a plan?"

"I have a plan nobody knows about."

"You've made yourself some good money the last few days."

"What did you tell Hooper about me and my new truck?"

"I told him to quit giving out guns to bad guys. Really got him on that one. I caught him on TV a few days ago, telling the government he let a thousand guns slip through his fingers."

"By his own self?"

"The whole stupid agency."

"How come soon as I buy a truck from you the feds show up?"

Castro nodded. "What I was thinking, Clint, is that you might want to get out of the country for a while. And I've come up with a good idea."

Clint looked down at forty-four thousand by his feet. All his. What a country this was. He'd make sure MK really got a full dose of understanding of what she had given up when she betrayed him, the most promising young outlaw in America. That might be very damned enjoyable. "I'm standing here waiting to hear this idea."

"I have friends in north Baja who have invited you down to stay with them. They would keep you out of sight. You could leave right here tonight, out of Jacumba. I know the tunnels and the trails and the patrol schedules. One word and I can have people waiting for you on the other side. Capable men. A few hours later you're in a guarded compound with more capable men. And some very lovely women."

"Same friends that buy my Stingers?"

Castro shrugged.

"They gotta be, since nobody is dumb enough to do business with two different cartels at the same time."

"No, you're right, Clint. Nobody is."

Wampler did some quick math, Castro style—offer babes and pennies to get the kid into capable hands, let the capable hands take his money and torture the Stinger phone numbers out of him, bury him in the Mexican desert and deal direct with the Pendleton wholesalers.

One less middleman. ATF goes away. Save dollars. Save steps. He wondered, *What makes people treat me like this?*

"If you leave now, I can have the Explorer retagged and sent down to you. At least you'd be able to drive it. That cash in the bag ought to last you very nicely south of the border. The roll on the table is just for the señoritas. You can come back in a year, when things have settled down."

"Why do you like me so much all a sudden?"

"I'd like to do business with you for the next twenty years, Clint. I can't do that if you're on death row for killing a federal agent."

"That's right. You can't. Mexico sounds good to me." Clint lifted the duffel in his injured left hand and swept the roll of bills into it. Castro smiled and held open the office door for him. "You first," said Clint.

"Fine with me."

"Why wouldn't it be?"

"That's another reason you should take a vacation—so I can get a break from your froggy bad attitude."

Clint followed Castro down the hallway and through the kitchen and into the back lot. They stood in the pale wash of a security light fixed high on the wall. Castro's beat-up truck waited by the Kia and the two stout Mexicans leaned against it, their arms crossed and their white hats tracking Clint in unison.

"Well, my amigos," said Castro. "You'll be going to Mexico to-night. As protectors of our fine young friend, Mr. Wampler."

Castro turned and spread his arms as if for an embrace and Clint dropped the bag and drew both guns from the peacoat and shot Castro in the heart with his right hand, braced his left and shot the others. Twice each, center shots, tightly grouped, a belch of chaos lasting only an instant. Clint felt disembodied. Through the smoke he watched one of the Mexicans writhe and fumble for his gun, and he thought, *It's amazing how fast I am.* He looked down at Castro flat on his back, trembling and gasping and staring wide-eyed at the moon or whatever you stare at your last few seconds.

He kept an eye on them as he loaded his money and the Stingers back into his Kia, then hit the road.

Back in Imperial Beach, Clint brought the missiles inside through the garage, then took a cold sixer to the deck and sat back in one of the chaise longues. In spite of the blustery cold, he felt warm on the inside, prosperous and accomplished, though still furious at MK for her betrayal and at Hooper for what he'd done to his finger. He peeled off the dirty white tape and threw the wad over the balcony to the sand. The cut oozed watery blood and pus again and the whole finger still throbbed every time his heart did. *Should have gotten Israel's house-call doctor before I shot him*, he thought. He wondered if he could risk an emergency clinic visit, what with his new hairdo, but decided not.

The beers went down swiftly and Clint listened to the waves and the quiet spaces between them, then the next crash and hiss. *Too bad about Mary Kate*, he thought, because this is the kind of time you want your honey around, when you've had a long hard day and you want to relax and feel good. The sky opened and the rain fell hard. He sat for a moment and watched the drops pelt the wet sand. He went inside and browsed the late-night porn titles on TV but what fun was it watching what you couldn't get none of?

He surfed way up in the channels where he never watched, clicking through them fast. It was hard to believe people paid to watch this stuff. Junk jewelry and online college courses and something to keep the spices in your cupboard from tipping over. When he came to diamond-fanged ATF agent Charlie Hood on *Fox News at Eleven*, admitting to losing a *thousand* machine guns, one of which had been used in the killing of Representative Scott Freeman, Clint knew he'd had more than enough of this guy. He'd be doing the country another favor if he just took him out.

He looked at his watch: eleven hours from now, Glitter Gums

would be waiting for him to pick up Mary Kate Boyle at the Greyhound station in San Diego, based on MK's fine acting and Hooper's gigantic stupidity. Of course, Mary Kate was already *in* San Diego, at a different hotel, that ratty-looking Regal, down in the Gaslamp District. You really fooled me, MK. She'd looked a little rattled walking down the street the other day, talking on the phone. To Hooper? Hatching some crafty little plan? Probably. It had been much easier for him to watch unnoticed from the Kia than a brand-new cobalt blue SUV. Clint wondered how many agents Hooper would bring to bust him at the Greyhound station. He wondered what a Stinger would do to them. He wondered what a Stinger would do to the Imperial Bank building that housed the ATF office in Buenavista, to all the other offices inside, and to the little café that had so many people in it that evening when he'd seen MK and Charlie Hooper come out together and walk across the street. He could tell by the way she walked and looked up at him that she was trying to get his attention. *You got alla my attention, Mary Kate. Then some. My stuff is all ready. Clint's on his way.*

40

Hood woke up with first light and listened to the rain roaring down on his roof. He pictured himself on the TV the night before, answering Theresa Brewer's questions with his usual lack of guile. *I am what I am*, he thought.

Beth lay beside him, breathing slowly and quietly. Her honey hair was a tangle and the bare curve of her shoulder showed from under the sheet. For a while he lay still and was thankful. Four and a half hours until the Greyhound station, he thought. Clint wouldn't show, but Hood knew that he himself *had* to show, just in case. Was Wampler crazy enough to try something with thirty lawmen waiting for him to show his face? He has to know we are on to him, Hood thought. *He has to know.*

Through a kitchen window he watched the raindrops boil on the desert rocks and waited for the coffee to brew. The sky was gray and the wind was strong enough to shiver the yuccas and sway the paloverdes.

Beth came in with her warmest robe and shearling boots. She came around the counter and they hugged. "I thought you were awake," he said.

"I couldn't sleep again."

"It's been a while, hasn't it?"

"My head is full of worries."

"Thomas is healthy and good."

"I love him and he's only a day old. What was all that with you and Bradley? What's going on?"

Hood watched the rain roar down. "Mike."

"Somehow I knew that. What did big bad Mike do now?"

"He wants to decide how Thomas is raised. He's wants Bradley and Owens to raise him. Not Erin."

"She'll fight to the death to keep him."

Hood gave her a joyless glance.

"He wouldn't . . ."

"No. Not directly. But he can persuade and manipulate and get people to do things for him. I've seen the aftermath of what Mike does, Beth. It's ugly stuff."

"So, now more than ever, you want to lock him up."

"I'm going to do it."

"Good heavens, Charlie. *God.*"

Hood poured coffee and added the milk and gave Beth a cup. She sat on a stool at the breakfast counter and Hood sat beside her. Outside the rain slackened and the daylight grew slightly. From her robe pocket Beth brought a wadded tissue and wiped her eyes. "I'm sorry, Charlie."

"For what?"

"For being what I am. A scientist. A humanist, I'd like to think."

"I love you for those things."

"You can't blame Mike for everything bad that happens to people you love."

"No, not everything at all."

"Any of it! It's irrational, Charlie." She studied him and wiped her eyes again with the tissue. Beth was a woman who usually tamped down her emotions, but when she decided to let them go they would rise and burst like fireworks.

"Can I tell you something I've never told anyone? It's not easy to admit."

"I want to know."

"When I was a little girl, I went to church and I believed. It felt so good. Then, when I got to be a teenager I looked around and I started doubting. Then, when I started studying life—biology, for my medical training—I came to see that life multiplies and sustains itself without any help from God, and it ends without any help from Satan. And the more I looked, the more I saw that there is no God and no Satan, no heaven or hell. These are stories we've told ourselves to answer the fear and mysteries of death. I'm an atheist, Charlie. Right down to my godless marrow. I haven't believed what you believe about Mike since I was a little girl. But I've done what you wanted. I've tried to make you happy. I love you. I wanted to be with you. So I gave up my home for yours, and I've taken care of Erin and Reyes and you. And now, you want to trap another human being and lock him up? Do you not see how crazy that is? How can you not see it?"

"I believe. I've seen and heard."

"I know. I respect it. It's irrational but I respect your beliefs. I told you four months ago, when I moved in here with you, that our relationship was day-to-day. I still feel that way. I'm moving home, Charlie. I don't want to lose you. But I won't be a part of this. I will not."

She leaned over and kissed him. Hood could smell her tears and taste the salt in them. When he spread his hands against her cheeks, they were wet and he brushed the tears into her hair. She stood, went back into the bedroom, and shut the door.

Later, out in the kitchen for more coffee and radio news, Hood called Mary Kate. He was fairly sure he'd awakened her. She told him she'd called the play director and they'd been able to postpone last night's rehearsal for two days. He warned her again not to go outside her room unless she absolutely had to. She joked that he was no fun to work for anymore. She said she had a decent view of the street from the Regal, and she'd not seen the blue SUV since she'd checked in sixteen hours ago. She had not left the room and it was getting smaller and smaller. She teased him about getting up so early just to listen to the radio. How could he leave a nice warm bed to do that? What, no one there to talk to? He ignored her and told her to stay alert and rang off just as the next news story came on.

"Imperial County businessman Israel Castro and two other men were gunned down behind Castro's Jacumba restaurant last night by an unidentified gunman who is still at large. Kitchen workers at Amigos Restaurant heard . . ."

His phone buzzed and Hood saw Soriana's name on the screen. "I just heard about Castro," he said.

"Forget about Castro for now. Charlie? Hey, look—Lansing called a few minutes ago. You've been let go by ATF. I'm sorry." Hood said nothing. "The attorney general's going on *Face the Nation* tomorrow morning. He's going to announce that six ATF agents have been terminated for the Love Thirty-twos that went to Mexico. Negligence and dereliction of duty. Nothing criminal. Then he'll talk about sweeping changes at ATF. I don't know what they've come up with at Justice. I'm not sure I want to know. Lansing doesn't have the balls to call you so I am. Don't shoot me, Hood, I'm just the messenger. You were a good agent and you deserve better. LASD is probably a better gig anyway."

Hood felt his heart in his throat and didn't speak.

"Take your gun and badge and ID to the field office in Buenavista. That would be easiest. Yorth will be there this morning. There's some paperwork. Lansing wants it all done ASAP. They want the laptop but you can keep the Charger 'til the end of the month."

"Who else got sacked?"

"Two from Arizona and two from Texas. And Bly. After the House hearing she told off Lansing in front of his people. Really chewed him a new one. So, she kind of volunteered for this. I feel terrible. I want you to know that."

"Nobody from Arizona or Texas even worked the Love Thirty-twos with us."

"It's politics, Charlie. That's all it is. Point finger. Distribute blame. Wash hands. Forget."

"I won't forget. Who's going to meet Clint Wampler at the Greyhound station?"

"I've got Velasquez and Morris doing a homeless act, and three more from here with armor and weapons. San Diego PD is on board with the helo if we need it, and two tactical teams. It's a mean little army. You don't really think he'll show up, do you?"

"No. But we have to."

"How's the girl?"

"I just talked to her. She's in the wind but fine."

"She's either brave or not too bright."

"Anyone get a look at who shot Castro?"

"A dishwasher saw someone with Castro a few minutes before the shots. Caucasian, twenties or thirties, medium height, slender, white hair. A heavy coat."

"Anyone see his car?"

"No info on a car."

"It's Clint Wampler, Frank, right down to the heavy coat."

"Possibly. But it could have been a down jacket, or a ski jacket or any winter coat. And the hair is wrong."

"Dye costs ten bucks and takes half an hour. I'd move on this, Frank."

"Move where? Wampler's got a gift for disappearing."

"Get his picture out there to the media again. Now he's a suspect in three *more* murders. Someone's going to notice him."

Soriana was silent for a long beat. "Thanks. I'll get the word out. Maybe Wampler will show up to greet his honey after all. And we'll slap four murders on him."

"Don't bet on it."

"Look, Charlie, I'm sorry about this. You need a recommendation, you need anything from me, and it's a done deal."

Hood punched off and poured some coffee and watched the rain come down. Suddenly the roar on the roof decelerated to a thrum and he could hear the runoff clanging down the metal downspouts.

Half an hour later he had showered and shaved and kissed Beth good-bye. He said nothing about the firing. He carried the laptop and his war bag to the car. He wore his own .45 on his hip and a two-shot .40-caliber derringer—a gift from Suzanne Jones—on his ankle. He kept his head up and his eyes busy. If Theresa Brewer could get his home address, why couldn't Clint Wampler? Oddly, to Hood this felt like any other workday—starting early, trying to anticipate, assessing available luck. He thought of Beth and of Erin and Thomas and Bradley. Of his mother and father. Memorial service soon. He thought of Suzanne. He tried to think of life without ATF and found it vague. Back to Los Angeles and the sheriffs? What about Beth?

He made downtown Buenavista in five minutes. He stopped at his usual doughnut shop. For a while he sat in the small bright-orange-and-yellow booth and watched the working people file in and out, on their ways to make their livings, Saturday or not. He wondered how many times he'd been in here since joining Blowdown four years back. He didn't think he'd miss this place but he did feel that with his firing, a large door had been closed, and that a long and meaningful chapter of his life was over. Would Beth come to L.A.?

He parked in the underground lot, made sure no news crews were lurking, then carried his war bag and laptop toward the back entrance of the field station. He swept his ID across the sensor and pushed open the door. He wondered if he'd miss this, too: the hugger-mugger of ATF, its insularity and self-propelled intensity, its accomplishments and mistakes, and, well, certainly his agent compadres.

41

Clint sat in the Kia and watched the front of the Imperial Bank building from down the street. He wore a new Cardinals baseball cap and sunglasses and his peacoat. His new binoculars were powerful and they brought up the lobby so close it was like he could walk right in. He saw that the bank was closed up and most of the offices were not open yet. There were a few people in the café. The girl making the coffee drinks was pretty. The same big blue-shirted security guard he'd seen before was at his station, sitting behind what looked like a marble desk, reading a newspaper. Clint didn't know exactly where the ATF office was, but the building was only two stories high and not very large. The reflective glass would be no match for the Stinger.

He glanced into the backseat at the bright Mexican blanket and the shape of the Stinger, armed and ready.

When the black Charger stopped at the entrance to the parking structure Clint understood that God himself had just singled him out to perform a miracle. He held the glasses absolutely still and watched the window go down and Charlie Hood push a card into the reader. The arm rose and Hooper drove in. Clint felt his finger throbbing but he smiled anyway. Should he wait for Hood to drive back out? How long was he going to be in there? What were his chances of hitting the Charger compared with hitting the building? After all, he'd never fired one of these things. Bird in the hand?

42

Yorth began to process him out and Hood could tell the man was embarrassed and angry. He seemed to be taking more time than he had to. In his few short months here in Buenavista, Yorth had lost weight and his hair was thinning. The death of one agent and the firing of two more agents under his command would not play well in his file or his soul. Yorth checked his watch. "Hour and a half until Wampler is supposed to show at the Greyhound station."

"That's the last place you'll find him. He knows we'll be there and he's not foolish."

"You think he shot Castro last night?"

"I do. My guess is Castro wanted in on the missiles."

"He must have wanted in on something. How's Mary Kate Boyle?"

"She's staying real low."

"She won't talk to me. She only talks to Velasquez and Morris now. And you."

"She's got a real stubborn streak."

"Reminds me of my sister." Yorth shook his head and sighed when Hood emptied his ATF-issue Glock and set it on the desk, focusing on the gun but not looking at Hood. Hood began signing the stack of forms and a few minutes later he walked out.

Down in the parking structure he had just aimed his key fob at the car when a sharp blast shook the ceiling and shivered the walls and rocked the Charger on its shocks. Chunks of concrete exploded through the glass walls of the elevator bank and skidded across the floor. Then alarms and human screams. Seconds later Hood ran through the blown door of the ATF offices. Inside, the screaming was more and louder, and water from the fire sprinklers rained down. He smelled smoke and explosives and he fell in behind Yorth, who was bleeding from his forehead but charging for the emergency exit with his gun drawn. Smoke had already drifted into the exit hallway. They burst outside to a narrow alley and ran through broken glass around to the front of the building, toward the screams of sirens and people.

The lobby plate glass was blown out and the far lobby wall was demolished and the reception desk was blown to splinters. Oscar lay twenty feet from his station, on his back near the elevators, and Hood saw that the middle of him was mostly gone, just a huge ragged hole below his chest. Hood followed the screams to the café. A woman with a bloody face knelt over what looked like an elderly man, and beyond them, through the glassless storefront, Hood saw two more women, one screaming and one staring ashen-faced back at the destroyed lobby while her leashed terrier barked furiously at a loose Chihuahua. A big shard of window glass detached from above and whistled down and burst on the sidewalk in front of Hood. A man crouched through the shattered front door of the accounting firm, holding his laptop over his head with both hands. Some fled the building and others ran in to help. The traffic on the boulevard had slowed and there were already gawkers pulled over to record the calamity on their cell phones. Hood watched a red Honda rear-end a black Denali and both drivers spill out with their phones already raised. His attention went to two small boys on the other side of the street who were touching what appeared to be a burning storefront wall. Distant sirens sounded as he ran across the boulevard and waved away the boys, who scattered in opposite directions, laughing. Hood saw that the backblast of the missile had blackened the storefront and the scorched bricks still smoked. He looked up and down the street, trying to spot a new blue Explorer or any young man who resembled Clint Wampler. Anything. He ran to the parked cars and the gathered spectators, yelling questions. One young man said he saw someone standing beside a white car with a "funny-looking bazooka-kind of thing over his shoulder, and the next thing I know there's a blast of white smoke going backwards out the tube, then the lobby blows up!" The witness could not describe the shooter or the car near which he was standing. When the smoke cleared, both were gone. The other answers Hood got were all no's and the looks he drew were dubious and fearful.

He sprinted back across the street to the Imperial Bank building and helped the bleeding woman walk the elderly man outside. He seemed stunned and possibly unhurt. The girl who worked in the coffee shop hugged herself, trembling as she ran through the shattered glass. The first cop car skidded to a stop out front, lights flashing, then a fire department engine screamed up behind it. Hood walked back inside the demolished lobby. The hole in the rear wall looked big enough to drive a car through. Yorth stood over Oscar in the sprinkler rain. He looked at up Hood, a trickle of watery blood still coming down his forehead and a coldly furious expression on his face. "Clint," he said. "Goddamned Clint."

A moment later the Charger screeched from the parking structure, leaving a billow of white smoke in the clean desert air. Hood circled the bank building in a series of right turns, expanding each time, hoping to spot Wampler. Fruitless, he worked his way nearly to the interstate, then back again toward downtown Buenavista and the Imperial Bank building. Two more fire companies roared around him, lights flashing and sirens wailing. Hood pulled over to let them pass, then gunned the Charger onto the on-ramp of I-8 west, toward El Centro and San Diego. He called Mary Kate and told her Clint had just blown up the ATF field office in Buenavista.

And not to open the door for anyone. *Anyone.*

43

An hour and forty minutes later, Clint was parking the Kia at the red curb in front of the Regal Hotel. The missile attack on the Imperial Bank was all over the news—at least one dead and several wounded. His pulse was good and slow and the world was in terrifically sharp focus. When he'd let that Stinger go at the bank building, he had felt a surge of adrenaline go through him, like the missile had actually released it, but by the time he'd dropped the launcher into the trunk and gotten back into the Kia and watched the aftermath of the explosion he was already beginning to feel calm again. The only problem was the finger, swollen and burning with pain.

He went inside the Regal and the man at the desk told him he couldn't park there. It was the law. The man had one of those goofy accents that make everything a question. RAKVI, said his name tag. Clint said he'd just be a minute and what room was the girl with the black eye in? The clerk scowled darkly and shook his head. Nimble as a chimp, Clint swung himself over the counter, landed lightly on his feet and rapped the clerk hard on the forehead with the blackjack. Rakvi dropped and started moaning. Clint pressed his boot to the man's mouth to mute him while he fiddled with the computer. It didn't take long to find the room assignments, but no listing for Mary Kate Boyle. There were eight rooms taken by women and Clint saw that parking charges applied to five of them. Mary Kate had no car. Of the remaining three, two had given credit cards and one, Jennifer Logan, was a cash customer. JL, Clint thought. MK loves J-Lo. Room 6. He lifted his boot off the clerk's mouth and put Rakvi's wallet in a back pocket of his jeans.

Room 6 was first floor. No spy hole. Clint knocked softly on the door and tried to mimic the clerk. "Miss Logan? This is Rakvi? The manager. I have a letter for you from a man named Charlie Hood?"

Mary Kate slid the deadbolt and Clint barged inside and hit her with the sap, top and middle of her skull. The book she was holding fell to the floor and Mary Kate slumped but he caught her before she hit. He slung her over his shoulder. He found her cell phone on the desk by the TV and used his free hand to slide it the front pocket of his jeans. He walked back into the lobby where he got her upright. She couldn't stand on her own so Clint clutched her tight around the waist and half-danced, half-dragged her to the car. It wasn't easy to swing open the door and get her in but he managed. A passerby said it was kind of early to be that wasted and Clint told him his wife was a diabetic so go to hell.

He left San Diego, navigating wide around the Greyhound station, which was only a few blocks away. She was out, her head lolling against the door and window. Her eye was still discolored. When he was away from the city, down south on Interstate 5, he pulled off and found an out-of-the-way place to park and taped up her hands and ankles. She didn't open her eyes. He snuck a kiss when he was done. He didn't make the tape too tight, didn't want to hurt her. He kissed her again, fully starved for some home-cooked love but he couldn't do that to a girl in this condition. *I got standards*, he thought. *Clint's no rapist.*

She hardly moved as he drove the interstate south toward Imperial Beach. In National City, she started to wake up. Clint pulled off again and parked in a strip mall parking lot and rolled down a window. He listened to the radio. It was all about the bombing in Buenavista. But they couldn't even figure out how many rockets had been fired. No wonder this country's so messed up, Clint thought. A few minutes later Mary Kate raised her head and squinted at him through her mess of hair. "Ouch," she whispered, raising both taped hands to her head. "You hit me, Clint?"

"Not with my fist. With a secret weapon."

She lowered her hands to her lap. "And you got me all taped up?"

"Just don't scream or say nothing to nobody. I don't want to tape up your mouth so just stay quiet, will you?"

"Oh man." Mary Kate was still whispering. "I got such a headache . . . if I screamed my head would explode."

"Then don't and we'll both be happy."

"What are you doing?"

"I got it all figured. I know you been with Charlie Hood, Mary Kate. I seen him walkin' you out of the ATF place and I seen the way you looked at him. I know he was telling you what to say to me on the phone. And I know you thought you were fooling me but you weren't. You betrayed me after all that time I was secretly in love with you. I been mad enough to kill you, MK. I was gonna and I still might. But seeing you in person has beaten down the hardness in my heart. Mostly. Hooper's another story, though. Hood I'm gonna waste."

Mary Kate closed her eyes and slowly let her head settle back against the door frame. "I wasn't ever *with* him, Clint. He's a nice enough guy but he didn't have the time of day for me. I think he's got a girl stashed somewhere."

"Or a boy."

"What did he do to you?"

Clint held up his left hand. "This is all consequential of what he did to my finger, Mary Kate."

"That's just a hurt finger, Clint."

"It's more than that. It's the whole stupid thing about me being stupid."

"Goddamn, you hit me hard. I can't open my eyes without it hurting worse."

Clint gave her a sweater for a pillow and got back on the freeway. The day was bright and cool and the shipyards rose high at the edge of the Pacific, cranes and booms fussing over the huge navy ships and tankers, mile after mile of them. A California Highway Patrol car passed him going close to ninety, didn't so much as look at him, which pleased Clint. Probably headed for Buenavista. Nobody was looking for his little white Kia and that was just the way he liked it. He kept stealing peeks at Mary Kate Boyle, dazed or asleep with her head on his sweater, and he felt bad for hitting her so hard but he couldn't have a scene getting her out the hotel and into his car, now could he? She had a small upturned nose and pretty lips and he even liked her ears. He wondered what her scalp looked like where he'd walloped her. No blood, because a good sap wouldn't cut if you hit flat with it. And his was a good one, made it himself out of bull hide and a hearty slug of lead he'd cut from an ingot using a coping saw. Sewn by his own hand. He'd tried it out on one of Carl Blevins's young hogs out by Alley Spring back in Missouri, and that porker had collapsed like the rug had been pulled out from under it. Woke up about a minute later and ran around in circles, snorting.

He worked her phone out from his pocket and flipped it open and scrolled down the contacts.

44

Hood's phone vibrated and he answered. "Hood, this is Clint. I got your number from our mutual friend, Miss Mary Kate Boyle. MK? Say hi to Twinkle Tooth. Then I'll tell him how it's gonna be."

Her voice was faint and flat and almost choked up. "I'm so sorry. He was following me on foot yesterday when I called you. While I was looking for the damned blue SUV. I'm so sorry, I got fooled and conked and am now adding to all your troubles."

"Has he hurt you?"

"He hit me awful hard."

Hood heard static, then Wampler again. "How'd you like the explosion at ATF?"

"You killed a nice guy and hurt a bunch of innocent people."

"I'm weepin'. Were you in the office when the rocket hit? What'd it sound like?"

"A rocket hitting, Clint. Where are you?"

"Hood, I'm going to take Mary Kate to the ocean for a picnic. We'll be at the TJ River south of Imperial Beach. Waiting on you. I'll be able to see in all directions on account of it's a flat beach. Which means you come alone. Which means if I see another human being or car or even a damned helicopter I'll kill her. You know I'm capable of this. Come alone, Hooper. We're gonna settle this like they used to, before the whole country turned queer like you. I'll have my pistols in my pockets as is my style. You can pack anything any way you want—it ain't gonna matter to me. You can call it a gunfight although it'll be more of an execution. But it'll be fair. Clint don't cheat. The winner gets MK and the loser gets dead. All of this is subsequent of what you did to my finger. Where exactly are you at right now?"

"Five miles east of San Diego. You beat me to her."

"When you get there, head south, amigo. Walk out on that beach alone. We'll be there. You got exactly half an hour."

"Clint, this is stupid, even for you. Let Mary Kate go. She's a sweet girl and she never hurt you. Just drop her off and keep on driving. Go back to Russell County or wherever else you want to be."

"Where I *don't* want to be is on death row, for that fed I blew away in El Centro. I'm not too stupid to figure that out."

"Blowing away another fed won't help you."

"Me and MK are already making plans for our future. Aren't we, cupcake? You better show up alone, Glitter Gums. You're down to twenty-nine minutes."

Hood trudged through the rain-soaked sand, south along the Pacific. The sky was dark gray and stacked with great columns of pale gray clouds. The water heaved and chopped and the wind sent spindrifts off the crests. There were no surfers out and no one on the beach. Ahead of him was the river and beyond that the hills of Tijuana, faint in the distance. He zipped his jacket up against the biting wind and snugged its elastic hem between his holster and his hip, popped the strap and turned it down and out of the way.

Soon the estuary was on his left and the ocean on his right. Hood continued down the wide sand beach, the shoreline eroded by the recent storms. He saw two young lovers wrapped in a blanket, leaning into each other and picking their way down the beach toward him. A flock of seagulls stood in the sand close together and all facing west as if waiting for something to come in on the water. The slough glimmered and its surface rippled in the breeze. Another quarter mile down the beach the dunes were deeper and sharper, and he saw that Clint could be watching him from one of them and be very hard to see until Hood was close upon him. He stopped and looked back to the last buildings in the United States, then ahead to the tall iron border wall jutting into the ocean. A woman in sweats and a hooded raincoat ran up the shoreline toward him.

"Hooper."

Hood turned and saw Clint Wampler climbing out of a dune. He was holding Mary Kate Boyle's arm and she was having trouble getting up the slope of sand. Wampler pushed her along in front of him with one hand, keeping her body between himself and Hood. His other hand was in the pocket of the peacoat. Hood could see by Mary Kate's brief, dispirited struggles that she was exhausted or injured or both. Her hands were bound. They stopped a hundred and fifty feet away and Clint pressed her down into the sand. Her knees buckled and Hood heard her cry out. Wampler took a knee beside her and he seemed to be giving her instructions. He gripped her face in one hand and turned it to him.

Wampler then stood and took a few steps toward Hood and stopped again. He had both hands in his coat pockets. He looked back at her and said something and she nodded. "I think she's pulling for me!" he called out. "Mary Kate just has trouble showing her feelings."

"Let her go, Clint. Get to your car and get out of here. I'll make sure she's taken care of."

"She'll be coming with me. Don't you get that? I *want* this chick." Wampler started toward him. "Make your move when you think you can hit me, Hooper. I'm going to do likewise. This is what you get for treating another human being like you treated me." Hood used his left hand to pull the tail of his Windbreaker taut. He could feel the cold wind through his shirt above the holster but he knew the grip was unencumbered now and he knew exactly where it was. Don't hurry, don't miss. He took a deep breath and thought, *Help me.*

Hood walked. He heard his own breathing and the soft crunch of sand under his feet. Wampler's hands were deep in his pockets as he ambled forward. Hood concentrated on Clint's shoulders. At ninety feet the shoulders rose.

Hood began his draw but he had scarcely touched the grip of his weapon by the time Clint had fired twice, then gone down with a sharp yelp. Hood never saw his gun and his first thought was, *Someone must have shot him in the back.*

He charged, gun steady before him in both hands, Clint still down and screaming. At twenty feet, Hood crouched into a shooter's stance and held the sights steady on Wampler as he struggled to stand, one hand waving high for balance. The other hand was still stuck in the pocket and Hood knew the gun had caught on something. He saw Mary Kate running at Clint from behind, weaving in and out of his line of fire.

Hood was scrambling for a safe shot when Clint finally cleared the gun from his pocket. Then Wampler collapsed, Mary Kate attached to his back, her still-bound hands clinched tight around his throat. Hood ran and tore Wampler's weapon from his hand and threw it out into the sand. Clint wailed again, his cry partially strangled by Mary Kate's grip. Hood threw Wampler's other gun over by the first. Clint writhed in the sand, trying to twist himself free of her grip. Hood whacked him hard with his .45, and Mary Kate swung her arms over his head and rolled away.

Hood smelled the blood before he saw it, then he saw it everywhere—red and fresh on Clint's legs, encrusted with sand, pools and splatters everywhere. He wrestled Clint facedown and managed to get a plastic tie around his wrists. Wampler was groaning and half-choked by sand by the time Hood pulled him onto his back. Hood stood and Wampler kicked at him, but Hood caught the cowboy boot and pushed the blood-drenched thing back down. Then he dragged Clint a few feet by the shoulders of his coat and propped him against a dune. Wampler's left calf was gurgling up blood. It took Hood a moment to figure it out.

"You shot yourself, Clint. *Twice.*"

"The left gun got caught on my sap so I shot my foot on accident. Then I flinched and the right one fired, too. Foot hurts the worst. God, it goddamned hurts! *God, it hurts!*"

Hood looked down the beach at Mary Kate, who was running across the dunes toward two joggers loping south along the shore.

"Look at all that blood." When Clint raised his foot in the air, the blood poured from the boot and splattered onto the sand.

"She's calling cops and paramedics," said Hood.

"Shoot me before they get here," said Wampler.

"Can't help you."

"Because you're a queer."

"If you say so."

"And a fag homo fairy piece of shit, too."

"Right, Clint."

"And a women's liberal who voted in a half-nigger president who wasn't even born in America. Probably voted for him *twice*. I'm getting death for whacking that agent, Hood. So why don't you get the satisfaction of offing me right here and now? You get to be a hero instead of someone everybody hates. And I don't have to sit on death row for ten years."

"You *should* sit on death row for ten years."

"Dirty Harry would shoot me. He'd scowl, and he'd pull the trigger and feel good about it."

"Times have changed."

"What's changed is you're a sorry excuse for not having a single hero nationally remaining. *Ahhh! Ahhh damn, this hurts!* You think I'll bleed to death before they get here?"

"Fifty-fifty, Clint. I can see Mary Kate talking on a phone right now. You hold still, I'll cinch my belt around your leg and yours around your ankle.

"Don't touch my belt buckle, you fruit."

"You try to knee me or a head butt or something, I'll hit you again."

Clint threw his head back against the side of the dune and bellowed in pain and frustration. Hood cinched his belt tight below Wampler's knee, keeping an eye on him while he worked the end under the wraps. When he was finished, the bleeding slowed.

"Don't touch my belt."

"Have it your way."

"My way is you shoot me. I can't live in prison the rest of my life. I can't. I'm going to stand up and kick your ass into that ocean. So you'll have to shoot me."

Hood took a step back and drew his gun and waited for Clint to get upright. Wampler stood and struggled up the flank of the dune, cursing, the muscles in his neck and face flexed. He stood wobbling for a moment, then charged Hood and lunged head first at him. Hood stepped aside and let Wampler land facedown in the sand. He lay there, panting and groaning, and after a few moments he rolled over and looked up at the low gray sky, his face encrusted with sand. "Who'da thought Clint was so fast he'd shoot Clint?"

Wampler heaved himself up to a sitting position, legs out in the sand. He looked at Hood and shook his head. Hood looked north toward Mary Kate Boyle, who was now walking slowly up the beach toward him. A moment later a black-and-white SUV came whining past her, water and sand shooting out behind it.

45

Bradley drove his Cayenne fast up the dirt road, leaving the Buddhist meditation center in the dust. As the road climbed into the rocky hills and narrowed, he was forced to slow, and miles later it went from bad to nothing and he parked and stepped out. They stood in a small prairie of mine tailings that glittered blue and green.

"Well, it's pretty country," said Owens.

"We have a bit of a hike. It's good you wore the hiking boots."

"I don't get why we had to come this far to talk in private."

"You'll see." Bradley got his phone out and found the GPS coordinates he'd surreptitiously recorded shortly after meeting Beatrice. He'd memorized them but this was a double check, and his memory was good. He called Erin, who sounded well. Then Reyes, who was stationed outside Erin's room at Imperial Mercy: Nothing unusual there in the maternity unit.

He worked on the backpack and took the coiled rope. "Bring your jacket. It'll be cold and windy up there."

"You still haven't told me where we're going, or why."

"I'm about to commence. Let's walk side-by-side. Do you know what Mike is?"

"Well, of course I do. He's very honest."

"I'm going to show you what it leads to."

The angle of ascent was slight at first, and there was a well-worn game trail to follow. The trail gradually vanished and the sand became gravel and the gravel became rocks and the rocks became boulders. They stopped on top of a hillock and looked back at Highway 395 stretching out of sight to the north, and miles east, the acres of bright photovoltaic mirrors facing the cloud-dampened sun, and the dome of the prison tucked into the distant hills.

"I wonder why he never told you about Beatrice," said Bradley.

"Who is she? Is she meeting us way up here?"

Soon they were climbing between rocks that were far taller than they were, great boulders piled with haphazard grace, some of which looked perilously out of balance. Bradley remembered some of this and he pictured Mike in his bright golf garb, nimbly scaling the mountain ahead of him, chiding him about getting back to the gym. He heard Owens breathing hard and he waited for her to catch up. Even in jeans and hiking boots and a flannel shirt and a ball cap, she was soberingly beautiful. She looked up and smiled. Hard to believe that Owens had once been willing to kill herself, only to be plucked from death and later partnered by Mike Finnegan. They picked their way up around the towering rocks. Finally they found themselves on the small level plateau. The wind was strong and cold. Owens pulled on the sweater she'd tied around her waist. Bradley looked to where the doleful iron girders of the mine entrance slouched, framing the sudden blackness beyond and below. "We're here."

He set the coiled rope and his backpack on the same boulder where Mike had set his cooler, then went to the opening of the mineshaft. He got as close as he could, bracing both hands on the rough rusted girders. "Beatrice! It's Bradley Jones here. Mike's partner."

"Bradley! Are you alright? Is he with you?"

"I'm fine. Owens is with me. She's another partner of Mike's."

"Owens, he never told me about you. You have such a beautiful name!"

Bradley turned and looked at Owens. Her face had gone pale and her lips were parted as if she were about to speak but she said nothing.

"She's an angel," said Bradley. "Mike threw her down there ninety-four years ago. In six more, he has to let her out."

"I've never seen an angel."

"You're about to."

"I feel very light and strange right now."

"Answer her. About your beautiful name."

"Um, yes, thank you, Beatrice. I was named for the Owens River because my great-grandfather was a fisherman who loved it."

"I love fishermen and fishers of men. Does Mike know you two are here?"

"No," Bradley called down. "He'd have a conniption if he knew."

"That word was so popular a short century ago. I do miss it. But . . . why are you here? Did you bring me beer and meat sticks?"

"I've got something better."

"Pork rinds?"

"A rope to get you out."

"Oh dear. Father in heaven. *DEAR FATHER IN HEAVEN!* Bradley and Owens, you will be blessed for this! Give me just a few minutes to get ready. I've been saving a dress."

Beatrice was a filthy bag of skin and bones and she smelled terribly. Her dress was brittle and decaying and had once been some shade of blue. Her skin was startlingly white beneath the ground-in dirt and her reddish brown hair had grown to twice the length of her body. She was tall and her arms and legs were emaciated and her head seemed too large. When Bradley first took hold of her outstretched hand, he thought the bones would break. He guessed her weight at eighty pounds.

They sat on boulders in the cold sunshine, far enough apart so that Beatrice's stench didn't offend Bradley and Owens. Bradley broke out the snacks and Beatrice ate rapidly and quickly finished off three beers. Owens ate nothing and said little but Bradley saw that her color was beginning to return and that she seemed deeply troubled. Her posture was different. She kept looking at the angel with a combination of shame and doubt that Bradley had never seen in her.

Bradley couldn't tell the color of Beatrice's eyes because the sunlight, after ninety-four years of her going without, was too intense to allow her anything but an occasional, tearful squint. She'd bitten off her nails at about one inch, and sanded them on the rock flanks of the mine, she explained, and she thought they looked pretty good. She had kept her teeth from growing too long for lack of use by gently sanding them with a smooth, hard rock, and she'd brushed them with an unneeded undershirt until it decomposed, then afterward, for a decade or two, with her fingers. Bradley saw that she was vain and proud of her appearance, given the challenges.

They talked a little about automobiles and current events, but mainly Beatrice ate and drank. She lowered the dress modestly but enough to let the sun hit her neck and shoulders. He body hair had grown out in all of the predictable places. After a longish silence she licked the cheese-snack dust off her fingernails, then shaded her eyes with one hand and squinted at Bradley, then Owens. "Let me see if I have this right," she said. "You, Bradley, are recently partnered with Mike. You are a recent father. Mike of course wants to influence the child, raise him as the son of a devil. Correct?" Bradley nodded, though he had no idea how Beatrice knew this, unless she had the same thought-reading powers that Mike had. "Yes, that's exactly how I know. You, Owens of the river, have been long partnered with Mike. You have done his asking. You have been loyal. Faultless. Even slavish. Now, Bradley wants to break with Mike and betray him to one Charlie Hood. Some kind of religious leader, I suspect. Oh, a lawman? Then the reason, the real reason that Bradley has brought us all together here, is that he needs our help. Count me in, Bradley. I'd love to go after Mike. But, Owens? I sense your profound divisions. I must assume that Mike has enlisted your help in taking over management of the son, Thomas. So, you are hurt that Mike would strip you from his daily life and assign you to Bradley as a wife, stepmother and . . . guardian. Hurt, because you love him. You truly, genuinely love Mike because he met you at death's door and pulled you back inside the house of the living."

"Enough," said Owens.

"Would either of you like these last few crackers? No? Who is this Hood and why do you believe he can handle Mike? 'Taking him down,' as you apparently like to say now, is not going to be easy. He's as strong as ten men, and you cannot kill him. Just for starters."

"We can deceive him," said Bradley. "That's how we do it."

"Difficult at best," said Beatrice. Then she squinted again at Owens and nodded impatiently. Bradley was impressed by the limber velocity of her mind. "But *you* can deceive him, can't you, Owens? Because he loves you, too, as you love him. And he trusts you."

Owens fixed Bradley with another strange stare. "I don't know. I need time to think."

Beatrice noisily bit into an apple. "This project could be very, very satisfying. I am so tired right now. This is more activity than I've had in nearly a century. All I've really been able to do is pray and learn how to sleep. And talk to myself to keep my vocal chords from fusing together. Keeping up my appearance took some time, but it's amazing how long twenty-four hours are. I'm really tired of all those Psalms."

"We've got a long walk," said Bradley.

"My feet will be tender and I'll have to carry my hair in my arms. But I'm sure I can manage."

"I brought you a pair of athletic shoes and a dress. But you already have a dress." He dug deep into the backpack and held up a new pair of shoes, white with pink trim, still linked by a plastic tie. He had come *that* close to shoplifting them from a busy sporting goods store the day before, then caught himself and paid full retail, in cash, with money he'd earned as an LASD deputy.

"Bradley Jones—you angel you."

They headed for a Target in San Bernardino for basics. Beatrice was impressed by the speed and comfort of modern cars, and their numbers, and the staggering human population. "This was mostly cows and crops in nineteen-seventeen," she said. "Now it's so much more interesting." The wide aisles and bright lights and abundant merchandise of the Target amazed her. She lifted and piled her hair into one of the red plastic shopping carts and aimed it straight for the television screens flickering away back in Electronics. A security guard approached and asked her for ID and Bradley badged the older man and told him to get lost. Then off to women's clothing.

Beatrice drew more than a little attention in the store so they bought shears and pulled over in Norco, found a park, and Owens cut off her hair well above her shoulders. Bradley placed a length of the shorn hair on the ground and paced it off: twelve feet, approximately. He couldn't quite see leaving it behind so he collected and laid it all out lengthwise, then took one big handful at a time and coiled it, hand around elbow, twisting it tightly, just as he had coiled the rescue rope, then tightly knotting the ends. The hair made five thick cables, which he lay in the back of the Cayenne. Beatrice bathed in the park restroom with a new bar of soap and a new towel and came out a few minutes later in new clothes of her choosing: Dickie's work pants and a blue fleece vest over a tie-dyed T-shirt. She reeked of Heaven Sent. She slept in back all the way to Buenavista.

Outside the hospital room Bradley introduced Reyes to Beatrice. The old snake-bit cop studied her skeptically, then limped off to get coffee. In the room Bradley introduced Erin to Beatrice, who touched Thomas's cheek lovingly and gave Erin a long hug, then asked where the cafeteria was. Owens went into Erin's room and closed the door behind her. Bradley and Beatrice went to the cafeteria and took their food trays out in the hospital courtyard so she could get some of the mild desert sun. They sat with Reyes. "Hospitals haven't really changed that much," she said. "I don't recognize much of the medical equipment, but the atmosphere is the same, and the smells and the general sense of gravity and efficiency. More buzzers. More female doctors, thank heaven. The food's better, too. Why do you limp, former Chief Reyes?"

"Rattlesnake."

"Oh? One fell into my mineshaft a few years ago. *Crotalus mitchelli.*"

"Sounds like that movie," said Reyes. "Did it bite you?"

"No, the poor thing was stunned. I grabbed it behind the head and ate it."

Reyes laughed, then suddenly stopped. Nearly an hour later Owens came outside with a tray of her own. She sat down without a word and ate while Beatrice examined Bradley's cell phone. At first she thought he was teasing her about its alleged powers. Bradley dialed and Owens's phone buzzed and when Beatrice answered it, it was indeed Bradley, simultaneously speaking from the phone and from three feet away. "Electricity has come a long way. I've got so much to understand."

"That's nothing," said Bradley. He shot video of her and played it back and she was speechless.

"I'll do it," said Owens, interrupting. "I can't let anyone ruin Thomas. Not even Mike."

"You chose the right thing," said Reyes.

On that chill evening they brought Erin and Thomas back to Hood's home in Buenavista. On the radio news Bradley heard that the suspect in the slaying of an ATF agent in El Centro and the bombing of the ATF field office in Buenavista was expected to survive his gunshot wounds, apparently self-inflicted.

46

Two days later Bradley and Owens walked along the lily pond at Balboa Park in San Diego, surrounded by the old buildings, stately and ornate. The day was brisk. Bradley pushed the stroller and Owens held his arm and a picnic basket. Thomas's head, barely visible within the blankets, rocked gently with the motion of his ride. They passed a mime and a juggler and a young man with no arms, playing a guitar with his feet. He was very good. They stopped and watched and Owens tipped him two hundred dollars when the song was over.

Mike rose from the bench and waved when he saw them. Bradley steered the stroller his way. Bradley felt his pulse speed up and he tried to talk it down. Owens had briefed him on the Method, where an actor recalls something from her personal past to help make her acting more convincing in the present. Looking at Finnegan from fifty feet away, Bradley's first impulse was to draw the sidearm from the crook of his back and riddle the man with bullets. But his purpose now—perhaps the most important in his young life—was not to injure Mike but to deceive him, to convince him of Bradley's happiness here in this moment. So he pictured the first time he'd seen Erin, onstage and in the lights . . .

Mike was dressed in sporty black warm-ups and bright-yellow-and-green soccer shoes. He wore gold chains around his neck and a monstrous gold Rolex encrusted with diamonds. *Ridiculous, as always*, thought Bradley, but he knew by now it was a ruse. Mike swept up Thomas, blankets and all, and smiled down into the newborn's pink, doubtful face. "Beautiful is not the word," he said. "The word, to my knowledge, has not yet been invented. My *goodness.*"

Owens let go of Bradley's arm and hugged Mike rather stiffly, then returned to Bradley's side. He gently gathered her against him, smiling at Mike and picturing the first time he'd introduced Erin to his mother. Mike gave him an inquisitive look. "It's heartening to see two of my favorite people, together. Bradley—it must be nice to be loved for who you are, rather than resented for who you are not." Then he returned his attention to the baby in his arms.

Bradley said nothing. He absently stroked Owens's arm, calling up another pleasant memory, this time of fishing with his little brother in the Valley Center pond. Jordan. He was way over in Hawaii now, living with Ernest, the father of Suzanne's last child. Bradley had been texting both of his brothers lately. Jordan was so smart he was kind of scary. Kenny was growing up.

"And you, Owens," said Mike, glancing up at her with a gleam in his eye. "Something seems to have agreed with you. You look more lovely than ever. And that is saying quite a lot. I've always loved that dress, as you know." The dress was a simple sleeveless shift that fell just above the knee, a white background with red chilies and green leaves. Her espadrilles were red and her bracelets were miniaturized, brightly enameled pieces of fruit.

Bradley heard the breath catch in her throat. "I loved you, Mike," she said softly. "I always will."

"Oh, out with the old and in with the new, Owens! You are doing a good thing. Bradley, have you told Erin?"

"Are you kidding? It's going to be awhile. Right now, it would just infuriate her more and she'd try to run off with Thomas."

"We can't have that."

"I won't let her take him," said Bradley, recalling his first sight of the man who'd shot and killed his mother. Such anger he'd felt then. And later, cold revenge. He felt it again. *Hear it, Mike—my anger at Erin.*

Mike smiled at Bradley, then Owens. "Which leaves time for you two to learn about each other. You have such galaxies to explore within. I'm so proud to have introduced you. You will have very long and very exciting lives."

Sitting near the handsome latticed Botanical Building, they ate the lunch that Owens had packed. By then the March sun was just strong enough to warm Bradley and he purposefully recalled moments of strong emotion that he hoped Mike would misconstrue. But except for that one interrogative glance early on, Mike seemed convinced of Bradley's attraction to Owens. Not that he had to create that from scratch. He set a hand on her warm bare arm as she rearranged Thomas's blanket just so.

47

"Bradley doesn't have to touch her like that," said Erin. She rotated the focus on the binoculars. Hood and Erin stood at the window in a the third-floor office of the California Building Tower, looking down on Balboa Park. This hidden vantage point had been arranged by one of the Museum of Man curators, Erin and the Inmates having performed a gratis fundraiser for them just last year. The curator had secured a couple of hours for them, no questions asked, though he loitered in the break room with coffee and his laptop.

"I'm sure he's thinking of you," said Hood. Bradley was making his act look pretty easy, he thought.

"He better be. Look at Thomas. How small and perfect he is. Does he look like me? I'm a nervous wreck with him being so far from me and so close to Mike. I want Mike stopped. I want him . . . whatever it is you're planning to do with him. Do it, do it, *do* it."

Hood lifted his big camera and zoomed in on the picnic below. Mike was animated, gesticulating with a drumstick in one hand, his other hand outstretched, apparently mid-tale. His shoes were brand-new and very bright yellow and green. Bradley had already finished his lunch and he now slouched on the bench with swaddled Thomas in the crook of one arm, ignoring Mike. *A born actor*, thought Hood.

"Soon, Erin."

"Not soon enough. Maybe you can get Mike to shoot himself in the foot, like Clint Wampler. I'm so glad you stopped that rocket wacko, Charlie. Oh, *look* at my baby down there. He's so *cute*. They say a woman's IQ drops dramatically right after birth. I know mine has. What do you think, Charlie?"

"It'll come back."

"I hope so."

"What are you going to do with Bradley?" he asked.

She lowered the glasses and studied him. "I really don't know. Right now all I care about is Thomas. Do you know what Bradley has planned for later?"

"He won't tell me. He just wants us all there in Valley Center."

"I hope he doesn't think we're coming down to Valley Center to stay."

"You made it pretty clear you're not, Erin."

"I want to stay on with you in Buenavista," she said. "Can Brad spend some more time there with us? I know it's a lot to ask. And it's up to you and Beth, not me."

"Beth has moved out. She wants no part of what's coming. It's best for everyone, I think."

"Then it's up to you, Charlie."

"You're welcome in my home. All three of you."

Erin studied Hood, then lifted the binoculars and looked down through the opening. Hood watched her watch, her hands on the glasses and her profile and the red cascade of her hair. He knew that in another time and place they would have been good together but he also knew this fact was useless at best. "I love him but I can't love him," she said. "And I resent him. What am I supposed to do with all that, Charlie?"

"You'll know when you have to know."

"Do you really, *really* think he's changed?"

"I think he'd give his life for you and Thomas."

"But do you think I can trust him?"

"I'd give him one hour at a time."

"I'm serious."

"I am, too."

She lowered the binoculars and looked up at him. "You want him to pay for what he's done, don't you?"

"He will." Hood nodded and lifted the camera.

❊   ❊   ❊

That evening Hood parked his Charger outside the Valley Center ranch house. Bradley was standing on the deck with Call by his side, while the lesser dogs boiled around Hood's car. Hood and Beth got out, and Beth held the door for Erin, who stepped into the cold and pulled her Navajo blanket coat tight around her. She put one knee on the seat and leaned in to work her sleeping son from the car. Bradley came bounding down the steps to help her. He wore a pale suede duster and moleskin breeches and a jacquard shirt and his polished boots caught the porch light. Hood wondered what the occasion was. He wondered if Beatrice had finished off the rest of the food in his pantry yet. He hadn't figured on meeting an angel in his life, especially one with such a voracious appetite. A moment later Reyes and Owens pulled up in Gabriel's pickup, rekindling the dogs.

Hood looked at the ranch house and thought of Suzanne, standing on that deck, summer of '08. He was just a patrol deputy with a few questions to ask her about an investigation he'd been assigned. Her hair had been a mess and her nightshirt was periwinkle colored and revealed little while suggesting much. It was a Saturday morning and she was here at home with her boyfriend and three sons. Later that morning she'd flirted brazenly with him. She'd told him she was an eighth-grade history teacher, but was not like any eighth-grade teacher he'd ever had. First and last warning, she'd said. Later she teased him about his ears and almost touched her nose to his cheek. But not quite. He could hear her inhale. He felt judged. A minute later she excused him with a funny little backward wave as she walked away. The wave that said, SEE YOU LATER IF YOU'VE GOT THE COURAGE. Turns out, he did. He had met Bradley that day. And Jordan and Kenny and his father, a big Hawaiian man named Ernest. And just a few short weeks later, Erin. More past that's not even past at all, he thought. Thanks, William. You were right.

*   *   *

Now it was early evening and the sun was down. A rosy tint brushed the hills and lay flat and shiny on the pond. Doves creaked through the sky above them, disappearing into the big oak tree in the barnyard. Hood and Beth stood together looking to the oak glen beyond, where they had made love for the first time, in one of several tent cabins set up for Erin and Bradley's wedding guests. "That was a night," Beth said.

"And a morning and another night."

"Things were perfect then."

"Maybe again, Beth. How is it, back in your own home?"

"It's where I belong."

"Thanks for coming tonight. It means a lot to me."

"Remember at the wedding the absinthe bar was over that way? Remember the bulls getting drunk and stumbling into the lake and the guys on Jet Skis trying to round them up? And the dancing and the brawl? Now *that* was a wedding party."

"I was hungover for a week."

Hood saw that the barn door was slid all the way open and a strong light came from inside. He thought he saw a Ping-Pong table in there, then wondered if his eyes were deceiving him because the table seemed to be somehow suspended in midair. He blinked and refocused, but the table remained levitated.

Bradley got Reyes to help him set champagne flutes along the deck railing, then disappeared into the house. A moment later he came back with a magnum of champagne cradled in a towel and sent the cork zooming into the darkness. Some of the dogs broke off in chase of it, nipping at one another for advantage. Bradley motioned everyone to join him and began filling the flutes. "Look how responsible we've all become," he said. "Just a few years ago we celebrated our wedding with two days of food and booze and bull riding. Now, we toast our son with Dom Perignon. To Thomas Firth Jones! And to you, who helped bring him into this world. We thank you. We thank you!"

They drank. Then Bradley handed off the bottle to Reyes and led them back down the steps and, taking command of the stroller, walked them across the barnyard and past the big oak. The dogs followed with their usual sense of purpose. Hood saw the outline of the hills against the deepening dark and a white cuticle of moon already high in the late winter sky. There was a John Deere with a lowered front loader parked near the barn. Bradley stopped at the entrance and lifted Thomas from the stroller. "Charlie, can you hang on to him for a few minutes? Erin, will you take my hand? I won't bite. I have some things to show you all."

Hood gave Beth his champagne glass, then took the blanket-wrapped Thomas. He was very light and the blanket was warm with him. He wore the blue hospital cap and tiny blue mittens against the chill. Erin fussed with his cap for a moment and told Hood not to drop him, then they followed Bradley into the barn.

Inside the smells were of gasoline and vehicles and tools, not horses or livestock or poultry. Hood saw that what he had thought was a levitating Ping-Pong table was just that—held straight up off the concrete floor by two very large hydraulic lifts. He saw the MX bikes and the quad runners lined up against one wall, and the gas and oil cans and the tires stacked nearby. There was a Bobcat and two power mowers and a chipper and several generators.

Before they came to the Ping-Pong table, Bradley stopped and looked down. "Right here, you see this? This is where two of my friends were hacked to death five years ago. They were brothers and they lived next door. I found them. Mom thought it traumatized me but I said it didn't. I didn't sleep for eight nights. Then I slept for three full days. The doctors said I was fine. I think about those guys a lot. They were Rincon Indians, Herold and Gerald Little Chief. Mom had the concrete here replaced because of the bloodstains, then she thought their blood should be honored, not hauled away, so she had the new slab torn out and the rip-rap from the old one put back in. So that's why you see the stains and all the cracks." One of the Jack Russells nosed the floor, then looked at Bradley and cocked his head. "Come on, there's more."

They stood around the neat opening in the floor, above which the Ping-Pong table and section of concrete were suspended by the hydraulic lifts. Hood saw that the jacks were freshly greased and the welds were neat and ample. Stairs led down.

"The hydraulics came from city of Escondido garbage trucks I stole," said Bradley. "Two of them. They were surprisingly fun to drive. Now, watch your step coming down, guys. You dogs—*wait*." Hood watched as Bradley and Erin disappeared beneath the floor one step at a time. The dogs really did wait. Hood brought up the rear behind Beth, Owens, and Reyes. Thomas awoke when Hood stepped into the bunker. His eyes searched Hood's face and Hood had no idea what a three-day-old human being could see or think.

Hood snugged the blanket to him and looked around the vault. It was roughly twenty-by-twenty feet, with an eight-foot ceiling. The light was low voltage, bright and clean. It was cold. There were three floor safes and a gun safe. Along one wall was a workbench or a long table of some kind, covered by colorful blankets. Beneath the blankets were irregular shapes that Hood could not identify. Beth looked at him in frank disbelief.

"Did Suzanne build this?" asked Erin.

"I did, honey. It took six months. I excavated by hand so no one would know about it. I spread the dirt and rocks all over the ranch here where it wouldn't be suspicious. You never remarked on the patches of fresh dirt when we'd ride the quads, Erin. Did you wonder how they got there?"

"I never noticed the dirt. All I saw was you and all I heard was music. I was a fool. When did you come down here?"

"When you were working or asleep. Here, look what's in the safes." He knelt and spun the dial and threw open one of the doors, then quickly opened the two others. Hood saw the bricks of vacuum-packed cash, the jewelry and watches and loose stones. Bradley, still kneeling, stared into one of them as if hypnotized.

Erin stood above him, staring into the same safe, her hands raised to her mouth in disbelief. Her voice was a whisper. "Did you steal all this, too?"

"The cash was my cut of what I smuggled south to Mexico. Drug money, of course. The watches and jewelry and stones I took as payment or bought cheap from friends. I stole some of them myself, back when I was young and really idiotic."

Erin looked at him with a numb expression. She snugged the collar of her Indian blanket coat up against her neck. "You . . . your whole *life* was doing things like this?"

"There was also school and hapkido and football. And then the sheriff's department."

"Why?"

Still staring into the safe, Bradley stood and put his hands on his hips. Finally he turned to Erin and his look glanced off Erin to the others, one at a time, in turn. "I loved it. It was very intense and lucrative but mainly fun. Later, I told myself it was to provide for you and our family to come. But that was bullshit and I knew it. We could have lived just fine off your music and a deputy's salary. I don't love jewelry unless it's on you. Or fancy watches. And I don't really have anything to spend all this cash on. The *getting* of it was what mattered. It was a way to feel . . . alive."

"How did I make you feel? Dead?"

"Blessed. Chosen. Lucky beyond compare. After a job I couldn't *wait* to get back to you. You were my reward for the hard work it was to get this stuff. It's not easy working for a drug cartel. The first time I met Carlos Herredia I peed my pants. He's a demanding employer. You never know if he's going to hug you or shoot you. And stealing other people's things? It's not like anybody just lets you take what you want. Try taking a toy away from a two-year-old. And all the while I was trying to be a good cop. I really was. I wouldn't recommend that kind of life, except maybe to a few people."

"How about to your son over there, Bradley? Would you recommend it to him?"

Hood watched Bradley shake his head and look down. "No. Not after meeting him, I would not. Erin?"

"*What?*"

"There's more."

Bradley went to the workbench and pulled away one of the brightly striped blankets. Everyone crowded in to look. "All that stuff Mom said about her being a direct descendant of Joaquin? It was all true. These are some of his things. She died before she could show them to me, but I was a curious boy. All this stuff was hidden here in the barn. It wasn't hard to find. Even Hood found it. I didn't mean that as an insult, Charlie. What I meant was, even a relative stranger to our family was able to find it."

"That's ridiculous," said Erin. "It's not possible that Suzanne was a descendant of Joaquin Murrieta."

Hood watched as Bradley put his hands on Erin's face, looked into her eyes, and smiled. "After a lifetime of lying to you, I never thought it would be so hard to convince you of the truth. Look, honey—this saddle here was Joaquin's. And those are his six-guns and holsters. And his hemp lariat and leather bullwhip. He was very good with that lariat, known for it. That deck of cards belonged to him. He was a terrific gambler, used to deal Monte games in the Gold Rush country before they raped and murdered Rosa. His wife. My great-great-great . . . well, you know."

Bradley let go of Erin, lifted another blanket, and dropped it to the floor. "And that's his bulletproof vest. See the big dent in the middle? That was from Joaquin's own forty-four—the gun you see right here. Before paying for the vest, Joaquin ordered the blacksmith who made it for him to put it on. Then he shot him, to make sure the workmanship was high quality. Look! It held. And see the new pockmarks? The fresh ones that haven't tarnished yet? Those came during a gunfight in Lancaster two years ago, remember, the big car-wash shootout where two deputies and three drug runners died? That was *me* wearing the vest, Erin. Bradley Jones, direct descendant! See that, Thomas? That's what your daddy used to do."

"Not funny, Brad," said Erin.

"Erin, this is the last time he'll hear about any of this." Bradley looked back at Hood, then with a flourish pulled the last blanket from the workbench. The glass jar was just as Hood remembered it, the head pale and hairless and stripped of hope.

"Jesus Christ," said Reyes, crossing himself.

"Ouch!" said Owens.

"My *God*," said Beth.

"Don't let Thomas see it!" said Erin.

Hood sheltered the baby deep in his arms, hiding him from the world and the world from him. He watched Erin take a step toward the jar. She reached out her hand but stopped it short of the glass. "You came from *him?*"

"But tonight and here, all of this ends. It should. Mom couldn't decide if knowing was a curse or a blessing. It is not a blessing. And I won't let Thomas carry it."

Hood watched as Erin turned away from the jar and toward Bradley. She looked up at him for a long beat, then touched his face. Hood thought her hand looked like a blind woman's, touching an unknown face for the first time. Then she came past the others and took Thomas from him and climbed back out of the bunker. Owens followed.

Bradley spread his arms. "Hey, everybody! Show's over. Help me load all this stuff into the tractor outside. Everything on the workbench, everything in the safes, all of it. Right down to the blankets."

Within five minutes the tractor's front loader was heaped with the known physical history of Joaquin Murrieta, and the proceeds from

Bradley Jones's life of crime. Hood carried the big jar, as no one else seemed inclined. Reyes, his arms cradling bricks of cash, gave him wide berth. Hood came back and got the blankets, too. Bradley started up the clacking diesel and the dogs ran around the machine barking. In the faint moonlight Hood could see Joaquin's head bobbing with the rhythm of the engine. Bradley slowly drove the tractor across the barnyard toward the house. Hood saw Erin and Owens standing in the porch light.

At the water's edge Bradley stopped and reversed so the front loader bearing his past faced his home and his wife and son. He backed into water. Then he waved at Erin and shut down the tractor and jumped off. Hood saw the gas can in his hand. Bradley sloshed ashore, set it on the ground, and pulled out the nozzle, then lifted and upended the can over the front loader. Hood watched him drench it all, shaking out the last of the fuel before tossing the empty can up onto the barnyard grass where it landed with a hollow thump. Bradley waved back at Erin again, then turned to the tractor. Hood saw him bring his left hand from the duster pocket, and the motion of his shoulders, and a moment later the big bucket burst into flames. Bradley called the dogs as he backpedaled away and slipped and fell, then he was up again. The fire, momentarily confined and angry, roared and whirled upward, and Hood could see the writhe and curl of the blankets, and the journals sparking and smoking, and the quick surrender of the plastic wrap. It took some time for the densely packed cash to catch, but finally it did, with a sudden concussive *whump!* Bradley and his dogs had scrambled almost to the big oak tree when Joaquin's jar exploded and the sky was filled with burning fragments of him and fiery glass and bits of paper, all reflected in the water. Hood saw the lariat, aflame and uncoiling through the darkness on its way back to earth.

48

The next morning at LASD headquarters in Monterey Park, Hood was questioned by Chief Miranda Dez and Jim Warren. They were very interested in his transportation of alleged drug money to a known drug kingpin in Mexico. Confronted with the video and photographic evidence, Hood confessed to being the bag man in a kidnapping ransom payment. "It was a private thing, not a department action," he said.

"Everything a deputy does is a department action," said Warren. "Were Bradley Jones, Caroline Vega, and Jack Cleary involved, too?"

"They were part of it."

"Why don't they appear in any of this material?" asked Dez.

"Bradley edited them out so they could perjure themselves and avoid blame."

"Who was kidnapped?"

"Erin."

"His *wife*? Why didn't he tell us?" asked Warren.

"You know why he didn't. You just can't prove it."

"Charlie," said Warren. "More coffee? Something to eat? You're going to be here a long time."

At the end of the long time, Hood was suspended with pay for one week and ordered back to L.A. for desk duty, pending a full investigation by CID. Hood stood and dropped his gun and badge to Warren's desk. *Second time in four days*, he thought. "This job isn't worth the heartache or the paycheck. I'm out. I'll be at home if you want to arrest me for something."

Afterward he drove to Bakersfield and met his siblings and mother at Applebee's for dinner. They stayed up late, reminiscing. His brothers and sisters struck him as predictably advanced versions of what they had always been, and he was certain that he appeared that way, too. He slept in his boyhood bed. Lying in the dark in the small familiar room, he was effortlessly transported back through the years and he dreamed the dreams of his childhood. The next day they spread his father's ashes up on the Kern River, where he had loved to fish.

Back in Buenavista, Hood learned from Owens that Mike Finnegan had at least five residences in Southern California, her favorite being a remote cottage near Piru that backed up to Piru Creek and the Hopper Mountain National Wildlife Refuge. Ventura County, thought Hood—he and his father had fished Piru Creek when Hood was just a boy. According to Owens, Mike had purchased the cottage in 1887 when Piru was being developed as "a second Garden of Eden" by a wealthy publisher of Sunday-school tracts. Mike had told her that the nutcase publisher had planted the surrounding valley only with fruits identified in the Bible—dates, figs, grapes, olives, and pomegranates. Mike could see the original vineyard from his back patio. Owens said that Mike, even to this day, was still proud of his subterfuge in purchasing a home in the middle of enemy territory.

There in the cottage, she said, Mike now spent long stretches of downtime—reading, writing, researching on the internet, daydreaming, hiking the rugged hills, and swimming most mornings in cold, fast Piru Creek. He used a mask and snorkel and diving weights to get down and observe the fish and aquatic insects, often photographing them with a waterproof point-and-shoot camera. Owens told them that Piru was the only one of Mike's homes she knew of where he allowed himself to sleep—sometimes for up to two hours at a time. He slowed down and relaxed when he was there.

She said Mike believed that some places had certain powers and that these powers were determined by history. He had told Owens that the indigenous people of Piru—the Tataviam—had been free and spiritually advanced until their conversion to Christianity through the San Fernando Mission. He called that a tragedy. So, in Piru, Mike liked to let his mind ride back in time to before the King had ruined the Tataviam. He would sit out on the back patio of the cottage for hours on end, staring out at the fertile valley and the biblical flora and the more distant peaks of the mountains, a legal pad in his lap and his pencil held between his fingers like a cigarette. His eyelids would gradually close but never all the way. After hours of utter stillness, Mike would often suddenly sit up straight and start writing, filling page after page with his tight, clear print while he muttered and chuckled and hummed. Owens admitted to have peeked at the writings later in secret but Mike had never once written in a language she recognized.

Owens told Hood that Mike also had an apartment down in National City, two-level with a view of the shipyards; an active-seniors condo in Laguna Woods Village in Orange County where he played golf and made friends with older people; a little stucco 1950s tract house in Torrance; and a place somewhere on the Pearblossom Highway near Palmdale, though this was the one home he had never shown her. She suspected he had other houses though she couldn't be sure.

So Hood Google-Earthed all of the homes and saw that the Piru cottage would be the best place to surprise Mike. It was out of the way and tucked up tight to the woodlands and the creek. A good road in and out, a low chance of witnesses, and plenty of places to hide and stage. Besides, Mike would be in one of his pensive phases— resting and ruminating and daydreaming and swimming in the creek. The only thing Hood didn't like was the long drive back to Buenavista. He had friends with helicopters and light aircraft but he couldn't expose them to danger.

*   *   *

That evening in the kitchen, while Hood stood vigil over a prime rib and made up the horseradish sauce, Beth and Gabriel started in on potatoes, asparagus, and salad. Bradley came back from town with cheese, crackers, wine, beer, and various liquors and mixers, for which he took orders, then served with an unusual—for him—air of concern. Hood saw trouble in his eyes and noted that Bradley kept looking out the windows. Owens made an apple pie and a peanut butter pie, then set a boom box on the breakfast bar and found Mozart on the classical station. Erin hovered about with Thomas in her arms until he fell asleep, and she put him in the portable crib set up in the living room, close by, where she could easily see him. Daisy and Minnie lay down beside the crib. Bradley delivered a rather large glass of white wine to Erin and she took it with the first smile Hood had seen her offer him in recent history. Beatrice flitted about, "testing" the food and gulping zinfandel. With Thomas asleep, Owens found some rowdy Mexican music and cranked it up. "About time," said Reyes. "Does anyone ever get the feeling that just below the surface here, everything is crazy?"

"Duh," said Beatrice, who had heard Bradley use this current expression, and was quick to pick up on such things. "Gabe, would you teach me to drive a modern car while there's still a little light? I've never gone over twenty-six miles per hour."

"Easy on the wine, angel face," said Reyes. "Or you'll be DUI."

Hood and everyone else followed them out, Erin holding sleeping Thomas against her shoulder. Gabriel made Beatrice take the passenger seat of his pickup and when she had her shoulder restraint fastened he commenced an overview of the modern automobile. Hood looked out at the desert in evening light, the backlit peaks of the Devil's Claws touched with orange and their bases locked in purple shadows. He looked south to Buenavista in the middle distance, its nineteenth-century church with the bell tower jutting up just beyond the Burger King and the Blockbuster and the Chevron station. He thought about having quit the LASD. He hadn't planned to quit, but wasn't enough enough? He liked L.A., but he liked Buenavista better. But what to do? He wondered again about selling cars, and wondered whether, with the sudden death of Israel Castro and change of ownership at Castro Ford, a fresh salesman might be needed. Could a physician and a car salesman be happy together? If not, why not?

A minute or two later, Beatrice slid over and Gabe came around. She took forever with the power seat, moving it every which way and back again. She started up and jumped into reverse, tires throwing gravel against the undercarriage, then made a neat highway-patrol turn and accelerated down the rough dirt road. Daisy and Minnie ran alongside barking. Hood watched the dust rise behind the truck and the serpentine course she steered, left and right and left and right. Overcorrecting due to the power steering, he thought, then wondered if she was just doing it for fun. A half a mile out the truck stopped, then swung onto paved Sunset Rim Drive and the panting dogs came over the rise back to the house.

Dinner was the most unusual of Hood's life but one of the most pleasant. The women took over the conversation, all of them except Erin drinking briskly. Beatrice set the pace on the wine and out-ate the others, roughly five to one, including half of the peanut butter pie. She reminisced on the Portuguese in San Diego and the Apaches at Yuma. Owens told amusing Hollywood tales from her acting jobs and Beth became excited by her own ER stories and Erin described for them in fascinating detail the decaying castle in the Yucatán jungle where she'd been held captive by the drug lord Benjamin Armenta. Bradley continued to fill their glasses. Soon all four of them were telling four stories more or less at once, a layered narrative that reached Hood's ears as pleasant near-chaos: *Geronimo scalped him, then yawned and lay down in the shade and took a nap. Quentin takes my wrists in both hands and kisses them! I yell out two pints, stat—blood, not bourbon, you fool! The black jaguar looks at me again, and I swear he's sizing me up for dinner.*

Hood sipped a little wine and kept an eye on the windows. He put Mary Kate Boyle on speakerphone while he did dishes—she sounded happy and relieved, and the rehearsals were going well. She'd gotten back her job at KFC, no problem, just like Hood said she would. She still had headaches from Clint's blackjack, but less than before. She'd let him know about opening night. Hood thanked her again for her courage and good humor over the last weeks and she seemed disappointed by this.

Hood noted that Bradley drank nothing but coffee and was ankle-strapped and rarely had his back to a window or the front door. Reyes had a few beers but he made his limping rounds every forty minutes or so, flashlight in hand and .38 holstered to his hip.

49

Awakened by a dream in which Thomas was sold for one large silver coin to three faceless traders in a bazaar, Bradley lay on the long leather couch in Hood's living room and listened to the breeze hiss through the yuccas and ocotillos outside. He pulled on his pants and boots and heavy canvas barn coat and took the gun from under the pillow and put it in his coat pocket. He walked quietly back through the house and looked in on Erin and Thomas, both deeply asleep, touched by a faint band of moonlight. He went out the front door, triggering the motion lights. The giant and the two dwarves stood out by the stone wall on the other side of the carport. Bradley could see the twinkle of a vehicle down the roadside, parked out of earshot of people and dogs. He approached. "What do you ugly fuckers want?"

"We apologize for waking you up," said the giant. His voice was deep and clear; his tone was polite.

"I saw you earlier. You don't blend in."

Both dwarves motioned him down the road and Bradley followed, the giant so tall his head seemed to brush the sky, while the dwarves on either side of him were as short and stout as bookends. Fifty yards down all three stopped and turned to face him. "What we want to do is help you," said the giant. "Mike wants your son and he'll do harsh things to get control of him. We have differing opinions on how Thomas should be raised. We think there's only one person who can do it properly. And that person is you. Not Mike."

"Thanks for the vote of confidence."

"It's not confidence in you we have," said one of the dwarves.

"What we have is belief in nature's order. You are the father. And we are here to help you do whatever is necessary to secure your son. We are here for you."

"I don't want you here for me. I want you as far away from me as possible."

"Of course," said the giant. Bradley guessed him at close to eight feet tall. He wore a dark suit that fit perfectly. He brought a wallet from his coat pocket, and in his giant's hands, it looked like a child's plaything. But his fingers were deft and he extracted a card. Then, with two strides he covered the ten feet to Bradley. "My business card."

Bradley took it without looking at it. "I hit you, didn't I?"

"Yes. Fine shooting." The giant put back his wallet, then lifted his shirt and showed Bradley the small red slit, inflamed but apparently healing. "Still rattling around inside, too."

"I'd shoot you again if it would do any good."

The dwarves looked at each other and shook their heads in disdain.

"We feel pain," said the giant.

"So do we."

"Bradley, we watched the fireworks down at Valley Center last night. It was a spectacular attempt to escape your own past. We all know it can't work because you can't change who you are. That would be like a tree frog trying to become a tree. But we knew that the real point was to put your wife and Hood at ease, so I think the spectacle was a meaningful performance."

"It was not a performance. It was real. I am not what I have been."

The dwarves let loose a tight, vicious laugh.

"We did have the thought, though," said the giant, "that you might need some financial assistance to get started fresh. So, we'd like to offer you this. Just a beginning, of course."

One of the dwarves waddled forward holding up something flat and black and shiny, as if he were badging Bradley. Then he reversed it to reveal a similarly sized white card rubber-banded to its back. He turned the dark side to Bradley again and wiggled it to catch what there was of the moonlight. "A Visa Black Card," he said. "Their *best.*"

"There's a quarter-million-dollar limit," said the giant. "But if you need more than that, just call the number on the business card I gave you. We'll take care of it. And the CDL on the other side is genuine, though, of course Bradford Johnson and his personal information are not—quite. We have a much more generous budget than Mike Finnegan will ever have. But more importantly, we have far more progressive, forward-looking ideas about how best to serve our partners. We're part of an elite group. I am not bragging. Keep a hapless angel in a mineshaft for one hundred years? Inflict senseless cruelty on human beings we don't judge to be worth our time? Delight in human pain and chaos? We are not this. This is not how we behave. Think about it. Think about Thomas and what you would like him to become. Let your imagination run wild and let us help you make your dreams real."

Bradley took the credit card and looked at it and turned it over. The moonlight was just enough to reveal his own image on the driver's license, a picture he hadn't known was being taken. The giant went down to one knee and he spread his enormous arms. He and Bradley were roughly eye level now and the outstretched arms spanned far wider than Bradley was tall, and this freakish display brought him a woozy rush. "Bradley?" whispered the giant. "Fetch Thomas and Erin immediately. She's a key part in our hopes for Thomas, unlike in Mike's. Now. Bring them out. Save your wife and son, and we will help you build upon your life. *Don't throw them away!*"

Bradley looked at the kneeling giant, who was smiling now, and felt a shudder come up through him. He slipped the business card into the bundle and flipped all three back to the dwarf. They hit his chest, but he caught it before it fell. "Go to hell, all of you."

"I told you," said one of the dwarves. He snatched a rock off the ground and hurled it into the darkness and Bradley heard it hit far away. "A complete waste of time." He spun in the gravel and crunched down the road toward the vehicle, the second small man close behind him.

"Won't you at least take one of my cards? As a matter respect between gentlemen?"

Bradley pulled the Glock and aimed it at the great prow of skull above the giant's eyes. "Bradley—I am disappointed. But please know, no matter what you do or where you choose to do it, I will be looking in on you over the many years you will live."

"March."

"As you wish." He nodded and rose with a grunt, holding up a huge hand in appeasement, then turned and followed his associates down the road, his shoulders hunched, as if expecting a pesky bullet.

Angry and anxious but clearheaded, Bradley sat in Hood's living room until the first light of day came gray and faint through the blinds. He felt like a beetle caught in a spider's web. It seemed impossible to move without making things worse. He wrote a passionate letter addressed to Erin and Thomas and left it at her place at the table, then woke up Hood and Reyes and Beatrice and told them he'd be gone awhile.

By nine thirty he was in El Monte, being waved into Rocky Carrasco's property by a thin man with a big holster on his hip, cowboy style. Rocky's lair was a contiguous four-parcel spread with a large, aging two-story home on each parcel. The properties were surrounded by a single high concrete wall long overgrown with fragrant trumpet vines. With all of the backyard fencing removed, Rocky had built his compound—four apartments over the four detached garages, and a common area containing a playground for children and palm frond *palapas* for shade and a basketball court, horseshoe setup, and small swimming pool. There was also a small beach-style cantina made mostly of corrugated aluminum and metal beer signs, with steel-drum barbecues and plenty of tables and chairs, similar to those cantinas found around his favorite Mexican city, Mazatlán. All of this amidst lush palms and giant birds of paradise and plantain and huge agaves, some of which grew almost to the power lines.

Now Bradley and Rocky sat in this cantina in the morning sun. Rocky was a small knot of a man, heavily tattooed and bald, with a large bushy mustache. He wore a gold Kobe jersey and a pair of over-size athletic shorts. Bradley noted again that Rocky's skin was still prison pale from his years at Pelican Bay and his compulsively private, indoor life since his release. Rocky's idea of a good time was to watch basketball, *fútbol*, and boxing on the several large-screen televisions in his house—live broadcasts and taped events all blasting away si-multaneously. And of course *The Simpsons,* Animal Planet, and *Pimp My Ride.* This replica Mazatlán cantina was Rocky's only encounter with the outdoors that Bradley had ever known—inspired by a beach that Rocky had probably not seen in four decades.

"I worry," said Bradley. He could not remember ever having to choose his words so carefully, except perhaps when he was trying to deceive Mike Finnegan.

"That's what every new father does."

"Erin distrusts me."

"Maybe she is too beautiful for trust."

"I don't think it's that. I put her in danger. She no longer believes in me."

"But so long as she obeys you, then the belief and trust can come back."

"She's never obeyed me. I've never expected her to."

"America was ruined in the sixties."

"I want her back."

"Then you keep on trying, man. You get her back with good words and good actions. And if that doesn't work, you get a girlfriend."

Bradley nodded and looked out at the horseshoe court and the hoop and the brightly colored pots of flowers. "The watchdogs are all over me at work. They know I was down there when Armenta got it, but they can't prove anything. Yet. They're pretty sure I'm tied in with Herredia, but they can't prove that either. Yet. They know I rescued Stevie from the Salvadorans, so therefore you and I must have something going. Suspicion creates its own truth. You know what I'm saying?"

"How's it going with the Fords?"

"Fine right now. But I worry who's talking about me." Bradley watched Rocky's face for a reaction but he just stroked his drooping mustache and waited. "Warren knows things he shouldn't know. Is Cleary singing? Vega? I hope not. Rocky, let me be honest. I hope it's not someone close to you."

Rocky leaned forward. "He came to me. Warren. He wants to nail you, man. He wants to nail me. He keeps Octavio because Octavio talks. And talks. So what can I do? I say words. He knows about you and me and my son. So I say more words. He knows things, just like you say he does. More words. All words that say nothing. Even after years in Pelican Bay I never named."

Bradley sat back and looked up at the white spearlike blooms of the giant bird of paradise, so tall they cleared the vine-choked wall to catch the sunlight. "Thanks, Rocky. I want to raise my son."

"I get you."

"I know you do. I want to be like you someday. Sitting in a place I love with family and friends all around."

"Sixteen grandchildren, four great ones!"

"Well, maybe not quite that much like you."

Rocky smiled.

"But I can't go to prison like you did. I don't have the courage."

"Prison takes patience, not courage."

"Rocky, if you have to trade me for your freedom, or the freedom of someone in your family, all I ask is a warning. Give me that one small thing."

Rocky looked at him steadily and without blinking. His eyes shone with life and vigor, but Bradley saw the flat, blunt force in them. The man who wouldn't name, even in Pelican Bay, he thought. Rocky sat back, the big Kobe jersey hanging loosely on him. He crossed his muscular arms with the full-sleeve tatts. "I believe in Los Angeles. I was born in an apartment on Aviation. Eight kids. My padre, he worked as a janitor. My mama, she did other people's washing and made tamales. Thousands and thousands of tamales. They take time to make. She's ninety-three this month. She don't make tamales anymore. She lives upstairs in that house, right there. Papa wanted to live to be a hundred and he did. He died right there on the basketball court. Look at all this." Rocky unlocked his arms and held them out in a gesture of presentation, then let his hands drop to his knees.

"You've built a good life, Rocky. It's perfect here and you have everyone and everything you need. I believe in Los Angeles, too. And I've worked very hard, like you. But I think I'm about to get crushed, along with my wife and son. So, like I said—I worry. How *much* should I worry, Rocky? That's why I came here. Because you're wise and you know when to fight and when to get out of town."

Rocky nodded and stroked his mustache again. "You have the warning you asked for."

"Thank you. You're a true friend."

"I'm sorry, but I have my worries, too."

"I understand."

"Good luck."

50

Two mornings later Hood, burrowed like a dog into the cold mud bank of Piru Creek beneath the overhang of a willow, shivered in the darkness. He could see the roofline of Mike's cottage a hundred yards away, and the pale smoke rising steadily from the river-rock chimney. A rooster crowed to the north and Hood checked his watch: thirty-five minutes to sunrise.

Upstream where it ran behind the cottage, the creek gurgled and splashed through a rocky riffle. But then the water widened and deepened into a quiet pool nearly thirty feet long and fifteen wide. At the far downstream end of the pool stood several large boulders that formed a spillway through which the creek tumbled impatiently into a lower, narrower channel. Across from the boulders Hood was buried in the bank near the end of the pool, under the willow. Owens had said this pool was where Mike lingered longest—submerged, weighted, and masked—observing and sometimes taking pictures of the fish and insects. The boulders at the end of the pool were where he usually climbed out. One of the rocks was large and flat enough for Mike to sun himself on, in hot months. He never wore a wetsuit. Hood could see this pale rock in the darkness and he guessed it was no more than twenty feet away.

He looked out at the surface of the water, broad shifting concavities of black and silver. He felt unfamiliar to himself. He had a gun but no authority to use it, no badge. He still felt as if he was in law enforcement but he knew that he was nothing now but a mud-caked creature with a grievance.

He listened to the rooster and let his thoughts and memories roll past unexamined. More and more these days Hood enjoyed engaging the world as if he were not in it. He wondered if a light sink-tip fly-line would be a good way to catch the fish in this deeper pool. Maybe cast cross-stream from above the pool head and give it a mend and let it swing with the current, sinking. This was the kind of thing his father never tired of talking about, and in fact Douglas had been a very good angler in his day. Going through some of his father's things out in their Bakersfield garage after the memorial service, Hood and one of his sisters had found a heavy magazine-shaped journal with forty years of Douglas's fishing notes and sketches. The cover of the journal was leather and carved with a jumping trout. The notes were written in Douglas's unmistakable half-printed, half-cursive hand, developed in his early years as a drafting student. The drawings were clear and simple—water flow, structure, location of fish, cast direction and drift, etc. He remembered the look on Julie's face: *You should hang on to this, Charlie.*

Gradually the light coalesced and Hood could see the far bank and the willows and the upstream riffle. Smoke continued to waft out of the chimney. Apparently Mike had either gotten up during the night, or stayed up for most of it to tend the fire. Birds called, still deep in the trees and bushes, their songs meek and tentative on this cold winter morning. He looked at his watch again. Owens said that Mike was in the water just after sunrise during summer and early fall, but not until around eight A.M. during cold weather. *Two hours*, Hood thought.

He unbuttoned his coat and checked the Taser gun, body warm and dry in its holster. It was an X26c, modeled after the police-grade weapon, with fifteen-foot conductive wires and eighteen watts of what Taser called "Electro-Muscular Disruption" (EMD) technology. Hood learned that bare wet skin would provide enhanced "Neuro-muscular Incapacitation" (NMI) according to the Taser tech adviser, who also suggested sharpening the probes with carbide #8 sandpaper for increased penetration and hold.

Hood shifted within his half burrow, hoping to get the circulation back in his right foot. He'd worn full-length thermal underwear and wool socks and a good down jacket and his waterproof Red Wings, but his feet felt colder than in the snowstorm in Washington, D.C. He sipped the still-hot coffee from his insulated container, and dug some granola bars and an apple and string cheese from one of his coat pockets. He watched the house.

Just after eight, Hood heard a screen door rap shut and he saw Mike walk onto the back deck of his cottage. He wore red shorts and red rubber spa sandals, a short blue jacket with the collar turned up. He brought a mug of coffee to his mouth and looked out toward the Hopper Mountains. He took a call on his cell phone and listened for more than a minute, before speaking briefly and punching off. Hood shivered but hardly moved until Mike had gone back inside.

A moment later the screen door tapped shut again; Mike was back, barefoot and without the jacket. A diving mask with a snorkel rested just above his forehead, a pair of blue swim fins dangled from one hand, and what looked like a camera swung by a lanyard on his other wrist. He placed an orange-and-yellow beach towel over the railing. Strapped around his stout pale middle was a wide belt with weights spaced evenly around it, several inches apart.

He came down the steps and looked out again at the mountains, then turned downstream and stared directly at Hood. Hood remained motionless and watched through the dense willow branches that enclosed him. He wondered if Mike would be able to read his thoughts from underwater when he got closer. It didn't seem likely, given the reflective qualities of the surface water, and unless Mike was expecting someone during his morning swim in the remote solitude of Piru Creek. And even if he sensed someone nearby, maybe it would be too late by then—maybe the current would have already delivered him to within Hood's take-down range of fifteen feet.

Mike came down the wooden steps and stepped into the grass. His legs were stubby and muscular and tinted with red hair. His torso was powerful and compact. His head, which always seemed large, was now exaggerated by the mask and snorkel. He walked down to the waterline and stood on one leg while pulling on one swim fin, then the other. When the fins were on, he lifted the mask off and spit onto the glass and knelt while he dipped the mask in the river and worked his fingers over the surface. Again he looked downstream to Hood. Then he settled the mask over his face and took the snorkel in his mouth and waded in. He shivered and squealed like a little boy as he lowered himself into the river. By the time he reached midstream his body had sunk beneath Hood's vision. Hood watched the white snorkel with its orange tip slowly coming downstream.

It looked to Hood that Mike was taking his time, probably bracing his hands on the rocks to slow his speed. *Must be cold*, he thought. He remembered his father saying that most fish would wait until the sun was on the water to feed when the days were short and the weather was cold. So maybe Mike was photographing the still lethargic trout before they became too skittish. An internet search had told him that Piru Creek was running at fifty-one degrees. He wondered how Mike could stand the cold with no wetsuit, but Hood had experienced Mike's physical strength and it was remarkable.

Hood gradually worked his feet and legs free of the mud and rose to his knees and brought the Taser from under his coat. He checked the probes, which were clear of debris and shiny-rough where he had sanded the sharp points sharper. Crouching within the curtain of willow branches he released the safety and tested the laser sight along the mud bank beside him. He looked to the middle of the pool and saw the snorkel tilting left, then right, then back again, lazily making its way toward him.

He rose and climbed the low embankment behind him, then came back to the shore ten yards farther downstream, near the big boulders that framed the tail out of the pool. He crouched behind one and waited. The orange tip of the snorkel wobbled casually in its slow progress. Soon he could hear the faint sound of breathing over the rush of the water—long hollow intakes followed by wet exhalations as Mike inched along. Then the snorkel stopped and it was still, and Hood saw a muted silver flash beneath the water. The camera, he thought. Then slowly again the snorkel came his way. Another flash. Another few feet. When the snorkel came near the boulders it grew in length from two inches to nearly a foot, and Hood saw the white bulk of Mike's body rising through the dark water, then the back of his head and the strap of the mask, and then Mike was standing thigh deep in the creek looking through the glass at Hood. He spit out the snorkel. "Oh. Charlie."

Hood shot him in the middle of his chest. There was a fizzing electrical *crack* as the probes delivered the electricity. Bradley burst from behind another boulder with two hands extended and discharged both of his Taser guns into Mike's back and Hood saw the wires flashing in the young sunlight. Mike arched and grimaced but he was still upright, bleeding and sparking where the darts hooked his wet flesh. He growled viciously and his body spasmed. Behind the mask his eyes were wide and fixed on Hood. But with the clumsy swim fins still strapped to his feet, he could neither attack nor retreat, which left him rocking precariously on the slick boulders. Reyes barged out from behind a large black cottonwood and was practically on top of Mike before sending another set of electrical spikes into his thigh, the barbs sparking in the wet nylon of the swimsuit and the wires jumping crazily with current.

Mike quaked and slipped and crashed onto the boulders, hitting his head hard and knocking off the mask. The electrodes shorted out. The three men jumped in and held him under. His strength was great, but in the weakening seizures Hood could feel that Mike was not equal to them and the weights he wore and the numbing cold of the creek and the powerful volts of muscle-stunning electricity he had just endured. Five minutes after his struggling ceased they dragged him to the bank where Beatrice had already laid out, like fence railings, the five ropes that Bradley had made of her hair. They lifted and set him crosswise upon the ropes while Reyes reloaded his Taser gun and sent a fresh charge into Mike's unconscious body. Beatrice had to stumble away, weakened by Mike's proximity. *"But he feels me, too,"* she said. *"And he'll continue to feel me as long as my hair is his prison!"*

Bradley wrestled Mike's shoulders off the ground and Hood very tightly looped one of the ropes around his chest and arms, three times, then knotted it. Hood could tell its strength. Then they wrapped and tied Mike's belly and waist, trapping his arms and hands against his sides. Then his knees and ankles. The angel-hair ropes were nearly twelve feet long, providing enough wraps to nearly mummify Mike. Still he had not opened his eyes or made a sound. Hood pulled off the swim fins and threw them up on the bank. Reyes slid a needle into Mike's blue-cold forearm and slowly injected the sedative that one of his doctor friends had recommended, though at ten times the usual dose. Beatrice came sliding down the muddy embankment with a roll of weed-guard fabric, which was light and strong and was sold in a four-by-ten-feet rectangle ideal for this application. They packaged Mike in it, using his weight and the slight downward slope of the embankment to roll him tight, and duct tape to seal him in.

Bradley braked down the bank dragging a roll of rubber-coated chain link. They were all panting by now and their breaths made vapor in the morning air, but they managed to flatten the chain link and work Mike onto it. They grunted and heaved and used their numbers to roll him back up the embankment three times, cinching the chain link as tight as they could with each rotation. Then they affixed the heavy-duty rubber fasteners, seven in all, with shiny stainless-steel hooks at each end. Hood braced his feet and pulled with both hands to stretch them as far as he could before setting the hooks in the mesh.

A moment later the men bore Mike lengthwise on their shoulders like a canoe and Beatrice led the way along a trail in the brush to Reyes's brother's Denali. It was nearly a mile walk, uphill. Beatrice talked to herself for several minutes while devouring energy bars and Hood realized she was praying. Then she started humming. Mike was surprisingly heavy, even considering all of the material that enclosed him.

Hood was puzzled to hear himself laughing quietly as they walked, and he blamed it on the danger and stress. But then Bradley and Reyes began laughing, too, the same low-down, satisfied laugh, containing not only relief but wonder and fear. They loaded Mike into the back of the SUV and covered him with a heavy green tarp.

"May I sit up front?" asked Beatrice.

51

Late that afternoon Bradley drove from Buenavista to Valley Center. With March here the days were longer and the orange trees were in bloom and the air was filled with their sweet, clean aroma. With the birth of Thomas and all of the subsequent activity, Bradley had been away for five days. He'd burned up most of his personal time and traded out two shifts. Whenever he was away from Valley Center, Clayton the forger or Stone the car thief, old friends, would stay in the ranch house, tend the dogs, keep an eye on the property.

Clayton was here now but as Bradley pulled his Cayenne up to the gate he got that something-wrong feeling in his gut. There were tire tracks in the dirt just past the gate. Several sets. So rather than punching in the code, he pushed the intercom button used by visitors. Clayton answered and Bradley could tell by the tone of his voice something was wrong.

The gate rolled open but Bradley reversed away and continued down the dirt road along the creek and past the Little Chief's property, then climbed into the oak savannah hills to the east of his home. The road became narrow and overgrown and rutted from the winter rains, but the Cayenne was nimble and strong. Bradley drove down into a meadow where the road meandered through sage and wild buckwheat and Spanish saber and he saw a small covey of quail running ahead on the dirt road. Suddenly they burst together into the air, a percussive blast of wings. He dropped the Porsche back into low, then climbed up a hillock on the far side of the meadow. Near the crest he parked and got out, leaving the engine running. He climbed the last few yards to the top and squeezed between two large boulders and looked down on his property.

Clayton's old Stingray was there, parked up by the house, shining as always. So were two LASD prowl cars and a prisoner transport van and a slick-back black Police Interceptor that was parked up near the house. Jim Warren and Miranda Dez stood near the unmarked car, Dez in her uniform. Four uniformed deputies waited on the front porch, apparently satisfied that the front door was not going to open. Clayton sat at the picnic table bench, back and head leaning against the house, hands folded on the table before him in his Zen I-don't-hear-you posture. The dogs howled from the kennel in the barn. Two more uniforms walked from the direction of the barn. Bradley's phone buzzed and Cleary's number came up.

"Jack."

"They're on their way to Valley Center, Bradley. Search and arrest warrants signed by the judge and ready to serve."

"I'm looking at them right now."

"What do you need?"

"I'm okay." Bradley called Clayton and watched him pick up and put the call on speaker. The deputies came closer, and Dez and Warren cocked their heads toward the porch.

"Brad."

"Clay. I'm heading up to L.A. for the night. Little business to do. Can you hang another day?"

"Yeah. Everything's fine here."

Bradley rang off and watched and waited. Dez made a call on her cell phone. Warren looked bored, toeing the gravel with his boot. The uniforms broke into pairs and circumnavigated the house, then the barn, then the casitas up by the oak glen. The beauty of warrants was that they have to serve them to your person, Bradley thought. He crept back and turned off his Cayenne and got a jacket from the back and returned to his perch between the boulders. He watched. The deputies lingered patiently through a spectacular late-winter sunset

and the beginning of another cold night. They put on jackets. Finally
Dez and Warren got into the Interceptor and rolled down the road.
The prowl cars and van followed, and as soon as they were out of sight
Clayton picked up his phone.

"Clay, I'll be going away for a while but I need some things. Power
down the north gate sensors, pronto."

An hour later, when he thought it was safe, Bradley backtracked
through hills then picked up a good dirt road that looped around to
the north perimeter of his land. There he unlocked the decommis-
sioned gate and entered his property, then locked the gate behind him
and drove slowly toward the house. In the distance he saw the lights
of the barnyard, and his ranch house and Clayton's Stingray parked
out front.

Upstairs in his bedroom he kept looking out the windows and
checking his security monitors as he packed a suitcase and got the
briefcase of cash he'd secreted away under his bed, deducted from the
far greater fortune he'd sacrificed that night for Erin and Thomas. He
packed a Love 32 and two full magazines between the T-shirts and the
jeans, and made sure his LASD badge holder was in the pocket of his
jacket. He took his letter to Erin and slid it in next to the badge holder.

In the barn he let the dogs out of their run. They yapped and
leaped about and Bradley touched and said something to each one.
He knelt and rubbed big Call's throat the way he liked, then stood and
waved them back into the run. "Later, brutes," he said. "I'll miss you."
He felt a thickness in his throat as he walked away and they bayed
after him.

Back in the ranch house he told Clayton to stay here until he
called—it would be less than one week—and to keep his cell phone
on and play dumb with the Sheriff's Department. Out in the barnyard
he used his satellite phone to call Herredia.

He stopped in Escondido and mailed the letter. He was nearly to the border at Tijuana when he called Erin and told her he would be gone for a while, but not long, just a few days hopefully, maybe a little longer.

"What's going on?" she asked.

"Sheriffs were all over Valley Center trying to arrest me. They'll come to you and they'll do what it takes to find me. Don't tell them anything without a lawyer in the room. Call that one down in San Diego—he's good. They can't make you testify against me. And try not to worry."

"Not worry?" she asked quietly.

"I'm trying to do the right thing for you and Thomas."

"Was burning everything just a show?"

"It was to show you what you mean to me."

"What do you want?"

"Clayton's at home keeping an eye on things. You and Thomas can go there as soon as you're ready. You're safe from Mike now. Valley Center is your home and your property, Erin. Yours. Take it. Continue your life there. Make your music and love your son and give me a chance. Please give me a chance."

"When will we see you again?"

"You'll get a letter in a day or two. Please believe what it says."

She clicked off.

52

Hood watched Mike through the one of the grates. The grates were made of welded wrought iron, with heavy lids that slid open and locked shut with a penitential clang. There was one in a spare bedroom and one in the living room under an end table and one outside, flush with the concrete slab of the carport. The Mexican iron-monger who built the grates had the blood of Spanish and Moorish craftsmen in him, so his work was not only profoundly strong, but had an exotic Arabesque flourish. The grates were roughly the size and shape of the large, old-fashioned heater vents and because of this—and the vault soundproofing that Hood had installed months ago—he hoped they would not draw undue attention.

They had carried the still-unmoving Mike Finnegan down the stairs and placed him on the floor faceup in the largest room of the wine cellar, alongside the coffee table that sat in front of the sofa. Not willing to chance a surprise escape, they had left him bound in the angel hair, weed cloth, duct tape, and chain link, with the heavy-duty fasteners still in place. Mike did not appear to be breathing, and Hood detected no warmth at all when he placed the palm of his hand over Mike's forehead. Beatrice assured everyone that Mike was in the pink. Forty-eight hours later he had still not moved and Hood had no visual proof that he was breathing or even alive.

Hood looked down into the vault: one secondhand floral-print sofa, two mismatched, upholstered thrift-store chairs, a colonial-looking coffee table. There were shelves with a TV and DVD player that would play music CDs as well. No computer, of course. A few books and movies, some music. A wine rack with several bottles. There was a kitchen off to one side but no oven or stove, though it was plumbed for hot and cold water. Just a microwave and a small refrigerator, a set of plastic plates, bowls, flatware, and cups, one roll of paper towels. He could not see them from here but there was a good-size bedroom and a bathroom adjacent to the living area below, both visible from inside his house. There was central heat and AC.

By the middle of the third day nothing had visibly changed with Mike. He had not moved. Hood's dreams since Mike's arrival were vividly terrifying. He'd wake up throwing punches, shouting, sweating. Skinned knuckles, a broken bed-stand lamp, a shattered picture.

Now Hood dozed on a patio chair in the shade of the carport. The day was warm. Daisy napped fitfully beside him. She had been subdued and pining for Minnie, which reminded Hood of Beth, with whom he talked daily. Erin spent most of her hours with Thomas and her guitar and a portable keyboard, locked away in her bedroom writing. Hood could hear her from almost anywhere in the house, faint snippets of melody and lyrics. She came out with Thomas and sat with Hood a few times each day, then headed back for naps. Reyes, less needed now that Hood was here full-time, dropped by and spent most of his time talking with Beatrice. Beatrice cooked and ate and watched TV and borrowed Erin's car for increasingly long trips to unspecified places. She had gained nineteen pounds in less than a week and her skin was no longer alabaster white but a subtle rosy color. She bought larger clothes, and personal items and cheap jewelry. On the third day of Mike's incarceration she was picked up by a woman she introduced only as "Joan," and they set out for El Centro. She returned alone around two o'clock in a white Cube with Castro Ford plate holders and the pink slip that went with it. The large back cargo area was stuffed floor-to-ceiling with groceries.

Late on the third day, just before sunset, Hood was still sitting under the carport when he saw Mike's chest rising and falling. Hood heard a faint wheezing and noted that Mike's mouth hung slightly open now. An hour later Mike's head lolled to one side.

After dark, Hood put on a knit watch cap and a down jacket and got his one-million-candlepower floodlight and an extension cord. He aimed the ferocious beam through the grate at Mike's face. His head had lolled the other way. By midnight his eyes were cracked open. Soon his shoulders began to roll in a strange and rhythmic way and this went on for almost two hours. It looked to Hood like Mike was trying to scratch and itch or get his circulation going.

Around two o'clock Hood heard two startling wet cracks and Mike stopped moving. Then Mike craned his head hard to the right and over the next twenty minutes his left shoulder rotated one direction, then the other, rolling and rolling in ever larger circles. Finally it rose out of the encasement to rest flush against his cheek. Then the elbow popped out from the mesh, and the rest of his left arm flopped free. Mike was breathing hard. He craned his neck to the left and brought up his disjointed right shoulder and labored to free it, too. He wriggled and grunted and yelped. The shoulder and arm finally escaped. He wriggled more. When his body was free to the waist, Mike lay still and within a minute or two his breathing slowed to almost normal.

Then, one at a time, he shrugged the balls of his shoulders back into their sockets, drew the reconstituted joints up against his scapulars, and jackknifed himself into a sitting position. He was panting again by then but he unfastened the straps around his waist and legs and struggled out of the fencing material. He stripped off the duct tape and weed guard. By then he seemed weakened and Hood wondered if it was because of the newly exposed ropes of Beatrice's hair. Mike untied the ropes one at a time, deliberately, fumbling like a drunk to complete the simple task. But he stuck with it and had the strength left to coil and throw the hairy bonds to the other side of the room. Just after four o'clock he lay back in his red swim trunks and turned his face into the beam of Hood's light. He opened his eyes. "Owens," he whispered.

"Yes," said Hood.

"I was a fool. Our greatest weakness. Becoming sentimentally at-tached." Mike wiped his eyes with both hands, then let them drop back to the concrete floor. He sighed deeply and lay still for a long while. "Can you take the light off my eyes, please?"

Hood turned away the spotlight.

"First, Charlie, I'll need newspapers and periodicals and plenty of books. History, science, philosophy, social commentary, biography, poetry, and top-flight fiction."

"Nothing until you stop the dreams."

"Grim, aren't they? Agreed for now. Actually, an electronic reader would be cost-effective."

"No. You'd find a way to exploit it."

"I trust there are lights down here."

"Everything you need is down there."

When the cellar lights came on, Mike was standing by the wall with his hand still on the switch. "How long are you planning to keep up this nonsense?"

"Forever. I'll have a younger replacement lined up before I die. And so on."

"This won't look good on your résumé."

"Nothing much does."

"But you rounded up that simpleton with the missiles, now didn't you?"

"He pretty much captured himself."

"I'm open to negotiation, Charlie."

"I'm not."

"Just you and me?"

"Looks that way."

"Beth?"

"Back home."

"Bradley?"

"In the wind. Warrants issued, posse formed."

"Erin and my beloved Thomas?"

"Temporarily here. He's not yours, Mike. And he never will be."

"Going to move in on Erin while she's vulnerable?"

"She's tied to Bradley whether she wants to be or not."

"Charlie. Charlie. You are a good and honest and staggeringly disappointing man. I know full well what you feel for her. Whatever happened to the *take, take, take* that marks your human race? What happened to *you*, Charlie Hood?"

"I'll get what I want, Mike."

"But the odds are good that our beautiful Dr. Petty has already broken it off with you. Correct? She can't sit back and allow a fellow human being to be kept in a dungeon by her boyfriend. A violation of her Hippocratic Oath, just for starters. No. That won't play in her hot little movie house."

"I've got you, Mike. Right now, you're what I want."

"We'll see how long that lasts! Is that Beatrice's hair you bound me with? It certainly has her stunning aroma."

"Yes."

"She's long gone by now, knowing her."

"I think she's about to be."

Mike took a deep breath and dragged the ropes of hair over to the media hutch. He held his breath as he stuffed them into the bottom and slammed it shut. "You know we had a quake storm here just last month. Have you given any thought to seismic activity?"

"Some."

"Then you know the Yuma/Alvarado Fault runs right through here, between us and Buenavista. It's larger than they think, and very, very overdue."

"In geologic time. It could hold for hundreds of years. Thousands. And when it goes, it might free you and it might not."

"I guarantee you that Imperial County building codes are no match for the Yuma/Alvarado."

"Then we're both taking our chances."

Mike walked over and stood directly below the grate. With his foot he pushed away the roll of chain link, then looked up at Hood. He looked tiny and far away in his red swim trunks, a man easily contained by the walls around him and by the world beyond the walls and by the night beyond the world.

Then he squatted and sprang straight up and latched himself upside down and flylike to the grate. His white hands clenched the filigree and his feet clung to the ceiling, and he pressed his face hard against the iron. Hood hopped back a step. Mike's blue eyes peered at him from behind the thick iron. Hood saw the red stubble on his cheek. Mike was smiling rigidly and his breath was short and sharp. "Your walls cannot contain me, Charlie! And neither can the world or the night beyond the world. I will haunt your life and the life of your children and their children, and so on and so forth, forever and always, to the close of the age."

Mike hissed something in a language Hood didn't recognize, then let go. Hood stepped forward and watched him fall with his arms out and his knees flexed—ending the fifteen-foot fall lightly as a gymnast. Mike glanced up with pride, then brushed his hands together and went to the media center where he patiently studied the selections before putting a DVD into the player. Then he got the remote off the coffee table and lowered himself onto the couch. "*Manhunter*," he said. "I love this movie. That scene in the grocery store. The pictures in Will's head are much like your dreams, Charlie."

53

Six days later, Bradley called Hood and told him he was back home at Valley Center. He said they needed to talk—now—use the gate code from the other night, Charlie. Hood heard a rare doubtful waver in Bradley's voice, then he heard the clatter of the phone hitting something hard, and an explosion so loud it turned to static, then another. Gunning his Charger down the dirt road, Hood called the Valley Center Sheriff Substation.

When he got there, three San Diego County fire companies and half a dozen sheriff cruisers littered the barnyard and two helos hovered low over the hills. The barn was a smoking, blackened husk. Bradley lay sprawled faceup on the floor near the quad runners, most of his face and head gone and his entire body badly burned. A semiautomatic pistol lay close by. And a cell phone. And a steel military-style fuel can lay scorched in the rubble. Hood recognized Bradley's roasted leather duster and the remnants of the same fancy shirt and boots he'd worn here the night he'd renounced his life of crime. Now he was a scorched corpse with a face that had collapsed into the violently emptied space behind it. Hood figured two shotgun blasts. At least. Armenta's soldiers, catching up with him? Herredia's enemies here in California, finding him out? Or something Hood might know nothing about—an old score now settled?

Back outside he leaned against his car in the good sun and looked out at the oak tree and the house and the pond. He wondered at the journey that had begun here and pulled him and others through their lives and had now brought him back to this death. A cool breeze hit him and he understood that it would blow through here for centuries unending and he hoped this bloody smudge of history and the people who lived it would not be erased and forgotten. Bradley Jones had been twenty-two years old.

54

By late spring, Bradley had been buried for nearly two months. Thomas was growing fast and Erin seemed oddly hopeful considering what she had been through. Hood was impressed, once again, with her calm strength, and the way that she could turn the catastrophes of life into the beauty of music. She had seven songs ready for the next CD. She moved back down to Valley Center on the first day of summer, declaring herself ready for "the next chapter." Owens went with her. Hood watched them drive away down the dusty road and he saw both of their hands come up through the opened windows and wave good-bye.

Over the weeks Hood called acquaintances within the San Diego County Sheriff's Department for updates on the Jones murder investigation. The deputies were not trusting of Hood and they offered him little more than what SDSD gave out to the media: death by shotgun, the fire apparently set to destroy evidence, no suspects and no clear motive. LASD said publicly that Bradley had been "questioned" as part of a larger investigation of Mexican drug-cartel activity in Los Angeles County and this angle was well covered by the *Los Angeles Times*.

The story of his outlaw mother, Suzanne, was exhumed and revisited, complete with videos of Suzanne in action. Her self-proclaimed relationship to Joaquin Murrieta was given enthused but skeptical attention once again, with learned historians weighing in on its great unlikelihood. A university professor from Davis said that the Joneses "were a clearly troubled family but blaming their exploits on a notorious outlaw is flimsy rationalization at best." Hood thought of the head and gun and the saddle and the vest, of Suzanne's and Bradley's powerful lusts for danger and acquisition and lawlessness. A&E kept calling for an interview and Hood kept dodging them.

In the San Diego media, the flurry was over in less than one week, replaced by fresher woes and the county's irrepressible passions for the Chargers and Padres. Hood was able to extract one unpublished fact from SDPD, though it was of questionable value: Bradley's side-arm had contained nine of eleven possible shells and two brass casings had been recovered in the rubble. The two shells had been fired from Bradley's gun, but because of the ensuing fire, they couldn't say with certainty that he had fired them, and if so, when or at what.

In mid-July, Lonnie Rovanna was ruled unfit to assist in his own defense and housed in a high-security mental ward for treatment. Hood saw the video of Rovanna over and over, a staple on the San Diego news stations. They never showed any of the victims being hit by bullets, only Rovanna being tackled by Scott Freeman's hefty as-sociate. Hood's own name continued to appear deep in several of the newspaper and magazine articles, linking Rovanna's illegal possession of the fatal gun and a botched ATF operation. Dale Yorth kept Hood current on ATF musical chairs: Soriana bumped up to L.A., the L.A. Special Agent in Charge off to D.C., Fredrick Lansing demoted to a Justice Department job in Kansas City, Bly and three of the other fired agents filing a suit against Justice for wrongful termination. Hood enjoyed the information but didn't miss the bureaucracy. He felt less like a law enforcer than an unemployed citizen-kidnapper.

Clint Wampler was charged with five murders, including that of Federal Agent Reginald Cepeda. Clint's use of an explosive device in the bombing of the ATF field office, and the resulting death of Oscar Reitin, could qualify him for the death penalty. There was a news clip of Wampler also, limping into a room at the San Diego Superior Court, shackled at his wrists and ankles and held fast by two burly marshals. He looked as skinny and feral as Hood remembered him and he was ejected from his own arraignment for contempt.

*   *   *

Through summer Hood and Beth's time together trailed off. She admitted considering a job offer in San Diego, and to spending more time with friends and coworkers. She refused to set foot in Hood's home, telling him she'd either have to let Mike go free or call the cops so they could do it. She told Hood he would have to answer for Mike someday, then stopped mentioning him altogether. She spent two back-to-back, three-day weekends in San Diego, apartment hunting and bike riding in Balboa Park. She had such a blast. She implied that Hood should visit her often in San Diego, but the implication was faint and a direct invitation did not follow. She cried often and unexpectedly.

Beth left for her new position at Scripps Medical Center in San Diego late in July. It was a solid promotion and a vote of confidence and a nice hike in pay and benefits. A package arrived for Hood the day she left, a small rectangular box that contained a tissue-wrapped red apple and a note that said, "I love you."

Hood saw himself as freakish and alone. He remained proud and encouraging of her, though what he felt most of all was flattened. He imagined letting Mike go free, then hustling off to San Diego, maybe apply at some car dealers for a sales position. The fantasy would linger for a few minutes or hours, then be dashed the next time Hood looked through one of the grates at the little man reading, watching TV, listening to music, reading, reading, reading, writing, writing, writing.

I can do this a lot longer than you can, Mike liked to say. He often wore a wry smile and even from the Hood-to-Mike distance his eyes were blue and clear and merry. He'd grown a beard and mustache and favored plaid flannel shirts with the sleeves rolled up, which gave him a woodsy, lumberjack kind of look.

*   *   *

Over the summer Hood traded phone calls with Mary Kate Boyle once a week. Today it was her turn to call and she told him opening night was just a week away and she'd have two tickets for him at will call. She gave him the address of the Lowell and the box office phone number, just in case he needed it. She was happy to have been promoted to front-of-shop supervisor at KFC, which was worth seventy cents more an hour, and she'd bought a used car, the first car she'd ever owned. They talked about the car, then there was a long silence. "Charlie? Just so's you know? I'm not going to be badgering you or waiting around on you anymore."

"Please don't."

"Not that I've minded it. But I know what you're thinking. You're thinking I'm too young and dumb for you."

"You are younger and smarter than I am."

"I'm nineteen years old. Quick figurin' says I'm twenty-five and ready for babies when you're forty. And I'd be forty years old and still hot as a tamale when you're fifty-five. And so forth. The difference is the same year to year, but the relativity of it gets smaller. God, I sound like Clint."

"It's not that, Mary Kate."

"That I sound like Clint? I'm funnin' with you, Mr. Former FAT agent. I know what you mean. You mean it's not my age. So okay, then, what exactly *is* it?"

Hood slid the end table out of the way and unlatched the grate lid with his toe. He knelt and slid it open and looked in. "Move her right in, Charlie," said Mike. "Party *central*."

"Who's that?" asked Mary Kate.

Hood slammed the grate closed and set the latch and walked outside. "I want the *best* for you, Mary Kate. I want you to live and love and act and let your heart run free in the world. I want you to get your dreams. I'm sorry to sound so corny but I can't say it better than that."

"Dreams aren't corny! And what if you're one of my dreams?"

"Get a bigger one, Mary Kate."

"It is me, then."

They said nothing for a long while. Hood sat on the rock wall and looked out at the Devil's Claws and the downy white clouds in the west.

"Okay, Charlie. I'll put in for a dream upgrade but I'm still holding two tickets for you at will call. You bring whatever guest you want, and it can be a woman or a man."

"I'll be there."

"I don't *want* an upgrade, Hood."

Hood applied for jobs online so as not to be drawn away from his duties, but the rough economy and his questionable terminations didn't help. He did have a few thousand dollars left in the bank and wasn't particularly worried. There were security positions listed often, as well as janitorial work and a veterinary hospital night-attendant job that ran in the *Buenavista Beacon* classifieds every week. He figured that the job was noisy and stinky and sleep-robbing and difficult to fill.

Accepting Owens's offer to stand guard in his absence, Hood started leaving the house for an hour a day. He worked his way up to four and sometimes five-hour breaks. He'd go for a run or to the library and sometimes even a movie. He had the diamonds in his tooth removed and had his biannual periodontal cleaning. These excursions went without a hitch back home. His design of the vault, and the workmanship of the builders, had apparently been more than adequate. When he came home from hours away, Mike would sometimes glance up at him in irritation at the intrusion and continue his conversation with Owens, and sometimes ignore Hood altogether. The three had occasional conversations and drank some wine, Hood lowering the recorked bottle and a foam cup into the dungeon with a kite string. Of course Hood never entertained or invited anyone into his home, and at first he worried when the mailman came trundling up the road in his delivery Jeep. But the vault soundproofing was excellent and he would always leave the living room stereo on at some volume when he was gone. No calamities so far, though he truly missed Beth. Life was livable.

Mid-September Hood got a call from Erin with a dinner invite for the coming Saturday. The occasion was the nearly completed rebuilding of the barn. It would be her and Thomas, Owens, Reyes, Beatrice, the Little Chiefs from next door and the contractor who'd done the barn, whom she said she hoped Hood would like. Hood's antenna vibrated at this.

He drove out through the Imperial County heat and arrived at Valley Center well before sunset. The memories ganged up on Hood as always when he was here—and now he had the flamboyant shedding of Bradley's past, his unsolved murder, and Beth's departure to add to the canon. For a while they all sat in a circle on the thick grass in the shade of the big oak tree and let Thomas crawl from one pair of outstretched arms to another. He laughed and slobbered and the light in his eyes flared with young life.

Hood sipped a margarita and let Thomas climb on his crossed legs. The infant's hands seemed remarkably small and well formed. Hood could hear the contractor, Jason, spitting away with a nail gun inside the barn, still "putting on the frosting," as Erin put it. She said Jason had quoted six weeks for a complete rebuild, shown up with a three-man crew and brought the job in, under budget, in four weeks. Well, almost brought it in. She said he had some good ideas how to improve it, such as turning Bradley's old bunker into a wine cellar. Hood saw him come through the barn door, a man with square shoulders and big safety goggles and thick blond hair held back in a bandana. Hood handed his margarita off to Owens and stood Thomas up in front of him and let the boy stand upright, clutching Hood's thumbs for balance. Hood saw that Thomas had Erin's lithe frame and Bradley's head. Murrieta's head. *Don't start*, thought Hood. Don't remember. William had it only half right. Sometimes the past is dead and should be.

They ate on the big porch. Hood sat next to Owens and they talked about everything but Mike. She was working again, doing a series of commercials for Hyundai, where she appeared to be piloting a two-hundred-and-fifty-horsepower sports coupe through the curves of California 1 near Big Sur. She never actually drove it, just got in and out. Tonight she wore a retro dress of big black polka dots on a white background, and shiny black bracelets that didn't hide her scarred wrists. In the yellow glow of the bug lights her black hair looked touched by gold and Hood silently noted her beauty. He liked it that she wore her scars as trophies, not shames, because, as she had explained—she had finally chosen life.

Erin was more relaxed and happy than Hood had seen her since her kidnapping nearly a year ago. She'd gained a little weight. Reyes waited on her hand and foot, a hangover from the old days in Hood's Buenavista home. Beatrice ate with some semblance of self-control. She'd gained seventy-five pounds since her release from the mine and had slowed down her intake accordingly. Fully nourished, her body had regained its natural proportions and she was a tall, strong, and handsome woman.

Jason the contractor joined them late at dinner and left the table early. He was followed to and from by the dogs. Hood figured he was middle twenties at most and he was well muscled and had an unusually deep, clear voice. He sat at the opposite end of the table from Erin, ignoring everyone except Betty Little Chief on one side of him and Beatrice on the other. He appeared more interested in his food than in the conversation and he only looked at Hood once. For Hood it was enough. Soon Jason was gone and Hood heard the nail gun firing away across the barnyard and he looked out at the light from inside the barn forming a trapezoid on the grass.

Hood filled his wineglass, then walked under the oak tree to the pond, then over to the barn. Inside Jason was nailing pegboard to the drywall where the quads were kept. Hood stepped in and looked around. The inside of the barn was almost completely restored and the workmanship looked very good. Jason stood with his back to Hood, not twenty feet from where Bradley had died. The dogs whirled and dashed over to Hood and panted and yapped but kept their distance as Bradley had trained them to do. Jason turned and pushed the safety goggles up onto his forehead. Call ran his big head under Jason's hand.

"Nice work on the barn here," said Hood.

Jason nodded and pet the dog. "Glad you like it."

"Funny you called the vault a wine cellar. I used the same line when I built mine."

Jason smiled. His jaw was a little wider and his eyes had a soulful suggestion of innocence that was new. Fuller lips, by just a little. Subtle differences, Hood saw, but noticeable if you were looking.

"How long did it take you?" Jason asked.

"A few minutes," said Hood. "Who played you?"

"One of Herredia's victims. Plenty to choose from, any given week. The basic age and body type was easy enough. We didn't go out and take someone."

"What about DNA and fingerprints?"

"That cost me a pint of blood and a lot of money. Old acquaintance in the coroner's office. In the end it's just what the autopsy report and death certificate say. Then it was off to Tijuana for eyes, chin, ears, lips, and nose. Then Texas Voice Center for phonoplastic surgery. How did you know? What's the tell? It took Erin a while to believe it, even though I told her in a letter months ago. The new voice had her freaked out, being a singer."

"The circumstances gave you away, Bradley. Your last phone call seemed wrong. After I talked to the San Diego investigators I realized someone had fired your pistol at the bad guy *after* your head was allegedly blown off. But it was mainly just tonight—you hanging around Erin and the barn job taking a bit longer than you said. How the dogs behave. The way you looked at me across the grass when I was holding Thomas. Are you and Erin good now?"

"I told her I wanted to start at the bottom and work my way up. She's just starting to trust me again. Barely."

"Are you living here?"

"Tonight's my first official night. Erin wanted you to know the truth. I wasn't so sure, but I trust her judgment more than I trust my own. Thomas knows who I am, Hood—he calls me Daddy. Imagine that."

"I take it you skimmed off a little before you burned the bales of cash that night."

"Some."

"How much?"

"None of your business. I'd say just arrest me but you're not a lawman any more than I am. You wouldn't rat me out, would you?"

Hood considered but not for long. "No. That's my gift to your wife and son. I think you've actually got a chance of pulling this off."

"It's my only chance, so I'm going to work like hell at it. How's the little man?"

"It's impossible to tell."

"I think we ought to shoot him full of tranquilizers and package him up and throw him down Beatrice's mine. Just you, me, and Reyes. That way, he's trapped forever and you're a free man. Who's the prisoner now, Hood? I mean, what is there really to say to that sonofabitch day in and day out? He's going to wear you down or find someone and talk them into something, just like the serpent he is. Or he'll dig out or climb out or something. I feel like I owe you, Charlie, for helping get you fired."

"They didn't fire me. I quit."

Bradley smiled. The surgeon had changed that, too, but it was still a good one. "I'll *still* help you chuck him down the shaft."

"I like that idea."

"Beth still gone?"

"More and more so."

"You're about to hear from someone extraordinary."

"I don't know if I can handle any more extraordinary."

"You can handle this, my friend. I guarantee it." Bradley shrugged and went to one knee and rubbed Call's throat. He looked at Hood. "They got Joaquin's head but all they got off me was some of my face. It's evolution, Charlie. Mom would be proud. And guess what? I finally forgive you for falling in love with her. Given your situation, I would have done the same."

Later Hood walked down to the pond. The night was warm and a breeze scented with orange blossoms came out of the west. The moon was nearly full. He heard voices and laughter from the patio and he turned to see Owens and Beatrice exchange a hug. Owens then lifted two wineglasses off the railing and came down the steps and across the grass toward him.

"Feeling lonely, cowboy?"

"Depends what you and Beatrice are plotting."

She handed him a glass, then touched it with hers. "Splendid things. She's so good at reading my heart. She seems to know it better than I do." She drank, then looked up at the moon. "Remember years ago when I put my number in your cell phone and said I wanted you to call me?"

"And the way you turned my face left then right and studied it, and I felt like a dog being examined. And you said I'd have a reason."

"I think that time is now. We don't need the phone. Let's go up to the dock and take out the rowboat. I've never been on a boat in the moonlight and I want to be on it with you."

They followed the waterline north. The frogs went silent ahead of them, then splashed into the water as they passed. When they came to the dock, Owens stopped and Hood stepped into the rowboat and offered his hand. She climbed aboard lightly and smoothed her dress and sat in the middle of the fore bench facing back. Hood handed her his glass and untied the ropes, then took up the oars and pushed off. The boat made a sipping sound and the oars splashed softly. The moon lined up over Owens's shoulder and cast a widening silver ribbon on the water behind her and she was looking at him.

55

Hood sat in the October shade of his courtyard and saw Reyes's car coming up the road. Owens looked up from her book and lifted the floppy brim of her hat. "Are you expecting him?"

"No," said Hood.

"I'll batten down the hatches in case he's not alone."

Owens started with the grate under the carport roof. Hood heard the metal clang of the lid sliding and the squeal of the latch closing and Owens strode across the courtyard and into the house. Music came on inside and from new outdoor speakers disguised as rocks. The car ground up the rise and came level near the carport and Reyes pulled in and parked directly over the grate, next to Hood's new/used Camaro.

Gabriel climbed out and looked at Hood, then the passenger door opened and out stepped a stout woman with straight short orange hair. She wore a denim pantsuit and sky blue cowboy boots. She took off her sunglasses and gazed around with a formal air. Then they came across the gravel and through the courtyard gate, where Hood and Owens stood and welcomed them.

Reyes introduced her as Camille Gomez, city manager of Buenavista. Hood had seen her in the paper and on TV. She was short and heavily hung with turquoise, the centerpiece being a squash-blossom necklace that was half as wide as her torso and reached clear to her beltline. Plus turquoise earrings, bracelets, rings, and buttons on the denim jacket. Her eyes were green and surrounded by laugh lines defeated by her dour expression.

Reyes and she sat on a bench on one side of the courtyard picnic

table and Hood sat across from them. Hood heard the music get just
a little louder. Reyes asked after Beatrice, whom Hood had not seen
or heard from since September. Reyes seemed hurt that she'd vanished
without a word, but Hood figured she'd been doing it for centuries.
Owens came back with four glasses of tea and joined Hood on his
side of the table.

They drank and made small talk until Camille Gomez interrupted
Reyes mid-sentence. "I came here to offer you a job as the Buenavista
chief of police. Gabe here was good, but his replacement isn't . . .
confident. He has in fact received death threats from the North Baja
drug cartel, though I think pretty much every border cop between
here and Texas has gotten some kind of threat, too. Real or implied.
I need a man with hair on his chest. Or a woman. Maybe not that.
Anyway, it pays okay and the bennies are decent but nothing like the
old days. I can offer you a take-home car and—"

"I accept." Owens squeezed his leg under the table.

"I'm not done, cowboy," said Gomez.

"When do I start?"

Camille Gomez considered Hood, then smiled, the lines of her face
now fully employed. "Well, Mr. Hood. That was about the easiest
recruitment pitch I ever made."

Reyes toasted the new chief and they lifted their glasses and drank.

ACKNOWLEDGMENTS

Deepest of gratitude to everyone at Trident Media Group for your unflagging alliance.

And respectful thanks to Dutton for helping bring these stories to life.

ABOUT THE AUTHOR

T. Jefferson Parker is the bestselling and award-winning author of nineteen previous novels and a three-time winner of the Edgar Award. Formerly a journalist, Parker lives with his family in Southern California.